The
Double
Life
of
Daisy
Hemmings

A former broadcast journalist, political adviser and government speech-writer, Joanna Nadin is the author of more than eighty books for children and teenagers, including the Flying Fergus series with Sir Chris Hoy, the bestselling Rachel Riley diaries, and the Carnegie Medal-nominated *Joe All Alone*, which is now a BAFTA-winning BBC drama. She is also a lecturer on the MA in Creative Writing at Bath Spa University.

She has written two previous novels for adults, *The Queen of Bloody Everything* and *The Talk of Pram Town*.

Also by Joanna Nadin

The Double Life of Daisy Hemmings

JOANNA NADIN

PAN BOOKS

First published 2022 by Mantle

This paperback edition first published 2023 by Pan Books
an imprint of Pan Macmillan
The Smithson, 6 Briset Street, London EC1M 5NR
EU representative: Macmillan Publishers Ireland Ltd, 1st Floor,
The Liffey Trust Centre, 117–126 Sheriff Street Upper,
Dublin 1, D01 YC43
Associated companies throughout the world
www.panmacmillan.com

ISBN 978-1-5098-5305-2

3 5 7 9 8 6 4 2

A CIP catalogue record for this book is available from the British Library.

Typeset by Palimpsest Book Production Ltd, Falkirk, Stirlingshire
Printed and bound by CPI Group (UK) Ltd, Croydon, CR0 4YY

MIX
Paper | Supporting
responsible forestry
FSC
www.fsc.org
FSC® C116313

Visit **www.panmacmillan.com** to read more about all our books
and to buy them. You will also find features, author interviews and
news of any author events, and you can sign up for e-newsletters
so that you're always first to hear about our new releases.

For my dad and uncles,
who grew up sailing this estuary

Disclaimer:
The characters in this book are works of fiction.
But then, isn't everyone?

'Is insincerity such a terrible thing? I think not. It is merely a method by which we can multiply our personalities.'

Oscar Wilde, The Picture of Dorian Gray

Prologue

Jason, 1978

Here is the boy.

A seven-year-old, pale as milk and scrawny as his big sister is stout. And small enough, still, to wriggle onto his mam's lap or into the snug of her arm.

'Can you see them?' she asks, as they hang off the harbour, eyes fixed on the shallows. 'Look, there!'

Jason looks and spies a flicker of silver, then another – a whole shoal of them, dancing on the tide like starlings – readies his net.

'Ah, they're just babies now, mind,' she tells him. 'Let them grow before we fish them out.'

Disappointed, he pokes the end at a stubborn anemone instead. 'What will they be,' he asks, 'when they grow up? Will they be sharks?'

His mam laughs, and he feels a pip of indignation in his throat. 'But will they?'

'No,' she says, nudging him nicely, dislodging it. 'Too small for that.'

'What then?'

'Mackerel,' says his sister. 'Boring bloody mackerel.'

Jason gapes.

'Sadie,' snaps his mam. 'Language.'

'My dad says it,' she justifies.

'Your dad's not ten and, besides, he should know better.'

Sadie glowers. 'They'll still be mackerel,' she says.

'Can't they be something else?' asks Jason. 'Can't they be . . . be swordfish? Can't they be whatever fish they want?'

'Idiot,' says Sadie.

'Sadie!' snaps Mam, then turns to him. 'No,' she says. 'They don't get a choice. They just are what they are.'

'Do I get a choice?' he asks after a moment. He's thinking of his father, wondering if he'll have to work on the boats. Have to sweat and swear and get his hands dirty.

'Course you do,' says Mam. 'You can be whatever you want. You could be a doctor, or a teacher or—'

'Farrah Fawcett-Majors,' says Sadie. 'I'm going to be her. I'm going to marry the Six Million Dollar Man.'

'I think that job's already taken,' says Mam. 'But you could be a doctor or a teacher too.'

Sadie sighs. 'Gaynor Bates says they'll split up soon and get a divorce so I can marry him and I'll be Sadie Majors.'

'Don't listen to your sister,' says Mam. 'Sun's got to her.'

But he's not anyway, not really. He's too busy thinking: what will he do and who will he be? Too busy running through possibilities: tinker, tailor, soldier, sailor, rich man, poor man— No. He stops there, back-tracks. Rich man. He'll be rich as creases, whatever that means. Richer even. He'll live in a mansion and sit in a study surrounded by books, like that man on the telly in a wig, only he won't wear one of them. And he won't have filthy fingernails or stink of beer neither. And his mam can live with him, but not Sadie, nor his dad.

And so lost is he in his dream, he doesn't notice his net slip from his fingers and drift off on the tide.

'Jason!' squawks his sister. 'Dad'll kill you.'

'Oh, Jesus,' agrees his mam. 'Your dad.'

His tummy turns over as he thinks of his father. 'I'll get it,' he says and jumps into the water, sandals and all, soaking his shorts right up to his crotch; wades out and snatches the tip of the bamboo, before it edges past the slip-way and out into the wide, velvet estuary.

'Got it!' he calls, as if he's netted a monster.

'Dad'll still kill you,' says Sadie, smug, as they trudge up the hill. 'You're soaked.'

'Your dad won't know,' mollies his mam. 'You'll be nice and dry by then.'

But Jason doesn't care either way, not right now. Right now he's Dick Whittington, sitting in his fat future, counting his coins and his stacks of books besides.

And his dad? His dad's an ant, an emmet, so far away he's small enough to stamp on.

1.

James, 2018

Here is the man.

His days are practised, precise. Military in detail and execution.

He selects socks, black silk mix, from rolled ranks of identical pairs, striped cotton boxers from the folded pile; releases a pristine linen shirt from its plastic shroud. He eats rye toast, drinks a single espresso from a stove-top pot before switching to green tea, which he sips, pinched at the bitterness.

Forfeit, some might call it – have called it, in fact. But rigidity pays: his cholesterol is enviably low, his blood pressure steady, his waistline at forty-seven still a trim thirty-two. 'In your prime,' that doctor had told him. Pascoe, was it? Or Danvers, perhaps. And Isobel appreciates it, of course.

'Making up for a wasted youth?' she'd asked him once, when he'd turned down a rum-soaked trifle, an ironic nod at an East End restaurant that was all earnest Formica and art students.

'Hardly,' he'd said, and laughed, as if it were nothing, a moth of a comment to be swatted away. Then, later, he'd run four miles on the treadmill that stands in his lounge – No! Not lounge, living room – all the while pushing the packet of Dream Topping, the tinned mandarins, the stale sponge to the back of the imaginary larder along with the rest of his childhood.

Because he can do that now. Can corral, control it all – the mess of his previous existence. The spooling complications. Has had to. Has had to be as strict with his self as he is with his diet. Because obtaining that, maintaining that, requires twice the discipline of any six-pack.

And so, each day has a manageable form.

He rises at six, works out for an hour, showers and dresses according only to season and invitation, never whim, eats standing at the counter while skimming the papers – two broadsheets, one tabloid; it's his job, after all, to peer into the gutter. Then, his crockery rinsed, stacked in the stainless steel Smeg, he walks the four yards to his office, sits at his Ercol desk, and begins.

Such a strange charade, ghosting.

'Ghoulish,' Isobel had said, pun unintended, not long after they'd met, then compared him to a cuckoo or a thief. 'I know it's your job,' she'd continued. 'But still.' Then she'd laughed, faked a shudder, her polished bob flicking forward and catching on her lips.

'I'm only putting on their shoes,' he'd said, resisting the temptation to replace the lock neatly behind one ear. 'That's all.'

'But don't you ever lose sight of yourself?' she'd pushed.

Perhaps. 'Never.' And he'd shaken his head for emphasis.

He didn't tell her then, hadn't told anyone, that his posture was borrowed from a Saudi prince, his extravagant laugh a Whip's affectation, his habit of calling his few male friends 'Buster' the tic of a minor gangster turned grass. Because that's how it works: first he watches them, listens; next he mimics; then, like a magpie, he snatches the shine to keep for himself. He's a thief, yes. But it's no easy win – he can't relax, can't let up, even for a second, or he might be outed, the show might be over. And then where would he be? He shrugs off the thought.

Today, he's a retiring midfielder with a string of cup wins and caps, a game-show-host wife and a sideline in breeding pedigree shih-tzus. As well as a drug habit, two DUIs and a kiss-and-tell mistress, whom James has been forbidden to contact, has signed papers to that effect. It's a part he's played for seventeen weeks – an aeon in rush-publishing terms. But the finish line is a few days away, no more. Then he can give up thinking in dreadful Estuary, can go back to his own accent, received as it is from better men than this; can refuse to pick up the calls for the late-night cocaine confessionals, the morning-after retractions, the desperate, twenty-a-session texts to remind him to 'mention my mum', to 'big up the shih-tzus', to 'tell it so Laura's The One, you know?'

He knows.

So when the phone rings he's braced already, steeled for the same conversation he's had six times before, sixty perhaps.

'Tate,' he answers, swift and efficient.

'James!'

But the voice is a woman's and plum-brandy rich. His editor. His shoulders settle, his stomach releases its cinch. 'Lydia. Thank God.'

'Still fending off the footballer?'

'Regularly.'

She laughs, a deliberate thing, pitched to endear. 'Well, I think you'll like the next one better then. She's far less of a fuck-up.'

She, he registers. 'Christ it's not a Spice Girl, is it?'

Lydia's laugh this time is unfettered. 'Oh, way above their league, darling. Practically Madonna.'

'*Is* it Madonna?'

'God, no. That's gone to Hachette I think.'

'Again?'

'I know.'

'Thank fuck.' His relief, he finds, is genuine. 'So who then?'

Lydia pauses, vaping perhaps, or Facebooking; two in a myriad vices. 'Sorry,' she says. 'Where was I?'

'Who?' he repeats. 'Who is this almost-Madonna?'

'Oh, yes!' Her voice is a child's clap of delight, in its wake an inaudible drum roll as he waits for the name. But she's teasing it out, playing a guessing game. 'Actress,' she says. 'Big league. Once upon a time anyway.'

He fights the urge to sigh. 'I don't know. A Redgrave?'

'Close, but no cigar. RSC favourite. Played Juliet opposite Branagh in her youth. And some big film for Leigh. Or Loach. I forget which. Grim, anyway.'

His muscles tense, his throat constricts.

'Husband's about to stand for Parliament. Sacked off the hereditary title.'

'I . . .' But the words won't come.

'Jesus. You'll kick yourself,' she tells him. 'It's Daisy Hemmings.'

He doesn't drop the phone. That would be lax, amateur. But even seated he has to clutch at pale oak to steady himself, has to force himself to breathe.

Lydia is still talking. 'Hicks as was. Never understood why she took his name when she was already . . . someone. James?'

'Yes,' he says, though faintly.

'You must know her.'

'I . . . I do.'

'So is it a yes, then?'

He racks his memory for the question, slapping away the snapshots that battle for attention, turns up nothing. 'To what?' he has to ask.

'Biog, standard length, full access.'

'When?' He's going through motions now, answering by rote.

'As soon as.'

He shuts his eyes. Musters. Forces his voice to smile, if not his face. 'Can I get back to you?'

Lydia pauses. 'Of course. But close of play? Timing's tight.'

'Of course,' he echoes.

'Good. Now, back to the car crash.'

He flinches. 'Pardon?'

'The footballer?'

'Right. Yes,' he says. 'Absolutely. The footballer.'

Time stretches, elastic. He's unsure how long he sits for: a few minutes, perhaps fifteen, but in a rush it comes to him and he drops to his knees, is hauling open drawers in an aluminium cabinet, flicking through files of cuttings, of carefully clipped bylines, to uncover what he's buried like so much treasure. Like a telltale heart. The papers exhausted, he sets about the bookshelves, trying to remember where he might have slipped it after he'd taken it down from the kitchen mantel. He'd been worried it might fade, or gather a patina, or that Isobel might think his attention was elsewhere. Now he grabs at Nabokovs, pulls to the floor commemorative Penguins and a first-edition Amis (father, not son), before he spies it, snuck in at the end with the other lesser mentions: the trade paperbacks and tenth reissues. An unremarkable fifties Pan, on its cover a doe-eyed heroine in a cloak, clutching her fevered heart: Mary Yellan outside Jamaica Inn.

Trembling now, he spreads foxed pages, shakes them gently, feels the flap of it as it falls, face up, on the floor.

Not a still from a film, nor a head shot, all soft focus and sepia, but a small, square Polaroid of a girl. Nineteen and not yet known. Not yet talked about, lauded, at least not outside that small coterie of hangers-on and hopefuls. But in it her hair is tinted, her lips lacquered, her gaze already off-centre and hyperopic, radiating that air of indolence or exquisite boredom that she strived so hard to acquire. So that even then it is easy to anticipate the string of Oliviers and BAFTA nominations, the Oscar nod.

There is another version, though. A girl who wavered. Who wasn't sure who she was yet, or what she would become. But a girl who, though she doubted herself, believed fervently in him.

Believed he could be anything and anyone, if only he tried.

And, just like that, he is back there again.

In that house.

In that glorious, awful summer.

With Daisy.

2.

Jason, 1988

He falls for the house before he falls for them. Sitting stately, silent, sullen as he squats opposite in the damp, cramped, crap-pot of a quayside pub in Pencalenick, a backwoods backwater if ever there was one.

The first year after he was ferried, complaining, across the water from Fowey, he barely registered its presence. Grief still soaked his bones, the loss of his mother a wound as raw as if she were an organ that had been ripped sharply from him, not eaten slowly away over seven long months in a ward up Derriford. Then, when a second bitter winter softened to a salt-breezed spring, when he managed to widen his eyes to more than a reddened squint he saw the absurdity of it – this shrunken manor house, staring dead-eyed onto the estuary, shuttered stubbornly to the world. 'Like Wonka's Chocolate Factory,' someone – a regular – once said. 'No one goes in, no one comes out.'

It must belong to someone, though. Someone who pays old Minnow Rapsey to come clip the rhododendrons that dot the grounds, to mow the mossy lawn until it's shorn to a soft stubble, like the nap of a velveteen rabbit, or a child's nit-shaven head. In the middle rises a palm tree so that the effect is of an odd, tropical paradise, airdropped as it is on the edge of dense wood and dark water, its outhouse accessible only by a narrow slate path or, more probably, by boat. The whole lot shored up by a stone wall rising grimly from the river, twenty foot at low tide, ten at high, a steel ladder disappearing skew into inky depths. And on the gate, a faded, painted sign, proclaiming its name: Rashleigh.

'An impractical extravagance,' Mrs Mears called it, when she still came to clean at the pub, when she still put up with his father and his whingeing and his drinking. Always his drinking. 'He'll sup the pub dry,' she told Jason once, 'drink it under if you don't watch him.'

But there's no telling his father anything. He's learned that the hard way. And Mrs Mears is gone now so all that's left is him, a big sister itching to get out, and a man barely able to tell one end of a till from the other. But his father has friends – or acquaintances, maybe – enough to keep it ringing, keep the air in the saloon bar thick with smoke and swearing.

They're in there, all of them, when the call comes from the glass-voiced woman. It's Mrs Mears she's after, but there's no joy there.

'Gone,' says his father. 'And good luck to her.'

But the caller isn't choosy, and anyone, it seems, will do for this.

'For what, exactly?' His father stubs a cigarette out on the bar, the ashtray long broken.

Clean, it seems. Get the house swept and turned down.

'So someone's moving in?' says Sadie, interest mildly piqued.

'Just for a week. Kids, she reckons, from "college".' He spits the last word, then coughs onto the floor.

'So what did you tell her?' asks Jason.

His father nods at Sadie. 'I said *she*'d do it.'

Sadie bristles. 'Like bugger I will. Bad enough being a skivvy here.' She's got plans, big plans, has Sadie, and they don't involve a J-Cloth.

'There's a tenner in it,' their father retorts.

'And most of that for you, I bet.'

'Dealer's privilege.'

'I'll do it,' Jason says then, his mind on an album in Liskeard Woolies. 'I don't mind.'

'Like bugger you will.' The old man shakes his head. 'No work for a boy.'

'Not a straight one,' pipes up Fat Man Morris.

Jason flinches at first, but then steadies himself, lets the insult roll off him like water off a paddle, as he's learned to do with all the others. 'Someone's got to do it,' he says. 'Might as well be me.'

And four hours and five pints later his father relents, and, when the thick brown envelope arrives, Jason's the one who opens it, shaking out the key like he's shaking out Charlie's golden ticket.

Which it almost is.

He's spent idle nights imagining Rashleigh, concocting a strange amalgamation of *To the Manor Born* landed glamour and *Dynasty* kitsch, all polished mahogany, creaking teak and a vast, carpeted drawing room, then, suspended above it all, a glass chandelier that throws out dappling diamonds of light – a rich man's version of the glitterball his sister saw in Roxy's once and begged for her bedroom. Fat chance.

The truth is far less fairytale, less . . . obvious, but is still five times any house he's seen inside before. The hallway walls are papered a soft flock gold, the floor tiled in tiny triangles of black and white; elsewhere, off-white paint flakes onto flowered carpet or varnished oak; and, everywhere, ornaments line up to be admired – porcelain dolls and cut-glass ashtrays and Coronation china. A house waiting, holding its breath for someone to come in and love it.

In the glory-hole under the stairs he finds a grey globe of a Hoover and runs it round, sucking up the paint along with dust, dead flies and desiccated woodlice that appear to have befallen some kind of massacre in the pantry. In the kitchen he uncovers more evidence of uninvited guests – hard brown droppings behind a Baby Belling and, in the larder, the musty smell of the mouse who left them. He sweeps them up, sets a trap he finds under the sink, then switches on the fridge, eliciting an electrical buzz and, when he opens the door to deposit a pint of milk and pat of butter, a bright whiteness that pales his face to a ghostly glow. There he pauses for almost a minute, appreciating the luxury of something so simple as light, all too aware that the bulb in the pub's ancient Electrolux blew before they moved in, its own meagre contents – a block of cheap cheese; cost-saving bacon – resigned to fitting gloom.

Upstairs, he vacuums again. Trailing the cleaner behind him like a bored dog, he searches for dirt, and, better, treasure. He finds it, too, in a glass-eyed rabbit; a gold-framed map of the Fowey, its inlets all marked from Mixtow to Pont Pill; and, best of all, books. Cases and cases of them line the walls of the landing – their spines cracked, their pages foxed and dog-eared, but bursting still with words he wants more of. Because words, he reckons, are his ticket out. Must be, since his father's only reading matter is the *Racing Post* and *Razzle*; the only paperbacks the pub's seen, school set texts and, once, a second-hand romance that Mrs Mears left in the laundry, all heavy breaths and heaving bosoms, but he read it anyway.

He tilts one, pulls it from the shelf as if he's plucking a plum from a tree. *Jamaica Inn*, it's called; he's heard of that at least, knows it's up Bodmin way. His mum, he thinks, she must have mentioned it once, on a day trip to Plymouth – the bright lights of BHS and Dingles the closest he's got to the glittering West End, and the furthest he's been from home to this day. He checks the clock on the mantelpiece. Pub's shut for another three hours: his father across the river doing a 'job' for Alan Ransome; his sister's in town too, likely on the harbour wall with a fag in one hand and Alan's boy Barry in the other. Or back at Barry's doing something else entirely.

He baulks at the thought, can't understand what she sees in him, all tattoos and swagger; what she saw in any of them – Steve Saunders with his back acne, Neil Pearce with his slick lines and stolen Honda, Keith Figgis with his reputation for violence and a record to match. That boy from the fair once, too, spinning her and Julie Newton on the Waltzer till Julie threw up on her shoes and Sadie sent her home by herself so she could snog him behind the Rocket.

Maybe it's not them that's the pull but what they promise, he thinks: a way out of here, if only on the back of a bike or hauling a caravan. It's not that he doesn't want that too, just that he wants to go further. But, stuck at school for another year, the only places he's going are between the pages: Pemberley, West Egg, Wuthering Heights. And right now, though it's only twenty odd miles up the road, Jamaica Inn.

Checking the clock again to be sure, he sits on a single bed – one of twins in this room and four he's found so far, plus the double at the top – settles back against the struts of an iron bedstead, and begins to read.

When he wakes he can tell it's late and he opens his eyes half expecting three bears to be standing in wait, wondering who's been sleeping in their bed. But the house is silent, save for the hum of the fridge and the soft tocking of a carriage clock that tells him he's got just half an hour before he's due behind the bar.

He jumps up, pats down the duvet, pushes the book back in its place on the shelf, then, changing his mind, pulls it out again and pockets it. They won't miss one of hundreds, he reasons. And besides, he'll return it later, when they're gone, when he's called on to clean up, which surely he will be.

And, with that thought a nugget in his pocket along with the novel, he closes the door, turns the lock and heads the hundred yards along the path and across the slip home.

'Where the fuck have you been?'

His father's four pints gone and glowering from the throne in his corner court, Fat Man Morris and Alan Ransome his jesters or pages, paid in free beer to flank him. Behind the bar, Sadie's scowling, nods at the clock above the counter. It's gone six, he sees, his stomach slumping, and by a long chalk. He's been had, he realizes, held up by a lie of a timepiece, its gold casing nothing but a flash coat beneath which lurk slovenly works.

'Sorry,' he mumbles. 'There was more than I thought.'

'Well, make sure they pay us for it.'

Fat Man Morris grunts an agreement. 'Not like they can't afford it. Left that place empty best part of ten years. Who's got the cash to do that?'

Jason ignores him, nods a promise. 'I will,' he says. 'I'll get it off them tomorrow.'

'Tomorrow never comes,' says Alan Ransome, ever the devil's advocate.

Sadie smirks. 'It did yesterday.'

It takes ten tense seconds for it to sink in, but then they're roaring with it, heads thrown back in hop-heavy laughter, his father shaking so hard Jason thinks he'll piss himself in a minute. It wouldn't be the first time.

He leaves them then, picks up the empties and takes them through to the back for washing. And, standing there, in the strip-lit kitchen, he sees in stark detail the palace Rashleigh is, and that this pathetic place is not. Sees the surfaces smeared with chip fat, then gathering dust so that everything is layered with a gunge-grey winter coat; smells the sour taint of spilled beer, stale fags and faint disappointment. Beneath his feet not soft wool pile or sleek, clean slate but a sheet of transparent plastic over nylon carpet worn threadbare, though it still sparks static in his slippers so that more than once he's wondered whether he could burn it all down with the soles of his feet if he shuffled with enough determination.

Maybe he will one day. Maybe he'll set a match to it, a bonfire not of vanities but of shame and self-loathing. Watch it disappear in a crack and a flash and a worm trail of ash like a tabletop firework. Maybe he'll go too, escape in its wake.

Maybe.

He checks the cooker clock then. Seven fifteen. They might be here soon – the guests. Though it's a Friday and the bridge'll be chocker, so if it's London they're down from they'll be lucky to make it much before nine. And with that thought he sighs, resigns himself to the stilted wit and smutty conversation that stands in for a social life. For any sort of life.

For now.

3.

James, 2018

The anticipation is almost unbearable. His sleep – for so long an acceptable eight hours – has slipped to six or less. He's not cooked in two days, not eaten in one. Not been able to return Isobel's calls since Thursday. His girlfriend, or lover, perhaps – they don't live together, after all – but it's been three years, for God's sake, and he doesn't know what to say to her, how to act, is ashamed of himself. Because suddenly he's a schoolboy poised, one eye on the clock, waiting for the sweet release of the bell, or a pyjama-ed child on Christmas Eve, desperate for bed just to usher in the dawn yet utterly unable to close his eyes for more than a second. Or perhaps it isn't anticipation so much as dread that squats in his stomach like a grim homunculus, souring it, sending it slopping and sliding and him running to the toilet three times in an hour. Perhaps he's waiting on the hangman's call after all, readying himself to walk the green mile.

And all over a single word.

*

He wakes just before two then again gone four, his stomach a whirligig, alive with the beating of wings. He rises, treads naked across tessellated oak to check his diary, just to be sure. But there it is, in neat italics and Indian ink: Daisy.

That name! He hasn't dared so much as think it for years, but now he rolls it in his mouth, wondering what it will taste like on his tongue when he says it tomorrow – no, Jesus, today – out loud. Will it be soft, savoury like a fine Merlot or meaty olive? Or bitter-lemon sour; thin and difficult? Will he stammer? Will he slip up? Will he give himself away?

Perhaps his yes was a mistake; perhaps he should have told Lydia he couldn't fit it in, that his old paper was sending him on assignment, a long contract abroad. Another Japan. Or he could have claimed it wasn't his bag, such an obvious vanity case. But perhaps if she could find him a disgraced politician, a yesterday's woman or man with bills to pay, a habit to apologize for, a need for rehab, then he'd take the contract twice and happily.

But Lydia had pleaded and upped his fee, and in the end his desire for a healthy bank balance and his unhealthy curiosity had got the better of him. No, not curiosity. That implies his interest is mild, merely piqued. And this, this is a bigger need, as fundamental as sex, as desperate as it too. Despite the dreadful end of it all. Despite his numbered list of reasons to decline, there's a pull to her, a flame that burns as bright as sulphur, and he the helpless moth.

He goes to the mirror then, flicks on the sconce so that his face is bathed in pale, flattering light. He turns his head, inspects the changes: the hair, once lightened to auburn (the sun, he'd said), now, thankfully, silver; the nose and eyes altered, he claimed, for better breathing, better vision; the scar on his temple – the kiss of a Tonka truck thrown in rage – laser-erased now, but the skin beneath still dull and numb.

Satisfied, he tells himself now what he's told himself whenever he's faltered, whenever a flicker of doubt creeps darkly in: that that boy – the boy she knew – is gone.

She'd said it herself: 'Be brighter!' she'd told him. 'Be better. Be whoever you want to be.'

He hadn't believed at the time, dismissing it as the privilege of the already rich, the always beautiful. But Plato was right: necessity breeds invention, and so it was that he invented himself.

He failed to get himself right first time, of course. Like a child learning to walk or write or tell a joke he fumbled and made a fool of himself several times over. He was too desperate, then, to be just like *him*; too determined to ape his mannerisms, his mode of dress, his assumed magnificence. But, a fast learner, he realized swiftly that he could never compete in that man's league. Accents can be faked, an old school scarf bought online, but a history is harder to manufacture – the in-jokes, the rugger stories, the dorm acquaintances now ensconced at the Inns of Court or in the Commons. No, he had to be an outsider, and so it was to classless America he turned.

He rounded his vowels, softened his 't's to 'd's, developing just enough of an accent to sound as if he'd spent years dropping it. He worked up a taste for black coffee, took to carrying a copy of Kerouac in his back pocket, modelling himself on an ersatz Holden Caulfield by way of John Hughes. He knew how to avoid questions that would reveal too much. How to duck and spin and segue. He was as adept at misdirection as a magician pulling a coin from the ear of an unsuspecting child.

At first this anonymity thrilled him – he could slip in and out of corners and conversations without so much as a second glance. No taunts, no jeers, no 'charity case' or 'pikey' anymore. But all too soon insignificance irritated. He wanted to matter. He wanted to count. He wanted, simply, to be wanted. To do that, he knew he had to make himself indispensable. He also knew he needed money – more than he was getting pulling pints and washing pots. And so it was he found his vocation: he took up dealing. Two things: dope and words. The first he rarely touched himself. The second he inhaled as if they were the stuff of life.

From the back room of a bar in Oxford he hawked his wares: quarters and eighths in cellophane wrap alongside three-thousand-word treatises on Keats. While he limited himself to philosophy, the arts, his carte de menu was as wide and indiscriminate as his customer base. From freshers frantic to make their mark to weary final years who had coasted for far too long and found it far easier to plunder daddy's cheque-book than the shelves at the Bodleian. And once, an overseas PhD student, whose inability to use the definite article rendered his dissection of Chaucer as unreadable as the source material. That one kept him fed for a month, and paid his lump of a landlady up front for three.

So he gained a private education of sorts, funded, like Pip's, by benefactors unknown. And, though uncertificated, it was enough to allow himself a first-class honours on an already fraudulent résumé, to fund his move to London.

Like Dick Whittington he arrived, expecting streets paved with gold. But when all he got were gutters filled with dog shit it still didn't disappoint because here he could, finally, be the man he imagined.

The man she told him he could be.

When he wakes again at six it's not to the panicky flap of fictional insects but the buttery hum of Radio 4, and he is almost himself again. He works out, showers, picks his socks, boxers, a clean linen shirt. Texts Isobel to apologize, says he will call her, that he's been caught up with the bloody footballer but it'll be over soon. Everything will be back to normal.

'Normal,' he repeats, as if saying it out loud makes it so.

Because he has no reason to fret, he insists to his reflection, not really. He saw her once in a cafe off Fleet Street, fresh from a features interview and photoshoot, he assumed, from her immaculate complexion. He'd wandered in off shift and, seeing her, startled, dropped his coins in a clatter on the tacky lino. She glanced up and met his wide-eyed stare, but the smile she offered was not one of connection or even curiosity, but merely the surety of the adored, measured in a precise amount, as underweighed as Moroccan black.

So no, she will not know him. Besides, why would she pay it a second thought? Because that boy – the boy he was – wasn't just binned in a Jericho bedsit. That boy, as far as she knows, drowned in an accident almost thirty years ago. That boy is dead.

4.

Bea, 1988

It's half past six and Bea is seething.

Squashed in the back of Muriel's decrepit yellow Beetle is not how this was supposed to be. Playing gooseberry to Hal and her own bloody sister is not how this was supposed to be. Spending their twentieth birthday watching Daisy cavorting – always bloody cavorting, holding court, commanding his attention – while she sits, pith-bitter on the sidelines is not how this was supposed to be.

But nothing bloody is, is it. Not once Daisy strides in, takes the spotlight, takes over.

'Bloody *hell*,' Bea protests as her sister lunges across his lap to spit from the window, her skinny hip slamming into its twin. 'Just swallow them, can't you?'

'What?' Daisy demands. 'You were the one who said they were seedless. It's hardly my fault.'

'I thought you always swallowed, babe.' Hal smirks.

Daisy chokes on vodka, coughs with laughter.

'Seriously?' Bea demands, wiping her sister's saliva from her own sweat-sticky legs.

'Christ, just have a drink, will you?' Daisy proffers the bottle. 'Put us all out of our misery.'

But Bea doesn't need to drink at all hours – not like Daisy – and pushes it away, takes a grape instead.

'You could have called shotgun.'

Bea meets Julian's sneer in the rear-view mirror. 'Hardly,' she replies, looking pointedly at a half-cut, half-stoned Muriel, passed out in the passenger seat. A rivulet of spittle trickles from one corner of her crimson lips while her once artfully smudged eyeliner has smeared down one glittered cheek. With her naked legs wide and her mouth gaping open, she looks for all the world like a blow-up doll, Bea thinks, uncharitably. A butchered one. 'How much bloody further, anyway?' she asks, directing her stare out of the window, away from smug Julian, and the smugger couple.

'A couple of hours if we stick to this road. More if we take the bridge.'

'The bridge is quicker,' Bea argues.

'On a Friday in August?' Julian demands. 'I doubt it.'

Daisy sits up, leans over the gearstick. 'Oh, but we *have* to take the bridge.' She is emphatic. 'The bridge is the thing!'

'What thing?' Hal's full lips pull a cigarette from the soft pack he keeps stuffed up a T-shirt sleeve, fingers flicking a Zippo into life: Mickey Rourke meets Marx, by way of Marlborough College.

'Oh, *the* thing!' Daisy is primed, lit up, as if she is kindling and flame in one, or footlight and leading lady.

Of course, Bea sighs silently. All the world's a stage, and Daisy is centre of it.

'It's . . . it's transformative,' Daisy decides. 'It's a portal! Yes, that's what. A portal to a . . . another kingdom!'

'Like the wardrobe?' Bea suggests, sarcasm sprinkling her words like saccharin on a doughnut.

But Daisy is oblivious, too taken with her vision. 'Yes! The wardrobe. Exactly.'

'And Cornwall is, what, Narnia?'

'God, no,' chides Daisy. 'Not the whole of Cornwall. Just Rashleigh.'

There is a pause while Bea considers the absurdity of this analogy coming from her sister's lips, but any notion of retort is interrupted by Julian.

'Great,' he says. 'Frozen fucking woods and a talking beaver.'

'And an ice queen,' Daisy adds. 'Don't forget that.'

Bea wonders momentarily if this is a dig, but decides quickly there are no circumstances in which Daisy would relinquish such a lead.

'Sounds bloody wonderful.' Hal blows smoke over Muriel's shoulder and out the wound-down window. 'I bags Mr Tumnus.'

'"Bags"?' Bea repeats. 'You can take the boy out of public school . . .'

'Ha fucking ha.' Hal rolls his eyes. 'You can talk.'

Daisy ignores them. 'Oh, no.' She plucks the cigarette from Hal's mouth, pulls hard on it, a ring of pale pink shimmer sticking to the paper. 'You can't be Mr Tumnus. You'll have to be terrible Edmund with the Turkish delight.'

'Why the fuck can't I be Mr Tumnus?' demands Hal, all faux anger and accent again.

Daisy laughs, puts the cigarette back to his lips. 'Because Mr Tumnus is already there,' she says as if it's obvious, as if he's a doted-on but dim child. Then, relenting, she kisses him, drawing the smoke back into her own mouth and exhaling, extravagantly.

Bea mimes gagging as Muriel finally raises her head, her tangled curls for all the world an Aslan mane.

'I'll be Susan,' she manages. Then promptly vomits into the plastic bag placed judiciously on her lap by Julian. 'Shit,' she says, seemingly surprised, before spewing out another plume of purple Pernod and black, mixed with a packet of Fruit Pastilles and half a Mars bar, the only solids she's bothered with since breakfast.

Julian sighs. 'Are you quite finished?'

'I think so.' Muriel retches purposefully but pointlessly, pulling up nothing but a sour burp. 'Yes, definitely done.'

'Thank God,' says Hal. 'Get rid of it, will you, babe?'

'I suppose we'll have to stop now,' Bea mutters.

'Bugger that,' says Julian. 'We've only just filled up with fuel. I'm not stopping again until we get there. She can throw the sodding thing out of the window.'

'Actually, mate, I could do with a slash.' Hal stretches, testing his bladder, wincing.

'Are you driving?' asks Julian, raising an eyebrow as he sets a dare. 'No. Because I'm the only one willing to stay sober. So if I say we're not stopping, we're not stopping.'

'I'm sober,' says Bea. 'I'll drive.'

But no one is listening to her.

Hal snorts. 'Fine,' he says, smiling widely. 'You give me no choice, my man.'

Bea waits and watches, half in horror, half in hope, as he fumbles with his button fly.

'No!' Daisy shrieks in mock alarm.

'Don't worry,' he assures all occupants, 'I'm not going to piss on the floor.' He picks up a bottle, checks it's empty. 'See, I said starting early would make sense. Ladies and gentlemen, I give you the portable toilet.'

And with that he flops out his cock, sticks the tip to the lip of the bottle, and lets out a steady stream of stinking urine.

Against her better judgement, against all attempts to focus on the file of traffic heading east, Bea is transfixed. By the audacity of it, yes, the baseness, but more by the dick itself. An object she's spent far too long wondering about, given it's not hers to covet. She feels herself flush.

'Get enough of an eyeful?' Julian asks.

'Oh fuck off, Buchanan,' she tells him, adding a quick 'vile' for his benefit. And Hal's. Though 'vile' is a lie and she knows he knows it.

The last drips of piss plink into the Pernod dregs, and Hal sighs, satisfied, and puts his dick back in his pants. 'Better out than in.' He grins, then winks at her.

Helpless as ever, faced with his humour, Bea feels her own lips twitch into a half-smile. But before it can spread she forces it away along with her gaze. A moment later she hears the squeal of Muriel, the smash of glass on tarmac, followed by the thwack of a bag of sick.

And just like that, just like always, the moment is over.

Five miles pass in forty minutes, the Friday night traffic as slow as Julian said it would be, the car crawling past grim, granite terraces and, intermittently, the pathetic pretence of pebble-dash, intended to conceal sins but only succeeding in rendering them pock-faced and pimpled. 'Are we nearly there yet?' Bea asks, eventually, her voice pitch-perfect with child-like indignation and impatience.

'I hope so,' opines Hal. 'Or your sister might need to shit in a biscuit tin.'

'Charming.' Julian shakes his head.

As if Daisy would do any such thing, thinks Bea. Christ, she probably shits glitter as it is. If at all.

But no one is shitting or pissing anywhere, it turns out. They don't need to. Because less than a minute later Daisy calls, 'The bridge! I see it!'

'Don't be ridiculous,' snaps Bea. 'It's miles yet.'

Muriel, heavy eyes still only half open, peers into the distance. 'No, it's true,' she lisps in wonder – a lisp Bea is sure is entirely contrived, borrowed, all the better to play baby. 'Look.'

Reluctantly, Bea looks, and sees to both her dismay and delight that they are right after all; sees the concrete and steel suspension splendid in the late summer sun; sees the river beneath, wider than a mile, or so it seems, and studded with sailing boats like toy yachts on a pond. And, as they cross the chough-covered borderline midway on the bridge, despite Hal, despite everything, she believes for all the world as if she *is* walking through a portal, as if she is transformed, or about to be.

Daisy hoots. 'Do you feel it?'

Hal kisses her hard. 'I totally fucking feel it.'

But back down to earth, on the Saltash side, Bea sinks into the seat, and herself again. 'Well,' she announces to no one in particular. 'All I can say is that Mr Fucking Tumnus had better have our bloody supper on.'

5.

James, 2018

J ames sees everything.

'I am a camera,' he tells himself; his shutter open, always. Because that is how it is for ghosts.

While they slip, spectre-like, in and out of their hosts' voices, lives, worlds, they must not miss a thing: their walk, their talk, the words they choose, the way they say 'schedule' with a hard 'c', as if they are American. Every pixel, every pinhead-small detail must be noticed and noted lest its absence or abuse gives away the game.

And so he's grown, part flâneur, part scout. Like Baudelaire's dandy he contrives to idle through life, or so he seems to suggest, his wide, bland gaze roaming indiscriminate over all. But this loucheness, this laissez-faire is pure affectation, and underneath the surface he is hive-busy, his once-spindly legs a swan's, or a cyclist's, pedalling furiously to keep him moving, afloat. Because he cannot afford to get it wrong, is terrified of what might happen if he does – a Cinderella despatched back to rags.

But when he turns his eyes on himself this morning, he's pleased with what he sees.

He sees money – enough of it – in the cut of his cotton shirts, the thread count of his sheets: the spoils of stories and proceeds of pills. Though his dealing days are over, the sideline endured into early journalistic assignments, topping up paltry pay cheques and stringer fees to keep him out of the studentesque squalor of his stable-mates.

He sees elegance, practised perhaps, but note-perfect and sure.

He sees breeding, too, borrowed though it is from books and the bars of Oxford. But still the kind that will open, if not gilded gates, then at least the door of the Groucho or Arts.

And now, it seems, of her Camberwell home.

He takes a bus – two in fact, changing at Elephant. Not because he's cheap, but because in a taxi he will be forced to talk – to feign an interest in stocks or sports or, God forbid, immigration – when all he wants to do is watch, breathe it in – the world – like so much nicotine. So he can work it out, reset his place in it.

So that he knows the fat-ankled woman ate bacon for breakfast, the salty taint tangled in her extravagant Afro. That the boys with the buzz cuts are still Friday-night high, their pupils dripped ink pools, their skin sallow and sour. That the taut-stomached teenager who catches their eyes, flips them a finger, has a date or a death wish, sweating as she is into flamingo-pink polyester on a day that is already sending the mercury soaring. It's exhausting, really, all these Sherlockian deducements, but he cannot switch off, not anymore – is alert even against his own better judgement.

They're disgorged at the green a full fifteen minutes early, so, biding his time, he maunders along. Sees as he walks alongside the iron fence a boxer dog, busily indifferent as it sniffs and then squats; the woman who bends to pick up its shit indifferent herself to the child who claims he is hungry and hot, the chocolate on his chin and his thin vest belying his whines.

He sees as he steps onto her street the sashes and pale stock of once-suburban South London, the bricks mixed with stucco, that great plastercast equalizer. Levelling the land as it rendered, so that any grocer who dreamed might sculpt himself a marble facade. But in this rotten pocket, packed with pound shops and chicken shacks, it has cracked and crumbled leaving only a handful of roads in their intended splendour.

He wonders, now, why she chose it, this deliberate downmarket, when she could have sauntered down Sloane Street, or climbed Primrose Hill with the rest of her set. Was it Hal and his 'people' he so lauded and loved? Or a snub to the father he didn't? Or is this, in fact, all her own work?

He's halfway along now, counting down doors, and as he closes the gap between miles and years he feels like a child about to poke a toe in an enchanted forest, feels the crackle and snap of a strange kind of electricity that separates this world and hers. It is, he knows, he fears, the hum of possibility, of hope. And at this his stomach slackens and swirls. Because he knows more than any that it is the hope that kills you.

A first-year called Hurst told him that, as he bought a

quarter to go with his cant. Though if he'd bothered to read the painstaking pages James slid in front of him he'd have put it more eloquently he imagines, or in deeper detail. Pulled out Pandora's jar or, as James did, pressed Nietzsche into service. For Friedrich was right: hope is the worst of all evils, prolonging, as it does, the torments of man.

But, God, what exquisite torment.

Feeling a twinge, he adjusts the canvas bag hanging over one shoulder – a Herschel – heaves it higher, weighed down as it is with so much . . . well, Daisy. In the past week he's revised as if for a final. Has collected and hoarded snippets of information like silver or stamps. Picked through the gutter press and gossip mags for diamond-bright detail: that she favours black for the red carpet, lending her a gravity lacking in the upstarts and ingénues. That she eats two eggs, poached, for breakfast but rarely takes lunch. That she no longer smokes, but Moët remains her drug of choice. That and a Mars bar, or so the *Mail* claims, sliced into small pieces, the better to deceive.

From the screen he gleans more: that the fine lines that once feathered her eyes and furrowed her forehead have been cleverly faded so that she seems to be living her life in reverse. That her breasts are augmented, but tastefully so. That her tummy is, in all likelihood, tucked.

From the absurd to the ordinary he knows it all.

But he knows more too. The unusual and unspoken, at least to the press.

That she believes in a god, but not in a heaven. That she once ate a woodlouse to make good on a dare. That she is scared of the obvious as well as the obscure: spiders and slow worms, rat tails and rabbits, dragons and demons and dying alone. Or maybe she's outgrown them now, these nursery fears, has had to forsake them when faced with the world.

He hopes not.

But he's dithering now, dawdling awfully, so that when he checks his watch he sees he has less than a minute to make it on time and four hundred metres or more. So he speeds up – fast enough to rule out rudeness, but not so quick he risks a sweat, though his shirt is deliberately thin, his loafers sock-free. This last concession he sees now was a foolish one; his feet slip on the wicking insoles, and he has to stop to steady himself.

But this is all necessary. He cannot afford a single mistake. He has to be clear who he is.

My name is James Tate, he tells his faltering self. I am forty-seven years old. This is a job, nothing more. No different to Cameron. No bigger than Blair. And who is she anyway? An ageing actress, a has-been, yesterday's news.

He tells himself this, chants it over and over. But knows, despite it all, that the last line is a lie.

She isn't jaded, faded, fallen from grace. Not a has-been or a discarded headline.

She is Daisy, Daisy! Grown more luminous than he ever thought possible, than the already technicolour version he fell for that first night. So that, before he grasps the gilt, gaping mouth of the brass lion, he must wipe a slick of sticky salt from his clammy hand and swallow stale gum.

Then, solid as an ox, he knocks. Prepares himself for a lackey, or Hal.

But seventeen seconds later the door opens and it's not Hal, not a housemaid – do people have those, anymore? Perhaps he should check – no, there, in front of him, is Daisy. And he is floored, transported, by two hundred and more miles and thirty years to a smoke-thick saloon bar, and a boy who felt, for the first time, what true beauty meant, who understood, suddenly, Byron's cloudless climes, who saw what Sadie strived so hard to be and to chase.

'Oh!' she says, in delight or surprise.

He opens his mouth. 'It's—'

But she doesn't need telling, does she. 'James, isn't it?' she says with a smile. 'Well, you'd better come in.'

6.

Jason, 1988

He's clock-watching. Counting the hours, wondering when – if – they'll come, waiting for something – anything – to happen. He's heard the car all right: a coughing, clattering thing that pulled up or passed out at the top of the lane over an hour ago. He's heard *them* too – a pack of them clambering out, calling vague names and hunting for keys.

'What's got into you?' Sadie asks as he cracks a glass trying to stack it.

'Nothing,' he says.

But it *is* something. Though he can't explain what, can't fathom it himself, this want. This feeling of being on the crisp cusp of something. Maybe it's mere desperation; he's clutching at straws, clinging to a raft in the messy wreck of their lives. But whatever it is he's giddy with it, his feet tip-tapping the flags and catching static from the carpet so that Sadie flinches when he pokes a primed finger to her forearm.

'Fuck's sake,' she complains. 'Grow up.'

'Language,' warns their father.

'Hypocrite,' she flings back without thinking, then freezes, aware she may have struck a match.

It's Jason's turn to flinch now, waiting to see if his father'll rise to it, lift a finger of his own, or a fist. But he's too far away, and far gone as well. If he bothered, he'd probably miss.

'Fuck off, yourself,' he says finally to a standing, swaying ovation from Fat Man Morris and Alan Ransome.

They're still clapping when the door swings on its hinges, so hard it cracks against the granite surround, sending his father into a conniption of cursing and Alan Ransome clattering back to his seat. And rendering Sadie surprisingly silent.

Though he knows what's got her tongue. It's trapped his too, and caught him poised, pint glass midway from the pump, as he drinks them in.

Four of them, he counts: two boys and two girls – women, really, and men, too. Older than him but not by too much. Though they're worlds away in every other respect. The boys are as full of themselves as the bare-bellied townies but can back it up with money, he thinks. And the girls . . . one of them has hair like a lion, and make-up like a Falmouth tramp, or so his mam would have said. Though he can see Sadie eyeing it, green-irised. But that one's an irrelevance anyway, too obvious. All lipstick and glitter and a faint smell of sick. No, it's the other girl who matters, he can sense it already; her pale hair chopped off at the chin, her eyeliner neat, her smile wide and guileless.

And directed at him.

'If the wind changes, you'll stay like that,' Sadie says, pushing past now, pushing her tits out as well.

He comes to, sets himself right, sets the pint glass down on the bar. 'Len,' he calls.

Fat Man Morris walks wide-legged and wobbling, picks up his pint and heads back to his stool, spilling licks of it on himself and more on the floor.

'Free for all, is it?' asks the dark bloke, all bravado and swank.

'He's got a tab,' Jason says.

A tab as long as a six-year-old's Christmas list and twice as improbable, though his father stopped logging it a long time ago, let alone chasing it up. 'Jeanie's paying,' he sometimes says. But the life insurance has already been bled dry twice over, and the brewery will come calling soon. So Sadie reckons.

But these people are paying customers. Might be for a week. And big spenders, besides. And anyway, he needs them drunk and soon, the better to blur the damp and the dirt. The terrible dereliction of it.

'What can I get you?' he says then.

'Two pints of Flowers, two vodka and tonics,' replies Swank.

'Actually, I'll have a vodka,' the other boy says. The strawberry-blond one, stuck-up, with a nose to be looked down. 'Or I'll be pissing all night.'

'Fine. One pint, three vodka and tonics, and what food have you got?'

'Food?'

Swank looks at him as if he's a moron. 'Food. You know – scran.' He tries again. 'Scampi? Chicken in a basket? A sandwich?'

'Crisps,' Jason tells him. 'Plain, salt and vinegar, or cheese and onion. And peanuts.'

'Told you,' the other shouts.

Swank sighs. 'Four packets of crisps,' he says. 'Any flavour. Put them on the tab.'

Jason feels his stomach slacken, flicks a glance at his father.

'Tabs for locals,' the old man shouts over, then mutters under his breath, sending Alan into spasms again.

The girl – the bobbed one – turns, and he sees her bare back, the ridges of her spine, the black strap of her bra showing as if it's nothing, or a statement itself. 'But we *are* locals,' she insists. 'We're from over the road. From Rashleigh,' she adds, as if this will be the ticket.

It isn't.

'Tabs for locals,' his father repeats. And with that he's lost interest, gone back to his booze and his bragging and Fat Man Morris's farts.

'Like the Slaughtered sodding Lamb,' mutters Swank as he slaps a tenner on the top.

'Pardon?' Jason asks.

'It's from a film. An eighteen.' He grins. 'So you won't have seen it.'

And for that, and the rest, Jason hates him, though he knows he's not wrong. This strange place, cut-off and clois- tered, that stares down and scoffs at incomers, though they're the only ones keeping the pub open. And then, barely. Because he *has* seen it – *American Werewolf*. Though he doesn't mention the bootleg tape or Barry Ransome's back room where they watched it.

Instead he says nothing, just rings up the till and scatters a handful of change onto the sticky bar.

'Keep it,' says Swank.

'There's nearly a fiver,' Jason says.

'Call it a tip,' comes the reply, accent slipped from comp school canteen to high table and back. And, taking the pint and two vodkas he saunters to the corner, sets up his own court, his henchman and lion-headed concubine slipping in by his side.

But she – the other girl – lingers.

'Thanks,' she says, taking the last glass.

Then, she reaches out and touches his arm, not a trick this time, like his to his sister, but he snatches it back as if scorched anyway.

She laughs then, delighted as a child. 'It's all right,' she says, 'I won't bite.'

'I . . . I know that,' he mumbles.

'Daisy,' she says, and holds out a hand this time.

He looks at it, sees from its position it is meant to be kissed, not clasped.

It's a dare, he thinks. But does he? Dare. In front of Sadie? In front of his father?

He takes it, shaking, kisses it quick, feels the churn of his stomach as insects flap to get out.

'And you are?' she asks, still waiting.

'Oh.' Heat pinks his cheeks quick. 'Sorry, it's Jason.'

She stares at him for a second. 'No,' she says finally. 'That's not it at all.'

'It's not?' He feels moth wings soar.

'Oh, definitely not,' she replies. 'You're not a Jason. In fact, I know exactly who you are.'

'Who?' he urges, intrigued now.

'Why, you're my faun,' she tells him. 'You're Mr Tumnus of course. We *have* come through a portal after all!'

He doesn't understand, wonders if it's an in-joke, and at his expense. Though the way she stares at him isn't with spite, or scorn.

'Mr Dickhead, more like,' says Sadie, sticking a pin in a birthday balloon.

He drops the girl's – Daisy's – hand hastily and watches as she drifts to the corner, drapes herself across the dark-headed one.

Shit. He *is* a dickhead. Of course she's taken. How could she not be? Of course she's *his*.

Or he hers, Jason begins to think as the court turns its attention firmly to the girl. As she spins a tale, spools laughter from them like so much silk thread.

He feels Sadie watching them, the same way she watches all the emmets: with a mixture of envy and hate. Catches her flirting too, later, indiscriminate in her affections, a scattergun approach to sex that has served her well enough if the prize is a shag behind the boatsheds. She starts with the stuck-up one, giggling ridiculously when he lies and says he likes her T-shirt, then, not a political bone or thought in her, nods like a dashboard dog when Swank rants about taxes.

'It's fucking Thatcher,' he rails.

'It's always fucking Thatcher,' says Daisy, glancing at the bar, catching his eye again, claiming a conspiracy between them.

A conspiracy he clutches at like a gold coin.

'Look at the miners,' adds Swank, warming to his cause.

At that magic word, his father lifts his head from its slump. 'Miners are fucking martyrs,' he says. 'Martyrs. And Maggie screwed us all. Fucking Thatcher,' he repeats, drawing out the name as if he's summoning a demon.

'Used to be one,' Sadie explains. 'A miner, I mean. Tin. Till they cut jobs at South Crofty.'

Swank nods like he knows all about it – knows the thankless black pit like the back of his hand. Though it's clear from his fingers the only hard graft he's done is holding a pen or rolling a fat one. But that doesn't stop him. 'Cutting off our coal,' he says. 'Selling off steel.'

'You should do something,' says Sadie, breathless and pumped with possibility.

'I will,' says Swank. 'I am.'

'What?' she asks, wide-eyed, expecting a protest, maybe, political ambition.

'A play,' he tells her. 'Agitprop.'

He says it as if it is an Abracadabra. But it's no more than an absurdity, even Jason sees, and laughs. 'Theatre?' he asks. 'Really?'

'What's wrong with theatre?' Daisy asks.

He looks at her, panicked, sees the conspiracy hanging in the balance. 'I . . . it's just . . .'

But he can't find an answer that doesn't sound like his father, that hasn't been his father, jeering at him, calling him 'Juliet' for wearing tights. 'It's what they wore,' he'd said, desperate. But his father was having none of it and so he'd walked bare-legged onto the school stage that night and stayed off sick for the rest of the run, Simon Heap stepping up as Hamlet and getting the applause and the plaudits.

'How old are you, anyway?' asks Swank then, lighting up a cigarette with a flick of his wrist.

'What?'

'He's old enough,' Fat Man Morris pipes up, a stand-in himself for Jason's father who's gone outside for a piss, the toilet being a yard too far for his beer-filled bladder.

'Hal, don't start,' Daisy says, taking the cigarette from his lips and putting it between her own.

He holds up his hands. 'I'm not,' he insists, then turns back to Jason. 'Seriously, you can't be more than, what? Sixteen?'

'What's it to you?' Jason is on the backfoot, panicked, not sixteen, but still a year too young to be behind a bar. But what else is there to do?

'Leave it,' pleads Daisy.

'You've got rights, you know that?' He – Hal, is it? – pulls another fag from the soft pack up his sleeve, lights it. 'Laws to protect you. It's child labour.'

'Round here?' asks Sadie. 'Don't make me laugh. Kids are down the yard working cash in hand soon as they're old enough to get their end away.'

'Twelve then,' says Fat Man Morris, and roars at his brilliance.

Jason shrinks. 'I'm not a child,' he says quietly.

'Leave it,' repeats Daisy to Hal. 'Leave him be.'

'She's right,' the stuck-up one sighs. 'If we get chucked out the nearest pub's a ferry-ride away.'

'Or a swim,' says Sadie.

Hal raises an eyebrow. 'Is that a dare?'

She grins, thinking she's got him. 'Maybe.'

'I love swimming!' says the lion-haired girl then, sitting up as if she's just woken from a brilliant dream.

'Shut up, Muriel,' says Stuck-up. 'You're too pissed to swim.'

'Shut up, yourself, *Julian*,' she retorts, though half-hearted and through a smile.

'All of you, shut up,' Daisy says then. 'I can't hear myself think.'

'What?' asks Muriel, low-voiced, expectant. 'What is it?' As if she might produce a rabbit from a hat at any moment.

'A bottle,' she says instead. 'That's what we need. We can take it back to Bea.'

To be what? wonders Jason.

'You can come.' Daisy turns to him, as if she's heard.

But he can't, can he? Not until Alan Ransome and Fat Man Morris have sodded off. Not until he's got his father up the stairs and onto his mattress. Not until he's cleaned up and cashed up.

'I'll come,' says Sadie.

'No you won't,' says a voice.

Jason looks to the door to find his father zipping his fly as he flounders back in. Jesus.

'But—'

But nothing. 'Shut up,' he tells her.

And she does.

'Another time,' says Daisy, placating.

Sadie shrugs, and settles on serving Hal a half bottle of rum and a full one of Coke.

'Ta, love,' he says, all wide boy again. Then, downing his dregs, he leads his band to the door, not one of them looking back.

Not one.

Not yet.

Until – there! – she turns. 'Until tomorrow, Mr Tumnus,' Daisy tells him. Then, quick as an imp, she too is gone. And it's just him and his sister and a pissed trio of fools.

And that is the moment it both begins and is over, he thinks later.

The moment hope opens the door and slips through the chink.

The moment he falls for her. For all of them, perhaps, despite their pomp, their privilege, their silver spoons.

Against them he knows his life is thin and insignificant. Against them he is stretched see-through as cellophane; no more than a ghost of a boy.

But, still, she *sees* him. Sees something in him, he's sure of it.

As he collects up their glasses, wipes down their table, he's sure of something else too: that she has the power to change him, to colour him in. To take the clay of him and mould a better boy – no, a man. He's seventeen after all, not long off it, not a child anymore.

Then he spies it, slipped into a pleather crevice on the banquette: like the trailing tail of a mouse but glinting silver. He pulls at it, sees it's a bracelet – sterling – studded with charms: a dancing dog and a delicate bee and a two-faced mask of Janus. In his mind's eye he fastens it around a thin wrist, watches it catching the light and jangling when she claps with delight, when she pushes back her pale, bobbed hair.

And there he has it – the perfect excuse. He will go, in the morning, first thing. He will take back her treasure before she clocks it's missing; collect the cleaning money as well before his father clocks that. And, clutching the bracelet in one hand and that thought in the other, he calls last orders with a smile that is, for the first time, more than relief.

7.

James, 2018

Oh, he's seen her before, of course, but usually at one remove. On the screen, or, once, on a date he'd tried and failed to wheedle out of, from the cheap seats, so that her face was a mannequin, caked in panstick, and his, if she'd looked, no more than a blur.

But here she is – Daisy! – in vivid detail and extreme close-up for the first time in almost three decades. Thinner now, if that is possible; concealer covers the dark circles beneath her eyes, and her shade of blonde comes from a bottle these days, but there is no mistaking her. The elegant jut of her jawbone; the eyes, blue as a pool; the skin pale. And he recalls in an instant her coating herself in sunscreen, her legs shimmering as she lay out on the harbour wall.

Something burgeons in him. 'It's me!' he wants to scream. 'Remember?' But he is good at this, has had to be, at the tamping down of urges, the wetting of embers – though God knows it's cost him – and so he swallows and nods and follows when she says, 'This way.'

She leads him down a broad hall, unhung canvases tagged 'Saatchi' stacked casually against the wall, as if they're

ten-pound repros from the Walworth Road, or the kinder-
garten work of some unnamed nephew or niece. Though
there *is* a child. Grown-up now, but one who once crayoned
a face below the dado rail, a daub unnoticed or unworthy
of removal, or perhaps an installation in itself. It displays,
he thinks, the disregard for surroundings only the truly rich
or truly poor can afford. For, despite it all, this contrived
shabbiness, he can see the unmistakable sheen of inherited
wealth.

'Stop it,' she says, as two dogs – whippets, what else?
Their gaunt flanks as delicate as her own – scuttle from a
side room, follow her, tic-tacking their way thinly across the
tiles. Nervous, devoted things, one pushes a pointed snout
at her hand, whimpers, angling for attention.

'Oh, Egg, do pipe down,' she scolds, but pats him all the
same. 'Absurd creatures, my husband tells me.'

He scrabbles for words, for a smart retort or just an astute
observation. Manages, 'I like them.' Then chides himself
silently.

'The other one's Hobson. Not my choice.'

He laughs at the joke, realizing too late she hadn't meant
to make one. Sweat blooms on his back. 'I'm sorry,' he blurts.
'I didn't mean—'

'Don't be.' She dismisses it with a flap of her hand. 'It's a
daft name. My daughter's idea. And he doesn't care. Do you,
boy?'

They're in a kitchen now, all wide, off-white walls and
clutter; a sort of minimalist chaos. How very Daisy, he catches
himself thinking. Because everything about her seemed to

burst at the seams – ideas, tears, laughter – as if her tiny frame couldn't contain the enormity of her being. Here her life spills onto every surface: a fat-spattered stainless steel range; a mantel stacked with vague nudes in various shades; an ashtray overflowing with lipstick-ringed tips, proving she's lied to the press, a fact that delights him: that he, at last, is party to this secret.

'Tea?' she offers. 'Coffee? Or something stronger?'

He glances at the railway clock that vies for position with a pink neon shop sign. 'Oh, I'm fine,' he replies. Though it's tempting, he has learned the hard way he can't risk drink.

She tilts the half empty bottle of red – a decent Rioja – sets it down again. 'You're wise. Coffee, then.'

She clicks on a kettle, busies herself with cups, and he finds himself, again, lost for words. He, who practises small talk as if it were script for an audition. Who has written himself as many roles as Molière or Shaw, with him alternatively the wit, the enigma, the cad.

But now he's the fool, the pitiful Malvolio, reduced to a 'yes' to milk and 'no' to sugar, though at least he manages not to stutter out some laboured joke about one of them being sweet enough already. He's still weighing up whether and where to sit when she announces that she thought they should talk in the study.

'Of course,' he replies, grateful for the cue. And, like one of her dogs, hoping for a pat – a scrap of affection or attention – he trails Daisy limply again, back down the hall and into a dimly lit side room he'd assumed was for dining.

'Oh.' She stops short. 'I didn't know you were in.'

The dogs skitter through her legs leaving him standing awkwardly in the door, too far in to retreat elegantly, but far enough to see who she's addressing. His long hair shorn now, but still defiantly curling. His face weathered and unshaven, both deliberately so, James suspects. His single earring gone, though the ragged hole he made himself with a safety pin must surely remain.

Hal.

His heart jinks, a hare aware of a farmer, and he pulls back a fraction, though not out of sight.

'Where else would I be?' Hal snaps a laptop shut.

'Out?' she suggests, as she sets cups slopping onto a stained desk that seems to heave under the weight of paper. 'It is glorious after all.'

Hal ignores her, looks through her, at James. Sizing him up. And it takes all he has to stand straight, to remain steady against the beating of wings that brush his stomach. But Hal can't remember, James reminds himself. Back then the man barely acknowledged his existence. And, even if he does recall it, like everyone else – Daisy, Sadie, his father – he believes Jason to be dead.

And so, it seems, James passes the test.

'Hal,' he says eventually, and, like the gentleman he was raised to be, offers James his hand.

James steps forward and takes it, praying to a god he long stopped believing in that Hal cannot sense the tremor.

'So you're the writer?'

He forces a smile. 'I am.'

'What did you say your name was?'

'I didn't. It's James. James Tate.'

That name! Bland, two-a-penny, but like Christmas Day Turkish delight on his tongue, he marvels at it still; that it is his, all year round. Recalls the thrill of being able to change his very being. The overwhelming pressure too. Like being asked to choose only one food for the rest of his life, or one desert island record. It had to be perfect. It had to fit, and fit all purposes, too.

Of course he didn't pick just one. He couldn't. Like a child given free rein in a sweet shop he tested several for satisfaction. So he has been Thomas and Timon, Simon and John, and once, drunk on Bulgarian wine and vintage Waugh, Charles. But old habits were hard to shake and he found himself wondering who these strangers were when their names were called, taking too long to realize it was him being summoned. At least this way it's close enough that he turns his head in automatic response.

'James,' Hal repeats. 'Should I have heard of you?'

'I hope not,' he replies, repeating the well-worn answer. 'That's sort of the point.'

Hal looks back blankly.

'I'm a ghost writer,' he explains, patiently now, relief soaking his words, slowing them. 'If I stood out or . . . stood up to be counted then the whole charade would collapse.'

'Right.' Hal nods, though appears somewhat unconvinced.

James opens his mouth to embellish but she cuts him off, hands on her hips now like a cross toddler. 'So can we have the room?'

'You're starting now?' Hal looks at his wrist. 'It's Saturday.'

'Not starting, darling. Just going through the details. The small print.'

'I told her *I'd* do it, if she was that bloody determined.' He's talking to James again; trying to get him on side perhaps. 'But apparently I'm not good enough.' He smirks then, but James knows from old it's bravado, false.

'And I told him he's too close,' she says. 'And anyway, biography is so not his bag. Says it's self-indulgent.'

'It is,' Hal insists. 'The whole thing's a bloody indulgence if you ask me.'

'Well we didn't. And, Hal, please . . .'

'Fine.' Hal raises his hands in defeat, stands and gathers his laptop, an iPhone, a pair of horn-rimmed glasses – Gucci, James notes. 'Good luck,' he says as he trudges past.

'Thank you,' James replies, and finds, to his disappointment, he means it.

And then it is the two of them again, the air thick and bristling, as if the room has drawn in a breath.

She pushes books off a chaise longue and lies back on fading toile. 'Sit,' she says, nodding opposite at a wingback chair in fraying velvet.

Obediently, he does as he's told, the dogs also obliging, collapsing at her feet in an elegant faint, like underfed ingénues or especially fey guards.

For want of occupation he reaches to hand her her coffee but she waves it away as if fending off a tiresome fly so he finds himself ignoring his own, despite his craving for caffeine, even from a cheap, chipped, cafetiere, missing, as he did, his daily espresso.

'So why *am* I doing this?' he asks then, aware even as he says it that this isn't mere qualification but a pathetic quest for validation. God knows, he's asked himself the question enough times. He hadn't even wanted the job, has tried so hard to stay away all these years, and yet here he is, a love-sick seventeen year old again, risking everything for affection.

'Is that an existential question?' she bats back.

This joke is deliberate and his laugh almost genuine. 'No. I mean why *not* Hal? He is a writer, isn't he?'

'A playwright,' she says. 'And was, not is. And if he'd been any good at it, he'd be in rehearsals right now, not running for bloody government.'

A flicker of interest twitches in him, which he puts down to instinct, the seeking of story. 'You don't approve?'

'Am I on record?'

He panics, holds up his hands. 'No. I—'

'I'm joking,' she placates. 'Yes of course I approve. It was me who pushed him to do it.' She looks up at the ceiling as if for inspiration, or courage, then back at him. 'Between you and me, he should have done it years ago. Would have, I suspect, if his father had popped his clogs sooner.'

James shifts uncomfortably, though the sentiment is hardly alien.

'You think I'm being flippant?'

'No.' And this is gospel solid. He knows she isn't flippant. Just unwaveringly Daisy.

'You'll get used to me.'

'I'm sure I will,' he replies. Though this time it *is* a lie. Because, of course, he already is.

The terms are these: he may have access to her between the hours of ten and four, wherever she is, whatever she's doing. He may record all interviews, and copy anything he needs from her own personal archives. He may also, if he desires, interview Hal and, if she agrees, their daughter. Though that, Daisy tells him, will be down to him to argue the case and possibly pointless anyway, as therapy has 'skewed her view' and she still pretends to be an orphan when it suits her, though not, Daisy sighs, when it comes to paying her rent.

But if the terms are generous, the timing is less so.

'Two weeks?' he repeats. It's not long enough. Is it? Or perhaps it's too long. Perhaps he should grasp at this, a lily not a nettle, and be in and out as slick and quick as a burglar before she catches him.

'If you don't want the job . . .'

But he does. At the threat of denial he realizes, to his astonishment and dismay, that he *wants* to stay; he has a foot in the door and wants – needs, almost – to keep it there.

'No,' he insists. 'It's just—'

But he cuts himself off as Daisy is standing now, has heaved a pile of paper from the shelf and, to his astonishment, drops it on the floor, the thud sending Egg yelping and Hobson careering out of the door in a flurry of dust.

'Seventeen playscripts,' she tells him. 'Not one of them more than half-finished.'

'I . . .'

'Now you know why I can't ask Hal. He starts off at full steam then loses patience, or faith, or both. And I have neither the time nor the inclination to pester him anymore.'

'Isn't your daughter a writer?' He is testing now, checking, making sure this is watertight.

'Clementine? Hardly. She's an academic. All words like "liminal" and "hegemony". Hideous.' She opens a desk drawer, pulls out a packet of Camels. 'Besides, Lydia said you're good at . . . this sort of thing.'

He nods at the compliment. 'It's just . . .' He clutches for something. 'Two weeks isn't very long to . . . get to know you.'

'Oh, don't worry,' she says, flipping the lid of a Zippo, clicking the flint, 'I'm terribly shallow.'

'I doubt it,' he answers – another pat, a sop, though he knows it to be true. 'Then, yes,' he says, emphatic now, the word a party popper or rocket going off, filling the air with sparks and sulphur. 'I want the job.'

'Good.' Eyes closed, she breathes out a cloud. Then, opening them again, looks pointedly at him. 'But this –' she wafts at the smoke – 'is strictly off limits.'

'Of course,' he tells her. 'You'll get final copy approval anyway.' She laughs then and he wonders if she's been caught out before, indignant, suddenly, strangely, at this imagined slight. 'Really,' he assures her.

'Oh, it's not that,' she says, sitting back on the chaise, her legs crossed in such a way that her dress gapes and he has to look away to stop himself staring at her upper thighs and a glimpse of knicker. 'It's the whole thing.'

'I don't understand.'

'Maybe Hal's right. Maybe it is a bloody indulgence.'

He shakes his head, weak with relief, able as he is now to pluck a placatory reply from the file. 'It's clues, isn't it? People want to be able to piece celebrities together. You're doing it for them, really.'

'Am I? I thought I was doing it for the cold, hard cash.' He laughs.

She doesn't. And the slackness in him tautens whip-quick.

'It's not easy being older,' she says. 'I'm too old to be the love interest, too . . . too . . . vain to be the crone. And there's the house. And a campaign to fund now.'

'The party pays for that, surely.'

'Oh, please. You can't do what you do and be that naive.'

But he is. He is stunned she's funding him – this once heir to a peerage, this ex-public schoolboy. Unless the rumours are true and he was dropped from Daddy's will. Unless he's paying for his parliamentary selection in other ways.

Or Daisy is.

Of course she is.

'But let's not talk about him,' she segues. 'Let's talk about me. Isn't that what we're here to do?'

His shirt is sticking to his sweat-damp back now and he pulls at it awkwardly. 'I didn't think you wanted—'

'You did bring your thingy, didn't you? Your tape recorder?'

'Yes.' Always. He fumbles in his bag and pulls out the dictaphone, not trusting the technology of digital after one too many horror stories from colleagues, after his own fuck-up with a racing driver. Places it on the edge of the desk.

She smiles, composes herself as if on set, readying for

cameras to roll. 'So,' she says, projecting, polished. 'Where shall we begin?'

He clicks the record button, smiles too now, his next sentence word perfect. 'At the beginning of course.'

She laughs, at last. 'Well, where else?'

He nods, takes a breath, and begins with something easy, benign. 'What did you want to be when you grew up?'

She pauses, looks at him as if he is mad, or mistaken. 'Me,' she says. 'I only ever wanted to be me.'

At first he thinks she's misheard, or that he has. But slowly, like a hidden image in a magic-eye picture, it becomes clear. Is obvious.

'You think that sounds narcissistic?' she continues. 'Maybe I am. Or maybe I'm just happy with myself. Maybe I'm just honest.'

'Or lucky,' he says.

'And that.'

And, God, how lucky. She always inhabited her skin with a confidence bordering on arrogance. And for a brief, narcissistic moment of his own, he finds himself wondering if she pitied those who had to work so hard to shed theirs.

If she pitied him.

If she pitied her sister.

8.

Bea, 1988

'Oh, for God's sake. *Now* what's the matter?'

Bea shrugs. 'I just don't feel like it.'

'It's a pub,' says Daisy, incredulous. 'There'll be drink. Dinner, even. You said you were hungry.'

'In *there*?' Bea shudders affectedly. 'I'd rather not. Besides, I can make toast.'

'With what?' Muriel, curious, peers into a musty cupboard, wrinkles her nose, freckles and flecks of glitter concertinaing in feigned disgust.

Bea shoves it shut, sending Muriel squealing and scattering. 'There's butter in the fridge and bread in the bin. Aunt Alice arranged it.'

'A veritable feast then.' Hal flips the Zippo, lights a fag.

Bea snatches it from him, takes a drag. 'Reckon you'll get better in the Ferryside?' She taps ash into a saucer, hands it back to Hal. 'It'll be frozen bloody scampi in a basket at best.'

'And that's beneath you, I suppose?'

'It's beneath bloody all of us,' Julian interjects. 'But needs must. I haven't had a thing since that sandwich at Leigh Delamere.'

61

'Have I?' wonders Muriel.

'No, darling,' says Daisy.

'Oh.' Muriel is disappointed.

Daisy places her hands on Muriel's cheeks then, as if talking to a toddler. 'No. And what you did eat you threw up.'

'Yes,' Muriel ponders. 'So I did!' She appears pleased, though whether it's at her performance, or the fact she has managed to pull out a memory of it, it's impossible to tell.

Bea wishes they'd all shut up now. Shut up and fuck off. It's been five hours hemmed in with them – more if you count the hunt round the houses they were harangued into to track down Julian's dealer. She opens the fridge, pulls out the pint of milk and pops the gold top. Then, eyes on her sister, takes a deliberate swig.

'Jesus, Bea. You know milk makes me puke.'

'And me,' adds Muriel. 'I'm practically allergic.'

Daisy sighs, but indulgently. 'Everything makes you puke, darling.'

'For fuck's sake,' says Hal. 'Can we go now?'

'Fine,' says Daisy, dropping her hands.

'Last chance,' offers Hal to Bea as he walks backwards, a practised ploy.

Bea licks the milk moustache from her lip, eyes fixed on him as she thinks of a slick retort.

But Daisy is too quick. Daisy is always too bloody quick. 'Oh, leave her, Hal. She's just being . . . Bea.'

The word – the name – is pith when Daisy says it like

that. The plastic taint in a beaker of water. She flips a finger in response.

'Charming,' Julian remarks.

'Oh, she's the bloody queen of charming.' Daisy eyes her idly.

Hal laughs. 'Queen Bea,' he declares, and bows.

He looks ridiculous, she tells herself. He's a dick. An oblivious dick.

But as the door slams and the silence sinks and surrounds her like quicksand, dick or not, she has never wanted him more.

In the kitchen she sits, motionless, as if struck by a gorgon, or practising statues. Her lazy gaze is fixed on a drip at the lip of the tap, swelling then shrinking, then swelling again, threatening to drop but never quite managing it. She should move, should explore, she knows. But inertia creeps like morphine, keeps her glued to the stool so that she can barely lift her lids let alone her limbs. Besides, what would be the point? Nothing has changed. Six years, perhaps, since they visited, and still the mildew lingers, still the pantry smells of damp, the paint flakes, the clock runs slow.

If she enters their bedroom she knows what she'll find: cabbage-rose carpets, candlewick bedspreads and an unloved rabbit on one twin bed, its outfit intact, its factory eyes button bright, its fur pristine still, having never been clutched tight to a child's chest at night; never been dragged outside and dangled over the boat; never been anywhere at all.

'But it's just a rabbit,' she remembers telling her ten-year-old twin. 'How can you hate rabbits?'

'I don't know,' a defiant Daisy replied. 'I just *bloody* do.'

The word was a new one, on loan from the raisin-faced gardener Minnow Rapsey, who came to clip the hedges and water the lawn once a week in season, and both girls were using it in abundance before it had to be handed back at the beginning of term.

'If you like it so *bloody* much, you have it.'

And Bea had tried to love it. But something in it irritated like grit, and try as she might she could not come to care for this second-hand thing. And so, when the time came for the long trip back to London and on to school – a draughty redbrick thing in one of the more ambitious suburbs – the rabbit remained, propped on a pillow 'for next time', when it would be promptly ignored or pushed under the laundry pile, until, at Daisy's behest (citing theatre commitments, Italy trips, and the sheer giddy pull of London in the summer), they stopped coming altogether.

And that is it, Bea thinks, the root of it – this dull ache in her. Because this – today – is not how it was supposed to play out. This should have been a triumphant return, a new start with Bea at the helm, bringing Hal – *her* Hal – back to her childhood playground. Instead she is no more than the tagalong, the plus one, the green-furred gooseberry sitting on the sidelines while her sister – whose contempt for Cornwall once stretched to declaring it 'povvy' in front of Felicity Witter – plays at being lady of a manor she swore she never wanted.

At least there is Muriel, she supposes. Sweet, pitiful Muriel, whose mother barely remembers she is one, and whose erstwhile father's responsibilities extend only to money once a month and cards twice a year: one birthday, one Christmas, which is almost worse than nothing, Bea often thinks. Almost.

But even Muriel was Hal's friend first and Daisy's now really; hers only by default because that is how it is when there are two of you, when you are told that everything must be equal, must be shared. But it never is. Equal. There's always one whose smile is one teaspoon of sugar sweeter, whose waltz is neater, whose teeth are picture perfect so that the other, the second child, seems merely to drift in her wake like lint, or a mote of dust briefly glittering in the swirl of her sunlight.

Her limbs are pimpling in the chill now – the sun set beyond the folly. Though the house never really heats, not even at high noon. The woods and water and fat granite walls see to that. She should find a cardigan, but even as it occurs to her she sees her sister's eyes roll at the spinster sensibleness of it. So she tries another tack. 'What would Daisy do?' she wonders. Find a fur coat in the back of a wardrobe, comes the reply. Or light a fire.

Or find the boy her sister wants to kiss, and fuck him senseless on a single bed.

She stubs out a cigarette and squashes the thought.

Or run a bath. A bath is the ticket, she thinks, her voice someone else's – Muriel's – now. She has sweated for several hours cramped in the back of the Beetle, she must smell. And even if not, she itches with it – can feel crisp crumbs and fag ash and the faint taint of a makeshift toilet that has somehow seeped into her skin. And, as the drip finally fattens enough to fall into the sink, she slips down from her stool and, barefoot, steps cat-like, one paw in front of the other, out of the door, along the narrow corridor and up, up into the house.

The water is scalding, the air filled with steam so thick it drips down the crackle-glazed tiles and fogs the mirror, so that, as Bea undresses, she sees only a faint shape, tinted pink and pleasingly blurred. Sometimes she likes to look at herself head on, map the landscape, interrogate the almost invisible faults that separate them, Daisy and her. Hal says he can't tell them apart, but he is lying, of course, or why would he sleep with Daisy so quickly when he'd spent weeks – months – in Bea's company and not so much as touched her?

Paper dolls, their mother had called them once, barely a sliver of difference – just a mole and an inch of silvery appendix scar. Identical sprigged smocked dresses, identical brown buckled shoes, identical neat-toothed smiles that could be conjured at the click of a camera. But after Mummy went, the shoes became crooked, the outfits awry, and then Daisy stole an eyeliner from Woolies one Saturday so that now the distinction is painted on in tight, defiant detail – a line drawn in cheap Rimmel kohl: this is me and that is you and never the twain shall meet. Maybe that is why, tonight, Bea is happy to see herself disappear.

Naked now, she leans into the steamed-up mirror. 'Daisy'

she draws, as if writing it will make it so. And, for a second, caught in the fog of a fifties bathroom, and filled with something dancing between desperation and hope, it almost is. Then, swiftly, suddenly, she raises an arm as if waving a wand and in one swift swipe – puff! – the illusion is over.

It's a quarter to midnight when she's hauled from the water, scrabbling and slapping at her would-be knight. Or princess.

She'd been attempting to masturbate, one hand idly prying at her pubic hair as she tried to conjure him, tried to imagine it was his finger that stroked and coaxed and pleaded. But suddenly it was Julian's voice that urged her on, told her to turn over, to beg. And, chastened, she had given up and slipped beneath the murky surface. To stifle the sound. Nothing more. At least not at first.

She hangs over the side of the steep tub as it drains, spits something milky onto the floor: bathwater half swallowed in shock.

'What the fuck were you thinking?' Daisy demands.

Bea is aware of Muriel's thin-fingered grip on her arm then and yanks it away. 'Not what *you* were thinking, clearly. I'm not sodding suicidal.' She stands and snatches a towel from the radiator. 'What?' she demands. 'I'm not.' She holds out her pristine wrists for inspection.

'Well, what then?'

'I don't know.' And she doesn't. Just that the peace was pleasant, perhaps.

'I tried to kill myself once,' says Muriel.

'No you didn't,' Daisy replies. 'That was in a play. Remember?'

'Was it? God, aren't I awful?'

'Awful,' Daisy agrees, smiling. 'Perfectly awful.'

And Muriel beams.

'Where's Hal anyway?' Bea asks then, half disappointed, half relieved he was not her rescuer after all, however ill-judged.

'Still drinking,' Daisy says. 'You should come down.'

'We might play a game,' Muriel adds. 'And Julian has charlie.'

Bea twists her dripping hair over the sink, then shakes it. 'Maybe,' she replies.

But she doesn't of course.

That night she lies in her twin bed and listens to them fucking above her, their dead parents' headboard keeping time on the wall.

'Nice,' she says and turns onto her side.

But Muriel is already asleep it seems. And, emboldened, indifferent, she slips under the cover and imagines it is her up there, held down, pressed.

And this time, she comes.

9.

James, 2018

'You want to know how I lost my virginity?'

He nods by way of an answer, aware that he may be on the brink of discovery, but wary of what may be revealed, knowing from bitter experience that the amulet, the bright diamond he covets, may be no more than mica, or, worse, a vial of poison.

She laughs, a short, scoffing sound, then leans in to the tape recorder, whirring, purring between them. 'Me too,' she says.

They are three meetings and two boxfuls of TDK micro-cassettes in; eighteen hours of audio to be transcribed, edited, adulterated into what he believes she wanted to say. But so much of it – like this – is at best insinuation, at worst outright fabrication. She talks as if scripted, half her lines seemingly snatched from films or stolen wholesale from someone else's utterings or life. What truth she has told so far is no more than he could have gleaned from magazines, or a few hours spent trawling YouTube. 'How sad,' Isobel had opined two nights ago. 'To always be . . . on show like that. To act as if you're on stage.'

That had irked him, though he strove not to show it. 'Perhaps,' he said. 'Or perhaps that doesn't matter. Perhaps authenticity is overrated.' After all, he thought, who is he to say what's real and what mere smoke and mirrors?

But Isobel had dismissed it, him. 'It's . . . weird,' she'd managed, as she rolled over to click off the light. 'Thank God we mere mortals don't have to play charades.'

'Yes,' he'd replied, as he lay eyes wide open in the black-out-blind pitch. 'You're right. Of course, you're right.'

But here he is, no better than her. But no worse, perhaps, either.

'So not Hal then?' he tries now, a mealworm bait to coax her into confession.

'Hal? Hardly. I was nearly nineteen when I met him. Or did you assume I was a prude?'

'Not at all,' he assures her quickly, then fumbles for something to cover his gaucheness. 'I–I would have thought it foolish to stake a future on the first person you kiss.'

'So you won't think less of me if I say I truly don't remember?'

He shakes his head and finds it's not a lie.

'What about you?'

He starts. 'What about me what?'

'Your virginity. Who was she? Or he?'

If he is disappointed at her apparent lack of insight, he takes no offence at the insinuation. She isn't the first to suggest it, after all. 'Effeminate swank' F. Scott called it. Perhaps he was right. Perhaps it comes with the territory. James has never disavowed colleagues when they presumed to know he swung a different, or both, ways. But truly it's only women he ever wanted, at least sexually. And only one woman, back then.

Or two, perhaps.

'It— *She* was a she,' he tells her.

'And does *she* have a name?'

The vision is swift and vivid. Disarming. The pale face – *her* face. Eyes blue as a pool.

'No,' he lies. 'Or yes, but it doesn't matter. It wasn't . . . love.'

'Nor mine, clearly.' She pauses. 'It wasn't rape,' she clarifies. 'Or maybe it is now. It's hard to know what's what anymore, don't you find?'

He doesn't. But he says nothing.

'There was a party, you see, at school. Or rather, out of it, at one of the day pupil's houses. There was a drinks cabinet and someone else had got vodka. From the village shop, probably. They never checked for age back then. Do they now? I don't even know. How terrible. Anyway there were a pile of us in a bedroom and Miles . . .' She flaps a hand, grasping for an answer. 'I don't know, Miles Something dared me to dance naked on the bed and I did. I said yes. I definitely said yes then.'

She ponders this, lost in a memory for a moment, and he waits, patient, still, inconspicuous, while she digs around for more detail.

'I woke up back in bed. In the dorm. There was a bucket beside me and Bea . . . Bea had undressed me. And my knickers were ripped. They were Wednesday ones

71

even though it was a Saturday. Do you remember them? Days-of-the-week underwear? We both had a set and Bea never got them out of order but I was "deliberately obtuse" according to Aunt Alice.' She comes to, snaps her head back to him. 'But you're not here to talk about knickers.'

He's not and shrinks at the thought, that he might be seen as some pervert, or, perhaps worse, an amateur.

But she's quiet now, contemplative, and he doesn't want that – can't afford for her to clam up when they've already chewed through so much of his allotted time. When there is still so much left to find out – so much more than kisses and fripperies and days-of-the-week knickers. Because he's found he wants to know everything now, finds himself as eager, as gimlet-eyed as a gold-panner. He has had to shut her, her sister – all of them – out for so long. Had to pretend they did not share the same air, tread the same streets. Had to imagine they were nothing more than a passing acquaint-ance, as brief and meaningless to him as the boys who sat behind him in Latin, the men who lined up at the bar, the PRs who danced round him, flirting indiscriminately to buy a byline. But now he thirsts for it. For long stories, for deli-cious snippets, for diamond-bright detail about Daisy, about Hal, about—

But at that, he's always stopped himself, pulled up short. Though Daisy has slipped her into conversation, as casually as if dropping a coin or discarding used chewing gum. But he knows this is a front, an act, as fine as her Antigone, her Medea, her Helen of Troy. For that name, even after all these years, must surely sting. It hurts him to even think of it. Slices. Sends him scurrying back to the safety of premieres and parties and how Daisy prefers her Pimm's served. Because to say that name aloud is an acknowledgement that she existed.

And affirmation that now she doesn't.

He pushes the thought away. Rallies. Reminds himself that this is a job not a holiday. That he has a few days and then all this – this silliness, this indulgence – yes, Hal was right, indulgence – is done. And that he cannot get to the heart of her – cannot go back to Lydia – if he doesn't broach the topic, the elephant in the room it has become. So, as she sits rigid in the wake of her dorm room deflowering, he stammers out the words he'd shut in a cupboard:

'I— Tell me about . . . Bea.'

To Daisy's credit, she does not flinch. But he can see he's picked at the lip of a still-raw scab when she rises and pour herself a finger of gin, topping it up with the same of Schweppes.

'You want one?'

He shakes his head, his stomach soured enough. Besides, 'I'm working,' he says.

'So am I,' she bats back.

'I . . . No, thank you. I'm sorry, I shouldn't have . . .' But he can't say it – her name – again.

She shrugs, sits back on the chaise, lets the desperate Egg slink back into her lap. 'What do you want to know?'

He thinks swiftly of specifics – the daring, the dressing up, the demands on the night of the . . . the fight – but these are symptoms, not the essence of her. And so, desperate, amateur, says simply, 'Everything.'

'Very well,' she replies. 'Then I shall tell you.'

Two hours later and she has barely begun. He knows now that Bea drank milk from the bottle and ate pickles from the jar. Knows that she carried a stuffed monkey with her wherever she went, from the age of four until she fell ill at six. Knows that, even in remission, cancer left her weak, prone to fever and fainting. Her blood thinner, somehow, tainted. Knows too that the monkey was replaced in turn by a duckling, an imaginary friend called Collins and then, finally, by a black dog that crept in in winter, kept her in bed for days staring sullenly into the gloom.

'Such a waste,' she says then. 'A waste of a girl. You know, Bea was always the better actress.'

He shakes his head, used to self-effacement – genuine and gimcrack – from even the highest achievers. 'I find that hard to believe,' he says truthfully, though he knows she did not lack talent.

'No, no, it's true! I was just louder, that's all. Better at grasping opportunity, I suppose. Do you know we were once in a can-can line-up – some ballet school thing – and not everyone was flexible so Miss Wroblewski had us all kick at exactly four foot so we were in formation. Do you know what I did?'

He shakes his head, though can hazard a guess.

'Every night,' she goes on, 'every single night, I kicked at four foot four . . .'

'So that people couldn't help but look at you.'

'Exactly. Bea was livid. But you don't get noticed colouring inside the lines.' She pauses. 'You think I'm being vain again.'

'No.' And he doesn't. Not at all.

'I'm embarrassed, really I am. I was ever the stage school brat. Bea . . . Bea was the Shakespearean scholar. Or would have been.' She feels in the pocket of her capri pants for a packet of cigarettes. 'Acting's how she and Hal met. Did you know that? He put her in some play of his at Oxford. Godawful stuff it seems now. Amateur. But at the time we thought it was going to change the world. That *he* was.'

'But he hasn't?' he suggests, aware suddenly that an unattractive eagerness edges his thoughts if not his words.

She pauses, a Camel stained with vermilion lipstick smouldering between liver-spotted and lacquer-tipped fingers. 'Not yet.'

And in two words the subject is shut down and instead he has to second-guess, to surmise what it was that made her stay. Was it because in the wake of it all there was no one else to anchor her? Was it the baby? Did he come back and beg forgiveness, beg her to marry him when he found out?

He must have. Because here she is. Daisy has slipped into the role of doting, devoted wife as slickly as any West End part. But what is so sad, so upsetting, so insurmountable, is that she's not just convincing, she actually believes it herself. And this despite the evidence in front of her: this man – Hal – who promised marvels and has delivered nothing but mediocrity, the mundane. Isn't she disappointed? Doesn't she wonder 'what if?'?

Of course she must, for this question is what drives them both, ghost and actor alike, writer and player of parts. It is the stuff of life itself, the million-dollar question, the reason to go on, and on, and on . . .

But he cannot dwell on this. He has only an hour left before the sand runs out, and he intends to use it. Refuses to lose a single second when he can be in a room with her. Can breathe the same air as her, however thick it is with her Camels and the lingering stink of Hal's cigars. He'll have to drop those of course. Men of the people don't have fat Havanas and hundred-pound bottles of brandy with their 'kitchen suppers'. Not anymore.

But he's digressing again, spiralling, and must pull himself back, pull *her* in. He needs a trick, a sleight of hand, a grand act of flattery. And he finds one in his stockpile, grabs it with a flourish as if it is a bridal bouquet or even plastic flowers. 'You were identical,' he says.

She nods, solemn.

'But weren't you always the more beautiful one?' He waits before adding a throwaway, 'Everyone says so.'

Daisy stares at him. Cold and calculated. And for a moment he worries he's fucked up, overstepped, that he won't just be shut down but shut out for good, a wave of nausea sending his stomach into a giddy swirl. But then she laughs, guttural, her head thrown back in exaggerated effect. 'Did you hear that, Egg?' she says. 'He thinks that will get him everything.'

Then she turns to him, her kohled eyes B-movie-wide. 'And he is right.'

10.

Jason, 1988

He's up by nine, bathed and dressed, though it's taken four costume changes and an array of hairstyles to achieve anything close to satisfaction.

'As if,' says Sadie as she catches him reverse his parting for the seventh time.

'Fuck off,' he retorts, though with less venom than he's feeling. After all, he can't afford to wake the sleeping beast.

'I'll come with you,' she offers then, deceptively selfless.

But he knows her game. 'You're all right. Anyway, won't Barry blow a fuse if you're late?'

Sadie snorts, though whether it's at him or at the thought of what Barry might do is unclear. She slinks out anyway and five minutes later he can hear her sandals slap-slapping the slipway as she runs to catch the ferry, leaving him to the bathroom mirror and the sweaty snoring from next door.

It's a fine line he's dancing. If he leaves it too late he risks being caught by his father: snagged and sidetracked into washing and stacking, or manoeuvring barrels. But too early and he risks waking the guests, getting snapped at or sneered at or worse. Despite the practice, the sometimes nightly pummellings, his skin is still thin as the membrane on a new-laid egg. He weighs it up – his Hobson's choice – before landing on a third possibility that comes to him in a moment of unusual clarity: he will take the boat out. If he is seen, summoned, he can abandon ship; if not, if nothing else, it will buy him time and afford a view of Rashleigh he can only otherwise achieve by precarious trespass along the launch wall. And so, mind made up, hair set, he slips swift, sneaky, past his father's room, down the stairs and out the door into the bright, hot day.

The paint – pea-green – is peeling, and the outboard as recalcitrant as a cat, but aside from his meagre wardrobe and selection of records she is the one thing he can call his own.

Dolly.

He was going to name her for his mother, but she'd said he might as well stick a sign saying 'slap me' to his back, and besides, it was maudlin, 'cause she'd known even then she hadn't got long. Not long enough to leave proper, Sadie'd said. 'Cause if she'd lived she'd be long gone by now anyway, over the Tamar and far away. And so would they. Instead her life insurance has bought them a failing pub and a life sentence, or so Sadie said when she was in one of her better moods. 'Death sentence', when she was spitting.

He yanks the cord of the outboard, willing it into submission. He'll just do once up to Pont Pill, he reckons, if he can get the bastard started. Though that's looking less likely, and he's already regretting his plan, damp as he is. The weather's supposed to break before the regatta but the sky's blue enough to make a sailor suit and the sun hot enough to melt a Mivvi in minutes despite September creeping in. He makes a deal with himself: one more haul, then, if she won't co-operate, he'll give in, go back to plan A or B or whichever gets him indoors quickest. He should bother with the oars, has had to when he's had no cash for petrol, but then he'd be giving in to dark circles in his pits and across his back, though he supposes it might lend him a romantic air – an Odysseus or Dickie or even Joss Merlyn, smuggling secrets of his own in and out of coves. Though no sooner has the flame of thought snuck in he snuffs it. He's not a Joss, nor even a Jem. He's just Jason. Jason Pengelly: the scholarship kid with the dead mum and drunk dad. And fired with that furious thought he hauls once more with all his might. And this time his kitty cat raises herself up on her paws, yawns, and coughs obstinately into life.

He's barely coaxed her out off the mooring when he hears it: that voice like a sonnet.

'Can I come?' it calls.

And he turns, quick, nearly catching Ned Pauncy's launch in the process, scared she's no more than a will-o'-the-wisp and will disappear – puff! – swift as his own confidence. But no, there she is, atop the wall, one hand shielding her eyes against the sun, one on her hip, and wearing a white dress that turns transparent so that he can see the outline of her underwear and feel the flush of heat in his cheeks that follows.

Daisy.

'Yes, I— Hang on!'

But he's fumbling now, the tiller slipping in his slick palm, so that he has to snatch it back to steady her, slow her, so he can creep to the wall to collect this gem, this treasure that he hasn't even had to go digging for, can hardly believe has come hunting for him instead. But closer now, he sees something is off, odd. She's clearly the same girl as last night – the same lopped-off hair, the same skinny limbs, the same determination that sets her jawline just so – but it's as if she's washed-out, a blurred version. Beautiful, still, but less . . . splendid.

And somehow she knows it.

He pulls up to the ladder, lifts a hand, chivalrous, to beckon her, bring her on board. 'Here.'

She looks at him as if he's mad, or a dangerous stranger. 'I was joking,' she says. 'I don't really do boats.'

His buoyancy gone, stomach slumping, he lashes the boat to the ladder and shuts off the engine, aware that this is an almost guarantee that the oars will have to come out after all, if only to row himself the few yards home. 'Why not?'

'Not much call.'

Those words unnerve him, said as they are now with an edge that's as sharp as a Swiss Army knife or his father's slap, and the way she looks at him, into him, sends a needle of cold creeping down his back. He puts it down to drink, has seen it in his father – even in Sadie – enough after all. The light in her eyes when she's bathed in Bailey's, the love she declares for whoever's bed or back alley she's found herself in, then the regret in the thin, half-light of a February morning and rage of a hangover.

'You left something at the pub last night,' he says then, clutching at a connection, something to offer up, to elicit a grin.

But it fails, falls short or flat.

'I doubt it.'

He pushes his hand in his pocket, pulls out the bracelet dangling with charms. 'Here.' He holds it up to her, expecting her to reach down to the water to snatch it back.

But she regards it with something approaching disdain. 'Oh, that. It's not mine.'

Confusion bruises him. Was it the other one – Muriel – who wore it? No, it was her, this girl right here. He's sure of it. 'But—'

But before he can question her, demand an answer, she offers up the words that will tilt his world further off kilter. 'It's not mine,' she repeats. 'It's Daisy's.'

He's on the threshold again, dawdling in the doorway while this girl – Bea, she tells him, short for Beatrice – shouts up the staircase. 'Daisy,' she calls, then glances behind. 'A stray to see you.'

It's as clear to him now as if he's managed to somehow muddle chalk and cheese or a pea and a peppercorn. 'I'm so sorry,' he tells her again. 'I just . . . you're so—'

'Oh, everyone does it.' She cuts him off. 'Until they see us side by side.'

'But you're . . . identical.'

She shrugs. 'Apparently not.'

He stares at her hair, at the jut of her jaw and fails to see it, though he knows it to be true, can sense the minuscule difference even if he cannot see it.

She sighs. 'I've a mole on my chest and she a scar on her side. I drink milk and I like rabbits but I never eat peanuts. Allergic.'

A snapshot flashes then; a quick click of an image of Daisy with a packet of KP.

'Oh, and I . . .'

But he fails to find out what else separates them, because then, at the top of the stairs, as if by magic, Daisy appears in a pink silk gown and hair that defies styling.

'Oh!' Her face, at first a bland, sleep-lazy sprawl, pulls focus and rearranges itself into a wide welcome of a smile. 'It's you!'

The soar of butterflies is instant, and again he wonders how he made a mistake. 'You left this,' he says for the second time, but surer now. He holds out his hand, crossed with silver.

'Did I? God, probably.'

She saunters down, clapping a chip-nailed hand over a yawn; her robe – or kimono, perhaps – slipping so he sees she's naked but for a pair of knickers with the word 'Monday' embroidered along one side. 'But it's Saturday,' he has to stop himself saying, has to force himself to look down.

But then she's there, in front of him, so close he can smell the sleep on her, smell something else too. Sex, perhaps.

'Here.'

She picks the thing from his palm, dangles it curiously. 'I suppose I must have done. You could have kept it. I wouldn't have known. I'm not even sure where I got it.'

'Muriel gave it to you,' the other one – Bea – tells her.

'What for?'

'Our birthday.'

'But that's not for a week,' she says, almost put out.

She sighs. 'Last year. God, how much did you drink last night?'

Daisy ignores the question. 'Oh, very well.' And she slips it over her skinny wrist, so delicate he can trace the veins, blue beneath, as if she's not all bravado and brashness but as tender, as fragile as he feels. 'Is that all?' she asks then.

The insects in him flap in panic. 'I–no . . . Yes.' He can't mention the money. It seems beneath him, though he needs it, will have to get it somehow.

'It's all right.' She laughs. 'I have what we owe you. You don't have to be embarrassed.'

'I wasn't,' he lies.

'I'll find my purse.'

She pads down the hall, one arched foot in front of the other. He hears the sound of a bag being upended onto a table or kitchen counter, then a sudden, plosive, 'Bollocks!' followed by a plaintive, 'Bea?'

He catches Bea's eyes, sees weariness. 'Fine,' she snaps back. Then, to him, 'Ten, isn't it?'

He nods, and she slips up the stairs and disappears, a will-o'-the-wisp herself.

'Sorry.'

Daisy's back, dripping water from a pint glass slapdash on bare feet, and he feels for a moment as if he's caught in a deliberate trick, the pair of them playing him, trying to prove he's a fool.

'It's nothing,' he says. 'Not a big deal. I could've waited.'

'Nonsense,' she tells him. 'It's yours. Besides, Aunt Alice would be livid.'

'Is she . . . is this hers, then?' He gestures with his head at the house surrounding them.

Daisy swallows, coughs. 'This?' She laughs. 'You really don't know?'

He shakes his head.

She snorts, incredulous. 'I assumed our terrible reputation preceded us. How disappointing. I thought you lot loved nothing more than a gossip, a good tragedy.'

He bristles at that 'you lot'. At being lumped in with the likes of Alan Ransome and Fat Man Morris. With his father. 'I don't—'

'Oh, it's all right. I'm not including you. You're different.'

He brightens, caught in the shine of her, carefully directed as it is.

'We do,' she says then.

'I'm sorry, what?'

'*We* own it. Don't we, Bea?'

He turns to see the sister already downstairs, as if she can summon herself, phantom-like, to any spot.

She hands him a note, which he pockets roughly. 'We do.'

'We're poor little orphans.'

He swings back to stare at Daisy.

'Banished to boarding school, to the dread Mrs Munt. And to Aunt Alice in the holidays.'

He fumbles for something to say. 'That's . . . that's awful.'

'Oh, it could have been worse,' Daisy says cheerily. 'We could have had to stay in Saffron Walden the whole bloody time.'

'What . . .' he begins, trailing off before he can find the right words, the courage to ask them. 'What happened to them? Your parents, I mean.'

He addresses them both but it's Daisy who answers. 'One car crash, one cancer. Runs in the family.'

'Daisy!' Bea is imploring.

'What? I'm going anyway. Gasping for a fag. Where did Julian leave his?'

Bea sighs. 'How would *I* know?'

'Fine.' She slips between them and onto the stairs. 'Julian?' she calls as she climbs. 'Wake up, for fuck's sake.'

He glimpses knickers again, riding up over a buttock; feels heat in his cheeks and sweat pooling in his already-dank armpits.

Daisy turns, catches him, but instead of calling him out she smiles. 'Come back later? We'll have a beach party.'

He nods, incapable of any other answer.

'Good.' And with that she is gone, bare flesh and a flash of the forbidden disappearing down the landing.

'She does that deliberately.'

'Huh?' He turns to Bea, sees one eyebrow raised.

'Hitches her kimono up so her knickers are showing. She did it even when we were six.'

'I wasn't . . . I didn't . . .' But it's useless. They both know he saw it, looked for it.

As if to confirm she lowers her gaze to his crotch, lets her lips slip into a half-smile as she sees she is right.

'I should be going,' he says then.

'Oh don't go on her account.'

'It's not. I've . . . I've got work.'

'You will come back though, won't you? For the party?'

He nods.

'Good.'

'When?' he asks then, desperate.

'Oh, you won't be able to miss it.' She sits down on a stair then, looks up at him as if taking him in for the first time. 'I don't even know your name.'

'Daisy didn't tell you?' He is hurt, crushed, insignificant again.

And she knows it. 'Oh, don't worry. She was too fucked to say much at all last night.'

'Oh.'

Her 'So?' is expectant, pregnant with possibility.

'Right.' He thinks, for a moment, of plucking a new name from the ether, becoming a Heath or a Henry or Hal. No, Christ, not Hal. But something, anything other than his own. But how long would that last? How long could he get away with it? For a few hours at most. Until his father, or, worse, Daisy, laughed him out of the bar.

'Jason,' he says. 'It's Jason.'

Later, he marvels at the pair of them. At the idea of it even, having never seen twins for himself in the flesh. Though Sadie claims she snogged two Lawsons up Liskeard one

Saturday, but only by accident. She'd thought it was Gav she'd had in the car park but it turned out to be Darren. Not that it made a difference, she told him. Both as bad as each other, all tongue and no technique.

He's read about them, of course, seen them on screen, been mesmerized in turn by corpulent toddlers Tweedledee and Tweedledum, by precocious Hayley Mills besting her parents, by the delinquent double of Dr Henry Jekyll. He's wondered what it must be like to find yourself carbon-copied, wondered, as well, what pranks he might play. Though mostly, he supposes, it must be odd. Disappointing, even. Not to be unique – at least on the outside.

Though they are, of course. Unique. Bea was right: now he's seen them, side by side, it seems impossible he ever confused them. They are as unalike as a peacock and a pigeon. No, that's unfair, not a pigeon, but a lesser bird, somehow. No, that seems cruel too, and now he thinks of it even the peacock is wrong in its garishness, suggesting one is tawdry and one dowdy and drab. They're neither, but there's a difference, barely palpable, but there all the same, and not in their looks but in their very being.

And he can see it.

And he feels, then, as if he holds the key to the universe in his very hand, or, if not, at least a secret that Sadie hasn't got hold of yet.

He finds her in the bathroom, trying to cover up a love bite.

'Got any Colgate?' she asks him.

'Look in the cupboard.'

'It's all bloody Aquafresh and I can't go round with red and blue stripes, can I? Might as well draw a circle round it and be done.'

He shrugs, never having been in need of such an act of subterfuge, nor in possession of anything that might exact it. 'You could wear a scarf?'

'It's twenty-five fucking degrees outside,' she tells him. 'I'd look like a spanner.'

'Who says you don't anyway?'

'Oh ha bloody ha.' She dabs at her neck again. 'You seen them, then?'

'Who?' He feigns ignorance and indifference in equal measure.

'You know who.'

'What, Hal? No.'

'Oh.' She's put out, as if the man's absence is a personal affront. Assesses herself again, checking her neck, then squeezes her tits in tighter under the too-short T-shirt. She knows her assets and how to use them: DD cups – he's seen the bras on the line – and hair that almost hits her hips. That and a love of sex that's as expansive as it is indiscriminate.

He could tell her now. Blurt out Bea's existence. But he thinks better of it. He'll make her wait, watch her gobsmacked reaction, then drop in an, 'Oh, didn't you know?' But he's not without pity. 'I'm sure they'll be in later though.'

'Really?'

He nods. 'Definitely.'

He's never been surer of anything.

Nor more desperate. And not for the great unveiling to Sadie, the secret of Bea, but to see Daisy herself. Because no matter how hard he tries he can't stop thinking of her as the original. And not just because he saw her first, but because she's more . . . More what? He thinks, then catches it, the glint of it, like a gold bottle-top on the river bottom: she's more glorious.

And it *is* a glory, a brilliance he never imagined he'd catch sight of – not in the pallid faces of the grammar girls on the Plymouth bus, nor amongst the ranks of Sadie's preening mates. It's a brilliance he wants for himself and, for the first time in his life, he might be close enough to touch it.

11.

James, 2018

'Do you . . .' He fiddles with the dog-ear of his notebook, his backup, his rabbit's foot in case . . . in case of what? Not a technical fault. Perhaps just his own need to have something to do with his hands, or to feel the precision, the indelibility of words, scaffold as they are of his precarious existence. 'Do you ever go back?'

They've been talking for more than a week by the time he summons the courage to ask her, on a Wednesday strangely wet given the persistent heat. Because he needs to know, of course, needs to get to the nub of it. Tells himself he owes it to Lydia, to wheedle out the desperate revelation that might secure a red-top spread. But of course it is so much more than that – for Daisy and for him – and less, too. A selfish bid to shore up that scaffold.

So he's been skirting around the subject for two days, trying to ease the route, cut down the brambles and nettles that choke the path back to that night, back to Bea. So that she can find her way there without him having to drag her. Because God knows he's had to do that before – with politicians and pop stars alike – but with Daisy? He's not sure he's capable, still less willing. So instead he's teased out details: of Daisy's adored performance; of Bea's petty jealousy; of the ties that bound even when circumstance contrived to keep them apart. The months Bea spent in hospital, clinging on to existence, hovering in that netherworld between life and nothingness. Then the division of ambition when, despite getting into the same roster of top universities, Daisy, the determined drama queen (her words), chose to go to RADA and Bea – bookish, brilliant – Oxford, and they were separated by more than sixty miles and several trains.

But holidays they spent together, gleefully fleeing smalltown Essex for Hal's father's flat in Westminster – all ghastly salmon carpets and Whistler prints. Or, occasionally, Muriel's mother's decaying basement at the unfashionable end of Portobello, with its stink of patchouli and endless selection of undepilated lesbians. And devastating neglect, not least of Muriel herself.

Or, of course, Cornwall.

'To Fowey?' She laughs, brisk, dismissive. 'I was waiting for that.'

He fumbles for words, mumbles, 'I'm sorry, I—'

'Christ, don't apologize. You wouldn't be doing your job if you didn't at least ask. But no, I haven't been, not for a while. The house was sold, you must know that.'

He nods, he does know – has known since 1991 when it – she – made the papers, as Daisy so often did even then, infamy dogging her before true fame came wagging its tail.

'What about you?' she asks then.

He is thrown by a strange vertigo, worries for a moment he will throw up. 'I . . . Sorry?'

'Cornwall,' she clarifies. 'Do you know it at all?'

He opens his mouth, then closes it again, a gasping fish out of water, or back in it, in the confusing soup of a former self and a family abandoned.

That he had no choice is no mere lie he tells himself to make it better, to allow him to sleep. Because going back would have been betraying this new man, betraying James. And betraying others for a second time. His is, after all, a family who, to the best of their knowledge, laid him to rest nearly three decades ago, the coffin empty but the surety of the body – *his* body – sucked lifeless and out to sea.

And so he buried it all alongside that boy, has had to, or risk torturing this new version into an early grave. Has avoided stories that would have taken him any further west than Oxford with a diligence and determination normally afforded only to those who require trigger warnings for paedophiles or the otherwise perverted. Has turned down contracts – to profile a notorious sportsman, a fallen don, an actor once morbidly obese and now hawking healthy living from his Helford manor like snake oil – all deals that would have kept him in Savile Row suits for several seasons.

Is he scared? Is that it?

Of course. He is terrified.

Not of his father, not anymore. He's long gone and buried – oh, the pathos! – in a plot next to Jason's. And he felt not a drop of sorrow when he found out. Oh, of course he found out – while he has to be careful not to tread too obvious a trail in the ether, even a man as insubstantial as John Pengelly has left an indelible mark, his death announced with all the dignity it deserved on the *Packet*'s Twitter feed under the headline 'Tragic landlord found dead in Datsun Cherry'.

James was in Japan at the time. A fact that struck him as somehow fitting – a nod to the absurdity of the map of the world that hung behind that backwater bar: that his father who, in life, had not once crossed the Tamar, had in death travelled half the world and back.

No, it's not his father he fears, not anymore. Nor even Sadie, whom he assumes fled up country, riding pillion to Barry Ransome, or some other Darren or Shane with Dick Whittington dreams of their own, before settling for less than the West End she dreamed of in a semi in Clacton or Hastings or Penge. He may be wrong, of course. But there are no Sadie Pengellys still living in South Cornwall, nor any bearing a resemblance circling on social media. And no record of death, or marriage. So if she's changed her surname by deed poll or common law, he can only wish her luck, and hope she chose her new life as well as he. No, he is not scared of them. They're no longer a threat.

The ones he fears are much closer to home: Daisy and Hal, and himself more than any. For who is more likely than he to let something slip, to drop the facade for a second and render himself revealed, like a devilish magician's trick.

'James?'

He comes to, remembers the question. 'Only by reputation,' he says, deliberately vague. 'I think I visited once, as a child.' He finds he cannot lie outright, though whether this is self-preservation, to explain any obscure knowledge he may have or may still unwittingly reveal, or because it is Daisy to whom he's confessing, he's unsure. What he *is* sure of is that it's time to change tack, to escape the confines of that cut-off county and come at it all from another angle.

Breathe, he tells himself. Focus.

'Do you ever regret not opting for Oxford?' he asks.

The reprieve, though, is temporary, the segue incomplete. Because, less than a day later, Daisy is back in the dark woods, in no-man's-land.

He's packing up when she broaches it, flipping through his scrawled shorthand, labelling the last cassette.

'Oh, I've been meaning to tell you,' she says, as casually as if she's about to announce she fancies a pasty or will walk him to the corner.

He's still fiddling with equipment, doesn't even bother to look up as he asks, 'What's that?'

'My birthday,' she says. 'Only it's this weekend and we're going away.'

He stops what he's doing, running swiftly through the implications. 'You're not celebrating here?'

'God, no. August bank holiday in London? Appalling.' She musters a shudder at the very idea.

'But . . . for how long?'

'Three days. Four possibly. It rather depends on the weather.'

He calculates quickly. Their time together was due to end at four on Sunday and, panicked, his voice snaps. 'Where are you going?' He prays for the provinces, some hyped-up Home Counties hotel with a spa and silver service, close enough to drive to without requiring an overnight. 'I mean, I'll still be able to see you. Won't I?'

'Hardly. It's . . . rather far.'

He clutches at straws. 'Can I . . . call then? Or Skype?'

She pauses, pondering the possibility, perhaps, fondling one of the dog's ears – Egg, he thinks, though they are hard to tell apart until they whine, and Hobson's high pitch is evident. Then she claps, as guileless as a child, sending Hobson – clearly Hobson – yelping. 'Of course you must come!'

The world slows and sound seems to stretch, a yawning song played on the wrong speed. 'I–I–' he manages to stammer.

'I should have thought earlier.' She talks over him. 'There's a bunch of us. Hal's pals mainly. And Clementine, of course. So it wouldn't be . . . weird. You wouldn't be intruding. You'd enjoy it, I think.'

His hands are clammy and he has to resist the urge to wipe them on the back of his trousers. What was he thinking? He can't do this. Has to find a way out. 'It–It'll be too late, won't it? To book somewhere. On a bank holiday.' He almost sighs in relief at the treasure he's dug up in desperation.

But this is no diamond.

'Oh no,' she intones. 'That won't be necessary. You must stay with us. There'll be oodles of room.'

'You don't have to—'

'Nonsense. That's settled then.'

Fuck, he thinks. Fuck. Isobel will be livid. They're supposed to go to her mother's. He keeps putting off meeting her, even the words 'Tunbridge Wells' are enough to send him scurrying, claustrophobic, into his study, hemmed in by the thought of wagging tongues and chatter. At the endless questions about his schooling, his childhood, his family; demands for photographs he will have to explain, again, were lost in a move. She'll not forgive him, not again, surely?

But even this isn't enough to persuade him to stay.

'Will I need a passport?' At least spare him that, he begs, though the days of sweaty paranoia at border control are mostly over.

She laughs. 'Not yet. Though I won't be surprised if they manage it one day.'

His relief is palpable. 'And I should pack . . .?'

'Oh, bathing trunks. Shorts. Nothing smart— No, maybe something smart. A dinner suit.'

He doesn't know whether to be relieved she assumes he owns such an item or appalled at the prospect of sitting stiff-collared in some staid dining room with Hal and his 'pals'. 'So where *are* we going?'

'Oh, sorry. I should have said at the beginning.' She smiles, generous, his benefactor, or so he assumes she believes. 'We're going to Cornwall.'

His face flushes then drains, his complexion anaemic. But he cannot let this betray him, must be careful of his reaction. Must plaster on a smile that contrives to calm, to convince her that he is grateful, thrilled, even. Besides, it's a large enough county. And anyway, the house is sold, gone, out of bounds even if it weren't too tarnished by memories to trespass again.

So: 'Which part?' he asks, his demeanour settled, if not genuine. It will be the Scarlet, he thinks, hopes, above the steps at Bedruthan. Or St Mawes. Some Polizzi-rebuilt pastel pile with its own pool and private beach so they won't be troubled by the locals, or the locals by them. Or a rental in Rock; Chelsea-By-Sea with the rest of the Westminster set, playing pétanque at Daymer by day and eating Padstow out of Stein-branded chip dinners by night, before ferrying themselves back across the Camel on their private launch. And he's surprised to find this both appals and appeals in equal measure.

'Oh, I don't think you'll know it,' she tells him then. 'Unless you sail. It's a backwater, really. Except at regatta.'

His world tilts, shifts a full 180 degrees so that everything seems blurred and disturbing.

'Just a hamlet,' she continues, oblivious. 'Not even a pub to its name anymore, I'm told. Though there are a few over the estuary.' Then, as she says the word, names the place, tells him, finally, where they are heading, blood rushes from his head so swiftly he has to steady himself by stealth, leaning against the doorframe, as if idly interested, nothing more.

'Pencalenick,' she says. 'It's just across from Fowey.'

12.

Bea, 1988

It's a hamlet, really. Not even a village. Just the pub, their house and a few more rising hugger-mugger above it; a settlement premised purely on a ferry, then forced to watch its occupants spill straight off the deck and away up the hill towards bigger and better things.

There's nothing to see here, no one to be, and within minutes, it seems, Bea has exhausted all possibilities and is back where she began, on Rashleigh land. She could get plastered, she supposes. But the pub is shut and their own private bar stacked by the bin or left sprawling across the floor, no more than dregs. Besides, she's too old for minesweeping. She eyes the ferry then, a filthy, flat-bed thing, its ramp clanking as it chugs along its chains to Fowey, with its Co-op and corner shops and happy clatter. But it's hot, too hot to be caught in the Saturday crowd, and so, in the end, it's into the woods she goes, along the path that threads its way through the thicket behind the house then cuts along the cloistered coastline. A hard, parched trail, it is pestered by nettles and tented with hazel and oak and thin-needled pine, their roots rising from the dry mud like the exposed bones of a desiccating skeleton.

Picking her way past brambles and skirting dried-out dog shit she walks, until, despite the dank, she is sweating and sore-throated, and she remembers she hasn't brought water. She hasn't brought anything at all. And she sits, sullen as a sulking child, on the cornerstone of the odd cross that stands sentinel, lost in the forest. She wonders then how long it will take for them to wake and notice she is missing. Whether they'll come for her, calling out, or suppose she's stalked off of her own accord and simply skin up and wait for her to come crawling back. 'She's just being Bea,' she can hear Daisy say. 'Let her get on with it.'

And that is the truth of it. That she is not needed, not really. Not by Hal now, and not even her sister, not anymore. Where once Daisy would have entertained her foibles and fancies, tended her, begged her to explain, now she just rolls her eyes, downs another White Russian, and dances off with Muriel to have fun, fun, fun. And so, sighing silently, Bea stands and slinks back down the path, before they can notably fail to acknowledge her absence.

But she has dawdled, it seems, because by the time she gets back they are up, and out on the beach. No, not beach exactly, more a strand of muddy sand spanning the path up to the pub, the slipway and the short leap from there to Rashleigh's far walls. Only visible really at low tide, but useful enough for paddling, if you are that way inclined.

But Bea is never inclined.

Instead, a beaker of tepid tap water in hand, she squats on the rocks to one side of the ferry landing, the tips of her toes sending eddies across the depths, one hand shading her eyes, watching Hal and Julian fooling about with a frisbee, flicking it half-heartedly to one another whilst still managing to swig from tins of what must be warm beer. While Daisy, dishevelled and wet, and still half drunk, Bea suspects, stands on the top of the ladder like she's queen of the bloody world.

'Watch me!' she calls, arms outstretched as if she is an angel, or dragonfly, perhaps, its glistening wings picked out in a pair of silver bikini bottoms and two tiny triangles of gossamer top.

Muriel sits beside her, smoking, naked but for a pair of knickers (her packing, while including two hats, a feather boa and a pair of cowboy boots, has deliberately, or so Bea believes, omitted a swimsuit of any sort) and a string vest that gives glimpses of nipples, hard and brown as nuts. She looks up. 'I'm watching,' she insists. 'You can go now.'

But Muriel's undivided if hazy attention isn't enough. 'Hal!' she hollers. 'Watch!'

Hal spins quick, forgetting the pink plastic frisbee, which clips him across his ear, so that he ducks, clutching himself, and lets out a yelp just as she leaps, arms and legs pointed, body swan-like, out into the water.

She surfaces with the slick, dripping grace of a mermaid and the ire of a siren. 'For fuck's sake,' she spits. 'Can't you two grow up?'

'It was Julian,' Hal tells her. 'He can't bloody throw.'

'You can't catch, more like.'

Hal snorts.

Daisy seethes.

'Look, just do it again, babe. I'll watch properly this time. I promise.'

Bea can see peace is about to be brokered, sealed with a kiss, when a shadow, a black imp of a thing, slips across the spit in front of her, and sidles up to Daisy.

'You should be careful,' he tells her.

'Of what? Monsters?'

He smiles, despite himself. 'No. Just, it's not safe.'

It's the boy from this morning. From the pub. Jason, isn't that his name? As she says it to herself she sees Aunt Alice wrinkle her nose and look down it. 'How common,' she says. 'You must stay away from common boys.' But before she can tell the fictional Aunt Alice to fuck off back to Essex, Julian has weighed in against Jason.

'Bollocks,' he says. 'She's a brilliant swimmer.'

Daisy feigns humbled.

'That's not the point,' says Jason. 'It's . . . there's rocks. If you don't know where they are—'

'She knows where they are. She's been here before.'

'Anyway' – it's Hal's turn – 'don't people swim across the estuary?'

'It's true,' Daisy assures him. 'I've seen it before.'

'Oh, let's do it!' Muriel squeals, waving her legs over the wall like a toddler.

'You can't now,' Jason insists. 'The tide's still going out. At least wait until it turns.'

'God, you're such a spoilsport,' Daisy tells him, swiping the smile from his face so that he seems weak, defeated – though her own suggests she is merely teasing. 'Hal?'

'What?'

She turns to the house, walks up the path, doesn't need to look back to check he's following.

Of course he's bloody following. There's a fuck on offer.

Bea turns back, catches Julian catching her in turn, feels his eyes on her as he scales the wall then jumps, wildly, widely, into the water, sending it soaring up and onto Muriel, who giggles idiotically.

'Come on, Bea,' he calls when he comes up for air. 'You know you want to.'

'You know she can't,' Muriel replies.

Julian tilts his head at her, as if she is a child, or a moron. 'If she never tries, she'll never learn.'

'I'll come.' Muriel, either astute enough to step in or, more likely, high enough not to give a shit, decides she wants to play instead, and hauls off her pathetic vest, revealing skinny hips and her hard, high tits, barely more than a boy. 'What about you?' she calls to Jason. 'Or can't you swim either?'

Jason's already red face flushes. 'I said not now.'

Bea sighs, tiring of all of them, the heat closing in like four solid walls. She needs to get out, again. But the house is full of fucking and out here is him. Julian. His goading, his gloating, his tongue that once licked her cheek like a dog. And so it is back she has to go. Into the woods. But not up this time, where the tourists trail the Hall Walk with their sandwiches and sensible boots and yappy dogs that crap on the path. No, this time she knows precisely where she is heading, and there will be no one to disturb her at all. And so, glancing once back at Jason, an almost-invisible signal to the out-of-bounds boy, she treads along the wall and across the lawn and through a rusting gate that whinges on hinges that have not swung open in six years or more.

And does he follow?

Of course he does.

13.

James, 2018

He packs with the same exhausting precision as he selects his wardrobe: linen in neutrals, T-shirts in navy, a single pair of charcoal shorts that suggest elegance or necessity rather than sport. Nothing is garishly branded but neither is it high street – Marks and Spencer staples, or, worse, Next. The sort bought in store-born panic, or by indifferent wives.

He wonders what relief it might bring to slip sometimes. To wear . . . just anything. But he knows, to his woe, that he cannot afford such a lax attitude. Clothes maketh the man, can alter him, form him, rebuild him anew. As a gawky adolescent he understood this: knew what a Cure T-shirt could cost him, a piercing, a pair of blue suede shoes. And what they could buy him, too. And never so much as now.

Because this, this is a test of what he's become. *Who* he's become. Because he's not that child anymore. He's better now. More. More than the boy who was spat at and slapped for his scholarship as much as his Docs. More than the boy who was scorned for his poverty as well as his ambition. More than the boy who swore he'd show them, all of them – the rat-faced locals; the fat-lipped public schoolboys; his father, the most talented bully of all – just who he could be. And look who he *is*! He has walked among giants; has talked to prime ministers and presidents and once, a ginger prince. To paupers, too, the common people. He is the epitome of Kipling's *If*. Or so he tells himself to calm the sweats, to soothe the roiling stew his insides have become.

Isobel, dithering in bed, watches as he folds and rolls and packs his case. 'I love Cornwall,' she tells him. 'We should go. Once we've got my parents out of the way.'

'Yes, definitely,' he placates, his mind on his socks and how many and where.

'Then perhaps America?'

He looks up. 'Why America?'

'Visit your old haunts.' She pauses. 'Or not?'

'Oh.'

He sees the slip, feels a hit tarnish his steeled skin, must run the story in his head. Of course, he is American, or partly, brought up between parents, both dead now, in Hampshire (town unspecified) and the Village. A bohemian mother allowing him to run amongst drunks in Washington Square Park while she sat on the steps of Wharton's old building and smoked dope with a black drag queen called Vesuvius Brown. It is, of course, a past he can be both ashamed of and thrilled by. A past he can struggle to divulge, and legitimately wish to change the subject. Which he does, right now. Plucks out a detail, paints it fine-lined to convince. 'Square's been ruined,' he says. 'Cleaned up. Besides, Trump. But' – he snatches for something to offer her instead, the clever swap he's had to become adept at – 'maybe Madeira? In the autumn, when the tourists have gone.'

Isobel smiles, and relief sweeps through him. Perhaps this trip won't be so bad, he tells himself. Perhaps no one will ask or, if they do, he can sidestep enquiries as slickly as this. Perhaps he can simply stay in his room, claim deadlines or a dicky gut. Or perhaps they won't even come to it – their pasts, shared or otherwise. Will be too consumed with drink and the great tomorrow to go raking up what's done.

Perhaps.

When he arrives, in a cab this time, Hal is packing the car – a silver Saab that has seen better days, and not a sponge in months, possibly years, it seems – hauling a heavy, leather-edged suitcase into the boot, where it nestles between the optimistic holiday roster and detritus of family life: a crate of champagne, a pair of barely worn Hunters, and a deflated, faded carton of Ribena, a relic from a school run, presumably, that ended decades ago.

He breathes deep, commissions a grin. 'So,' he says, bright as a Coke-cleaned penny, 'the big birthday weekend.'

Hal looks up, half-smiles and harrumphs. 'God helps us.' He heaves up another box, this one filled with groceries, as if Cornwall might not stock Marmite or rice cakes or even wine. 'Here.' He gestures at James's hard-shell hand luggage – black Samsonite with a laptop pocket.

James winces as he scrapes it along the pavement then smacks it on top of his own with all the ceremony of a rotten corpse. 'Shall I?' he asks, as Hal makes to manhandle it again.

'Be my guest.' Hal stands back, amused, as he attempts to arrange the contents with a vague tessellation and without further injury. 'You're wasting your time. There's Daisy's cases yet. And the bloody body boards.'

'But there's no surf,' he corrects, unthinking.

'You know it then?'

He jinks and fishes for something quickly, finds it, presents it with a flourish. 'I googled it.'

'Ah. The armchair explorer's best friend.'

'And journalist's,' he replies, self-effacement high in his toolkit. 'At least these days.'

Hal is about to pronounce his considered opinion when a call comes from the doorway.

'Darling!'

Though he knows it's not aimed at him, James turns anyway to see Daisy dressed for all the world as if it is the French Riviera and 1953 to which she's heading, and in an open-top Alfa, not a rusting estate: black Onassis sunglasses, some sort of kaftan, and a headscarf tied not behind, hippyish, but, regally, under her chin. She's playing a part, though whether it is herself, Bardot or even a young Lumley, he is struggling to tell.

She slaps down the path in stacked sandals, straps buckled around her ankles. 'James!' she proclaims, definite in her affections this time, effusive, expansive, arms flung open as if he is a long-awaited houseguest, not a hired hand. 'You came.'

And in those words, that action, the sour taint of worry slips into syrup sweetness. 'Of course,' he says. 'How could I not?

'You'll have to take the back, of course. Hal's called shotgun.'

He bristles at it, then thrills. 'Shotgun', as if she's Thelma or Louise or the Sundance Kid.

'Don't look so worried,' she tells him then. 'I almost never crash.'

'Oh, I wasn't—' he begins quickly.

'Really.' She stops him. 'This is supposed to be fun! A holiday.'

'Florida's a holiday,' Hal says then. 'Or Corfu or Crete. This is . . . I don't know what this bloody is.'

'Hal, please!'

But he doesn't please. 'If you ask me, it's maudlin. But what Daisy wants, Daisy gets.' He turns to James, as if seeking a second opinion, backup.

But James shuffles in his already sweaty shoes, desperate to segue. 'Shouldn't we be leaving?' he asks, adding an explanatory, 'Traffic.'

'Thank you,' she says, smiling, munificent. 'Yes, we should.'

And he feels it as solid as if it were a pat on the back or a squeeze of a hand.

But Hal snorts. 'It's you we've been bloody waiting for. Have you even brought the bags down?'

She turns to James. 'I do apologize for my husband. It's the heat.'

James shakes his head. 'You don't need to—'

'Bags?' Hal snaps.

'Yes, yes.' And the moment is broken as she turns back

to Hal. 'The bags are in the hall. And the boards . . . God, where are the boards?'

'There's no surf,' Hal says. 'Apparently.'

'Nonsense. I'm sure there must be.'

'Even if there was, would you honestly go in?'

James interrupts. 'Could I use your loo?'

'Oh! Please do. You know where it is.'

He nods, and slips quickly up the path, along the hall and into the shallow black of the downstairs lavatory, letting out a disappointing trickle of piss. But that was hardly the point; he was merely keen to avoid any more argument or arbitration, not unnecessary pitstops. Though the journey, he suspects, will be a drawn-out and desperate affair, even without the bickering. West London crammed with carnival traffic, the motorway clogged with caravans, and their own tin box taut with Hal's arrogance and his own bleak fears. And something else.

The striking of a match. A flickering. The beginnings of desire.

He tamps it down quick. 'Concentrate,' he tells the now apparently haggard man in the mirror. 'Just get through the next three days without fucking up and you'll be lucky.'

He thinks, then, of the life he's built. The flat in Marylebone, the pile of bylines, the shelf of embossed books slyly acknowledging his 'contribution'. Thinks of Isobel, brilliant Isobel – an editor herself – senior commissioning, at a mere twenty-seven. Thinks of her patience, her willingness to forgo living together, children, history; happy, for the most part, to be in the moment. And braced, believing again, he flushes, washes his hands, and walks out to the car.

He was right about the traffic. They crawl through South London, six miles stretching to more than an hour, the Embankment jammed with roadworks and red lights and a cycle lane that seems to have sprawled across more than its fair share of tarmac. And all the while he sits in the rear, staring from the side window like a moon-faced child or world-weary teen. It's one thing being in the back of a cab, as commander, the shamelessly chauffeured; quite another to be relegated, the third wheel in a party of three. Or – an awful thought occurs to him – the help. Though at least he's spared the indignity of the dogs – kennelled as they are, banned apparently, for fear of soft furnishings – if not their hair and dried-out spittle, which adheres to his trousers and, unlike its owners, refuses to be shucked off—

'Fuck!'

Daisy slams on the brakes and he is flung forward as they come to another juddering halt.

'I said we should have left yesterday.' Hal is hot, and harried, the air conditioning not up to much, or not enough, at least, despite his renewed efforts with the controls.

She slaps his hand away. 'Well it wasn't an option. And we could have got up at five but you pooh-poohed that. So here we are.'

James smiles at last, for who but Daisy would 'pooh-pooh' anything? And then settles, for now, along the A4 at Earls Court as they pass a vast Tesco, through Hammersmith with its land-locked ark, and then up onto the flyover, the M4 opening out in front of them, a six-laned yellow brick road taking them – God, Daisy – home.

They're past Reading and submerged in the murmur of radio journalism when he musters the courage to broach the fine print. 'So who else is coming?'

It's Daisy he's looking at, hoping to catch her gaze in the rear-view mirror, but her eyes are on the alleged fast lane, and it's Hal who answers. 'Old friend of mine,' he says. 'Julian Buchanan. Heard of him?'

James's smile is rictus, his reply a lie. 'Only vaguely.'

He's a Harley Street surgeon now, specializing in plastics – of course, plastics. Responsible for a double-page spread of celebrity nips and tucks, including the breasts of a countess, the lips of an International cricketer, and, if the *Mail* is to be believed, Daisy's own less-than-furrowed brow. Married once upon a time, but now rumoured around Fleet Street to have had several male 'companions', some of them paid. But the picture in James's head isn't of the Armani-suited silver fox he's seen paparazzi-snapped, but a swaggering strawberry blond, with a plum in his mouth and a hard-on in his shorts – a hard-on for Daisy that not even her sister, nor his tumescent homosexuality could shake off – and a chip on his shoulder at James's – no, Jason's – mere existence.

Jesus, what am I doing? James wonders. Why did I come? Why am I risking it?

He almost didn't. Typed and deleted an apologetic text three times before switching the bloody thing off and seeking solace not in gin but in the steady thud of feet on a running machine. But almost is no good to anyone and here he is – unable to let sleeping dogs lie, after all – so fucking buck up.

He smiles. 'I didn't know you knew each other,' he adds for effect.

'Julian's got his eye on a peerage,' says Daisy, uncharitably. 'So he's hanging around like a bad bloody smell at the moment.'

'Charming. If anyone's the bad smell it's Muriel. All that fucking patchouli.'

Another vision appears: a lion-maned waif, dazed and confused but endlessly enthusiastic. And devoted to Daisy of course. He wonders what has become of her. Of all of them, she is the one he's not bothered to follow in these last few weeks, so low was she on his radar. Perhaps she went back to Notting Hill – that flat must be worth more than a million these days. Or ran off to a commune or a red tent in Wales.

But now he's about to find out.

'She's coming. Did I tell you? And Luna.'

'Fabulous,' Hal sighs.

'That's her daughter,' Daisy says, for James's benefit. 'She's rather a handful and her father is . . . well, he isn't, basically.'

'And your daughter?' James asks, scrambling back to safe territory. 'Clementine? She's coming too?'

'Eventually. She says she's stuck at work, though what could be so urgent about her research I don't know. It's not as if she's curing cancer; she's a philosopher for fuck's sake.'

He realizes, then, he has neglected her – Clementine – too, makes a mental note to google her, or check her Facebook page. That's the trouble now, there's so little mystery. These twenty-somethings who carefully curate themselves but forget they are tied to facts and faux pas, dogged by the blogging and mindless tweeting of their younger, vulnerable selves.

'Good of you to come,' Daisy says then. 'I do hope you're not missing anything important on our account?'

'*Your* account,' Hal corrects.

He thinks of Isobel. Her initial belligerence. 'But I don't understand,' she'd protested. 'Why do you need to go? Why would she even invite you?'

'No, you don't understand,' he'd agreed, defensive despite his own misgivings, or perhaps because of them, convincing her to convince himself. 'It's just . . . how it works.'

Is it working?

'I should have asked,' Daisy adds. 'You could have brought . . . someone.'

The kindling catches again. Is she checking, he wonders briefly, the lie of the land? Does she know about Isobel? No, she can't do. But the thought of it – introducing the pair of them – is unimaginable, would border on cruel. So he comes up with a nothing answer anyway, all sidestep. 'I'd only have worked if I'd stayed at home.'

'How dedicated you are.' And then she does it, she catches his eye in the rear-view mirror and offers up a smile, small but private.

And his pathetic heart soars, briefly, before guilt picks at him.

Hal begins to fiddle with the air con again.

'Jesus, just leave it,' she pleads, winds down a window. 'That's better.'

Hal takes in a lungful. 'Mmm, motorway air. Bracing.' But he's playing, feigning now, demob-happy perhaps, now London and Westminster are far, far behind.

Daisy laughs. 'Remember that Beetle?'

'Christ,' Hal says. 'That thing.'

'You peed in a bottle.'

'I did not.'

'You did too.'

James stiffens at this. Not their memory so much, though he is troubled by the slip into the past, but the closeness. He resents it, he realizes, the conspiracy of it; the pair of them – Hal and Daisy – bound by their shared story, their shared selves. And, emboldened by hope, however brief, he swiftly insinuates himself, stakes a small claim. 'Which way?' he asks. 'Into the county, I mean.'

'Hal?'

Daisy defers to her husband but James slips back in quick. 'Plymouth will be packed. I've got it on Google Maps. We could cut up via –' he appears to peer at his phone – 'Gunnislake or stay on the A30 then drop down before Bodmin.'

'Don't be ridiculous. We have to take the bridge.' She catches his eye again, smiling – smiling! – brightly. 'The bridge is the thing! It's the portal!'

And sudden as thunder he recalls it. 'A portal after all,' she'd said. And he, he was her Mr Tumnus, her poor faun.

He hadn't understood it then. Only later had grasped the Narnia reference. But four hours later, as they cross the Tamar, and Daisy howls as if she's a rabid hound or hawk, he lets her have that one. Maybe this bridge *is* a portal, a door. But not to a pleasant netherworld.

No, Cornwall is not Lyra's Svalbard nor Bilbo's Middle Earth, nor any of your fantasy lands.

But it is a test of mettle, a task to be passed. And pass it he will. Though it pains him, pins him rigid to this sticky seat in fear and loathing.

For he's no longer the pauper in this story, the pub boy. He's a hero, a knight, a prince of sorts, perhaps; handsome enough, if not charming. And once this ordeal is done, once he has slain dragons, and even – dare he dream it? rescued his princess? – then he will live happily and ever after in his own hard-won kingdom over the hills and far, far away.

14.

Jason, 1988

He's seen it before, of course, but only from the boat. The single storey in sullen granite set almost on the water, its roof sagging, half its tiles slipped or missing. Fat Man Morris once told the assembled it was part of a gunpowder plot, a store for smugglers, or soldiers, perhaps, rebels fighting the stannary tax. But Jason knows better, knows it was pilchards it kept hidden, or cold, at least. So the parish records say.

There's still glass in one window, and it's there he catches her, mouthing to herself in the makeshift mirror. A cuckoo, he thinks, speaking stolen words – Daisy's words. And uncannily accurately, her voice a pitch higher, a touch louder, her eyes exaggerated, her gestures wild. And then he is mesmerized, not fooled, for he's followed her, knows it's just Bea in borrowed clothing, but at that moment she could be, to all the world, her sister.

'What are you doing?' he breathes.

She spins in indignation, sees him hidden in the gaping hole where a door once hung, then slumps, disappointed, back to herself. 'Nothing.'

He stammers out a sorry. 'I–I didn't mean to . . .' But trails

116

off before mustering, plucking up the courage again. 'Will you do it again?'

She eyes him. 'No,' she says eventually. 'What are you doing here anyway?'

'I . . .' He's thrown, thinks he misread her. 'I came to see you.'

'Right.'

'I did, I . . .' He clutches at something, anything to tell her. 'Did you know smugglers slept here?'

Her eyes flicker, finally, with interest. 'Really?'

'Yeah.' He nods, warming to his theme. 'They stored all sorts. Gunpowder, even. Under the floor.' He scuffs his foot in the dust for effect, sending it billowing.

'Might still be down there.'

'Could be,' he tells her, then lowers his voice for effect. 'Could blow at any moment.'

She steps forward, is inches from him now, her eyes level with his eyes, her breath – minted – mingling with his breath. 'Actually,' she whispers, 'I think it's a fish cellar. But that's not interesting, is it, Jason?'

Shit, he thinks, and makes to confess but, indifferent, she's wandered into a corner, and now leans against a salted wall, the stone stippled with crystals; efflorescence leached out over years.

'Why won't you swim?' he asks then.

'None of your beeswax.'

He's startled, not just at her rebuff, though that smarts, but at her words, stolen, as they sound, from the pages of Blyton, or from black and white films.

But before he can repeat his apology she softens, smiles in the thick dimness. 'Actually, I can't.'

The admission trips from her tongue as lightly as if she's telling him she doesn't like lions or spiders or soup. But growing up here – at least for half the summer – and not being able to swim is a big thing, monstrous, almost. To him, anyway. Because what else is there to do in this ridiculous village?

'I was ill,' she explains. 'For a while. I missed lessons. Then, afterwards, they were too scared to take me, I suppose.'

'Who's "they"?'

'My parents. Aunt Alice.'

'Didn't Daisy make you?'

'School did. For a while. Told me it was compulsory. But I . . . begged to differ.'

And at this, his awe and adoration slip into something like pity. Pity, and a desperate desire to be a white knight.

'I could teach you,' he blurts. 'I mean, if you wanted. You probably don't . . .' He trails off. She's probably tried five times over, is done with doggy paddle and the grunting instructors who goad her to float, a black swim-suited star on the surface of a bleach-stinking indoor pool.

But while his imagination is vivid, it is, it seems, wildly inaccurate. 'Where?' she asks. 'Not here.'

He rallies, thinks. 'I know a place. It's safe,' he adds. 'Sandy. And away from . . . them.'

She nods. 'When?

He is eager, too eager. 'Whenever. Now?'

She ponders, shakes her head. 'Tomorrow morning,' she tells him. 'At ten.'

It's not quite what he hoped for. She's not quite what he hoped for. But she's here, and as close as he can get and it will be a good thing, this swimming, a staggering act of selflessness.

Though of course, it's himself he's thinking of.

Because he'll be a hero not just in Bea's eyes, but in Daisy's too. A benevolent benefactor, and talented to boot. And he's buoyed by it, bigged up. 'Do it again,' he begs then.

'Do what.'

'Daisy.'

She pulls a smile, a wry, dry thing. 'Not now,' she tells him. 'Maybe later.'

But as she dips out of the doorway and back into the dappled sunlight, there is something in the way she flicks her hair that shows she is posing, she is being, for his benefit, her twin.

And he is thrilled at the kindness.

And the likeness.

15.

James, 2018

He's fought it for years. Battened down hatches and built vertiginous barriers over which he believed nothing could summit. But the slightest, strangest thing will split his veneer: the curve in a flock-papered wall, the clank of a pint glass against a tap, the crackle of taffeta worn out of season. And then through this gap memories march like ants on a careless drip of jam.

And oh, how they parade now.

He'd anticipated a maelstrom; a hot swirl of expectation tempered with watery disappointment. But, as the Saab rolls down the hill, as he spies the red-sailed boats bobbing, the shimmer of sunlight on high tide, it is more contained than that. He is braced, primed for a fight, perhaps. His sinews tight, his midriff rigid, his fingers balled into white-knuckled fists that, thankfully, fall out of view. But all the while the images come, fragments of snapshots, stealing into rooms previously sealed off and throwing open the curtains, unlocking the doors.

He see himself, a boy in uniform, his blazer badge resewn from deliberate rips, his trousers hand-me-downs that came in a brown-papered parcel from the Varlows along with checked shirts and wellies and a folded dose of shame in the shape of underpants. 'Barely worn,' Mrs Varlow had told his mother. But she, to his joy, bundled them in the burner as soon as the door was shut, and before his father got back and got wind. The trousers remained, though, the turn-ups adjusted so many times they resembled nothing more than a pinholed height chart, a testament to their appalling poverty.

He sees the pub, too. Its mantels thick with grease, its cupboards stacked with cracked crockery, its windows spattered with a vague spray of something that Sadie squirted then failed to buff up.

He sees the slipway iridescent with petrol from the ferry, the bladderwrack surrounding it tangled with plastic and the wooden sticks from so many summer holiday lollies. A village tribute to neglect and disregard and an astonishing lack of ambition.

And he sees Daisy, drifting in like a jewel in the jetsam. Or dropped, perhaps, like bicarbonate of soda into cheap lemonade, sending that flat, pitiful world frothing and foaming and bursting out of its bottle as she flung open the doors to Rashleigh and beckoned him in.

Rashleigh. Because that is where they land, of course. Of course! Its two-foot-wide walls white-painted now, but its garden still signed and gated, its rhododendron-studded lawn still shorn as short as the nap on a rabbit. It sends him reeling, a rush of recognition as intoxicating as vodka, as sobering as a shot of coffee. Though it comes as no surprise. He doesn't know what he hoped for – a rental up near the church perhaps. Or Mrs Goggins's old cottage, with its sprawl of unused rooms, long vacated by various daughters – but he knows what he expected.

'I thought it was sold,' he says.

'It was.' She spins round and grins. 'I rented it. Two thousand for the weekend. Can you imagine?'

He shakes his head, though he can imagine, has imagined. And now, here they are, standing at the edge of a precipice, at the bottom of which lie two pale, sorry bodies. His own, and her sister's. 'Daisy . . .' he begins.

But she's gone, clambering out quick as a cat and off to investigate.

'Don't bother,' Hal says as he opens a groaning door, stretches legs that have been trapped for four hours amid bags and odd boxes. 'She wants, what? Catharsis? Closure? Whatever you want to call it.'

'I . . .' But he can't find the words.

'You know about her sister, right? I mean, you must do by now.'

He swallows, nods. Knows everything and nothing. Nothing at all. 'But . . . on her birthday?' he manages at last.

Hal shrugs. '*Because* it's her birthday, I think.'

And then he gets it. Of course for her birthday. Because it's not just hers, is it? It's Bea's, too, or would have been. Fifty, the pair of them. And for the first time he wonders – allows himself to wonder – what would have become of her. Daisy claims Bea was the better actress, and he has seen some truth to this, but would she have bothered to follow in her sister's glittering, stilettoed footsteps? Or would she be sitting in a dusty office in Oxford, a professor by now, one of those fearsome Hildabeasts that send men sneering while secretly they quake in their Loakes?

No, she was too astute for that, too inscrutable. Rather, he imagines a Plath, a whey-faced poet, driven by brilliance but plagued by self-doubt and the advances of her own coterie of Ted Hugheses. And, for a moment, he almost laughs at the vision he has created. But then, it soaks him – the truth – as cold as the Fowey. That these possibilities are pointless, cruel, even. Given that she never had the chance to become anything other than a female Peter Pan, destined never to grow old.

'The key's over the road apparently.' Daisy interrupts him and he turns, grateful, to see her stalking across the lawn, scarf undone and swathed around her shoulders, sunglasses pushing back her still-blonde bob. She brandishes her phone. 'I called the company and they swore they'd told me but I'm sure they've got it wrong.'

'Does it matter?' Hal is agitated, sore from the Saab and the strangeness perhaps. 'As long as we get in.'

But something prickles. Something does matter. 'Over the road?' James asks.

'I think,' she says, her forehead beguilingly lined for once, 'they must mean the pub.'

They do mean the pub, or what's left of it. Because gone is the grease and the smeared window; gone the optics and bottles, the brass, and the brash, blinking lights of the fruit machine; gone the swinging picture, a faded painting of a crabber on improbably high seas. Gone, even, the notice above the door: 'John David Pengelly, licensed to sell intoxicating liquor'; the sign Sadie and he so loathed, so derided, laughing at the language, the suggestion that selling even came into it. 'Licensed to get pissed,' she'd corrected. And he would curl up in mirth, though both of them knew it was so far from funny.

She'd laugh at this, though, Sadie. At this holiday home, this house with a name; a dream posthumously fulfilled for their mother who longed for a Lodge or a Honeysuckle Cottage. 'Go fuck off up country then,' their father said once, who thought house names were arrogant fancy, were 'la-de-dah'. And he thinks of him, then, feels his sweating presence as he peers in the window, sees his reddened eyes rove over the rustic granola in jars on the grey-painted windowsill, the red gingham cloth on a sanded-down dining table, the blue-striped Cornishware already set for breakfast. 'Cornishware?' he hears his father scoff. And for once, he is with him, knowing the truth was cheap melamine and Formica and a bowl of Frosties if they were lucky, own brand cornflakes if not. But then down comes the hand, swiping the bowl and its contents to the floor, sending a puddle of milk splashing up his legs and pooling into the cracks. 'What are you going to do? Cry over it?' And the laugh that follows is almost as harsh as the slap he gets later.

*

They collect the key from the cleaner, a bloat-faced woman in a cartoon T-shirt and what can only be called 'slacks'. She tells them she does all the houses from here to Polruan.

'Must be big business,' says Hal.

She shrugs. 'For some.' Then, mindful of time, maybe. 'Check-out's at ten. No later. Not with all them rooms.'

'Of course,' says Daisy, touching her hand. 'June, isn't it? And thank you.'

And, as simple as that, the stiff grimness is lifted, her day made with the fleeting touch from a film star. 'Be seeing you,' she mumbles and shuts the door on herself, stranding them on the slipway, saltwater lapping at sand-silted concrete, the clank of the chain ferry a song across the water.

'Isn't it glorious?' Daisy demands.

'Glorious,' Hal confirms, though he's squinting irritably, and fiddling for a cigarette.

James looks out at the estuary. At the rocks stacked in grey slices like stale bread. Yellow lichen and gallons of gull crap standing in for pin mould. He remembers its proper name: guano; a word copied in longhand from a textbook. But no one round here ever called it anything but what it was: shit.

No one but Bea.

He swallows the swarm that flaps up inside him. Remember your name, he tells his quivering self. Just play along. Be the hack they think you are. But it's hard, so hard, when there are things he wants to know, to understand. And he has to ask, doesn't he? He has to help her remember, for the book. So he needs the truth of all of it. Of what she thought of Bea. Of what she thought of that boy, wanted from him.

And, even – he thinks of the glimpse of it in the car, of what it is to be caught in her attention, trapped like a fly, perhaps, or a light-dazzled moth – what she wants from him now.

And so he speaks. 'Was it always like this?' he asks. 'The pub I mean.'

'Oh God, no,' she tells him. 'Not at all.'

'It was a shithole,' says Hal.

James blanches. Shocked not at Hal's honesty but at his own embarrassment, even after thirty years.

'Oh, it wasn't that bad,' she says. 'Well, sort of. But I rather liked it. It was . . .' – she searches for the word, plucks it, ripe as a cherry – 'quaint.'

If it is faint praise, he is markedly un-damned; more flattered, perhaps, or relieved that his reading of her was right, all those years ago.

Of Hal, too.

'It was a dump run by a drunk. Hardly surprising it didn't last.'

'Happening more and more,' she says with a sigh.

'Not if I have my way,' Hal replies. 'One man's shithole is another pisshead's paradise.'

She turns to James. 'The people's pub,' she tells him. 'It's a thing. Communities buying them up and running them themselves. Hal's on a mission, you know. That and the homeless.'

James doubts Hal has squandered more than seconds lamenting the lot of rough sleepers, but it will play well in his constituency, winning plaudits from all sides – the bleeding hearts and stone-cold ones who place great store on being able to catch a cab or use the cashpoint without being harangued for loose change. 'How admirable,' he says, though he means it, more, in Machiavellian terms.

Hal nods. 'Can we get a move on? I'm dying for a piss and I'm not sure flopping my cock out on the lawn will go down well in the papers . . . Or maybe it will.' His grin is lascivious now.

'Hal! Don't!' But she only half means it, and James feels the spin beginning, a dizzying dance between wanting to get through this unscathed and wanting to stand up and shout, 'For fuck's sake, pick me.'

'I'm serious.' Hal's hand hovers at his fly. 'Give me the key or I'll piss here.'

'All right.' She holds up a hand. 'Here.'

She tosses the key and Hal catches it, snatching it from the air as if it were a mithering fly, and strides up the path, while she walks backwards, clattering wide-armed in his wake, no more than nineteen, it seems. 'Last one in's a loser,' she goads.

But when she spins back, he senses her smile slip, feels her falter. Because, though she pauses only for a moment, she doesn't then rush, doesn't even pick up pace. She walks slowly, in measured steps to the greige-painted door that now sits wide, gaping like the mouth of a cave, luring Aladdin to the treasure within.

For *this* is the portal, of course, not the bridge. This is the door that leads back to that Neverland. That Narnia.

Back to her. And to him.

And to Bea.

And to that summer when their lives flipped and floundered like fish in a net.

And as he lets that thought slink in and settle, it takes every fibre, every sinew, every steeled nerve for him to follow, rather than throw up and run.

16.

Jason, 1988

He's fucked up. Should never have offered to teach her to swim. Her, of all people.

The reasons he reels out to himself as he dithers by the mirror are manifold if tenuous.

Because she'll be hungover. Has to be. He listened to them last night: Hal herding them onto the ferry at seven, then leading them off some local's launch gone half eleven, last orders already called, singing and swearing and daring each other to skinny dip as they tripped up the slipway. Though none of them did. Least not here.

Because, even if she's sober, who is he to school her? Not like he's qualified. Not like he's even the strongest swimmer. Not at the galas in the blue-tiled pool at school, not across the estuary either – that prize goes to Robbie Cox, slick as a seal, and fuelled, he claims, by fairings.

Because what if she's weak? She was ill before, she told him so, and who's to say this won't bring it on again? And he'll be to blame, you can count on it.

But top of the list is this: that instead of waiting for him to meet her by the water like he told her, she's only gone

129

and knocked on the sodding door, sending his father swearing to get it.

'All right!' Then, mumbling, 'Bloody coming.'

Jason, rigid, winces as it creaks on its hinges, waits for his father's bafflement. Or belligerence. Or sheer bloody-mindedness.

'Oh, it's you. Who are you again?'

There's a pause, which Jason paints in with mutual confusion. Then, 'Beatrice Hicks,' she replies, without a hint of irritation. 'I'm here for Jason.'

Another pause, then amusement. 'Are you now? Well you'd best come in then.'

The door shuts, and two sets of steps trip-trap into the back. At that, he finds his own feet, frantically scrambles down the stairs, taking them too many at a time, slips and has to right himself before he falls to the floor in front of them both.

I'm a dick, he thinks. 'Bea,' he says.

'Hello.' She smiles, though he's convinced it's tinged with disappointment.

And no wonder, in this dingy kitchen. He sees her eyes alight on it, the grime and the tat, even the ornaments – his mam's china figurines that dance along the windowsill – all cheap gimcrack stuff, none of it fit even for charity. Sees her take in his father as well, just five foot nine but filling the room still; his white shirt yellowing, his teeth too, and one of them chipped. Jesus, the look of him. The smell of him.

'We should go,' Jason says then. Before she clocks any more. Before his father tries to invite her to stay or says something excruciating. But he's too late, and too stupid to realize he won't get away that easy.

'So where're you off to? Church?' His father cracks up at his own joke, a great hawking caw like a gull.

Jason's just glad he's not had a skinful. Not yet. 'Swim.'

His father snorts. 'A likely story.'

'Oh, we are,' Bea insists. 'Well, Jason is. I'm only splashing about.'

His father nods at him. 'Where's your trunks?'

'I'm wearing them.' Praying he won't have to offer evidence, he turns to Bea, begs her mentally to aid their escape. 'Are you ready, then?'

She tilts her head, thinking. 'I don't suppose you've got any food, have you? Only we forgot to go to the shops and Julian ate the last of the cheese.'

'I—' he begins.

'You wanna get over to town,' his father intervenes. 'Only Devlin's'll be open, mind, and only till four. Or you could pop up Lostwithiel, I s'pose, or over St Austell.' His hands are on his hips, his eyes shining like he's offering salvation not stale bread and sausages.

'Thanks,' she says, making it sound like she means it. 'I'll do that.'

'I think there's some biscuits,' Jason says quick, not wanting to stand around long enough to make a sandwich, but not wanting it to seem like they've nothing to offer. 'For now, I mean.' Though, truth be told, he's not even sure of that, so long has it been since anyone stocked up. And he has to cross his fingers as he pulls the Crawford's tin down from the pantry shelf, rusted round the edges and musty with it. The rattle's promising, but when he finally prises off the tight-fitting lid he finds only digestives that have seen better days. But then, a flash of red! A foil-wrapped Penguin that might have survived, and he snatches that gladly. And, inspired, thinks of the crisps in the bar and bargains for two packets of salt and vinegar.

'It'll come out of your wages.'

He shrugs. There's no pay packet to speak of in the first place, just the odd fiver blagged for pocket money when his father's in a rare beneficent mood. Besides, Sadie survives on pub peanuts half the time and no one's noticed, or got the nous to stocktake.

He pushes the swag into his backpack, along with a tube of congealed sunscreen and a fraying bathroom towel, the lavender pile worn to no more than thin cotton. 'Come on,' he urges, reaching for the door.

'Thank you.' Bea turns to his father and so wide is her smile it's as if he did indeed save her.

Not that the man's bothered. 'Back by two, you hear me? Be a few in after church so there'll be pots to wash.'

There'll be two. Fat Man Morris and Alan Ransome. Maybe Ned Pauncy. But hardly a crowd. Besides, can't he pass the buck to brethren? Isn't it her turn? 'Where's Sadie?'

'Gone up Liskeard for a job.'

'On a Sunday?'

His father shrugs. 'So she reckons. Says Spar's hiring.'

He pictures her in a checked uniform, pricing tins of cling

132

peaches. Then sees her straddling Simon Greaves who works the bar at the Webb Hotel. Knows which scenario's the more likely.

'Two,' he agrees.

Then, letting out a breath as vast as the harbour, he ushers Bea out, shuts the pub door behind them and steps into the day.

When they get to the mooring he remembers, though. 'Are you okay in the boat?' And he's surprised to find he's hoping for a yes, no longer grasping for a get-out clause.

She eyes him wryly. 'As long as we don't capsize.'

'Just, you said . . .'

'I say a lot of things.'

He nods, and gets on with it, pulling a pleasingly compliant *Dolly* alongside the slip so Bea can clamber on board.

'I haven't got a life jacket,' he says, half to himself, in realization. 'Sorry.'

'I trust you.'

He's pathetically thrilled even with that morsel, lets her settle in the prow. But the weight of it troubles him, squats on his shoulders, and as he turns the tiller, feels *Dolly* prod forward, he glances at Rashleigh and nods it a promise.

The water here is brackish, murky from the churn of sand and silt, the flotsam of dead leaves. But, undeterred, Bea lets her fingers trail in it.

'It'll clear once we're past Polruan. Before, maybe.'

She smiles. 'I don't mind.'

'So where's Daisy?' he asks, then corrects himself quick. 'I mean, what did you tell them?'

'Nothing. She was in bed. They all are.'

He chances a glance at the house again, sees it sits empty-eyed. 'You didn't need a lie-in?'

'Are you saying I look tired?'

His cheeks pink. 'No, I . . . Not at all. You don't.' She doesn't. At least no more than yesterday.

'It was a joke.'

'Oh.'

'I can handle my alcohol,' she expands. 'Or abstain. Unlike others.'

'Me too,' he replies, eager to distance himself from both Hal and his father. Then panics she'll think him a prude. 'Not that I don't. Drink, I mean.'

She shrugs, indifferent. 'What's with all the tins?'

'Huh?'

'In the pantry. Larder. Whatever you call it.'

He pictures it then, the serried ranks of canned hotdogs and war-hoarded sardines, the bland stacks of beans, peas, even potatoes. 'I—'

'Are you planning for nuclear attack?'

She whispers it, a conspiracy between them, so that he almost tells her yes. But the truth slips out unbidden. 'My mam used to do it.' But not because of war. She was worried, he supposes. That they would starve. That his father was incapable of something as simple as writing a shopping list, filling a trolley. And then, when they'd moved, Sadie'd carried it on. Just in case.

Now she's the one that shops. Though it's only the staples – bread, milk, cheese. Once a week they eat processed pies, heat up a Fray Bentos in its foil tray, then boil a sponge pudding in its pricked tin, the water somehow not seeping in, as if it's magic, not syrup inside. Other days it's stale cakes and pasties sold off on the cheap and brought home in his school bag. Though, when he can, he buys himself oranges on the sly, so scared is he of the teeth-bleeding scurvy he's seen in his *Illustrated History*.

'What happened to her? Or is that prying? You don't have to answer.'

'I don't mind,' he says, finding, to his surprise, he doesn't. 'She had cancer. Died two years ago. That's when we came here.'

'Oh. I'm sorry.'

'Not your fault.'

'I know. It's just . . . what you say, isn't it?'

He nods a reply. It's what everyone said. Says. If they speak about it at all.

'That's why I don't recognize you then. From before.'

He frowns. 'I don't . . .'

'We were taken to the pub when we were small. Well, the garden, anyway. For bottles of Coke. But I don't remember any children. Just an old dog with rotten teeth.'

He shrugs. 'I lived over Fowey then. My father, he . . . he worked up the boatyard for a bit. On and off.'

He wonders, then, what her father did. A lawyer, perhaps, or a slick politician. Rich, whatever. And he bets a fictional

135

fiver her mother didn't work. Least not in a pinny waiting on other men's wives.

But if she's looking down on him she doesn't show it. 'So we could have bumped into each other then. Been on the same beach.'

He nods, indulging her, though he doubts it. Beaches were for out of season and besides, he'd remember twins, especially such golden ones.

'So where *are* we going?' she says then. 'Not Fowey?'

He shakes his head. 'You'll see.'

The cove is deserted, as he knew it would be. There's no road, after all, just a hollow way trodden alongside the hedges on Dennett's land. Otherwise the only route in is the one they came by – boat. Though there's litter on the sand – bottles, the burnt carcass of a barbecue – that suggests someone's made the effort.

He takes *Dolly* in as far he can, anchors her. 'You'll have to wade, I'm afraid.'

'I'll live,' she claims, as she hitches her dress to climb over the side and into clear water.

But her hand, when he takes it, is damp, and he feels the faintest of tremors. And not, for once, his own.

'You should eat,' he tells her once they're on the shore. 'Before we start.'

'Yes, Mother,' she replies, not bothering to apologize, as others do when they raise the spectre.

It's strangely satisfying, sweet even, and he smiles as he hands over the Penguin, a packet of crisps, watches her wordlessly as she picks her way through the latter, then licks the biscuit, until the chocolate coating is gone, before burying the remains.

'Done,' she says, then stands, slips her dress over her head and drops it on the sand to reveal the same bikini her sister wore the day before.

'Isn't that—'

'So what if it is?' She dares him.

'Nothing.'

'So come on then.'

He undresses with his back to her, as if that will minimize it, his thinness, his paucity of body hair. But when he turns back she's not even watching him, but the water.

'How far will we go?'

'Not far. Not out of our depth at all.'

She turns to him. 'Good. Last one in's a loser!' Then runs into the sea, screaming as the chill hits her midriff, only stopping when it does.

'Fuck, it's cold,' she announces.

Emmet, he thinks; his father, or Sadie, maybe, whispering words into his head. He pushes them out, chip-chop, follows her into the water, wincing himself as it washes over his balls.

'It's fine,' he says, though as much to himself as Bea, as he makes his way over.

He cannot fathom her – her flips in mood: the reticence one moment, then artless bravado the next. It's hard to tell which is fact and which face. And when he reaches her – loser that he is – she is rigid and goose-pimpled, and not just from the shock of the cold, he thinks.

'So how does it work?' she asks.

'I'm . . . God, I'm not sure.'

She pulls a face and he racks his memory, sends it back to school and the pre-prep boys, wallowing in the shallow end with wig-headed Mr Morton. 'No, wait. You float, first of all. On your back. And I'll hold you.'

'Fine,' she says, though he can see she is far from it. 'So do I just lie back or do you go first?'

'I . . . Here.' He sinks into knee-scratching sand, holds out his arms.

She copies him, squatting, jinking at the chill, then waits for him to take her.

'Further,' he says. 'You have to lean back.'

But she's stiff, cannot bend that far.

'Relax,' he says. 'Really, you have to. You have to . . . trust me.'

She flaps at something, angry, and for a moment he's afraid she's giving up before they've begun. But then she seems to ready herself, lets herself sink back so that she rests across his arms, one below her shoulders, one – oh, Christ – one under her backside, so he can feel the smallest pudge of buttock and the thin sliver of fabric that barely covers it.

'Now what?' she demands, as if awaiting some sleight of hand, some grand magic trick whereby in moments she will float unaided, then swim out to sea.

Perhaps that's how it works, though. After all, Mr Morton seems to manage it just by shouting at them to lie back and raise their legs. And, while it's fair to say Jason lacks that man's menace, as well as moustache, he has to try something. 'Lift your feet,' he tells her. 'So they float too.'

She does as she's told and he takes the weight of her then, but she is board-like still. 'Relax,' he repeats. 'I've got you.'

And slowly, like the unfurling of a tentacle, she lets herself wash into the water, ride on its soft bob.

'There,' he says. 'You're doing it.'

'No I'm not.' She is matter-of-fact. 'You're still holding me.'

'Fine.' He lets his hands drift an increment. 'There.'

She panics instantly, thrashing her arms in a wild windmill as she tries to right herself.

He stands to grab her. 'I'm sorry,' he says, holding her shoulders.

She shakes him off. 'God, that was pathetic. I'm pathetic.'

'No,' he insists. 'I did it too quickly.'

But before he can offer to take it more gently she is on her knees again, waiting for him. 'I'll be fine, this time.'

He says nothing, just kneels quickly, lets her fall back and balance on him. This time he stays there until he feels the sea take over, feels her rise up on its slow swell. This time he says nothing as he lets his hands drop. This time he watches as she realizes it for herself and instead of wheeling she widens herself into a star.

'I told you so,' she says.

'What?'

'That's what you're thinking, isn't it? "I told you so."'

'Maybe,' he lies, playing along with the game. Though mostly he's wondering what to do next, and how he's going

139

to hold her on her front without feeling her breasts. Do they teach you that at swimming school?

In the end he gets her to grasp his arms, legs trailing behind her, and pulls her around in an arc.

'It won't work,' she says after a while.

'Give it a bit longer.'

'Not that.' She meets his eye. 'I mean trying to turn me into Daisy.'

He stops, horrified. 'It's not . . . I'm not.' Is he?

She lets her feet hit the bottom, lets go of him. 'It's all right. You wouldn't be the first. Even I try sometimes.'

He stands, awkward in the water now. 'Why do you want to be her so much anyway? What's she got that you haven't?'

'You want a list?'

He nods, though he's painfully aware he may be going through motions, saying what he knows he should. Because of course Daisy is different, though if he were asked to define why, he'd struggle.

'Hal,' she says.

He scoffs audibly, though again this is for her benefit. 'Why would you want *him*?'

'You don't even know him.'

He shrugs. 'Don't need to.' He knows the sort, has seen them at school, claiming the corridors, commanding smaller boys as if they're toy soldiers. Plastic. Snappable.

'It doesn't matter.' She stalks to the shore now, wraps herself in a fat, patterned towel and sits.

He follows, eyes his own mauve monstrosity, thinks better of it and flops wetly next to her. 'Tell me,' he says.

She sighs and he's concerned for a moment he's blown it. Though what, exactly, he's blown, he's not sure. What does he even want from her anyway other than an escape for an hour or so? He can hardly bray to Daisy now he's failed.

But she was buying time it seems, or mustering something. Because then she tells him, 'It should have been me.'

He frowns. 'What should have been you?'

She looks at him, then back out to the horizon. 'With Hal.'

A buzz runs through him as the hum of possibility begins.

'I mean, I found him first. He was my friend first. We would have got together only Daisy came to stay and she kissed him.' She pauses for incredulous acknowledgement, which he offers up gladly. 'He was pissed, of course. But he'd never even met her. So he must have thought it was me, do you see? Because you don't kiss strangers back, not like that.'

He nods. He does see. But he sees something else too. 'That's not Daisy's fault, though.'

'Of course not,' she replies, sarcasm thick as syrup. 'Nothing ever is.'

He thinks of something. Something key. 'Did she know?'

'Know what?'

'That you liked him?'

She pauses, thinks. 'Maybe.'

'Did you tell her?'

'When?'

'After she'd kissed him?'

141

'I could hardly tell her then, could I? That's all too coveting thy neighbour's ox.'

'Or being honest.' He doesn't know why he says it. As if he's able to confess anything.

She shrugs and, with nothing to encourage her, they sit in difficult silence.

'It's okay if you want her,' she says eventually. 'I mean, everyone does.'

He bristles at the insight, but will not answer; will not give her the satisfaction. Instead he segues. 'So she has Hal. What else?'

Bea thinks. 'Her tits are bigger.'

'No they're not,' he bats back. But he's too quick.

'How do you know?

He flushes, caught out.

'Anyway, they are. By a cup size. And she can swim.'

'So can you.'

'Not properly.'

'Not yet, maybe. But we can do this again.'

'You don't have to.'

'I know.'

She eyes him then, taking all of him in, so he has to look away before she can catch his flush. But she's seen it, or something. 'I know you're only doing it to impress her.'

'How?' he demands, diffident. 'She's not here. And I'm not going to tell her.'

'Only because I'm terrible.'

'No.' He changes tack to hide his lie. 'Anyway, why are *you* doing it? To impress *him*?'

'Hardly. So I can flounder around without drowning now. Big deal.'

They listen to the clamour of sand terns fighting for leftover Penguin. He thinks of his father then, and wonders at the time. But his watch is in his pocket, which is in his backpack. Not safe in the water. Not like hers. And something slips into him then, so that Hal-like, a swain, he takes her arm and lifts it to look. But when he sees the hands creeping to twelve and two, he starts. It's five minutes to curfew, and more than twenty back even if *Dolly* starts first time. 'We have to go.' He stands, not waiting for an answer.

She doesn't give him one. Doesn't argue, just follows him, coldly, quietly, back down the sand.

They're around the headland before she says a word. 'Can you drop me at Polruan?'

'What for?'

'I need an alibi,' she says.

'But it's an hour's walk.' And five extra minutes on the boat ride.

'My hair needs to dry. And you'll . . . you'll be fine.'

He won't but he doesn't say so. Just ferries her to the harbour wall.

'Here.'

She goes to hand him back a packet of crisps, but he shakes his head. 'You have them. For the walk.'

She shrugs.

'See you,' he tells her, then goes to turn the tiller.

But she pulls him back. 'When?'

He is blindsided. 'I . . . same time tomorrow?'

'Earlier,' she says. 'Make it eight.'

'Eight,' he says, regretting it instantly. Then, before she can try for seven, he turns, takes *Dolly* back out and up the channel, chugging for home.

Alan Ransome's swaying on the slipway, waiting for the three o'clock ferry. 'Your father's on the warpath.' His words are slurred, treacle-thick with Guinness and something else – rum, Jason guesses, by the taint of his breath.

'I'll bet,' he answers, refusing to rise, still brimming with the brilliance of the morning.

But Alan's having none of it. 'You're not too old for a hiding.'

He opens his mouth to answer, but words stopper up in his gob, slip back down his gullet. Because he'll never be too old, will he? Not if he stays round here.

And with that thought a cold, hard seed inside him, he walks into the bar.

17.

James, 2018

Does she see her in every corner? Behind every door? Does she see Bea?

He wants to ask Daisy this and more but can't. Because he knows the answer.

Of course she does.

And so does he.

He sees Bea barefoot in the hallway in a cardigan with too-long arms, sleeves pulled over her fingers, so that the overall effect is of a child playing dress-up.

He sees her sitting on the kitchen table, legs kicking idly, as she taps ash from a cigarette into a can.

He sees her sneak into the scullery, rich with mildew, to discover the damp has left a dusting of mould on the day-old bread like feathers on a fledgling.

Or maybe Daisy shuts her sister out, slams the door on her, as he does now. Then – oh! – then he sees Daisy instead. A slip of a thing – though she is barely more than that now – in a vivid pink bikini and some sort of ballgown or ballet skirt, dancing at the top of the stairs. He hears the song sometimes – Talking Heads – can hum the tune from memory, though the words evade him. Does she remember that night? He's sure she must. Though, if she does, she doesn't show it. But nor does he. For, though his insides swill and slop like porridge, he is capable, he finds, of affecting a smile. While Daisy, accomplished as she is, manages to appear far more taken with what 'they' (whoever 'they' are – no one has yet determined) have inflicted on the kitchen.

'They've buggered it,' she yells. 'Hal, come see!'

But Hal is upstairs, staking his claim, taking the master bedroom. And so, in his place, James rallies, happily – or at least readily – to inspect the mess.

The difference is stark. Gone is the wide, pine table and the buzzing behemoth of a fridge. Gone the discreet charm of the fifties cupboards painted that strange shade of caramel. Gone, too, the chipped sink with its missing plug and intermittent drip that no one even tried to fix. Instead there is clean Corian, neat Shaker shelving, a reclaimed Belfast basin that seems to gape, empty as it is of cheese-smeared plates and wine-stained glasses. And in the centre of it all, 'An island!' she exclaims – more fitting in Fulham than Fowey. At best it is inoffensive though, and he tells her so.

'I suppose,' she concedes. 'But the walls! They're so . . .'

'Clean?' he offers, before realizing too late that that necessitates them once being dirty – and him knowing it.

But she doesn't seem to hear it, laughs charmingly and smiles and says, again, that she 'supposes'.

They walk through to the drawing room then, admire the space and light now it's been knocked through, though it is a shame, she says, to have lost the formal dining space, in all its alluring gloom. The scullery is now a downstairs lav, which even Daisy cannot fault in its thinking, but upstairs the bathroom is 'too Tube-tile' and the bath itself a 'monstrosity'.

'The old one had this pipe,' she tells him. 'Instead of a plug you hauled up a tube, do you see? We were fascinated by it as children. "Waste" it said on the top. I always found that odd.'

It was odd. A relic, even then. Absurdly narrow and impossibly deep and made of some kind of thick tin that clanked and creaked when you stepped in it. While this one – all claw feet and pewter – suggests heritage while being, he assures her, 'more practical'.

'You're right, of course. Of course! Now, bedrooms.'

Hal has bagsed the master for them. Julian will have the blue room, Daisy decides, though when they troop in they discover it is now an insipid string colour, as are its neighbours. 'Farrow and Balled to fuck,' Hal maligns, forgetting his own hallway in Slipper Satin, the study in Plummett.

'What about Muriel and . . . what's her name?'

'God, Hal. It's Luna, you know that.'

'No I don't. I can't be expected to remember the names of all your friends' brats.'

'She's your friend too, and Luna's not a brat.'

Hal snorts. 'She's hardly fucking Mensa material either.' He turns to James. 'That is strictly off record.'

'Of course.'

Daisy sighs. 'They can take the front one. It's still got twins, hasn't it?'

She means beds, of course, though James is momentarily thrown by her apparent candour.

Hal shrugs perfunctorily. 'Fine.'

She strides down the landing, her footsteps oddly precise, clacking as they are on polished floorboards where they should be carpet-blurred. And he follows – of course – to find there are twin beds still, and a lined bookcase, but no sign of its former occupants or, indeed, the rabbit. And he almost sighs when he realizes this means he will be in the back room – his old room, albeit briefly. The smallness of it. The safety. But, when she beckons him, breath held, to look, he is floored to find it's now a second wet room.

'It's fine,' he lies. 'I can sleep on the sofa.' Though he hasn't done this since Jericho days, since his Oxford 'career', and has little interest in repeating that with its uncomfortable bumps and reek of ineptitude.

'You can do no such thing. There's an extension thing. I checked.'

'Really?' he asks. 'Where? Off the kitchen?' He imagines a modern box with some kind of IKEA contraption.

'Oh, it's not attached.' She pushes a lock of her hair over one ear. 'It's in the garden.'

'A hut?' He pictures a caravan or cabin, decked out in twee. Though even this is better than a tent, he supposes.

'Oh, much better than that, I'm sure,' she insists. 'Shall we go see?'

'I thought Clementine might want it, but she can take the back attic.'

He nods, though it is automatic, rather than any form of happy assent, so blindsided is he.

'It used to be a gunpowder store,' she adds with glee, attempting, he assumes, to sell it. 'Smugglers used it. It could have blown at any time.' She turns to him, quickly, her face painted grave. 'Though not anymore, of course.'

He places a hand on the once-salted wall, now slick with sealant, looks around at the day bed, the desk, the dove-grey floor. 'Of course.'

'Bollocks.'

They turn as one to see Hal in the doorway.

'It was a fish store. Pilchards or something. She knows that.'

Daisy glares. 'But that's not interesting, is it, darling? Not a story.' She turns to James. 'He's such a bloody spoilsport.'

'I don't care,' says James. 'It's fine— No, I didn't mean . . . It's perfect.'

'Isn't it! And because you're out of the house you can work,' she tells him, gushing now. 'Away from the hubbub.'

Away from her.

And stuck here with memories. Of that night— no, nights. First Bea. Then Daisy.

But he doesn't say it. Of course he doesn't say it. Instead he smiles magnanimously, and tells her that's 'splendid', says he'll be in for supper at seven as requested. Will bring the wine he packed.

'You didn't need to do that,' Hal says vaguely.

'Oh, I did.'

And he did. Because this isn't just wine, is it. It's a signal. A bottle that offers him a sort of salvation. That says he's arrived. That he is no longer the boy who pulls pints and drinks the dregs of whatever is left on the tables. He is a man who can distinguish a Petite Sirah from a Pinot Noir in the tilt of a glass, who can pinpoint a vintage by the veracity of tannin, who can tell you the hundred-pound Viognier you're tipping down your neck like it's bargain bin Chardonnay is nearly shrivelled to extinction, the recalcitrant panda of the wine world.

Yes, he is sculpted, schooled. He has the enquiring mind of a polymath and the equivalent of degrees in several disciplines. More care has gone into his creation than the ceiling at the Sistine, more thought taken with his form than Moore's monumental bronze. He is no Frankenstein's monster, no half-formed, fucked-up man of clay. He is a walking, talking work of art. No, more than that, a gilded triumph.

Or so he tells himself, again and again.

Because he has to. Even here in this back-story backwater. Because that – this – was only a chapter. No more than a blip. The caterpillar stage, the ugly duckling. And, besides, who is left to recognize him, to betray him? No addled father in the bar, no sister even, sullen in her pub purgatory. And the others – Julian, Muriel, Hal even – can have barely been sober or straight the few times they saw him.

Because he – Jason – is gone he reminds himself again, and James has arrived.

And he knows, in this instant, that whatever happens, it is over for him and Isobel. He cannot fool himself or string her along any longer. Because James was invented for one person only.

And that person is here.

That person is her.

18.

Jason, 1988

He catches himself in the darkened glass, his purpling eye a reminder of time, or his lack of ability to stick to it.

Sadie said nothing, just fetched the half-empty witch hazel, dabbed at him awkwardly with a ball of cotton wool. But she lacked her mother's hand and in the end he snatched the pad off her and pressed it down, letting the sweet-stink of the liquid soak into his lid.

'You should smack him back,' said Sadie then.

'Like you would.'

'I would, too.'

But their father won't give her the satisfaction or chance. Won't raise a finger to her, just his voice. 'Only villains hit women,' he said once, and he's no Hooded Claw, so he says.

But Jason knows otherwise.

He's been up here since opening, skulking. For his own sake, though, not his father's. He's gone out, see, over to Fowey to see a man about a dog, or a woman, Sadie reckons. Fat Man and Alan Ransome are in but they won't scold. Badge of bloody honour, more like. Some badge. He's had a go at it with his sister's make-up as well but not even thick, pink-tinted Rimmel could cover the worst of it and in the end he washed it off for fear his father would have him down as a 'tranny' and smack him again.

No, it's the others he's worried about. The lot from the house. Her, especially. Thinking he's weak or a prick. Though maybe it'll raise his stock. Don't they go for that, girls? A bit of rough? Barry Ransome reckons so, and his mam must've to marry Alan. Though Jason's no Barry, and his own father's no fair fight.

They're in the bar now, have been for fifteen – no seventeen – minutes. He waited for Sadie to call him down, to tell him his friends were here. But there's been no word at all, just a numb hubbub, and in the end the lure spins too silvery quick to resist – and the worry that Sadie will snag them for herself is overwhelming – so down the stairs he goes, braced for the Spanish Inquisition.

And for Daisy.

But on the former, only, he's almost disappointed.

'Oh, there you are!'

While her sister wears a thin gingham dress in nondescript green, Daisy is resplendent in a neon-pink bikini top and a lampshade of a skirt, the kind you might find at a ballet or in a Cinderella picture book. It is ridiculous.

And brilliant.

He nods at Bea, at the others, who take turns to clock his off-colour socket but have the breeding, or lack of balls, to let it be an elephant. Then looks straight, if sore-eyed, at Daisy. 'Here I am.'

She arches a brow, and he can see words teeter on the tip of her tongue but then she swallows them, saving them for later, maybe. 'I came looking earlier. But your dad said you were out.'

'Did he?' He wonders, worriedly, what else the man may have said, whether Bea's secret is out of the bag.

But Bea shrugs in answer to his glance and when he turns back to Daisy she betrays nothing, just asks, 'Are you coming?'

'Where?' he asks, blankly.

'To a party.'

His heart dances on tiptoe. 'When?'

She smiles. 'Now.'

He imagines his father, who dares him, just dares him, with his fat marrow hands and face like a ham. But for once, for the first time, he has a thought, a diamond-bright dare of his own, and that dare is: fuck him. Fuck him to the Lizard and back.

'Coming,' he tells her.

'Jason?' Sadie's standing, arms akimbo, eyebrows up beside the bar.

But it's not his night to be on, and not even legal, not according to Hal. And more than that, he doesn't really care. There's something in him, something keen and blistering, hornet hot, desperate for anything that's not . . . this. And so instead of an answer he offers a wave, takes his place in the Pied Piper's line-up and congas out of the door.

*

He's not been to a party like this before. Not been to a party at all, not since Tom Varlow's seventh, and he only got invited to that because his mam had made the caterpillar cake and the egg and cress sandwiches. She'd stayed in the kitchen in a butter-sullied housecoat while the other mothers, all sprayed hair and sipping spritzers, held court next door and, though he loathed himself for thinking it, he was glad of that, that she'd kept out of it. Not that he didn't stick out like a pin anyway when it came to present time: his cheap plastic beach racket sitting next to a plethora of Technic Lego and Star Wars toys. He still spasms with embarrassment when he thinks of it now.

But this? This will erase it, he thinks, send it packing to the past where it belongs. They sprawl on the floor, tapping ash on the carpet. No better than his father, really, stubbing out his fags on the bare table, in the place where a saucer used to stand. Until he . . . broke it. Yes, they disregard and deny their privilege with the same vehemence and desperation with which Jason covets it.

And oh, how he covets it. He itches to fit in, laughing when asked to, matching them drink for drink.

Four vodkas gone he's ready to confess.

'Don't tell me, you ran into a door,' says Daisy.

'I ran into my father's fist,' he replies, 'twice.' And pulls up his shirt to show her the sucker punch, a browning weal across his stomach.

'Fuck.'

She reaches to touch it and he flinches without thinking.

'Shit, sorry. Does that hurt?'

He can't tell her it's her fingers that are fire. 'It's all right,' he lies.

'Mine's the same.'

Expectant eyes turn to Hal.

'My father, I mean.'

'You show me yours . . .' says Julian, scornful. 'We've all been there. Christ, mine broke my arm once playing cricket.'

But Hal's not bragging about breaks or bruises. 'Cunt.'

Jason drops his top. 'What did he do to you?'

Hal fumbles for his Zippo, relights a joint. 'He sent me to Marlborough.' Clacks it shut, then clocks Jason frowning. 'Boarding school.'

Jason nods then, getting it, despite the gulf.

But Daisy, to his brief disappointment, then burgeoning hope, has missed something or misheard. 'Poor little rich boy.' She ruffles Hal's hair.

'Seriously, Dais?' Bea is wide-eyed, indignant.

'Scoff all you want,' Hal adds. 'He just paid someone else to dole out the beatings.'

Hastily chastened, Daisy puts out a hand and pulls him in for a kiss. 'I'm sorry,' she says. 'I didn't mean it.'

And just like that, it's all forgotten. But like an invisible spill, the chink remains, a wisp of a rift that he might step into. He sees Bea feel it too, and in their brief meeting of eyes it's as if a promise is made. An oath. To breach it, to cleave them, whatever it takes.

But it's hard to get Daisy on her own. Muriel is a limpet, whispering conspiracies, giggling inanely, and then, when she is prised away briefly by Bea, Hal manhandles Daisy to his lap. And so it's Julian he's stuck with.

'I don't know how you do it.'

'Do what?' Jason asks guardedly. Is he drinking wrong? Too much? Or not enough, perhaps.

'Live here. In this . . .' He doesn't say the word, but Jason can fill in the 'shithole' for himself. 'Aren't you bored?' he adds.

Jason shrugs. 'Sometimes.' Most of the time.

'Christ, I'd be crawling the walls. I already am. You know I could be in Goa with the Olsens?'

Who are the Olsens? Should he have heard of them? Fuck, are they famous?

'They're in his club.'

He turns to Daisy, pathetically grateful, and drunkenly wondering if she's managed to read his mind. 'Like a sports club?'

Muriel, back now, claps. 'Oh, is it? Do you play tennis? I played tennis once, with Sue Barker. At least I think it was her.'

Daisy shakes her head. 'Hardly, darling.'

'What do they do?' He's imagining both the terrible and magnificent, in wood-panelled back rooms, with whisky and, inexplicably, antlers.

She leans in to him, whispers. 'They wank each other off into a trophy.'

'Fuck. Off.'

'Oi.' Hal, sprawled opposite, kicks Julian's foot.

'They keep secrets,' Bea says then. 'Pull favours. Protect

157

privilege . . . What?' She holds her hands up at Julian's indignation. 'It's true, isn't it?'

'Like the fucking Freemasons,' adds Hal.

Julian is indignant. 'And what's wrong with that?'

'Nothing,' Daisy assures him. Then turns to Jason. 'If you're in it.'

'What about you?' he asks her.

'Me?' Her laughter peals out. 'Oh, girls aren't allowed.'

'No tits,' agrees Muriel, earnestly. 'Or twats. Twats are too scary.'

'Yours is.'

'Fuck off, Julian.'

'Happily.' He stands.

Hal looks up. 'Where are you going?'

'I think,' he muses, 'it's time to get this party started.'

19.

James, 2018

He wonders, worries, how she fails to see it – the boy in him. Though the hair helps – the colour fading to grey, mercifully, in his mid-thirties, and the curls cut Caesar-short into what his Fetter Lane hairdresser, Leon, reliably refers to as a French crop. And the nose, straight now, rescued from its break; the old scar gone too, and others – two thread-fine lines taking their place where his eyelids have been lifted, opened, where once they hung hooded, sullen, strange. Then there's the bulk he's managed to pack, going from a fey eight stone to twelve three now, and most of it muscle. Hard won, too, for he is naturally scrawny, inheriting neither his father's indulgent brawn nor his mother's practical width. No, he is nothing like that string bean of a child who could have matched Daisy rib for skinny rib.

What makes it all the stranger is that when he stares at them – all four of them now – they have barely changed; all of them so keen to preserve their precious selves it is as if they have been dipped in aspic. Daisy and Hal, their looks intact, improved even, with age. Muriel still perfectly Muriel: still lion-haired and tiny, still with the hint of a lisp, though her skin is lined and dry, her lips shrivelled, her insides, he imagines, corroded by filterless cigarettes and drink. Julian is the best of them, if youth is the measure: a perfect picture of Dorian Gray, kept in shape as he is by his colleagues' needles and his own precocious vanity. His hair is silver sand, dyed James doesn't doubt, but expensively so, and his skin almost glowing, stretched tight and translucent over cheek-bones he knows both Isobel and Lydia would die for.

But this perfection is only surface and, of all of them, he is the one James fears, for he has reason, form. He's called him – or called Jason, at least – an imposter before, charged him with fakery, with forgetting his class. And yet Julian of all people – this monger of plastic magic – must understand the drive, the desire – the, yes, even necessity – to remodel one's self. Yet as they sit, the six of them, Luna included, at the dining table, a mess of spaghetti on their plates and their full glasses fresh from toasting Daisy's upcoming birthday, Hal's campaign, the past, Julian says nothing, seems to see nothing, but Daisy.

'I can't believe you're going to be fifty,' he says. 'It's almost as if you've had work.'

'Well, you would know.' She smiles, malign. 'What are you again? Fifty-one? How does it feel, old man?'

'Touché.' He feigns an arrow to his heart. 'Though fifty's the new forty. Hadn't you heard?'

'Blue pills working, then?' Hal takes a mouthful of James's claret, swills it round, swallows and nods in approval. And the thrill he feels is as rich as the drink itself.

Julian shrugs, leans back. 'Don't knock them.'

'Oh, I had one once.'

All eyes turn to Muriel who is, fittingly, oblivious of her own daughter who is pushing pasta round as if it's art not supper.

'What? I did. It was marvellous! I can see why you boys like it.' And then – oh Christ! – she looks at James and winks.

He glances over at Daisy, appalled and embarrassed, but it's Hal's eye he catches, who gives him some sort of nod, as if he's handing over a brood mare. Or a whore. James turns away, seeks out something benign, lands on Luna – her mother's daughter in all but the colour of her hair, dyed a defiant pink. Still toying with her food with all the hallmarks of a seasoned anorexic. 'So, Luna, what do you do?'

She looks up at him, stumped. 'What?'

'School,' he says. 'What year are you?'

'Eleven? Well, twelve next week?' She has the irritating upward inflection of an Australian – a voice he once tried out for size, and he congratulates himself briefly for choosing better.

'She's just done her GCSEs,' Muriel adds.

'Oh, fuck! I forgot.' Daisy joins in. 'What did you get, darling? No, don't tell me. A stars.'

The look Luna shoots is thick with pity. 'They don't do that anymore? It's numbers? And I got 6s?'

'"B"s,' whispers Muriel, absurdly, given she can utter 'cunt' without flinching.

Hal snorts. 'Not everyone wants to go to sodding Oxford.'

'It's true.' Daisy places a hand on an arm so thin it seems

161

snappable, brings Luna into her conspiracy. 'Your mother didn't even finish uni anyway, did she tell you that?'

Luna manages a half-smile, flattered, perhaps, at being part of it, or just at being Daisy's god-daughter, though God, he supposes, never comes into it. And, thick with drink, he feels it again, the bliss that proximity provides.

'Oxford's overrated,' he says then.

'How would you know?'

Julian is poised, sly, and the claret sours in James's mouth as he wonders not whether to lie but which lie to tell. But before he can weigh up the options against his increasing ill-ease, Daisy decides for him.

'He went.' She turns to James. 'Didn't you?'

He nods, enough of an answer. Because he was there, wasn't he? So what if he never registered?

'Really?' Julian is bemused. 'Oh, wait. The poly. What's it called now? Oxford Brookes?'

It's that 'poly' that does it. Not even a question, but arrogant assumption. And this slick dismissal stokes something in him, pokes a wasps' nest so that instead of a get-out clause he is goaded into full-blown fairytale. 'St Hugh's,' he replies, plucking a customer from the back room of the Jericho pub – Andrew Harrington, a boy who spent his first year mostly stoned on a boat, but went on to head a hedge fund and is retired already, at the age of forty-nine. 'Went up in ninety-two.' The year Julian left; enough room to manoeuvre.

But he forgets Julian's old club, and his own clientele.

'Did you know a Scott,' Julian asks.

James looks back blankly. 'Scott who?'

Julian raises an eyebrow on a forehead that fails to crease. 'Not Scott anything. Jack Scott.'

He's stumbled, fucked up, has to scrabble for footing. 'Oxford's huge,' he offers.

'St Hugh's isn't.' Julian is digging, digging: an aye-aye poking a single spindly finger into the log to root out a weevil. 'Where did you drink?'

'The Bookbinders,' he tells him, truthfully, knowing it was bereft of medics; a haunt, in the main, of philosophers and goths. 'You?'

'Eagle and Child. King's Arms. Turf.'

James thinks of them then – not Julian, but his pals, his pack – piling out of the pubs in the centre of town, throwing up fifty-quid-a-go puddles of puke from the Moët and coke. Oh, he wanted to be them, wanted all they had: their Coutts' accounts; their clean, neat teeth; their breeding. But not for one minute would he have treated the world with such unedifying disdain.

'Where did you live?'

Round four.

'Off Great Clarendon,' he says, the truth again, before a lie. 'I don't remember the road. What about you?'

'Bardwell. Near the Dragon. And everyone remembers.'

James panics, flaps. 'It's all a bit blurry to be honest,' he lies. 'If you know what I mean.'

And it's Hal, Hal of all people, who comes to his rescue. 'Christ, isn't it?' he says with a snort.

Muriel nods furiously. 'I can barely remember me,' she says. 'Back then I mean.'

'Nice?' Luna sighs.

'Just being honest, darling. Anyway, isn't that what college is for?'

'What, getting wasted?' Daisy demands. 'Speak for yourself.'

Muriel thinks for a minute, 'No, I mean being new people.'

'Not me.' Hal leans back, surveys his faithful. 'I'm the same as I ever was. Same ideals, same politics, same massive . . . ego.'

'Hal!' Daisy slaps him, but playful, and again James is piqued at their closeness.

'Same shit taste in clothes,' Julian adds, eyeing him idly.

'Cheers, mate. Always reliable. Always a—'

'Bollocks,' Muriel calls. 'You were going to move up North. Manchester, wasn't it? Live in a squat, form a "theatre of the people".'

'She's right,' Julian says.

Hal holds up his hands. 'What can I say? Life happened.'

'You mean Clementine?' Muriel blunders in, dumbly.

But it's not her, is it?

It's Bea.

And at her entrance onto their small stage they all fall silent. Muriel's eyes when she realizes wide and white as hard-boiled eggs; Luna confused, her phone forgotten momentarily, her myopic gaze flicking instead from one adult to another, wondering what the fuck is going on. Hal fixed on his drink; Julian fixed on Hal.

Then there is Daisy, suddenly staid, and focused on a

corner of the tablecloth that she rubs between forefinger and thumb.

And all the time, James watches, nose pressed at the window, unable to speak, unable to spill.

But then she says it, pricking the balloon's stretched-thin skin. 'God, wouldn't Bea have hated this!'

Muriel practically heaves in relief. 'Oh, darling, why would she hate it? It's us!'

'Exactly,' Daisy explains. 'All this fuss. This . . . nostalgia.'

Julian shifts in his seat. 'Isn't that why we're here? To remember?'

'Yes,' she admits. 'Yes, of course. I just . . . Oh, I don't know what I was thinking. Muriel's right, I barely remember me back then.'

'You were dazzling,' Julian declares. 'Still are.'

'I was pathetic,' she says, her laugh the sharp clink of a champagne flute. 'Scared of everything. Dragons. Nuclear war. Even being sick.'

'I thought that was Bea,' says Hal.

She seems to stiffen. 'Bea what?' she asks.

'Scared of being sick.'

She shakes her head. 'Definitely me. Though I think Clementine did for that. Five months I was throwing up, and not just in the mornings.'

'Nice to know they're useful for something,' says Julian. 'She can shoulder some of the glory of keeping Hal from backstreet theatre, too.'

'Mate, thanks.'

Julian raises his glass. 'You're welcome.'

James's breath is tight in his throat, hardened to a nut as he sits looking for an in. 'And rabbits,' he says suddenly.

'Rabbits?' Hal asks.

'Daisy's scared of them. Aren't you?' he adds.

She frowns, albeit vaguely. 'Why would I be scared of rabbits?'

He feels a wash of cold water, sobering, a slap. 'I–I read it somewhere, I think.'

But then, 'No you were,' Hal insists. 'I'm sure of it. Their ears, I think.'

'How absurd,' she says, then laughs, looks at James. 'I'm absurd.'

'We all are,' James says, that 'we' dissolving the nut to nothing.

'Isn't she supposed to be here?' says Muriel then.

'Who?' Daisy asks.

Who? James thinks.

Muriel is confused. 'Who what?' She pauses, puts it together. 'Oh. Clementine.'

'Saturday,' replies Hal.

'Tomorrow,' clarifies Daisy. 'She's stuck at work.'

'But isn't she an academic?'

James nods, delighted at another in. 'That's what *I* said.'

Daisy shrugs off the snub. 'She studies the soul. Or the self. Something complicated like that.'

'How esoteric.' Julian yawns.

'How mysterious.' Muriel's bangles clatter in agreement. 'My soul is terribly complicated.'

Luna, amused, looks up from her phone. 'You don't have a soul?'

Muriel bristles. 'Harsh, darling. And of course I do. Noah, my yoga teacher, says I'm the most soulful person he's met.'

'Was "Noah" fucking you at the time?'

'Julian!' scolds Daisy, as Muriel slumps in a huff, ever the adolescent.

'What?' Julian feigns ignorance. 'Wasn't he?'

Muriel flaps a hand dismissively. 'Possibly, but . . . Luna!'

But Luna nothing. The child barely registers it, just rolls world-weary eyes and goes back to Snapchat or WhatsApp or whatever virtual world she thinks she inhabits. Besides, she's hardly silver-tongued herself, throwing around 'dick's and 'bitch'es; using 'fuck' like a comma. Though, as with all her generation, she litters her speech with 'like's, marking her out as the child she is when she thinks she's playing with the grown-ups.

Though not for long. Because swiftly Daisy slips out, then parades back from the kitchen, a pavlova held high like a prize.

'Pudding!' she declares.

Julian grimaces.

Muriel claps. 'That looks divine.'

'All my own work,' Daisy tells her, proud as a child with a pasta picture. 'Meringue from scratch.'

And James recalls the box in the boot, placed carefully, its precariousness questioned and corrected three times before she was satisfied. He'd assumed it was glass or some kind of fine china, but this is infinitely more desirable.

For some of them, anyway. Because while Hal and he compete to finish gluttonous bowls, and Muriel licks cream from the back of a spoon, Julian eyes the confection with all the distaste of a dentist, and declines, disappearing upstairs. Luna refuses too, excuses herself, citing tiredness, though she is glued to her screen every step of the staircase, typing furiously, and five minutes later he hears her on her phone, her every yelp, every 'omigod', every 'fuck' puncturing the floorboards.

Daisy goes to clear up but Hal grabs her hand, pulls her in for a kiss. 'Come with me,' he says. And, laughing, letting a plate clatter back to the table, she lets Hal lead her through to the drawing room, Muriel and James – red-faced, chastened – following along a few steps behind.

Hal turns on the stereo, and turns it up. David Byrne shouts a 'Hey' and jangling guitars kick into their riff.

'Oh!' Daisy exclaims.

Talking Heads, James thinks. God, *that* song.

'Little Creatures,' confirms Hal. 'Classic.'

Muriel, collapsed on a chaise, agrees. 'God, we *loved* this!'

'I know,' Hal grins, triumphant. He is King, again. Still.

And, it seems, Julian his scheming minion as, back from the bedroom, he holds up a tiny white envelope. 'Dessert, anyone?'

The jolt is as swift as a hit, the memory chemical sharp.

And the boy he was, appalling.

20.

Jason, 1988

Jesus fuck.

He is a god. A walking, talking – oh, so much talking – god.

Or at least a new man. Clever and confident and not a little cocky. But then so is Hal and look at him. Look where he is, who he is, who he *has*.

One fat wrap down and he is literally brilliant and anything, everything is possible. And all without even changing his clothes.

Julian has racked them up again: five little white lines on the flyblown mirror from the back bedroom. He grins, wide and wise and wicked as the Cheshire cat, then lowers his head and snorts, expertly, through a rolled twenty, then, eyes shut in glory, holds it out to Hal. Jason twitches. He's last in the pecking order but anticipation sends his legs itching with want and he's already half high on the next hit.

Muriel pauses, rolled note in her fingers like the world's most expensive cigarette. 'Did I tell you I'm fucking a lecturer?'

'Darling, you told us five times.' Daisy gestures at her to get on with it.

Muriel ignores her. 'But I am! He's ancient. Thirty-four. Can you imagine? I think his wife's a frigid bitch. I mean she must be, mustn't she? At least his balls haven't sagged yet.'

Hal snatches the twenty, takes his turn, hands it back. 'Wait until you're thirty-four and he's, what, fifty-something? Then you'll regret it. Testicles down to his knees.'

'Oh, I'll never be that old. Never,' she says solemnly.

Probably not, Jason thinks, as she snorts up a line, then with one wet finger wipes the mirror and licks it off like sherbet, as practised as Hal. But old is a long way away and right now they are alive. So fucking alive!

Except for one. Bea.

When the mirror comes round, passes her by, he pushes it back, wants her to feel like this, feel everything he feels.

'No thanks,' she repeats.

'Prude,' accuses Julian.

Prude, he thinks too. And he doesn't even bollock himself two seconds later. Besides, all the more for him.

He's astonished he's never tried it before – never tried anything but some rank dope he bought off Barry Ransome and had to mix with tobacco stolen from his out-for-the-count father. And that just blurred the edges, dulled it all down, made it fractionally smaller. But this – this makes everything pin-sharp and pretty, pulls the quick-spinning world into focus and puts him at the centre of it all, snapping with audacity.

'Shit!' Hal laments.

'What?' Daisy turns, concerned, and he thinks he might burst with the beauty and bloody unfairness of it.

Hal holds up the Moët. 'All gone,' he says, a hard-done-by child who can't recall finishing their own bottle of pop.

'How desperate,' says Daisy. 'How will we survive?'

But desperate he is and his heart catches in panic. Not at the lack of alcohol, but the potential end of the party. 'What about vodka?' he tries. 'Don't you have some of that?'

'Had,' replies Hal. 'We drank that earlier.'

'Beer? Cider.'

Julian grimaces. 'Jesus, we're not heathens.'

'The pub will have some,' says Daisy.

Julian scoffs. 'Will it fuck.'

'It'll have something.'

'Asti Spumante,' Muriel suggests. 'I drank that once in Bermondsey. It was surprisingly nice.'

Bea sighs. 'You think Viennetta is nice.'

'I do!' She claps, lost in ice-cream ardour. 'And rocket lollies, and those oyster things. How wonderfully common I am!'

'So, Jase, pub?'

Hal slaps him on the back, so hard he thinks he might cough or topple. But he pulls in a breath sharp, puts on his smile. 'Course.'

Of course. There is nothing he can't do right now, so high is he on life, on pure possibility.

And so they go, Hal leading the way but he, Jason – Jase! – in second place, across the lawn, over the slipway and into the jangling dank of the pub.

*

171

His father's not back but Sadie clamours around, clucking, preening like a prize hen, still indignant at the twin visions – she'd not suspected a thing! How could he not have told her? – chiding Hal for his part, too, but then finds them a bottle of Bordeaux in the back, a sample left by a seller, who didn't listen when the landlord told him there was no call for anything that fancy round here.

She clinks ice into the glasses and he flinches at the foolishness, flushes with shame at the ignorance of his own flesh and blood. But while Julian groans, Hal snatches his greedily and Daisy seems delighted by the daring of it, the invention.

'It's almost like a cocktail,' she proclaims.

And at that, he gets behind the bar, rummages in a jar of pennies and stamps and elastic bands, before pulling out what he's after: a pink umbrella.

'Here,' he says, balancing it on the rim of her drink.

Daisy smiles, kisses him on the cheek so quick he thinks he might have imagined it, were it not for the grease on his skin, the tremor in his legs.

The wink she gives him over her bare shoulder.

Julian leans over then, his vinegar-sharp breath hot on Jason's neck. 'Don't be getting any ideas.'

He pulls away. 'I'm not,' he insists, and for a second he almost believes himself, so addled is he.

But 'ideas' are what he thrives on, survives on, and so thick and fast do they come tumbling he can barely catch them all to keep them safe. He can be anyone, do anything, even claim Daisy. Besides, Hal barely clocks her, busy with Sadie and big ideas of his own.

'You should move,' Hal is telling her.

'Where?' she begs, practically panting; a dog with a treat dangled out of reach.

'London. Oxford. Wherever. You'll die here.'

She nods, falling for it. 'Where do you live?'

'Nowhere. Well, Oxford. For now. But once I'm done I'm heading North. Get some . . . reality.'

'Isn't Oxford real?'

She's stupid, Jason thinks. Doesn't get it.

But Julian muscles in. 'It's a fucking theme park.'

A theme park. Of excellence. Of men who will change the world and women who will love them. It sounds – it is – fucking wonderful when your sights are limited to, at best, a minor public school and a red brick.

But Hal's designs are wider.

He expands. 'The people. The people aren't . . . authentic. Manchester, Hull, Newcastle. That's people. Real people.'

'"People".' Bea seems to seethe. 'It's always about the bloody "people". Who are these mythical "people"?' She turns to him. 'What about Jason? Is he "people"? Why don't you ask him what he wants?'

He is embarrassed. Christ, even Hal is embarrassed, a pink tinge to his cheeks. But faint, and not enough to stop him. 'Isn't it obvious?' he says, gesturing at Jason. 'He wants what everyone wants. More jobs. Better jobs. Workers' rights—'

'No I don't,' Jason blurts. Then stops, checking himself, before realizing, yes, he *is* right. 'I don't,' he repeats. 'You know what I want? I want to be you. I want champagne and cocaine and . . . and this!'

Daisy laughs, astonished. Muriel claps. 'How adorable!'

Bea shrugs. 'See?'

'I . . .'

Hal begins to say something but, for Jason, it's lost to the touch of Daisy's hand on his arm.

'No you don't,' she tells him. 'You don't want that.'

He wants to agree but he cannot deny it. 'I do,' he insists. 'I want this.' He waves his arm wildly, taking in Hal, Muriel, Julian . . . Rashleigh, besides. 'All of it.'

And you, he thinks. I want you.

I want to fuck you.

His mind is steeped in it then. The certainty of it. Oh, he's fancied girls before in a half-arsed way. Entertained notions that one day he might get to undress one, but it was formed more from duty, desperation. He didn't love any of them, didn't know any of them well enough to even like them with any base of evidence. They were no more than faces and, though he maligns himself, tits he'd seen around town, on the bus, up Plymouth once, spilling out of C&A like a rainbow of knickers from a dresser drawer.

'Forget it.'

'Julian!' Daisy's defending him. Taking his side. Which only stokes his hope, his conviction.

But Julian sighs. 'I'm just being honest. Cruel to be kind. He'll never be Hal.'

'Who said I want to be Hal?'

'You did.'

He says nothing to that. Can't deny it. Instead he demands proof. 'Why not?' he asks. 'Why can't I be just like him?'

Julian sets down his glass on the bar, ice cubes melting in watery wine. 'Class,' he says. 'Pure and simple. You can try to deny it, defy it, but it will always out.'

'Bollocks,' Daisy says. 'Class means nothing. It's . . . bullshit.'

'Really? What's this?' Julian turns to Jason, holding up a sheet of white paper from the silver dispenser that squats next to the ketchup.

'A serviette,' he replies quickly, unaware of the trap.

Julian smiles, thin and obsequious. 'A napkin.'

'Julian.' Daisy's voice is soft now, pleading.

'What?' He holds up his hands.

'Stop . . . taunting.'

'I'm not. I'm just . . . saving him the effort.'

Daisy turns. 'You can be whoever you want to bloody be. Except Hal. There's only one Hal, thank the Lord.'

'Be who you want?' Bea snorts. 'Only people who have money say that.'

Daisy's eyes are still on him, with him. 'So he'll get money.'

Julian. 'Then what? That would change things? He'd still be a fucking hick.'

Daisy blazes. 'Fuck off, Julian.' She slams her hands into him.

His princess, his saviour.

Julian staggers back, knocks into Fat Man Morris at the fruit machine, who spills Special all over his shoes.

'What the fuck?' He swings round, fixing for it.

'Jesus,' laments Julian. 'Calm down. I'll pay for a new pair.'

175

Fat Man laughs, holds out his hand. 'Go on then.'

Jason waits, baited, not sure what wonder or horror might come next; not sure what he wants to come next.

'Julian.' Bea's pleas are loud now.

'Fiver cover it?'

It takes a minute for the slight to sink in. Then, like a sloth raised from slumber, or an elephant waking, it dawns on Fat Man. 'You wanker.' He throws a flailing fist.

Julian steps back, arms wide, still laughing. Hal grabs at him. 'Mate.'

Alan Ransome is fronting up now. Sleeves pushed up, 'come on' written all over his red face.

And Jason? Jason is dancing with it, drinking it in. The air so thick you could slice it like butter. So thick he can barely catch his breath. A gape-mouthed Sadie gasps, grabs at the lemon knife, as if this is *West Side Story* and she, Maria. He should do something, protect someone, and he lurches at Daisy just as the door opens and his father's swarthy form fills the frame.

'Oi, oi.'

Everyone stops. Stills. Even Fat Man, who brushes himself down, dignified now, defiant.

'Out,' orders his father. 'Now.' He gestures at them, the Rashleigh crowd. 'Not you, son.' He grabs at Jason, snatching his scruff like a mange-ridden stray.

Jason flails, wrestles out of his grasp but only as far as the fruitie.

Bea holds out a hand. 'Come,' she mouths at him.

He tries to find Daisy, waiting for a say-so, but she's

halfway out the door, hand clasped in Hal's, the dregs of the bottle in the other.

And he feels it then. Something is gone, washed out of his blood or fled through the door, perhaps, a rat from a sinking ship. And so he drops his bravado and his gaze, turns his blurry attention to the pots.

The party's over.

The door slammed, Fat Man back in his seat, his shoes still sodden but a fresh pint in his fist, his father swaggers to the bar. He doesn't smack him this time, just slaps down an order. 'They're barred. Do you hear me?'

Jason nods, eyes still sink-ward.

'Bloody upstarts.' He pauses, grabs his son's chin, peers into his eyes with his own bloodshot ones. 'Least you got blotto.' His father laughs then, an awful guffaw that rattles through his chest and sends him coughing. 'Maybe you'll get your end away one day and all.'

Jason says nothing, his mouse-fast heart still chemically charged, even if he can't feel the fun anymore. 'Maybe,' he says.

'Next fucking century,' says Fat Man, cock of the walk now the emmets have gone.

For a moment he thinks his father, silent, primed, might clock Fat Man instead. Fat Man agrees and braces, waiting.

But instead of a fist he throws out a laugh again. 'If he's lucky,' he says. Then, satisfied with his handiwork, it seems, he sits down at his table, signals at Sadie to bring him a pot.

'Parent of the year,' Sadie says when she sidles up to Jason after.

He shrugs. He's not bothered. Not anymore.

Not where he's going.

London, or Oxford, or even up North.

No matter whether they're real or not. He'd take fucking Narnia now. Anything over this.

He sees them again later. Naked, they are, four of them – Daisy and Muriel, Julian and Hal, dancing in and out of the water as if they're invisible, as if no one is watching.

But someone is. Because there is Bea, in a cardigan with arms far too long, knees pulled up as she squats on the rocks like a siren or seal. And there is he. Standing half-dressed himself, one hand on the curtain and one in his shorts.

Hard as granite and panting for it, he wanks as he watches her, her breasts high and pale, the 'v' of her dark and inviting and wet already, as if she is dancing for him, parading for him. Waiting for him.

Still tainted with chemicals it takes him a while but he's almost there, almost there when the other one catches him, looks up at the window and, oh fuck, smiles.

He drops his cock, drops back behind the curtain, deflated, distraught. He tells himself lies then. Maybe she missed him. Maybe she was smiling at life, at all the stars electric bright.

But when she wakes him at eight, it's not with a knock at the door but a stone to the window.

His window. And his heart falls as limp as his dick.

Though, if she cared what he was doing last night, she

wouldn't be here. Or so he tells himself as he hauls his barely
rested body out of sweat-sticky sheets, pulls on trunks and
a T-shirt, and trips quickly down to the too-bright morning
after the night before.

21.

James, 2018

He slaps the wrap down on the coffee table like it's a winning ticket or certificate of brilliance. Awaits the praise.

But Hal is rattled. 'Jesus, Julian. He's a fucking journo.'

Julian eyes James, dares him.

He shrugs. 'Strictly off record. Besides,' he adds, seeing an in for a dig, and for a golden opportunity to put himself at the heart of it all, 'do you really think you're unique?'

Muriel claps. 'Oh, do tell! Is everyone at it? Is it the royals? Or . . . who's that one with the tits and the kittens? From the advert – Daisy, you must know who I mean.'

'Muriel!' Daisy upbraids her, appalled. But—

'It's fine,' he insists. 'And no, it wasn't a royal or the one with the kittens. Who is that anyway?'

Muriel shrugs. 'I forget.'

'You forget everything,' says Julian, turns to James. 'So who, anyway?'

'Footballers, if you must know,' he replies. 'And a singer, opera not pop.'

'Oh, I know the one!' Muriel shrieks. 'I knew something

was up with her. No one who sings opera can be that thin, not normally. Not without help. How the fuck do you think I kept the baby weight off?'

'Muriel!' Daisy repeats. 'James, scrub that from your memory.'

'Really,' he says. 'None of my business.'

Or even of interest.

Oh, he has been there. Has been King of the World, soaring on chemical wings. But as it inflates the ego it loosens the tongue, and that he cannot risk. So when the CD case is passed around, the pristine fifty, he hands it straight over to Muriel, who, without even a glance at the ceiling, sniffs up her share and hands it to Hal.

'Daisy?' Hal, ever the gentleman, holds the lot out to his wife.

She pauses, and he wonders why, whether she's weighing it up or working out how hard to come down on him. Because come down she does.

'Hal, really.'

He shrugs, takes it back. 'Your loss.'

James's gain.

Because, three lines later, while the boys are bragging and braying and Muriel is absorbed in her own glory, an ageing Kate Bush wuthering wildly to old Bristol triphop, he gets the benefit of Daisy's attention.

'Having fun?' he asks.

But she doesn't dignify such an anodyne query with an answer. 'What were you like?' she counters instead.

'When?' he says, alert now, wary.

'Back then. Late eighties. You must have barely been more than a boy.'

'Barely,' he agrees, back-pedalling now, wondering what to admit, what to omit. 'A typical teenager,' he comes up with. 'Desperate to get out.' He doesn't say where from, assumes that will do. But he has underestimated Daisy's own probing.

'From where?' she asks.

Lie, he tells himself. Remember the story. But Hampshire flaps and flutters just out of reach while Washington Square gets stuck on his tongue. In the end all that comes out is, 'Home.'

'How very . . . evasive. Do you ever go back?'

He breathes with relief, then tautens again as he finds he has to pluck another truth from the shelf. 'Not for a long time,' he relinquishes. 'My parents are both dead. You know how it is.'

She nods, solemn, and then, in an act of grace, rests a hand on his thigh – only for a moment, but so touched, so taken is he, he believes he must glimmer with it.

'Maybe I'm the same,' she says then. 'Maybe I've avoided it. Maybe Julian's right. Maybe I haven't grown up at all.'

'That's not what he said,' he tells her, hard though it is to defend such a blunderer. 'He said you were dazzling. Then and now.'

'*She* was,' says Daisy quietly.

Now that, he knows, is a falsehood, and, though he wants to shake Daisy, to show her how she glows, still, he cannot belittle Bea. Not today, not now, not when she is at the heart of this visit. And so he lies. 'No,' he says simply. 'I'm sure you both were.'

She shakes her head. 'Maybe it *was* Bea who was scared of sick,' she says.

'Does it matter?' He attempts to placate.

But she ignores him. 'Paper dolls, my mother called us. No one could tell us apart. Except her, of course.'

'Bollocks,' Hal says, turning his attention. 'I could.'

'What's that?' Julian rubs his gums, joins in.

'Daisy says no one could tell them apart. Her and . . . Bea.' The pause before Hal says her name is paper thin, but there. 'Well, I bloody could.'

'And me,' Julian adds. 'Or did I accidentally fuck you too?'

James winces at the low blow, though knows it to be true.

Hal frowns. 'Jesus, Julian, really?'

But he snorts, laconic, leans back, pleased with his work.

James waits for Daisy to berate him, for doing that to the memory of Bea, for doing it to her in the first place. But she astonishes in her generosity. 'At least she wasn't your last,' she says. 'I'd hate to think that was what put you off.'

'Because *that's* how it works.'

'When *did* you swing?' demands Muriel. 'Because you never fucked me. Did you?'

'Sweetheart, I could never get past the queue.'

James switches it off, lets it wash over him, nothing but hot air. Hal is right though. They weren't indistinguishable, whatever Daisy likes to believe. Though it's true that Daisy has absorbed her, taken a part of Bea on. Maybe it's a subconscious trick to keep her memory alive. Or perhaps she has become nothing more than a dead limb, perhaps she'd rather shed her. But no, he cannot see any trace of a weight as, pulled to her feet by Muriel, she dances feather-light, her shoes kicked off, her back dappled by the glass lampshade. So young she looks, so, yes, dazzling. So . . . Daisy. Muriel rests her head on her and he feels his dick stiffen, as if it is him in her place, his lips grazing Daisy's shoulder blade.

'You've heard the rumours?'

Julian. And he says a silent thank you that the switch is dimmed, provides some sort of alibi. 'About who?'

'Muriel, of course.'

He shakes his head, relieved at her ridiculousness that so garners attention. 'What rumours?'

Julian seems surprised. 'That she once flatlined in some dump in Pimlico. That she shagged a cabinet minister.' He pauses. 'That she was into Bea. The sister. It's all bollocks, of course. Self-perpetuated. She thinks it makes her inter-esting.'

'I . . . I don't know what I'm supposed to say.'

Julian smiles. 'Pity and disdain are all it will elicit if you have any sense. But I'll tell you one thing.' He leans in. 'She's a fucking animal in the sack.'

James rewinds the conversation. 'I thought you hadn't been there.'

'Oh, I have. But she doesn't remember. The ultimate bloody insult. Or it would be if I gave a fuck about fanny anymore. But try her, do.'

James has heard it before, this soliciting, pimping – it comes with the class. But still it fills him with rancour. 'Thanks,' he says coldly. 'I'll pass.'

Julian laughs, a short, scornful sound. 'I thought what happened on location stayed on location. Strictly off record, you said.'

He shrugs, non-committal.

'Oh, wait,' says Julian, his voice brimming with it. 'Not Daisy.'

He reels – is it obvious? Or just assumption? – and says nothing. There's nothing he *can* say without incriminating himself or putting down Daisy.

But his silence, it seems, speaks the truth of it. How bloody ironic.

'Jesus? Seriously? Not a chance. Oh, she'll play with you, stroke your ego and your cock, metaphorically. But it's him she wants. Hal. Always has been.'

James's heart seems to plummet as he watches Hal pull his wife from a reluctant Muriel, claim her for his own version of slow-dance. 'I have a girlfriend,' he says then, trying to conjure some soft-focus flattering notion of Isobel, the kind that will glaze his eyes, render him a man besotted. Her bare-faced over breakfast, dressed in his shirt. Prone on the mattress, face deep in a pillow.

But his withdrawal fails. He doesn't love her; has resolved to end it. He's fooling nobody, least of all himself.

'Like that would stop her,' Julian replies. 'She's done it before.'

He's confused now. 'Muriel?'

185

'Daisy.'

He should ignore him. Should know it's just goading. Should retreat to the outhouse and the tapes he's still to transcribe, the shorthand he scrawled before dinner, noting her attitude, her thoughts on Cornwall. But whatever he has told himself, pressed himself to believe, he is a hack at heart and cannot walk away from a story. Nor from Daisy besides. 'What do you mean?'

Julian is primed, delighted. 'It was here,' he begins. 'There was a boy. A kid, really.'

Fear drips bitter and thick, sending his bowels churning, a soup of meringue and panic. 'When?'

'Thirty years ago.'

Fuck. 'What do you mean?'

'He hung around like a stray dog. But she encouraged him. Led him on like she was going to let him. Like fuck she would.' He pauses to enjoy his story. 'I felt sorry for him, really.'

James studies his face, looks for clues as to whether this is contrived or coincidence. But the face is smooth, unmoved, so he banks on the latter, feigning indifference, though that is a struggle. 'What happened to him? In the end?'

'You're a reporter, aren't you? I thought you'd know.'

He laughs, though it takes everything in him to force it out, to follow with the words, 'Obviously not a good one.'

Julian smiles, satisfied. 'Oh, he died. Trying to save her sister.'

The seconds he holds James's stare slow and slip into what

seem like minutes. But then it is over, dismissed, as swiftly as it was suggested.

'Drink?' he offers.

But James shakes his head. 'I think I'm done.'

22.

Jason, 1988

By the following Friday, a sort of appalling boredom is kicking in. Hal huddled in the shade of an immigrant cedar with his open notebook and the dregs of a bottle of red. Julian listless, medical textbooks littering the parched grass around him. Bea reading, another Virginia Woolf. Muriel still ignoring decency laws in favour of a strapless tan. But Daisy – ever the treasure hunter – finds glory in all of it.

'Isn't it funny how it all becomes ordinary?' she says.

Muriel sighs, turns onto her side. 'What?'

'Cornwall. Like we've lived here forever.'

'God forbid,' Julian says without even opening his eyes.

Daisy ignores him. 'I rather adore it.'

'No you don't,' Bea insists. 'You'd be desperate for Greek Street in weeks.'

'I'm not even missing it. Seriously, maybe we should move. All of us. You could set up the theatre here, Hal.'

Hal looks up from a page of scrawled playscript. 'And play summer stock for the yacht brigade? No thanks.'

Daisy sighs. 'Rich people need theatre too. You could

convert from the inside. An agent provocateur. How admirable.'

Hal snorts. 'I'm moving to Manchester, not playing fucking jester for a bunch of trust fund junkies.'

'Says the boy with the biggest trust fund in Christendom.'

'Shut up, Julian,' says Daisy.

'I wish I had a trust fund,' Muriel muses.

Daisy takes the cigarette from her, takes a drag. 'You do, darling.'

Muriel's brow furrows as she tries to fathom this possibility. 'Do I?'

'You know that money that goes into your bank account every month?'

Muriel nods.

'Where do you think that comes from? A mysterious benefactor?'

Muriel claps. 'Like Magwitch! Or Miss Havisham.'

'Jesus.' Julian rolls onto his stomach.

Muriel turns to him. 'I know it isn't really. More's the pity. I'd rather like a benefactor. Other than my father.'

Daisy holds out the cigarette. 'I'm sorry, darling.'

Muriel takes it, sighs. 'I'll live.'

And Jason? Jason takes it all in with the attention to detail of a court stenographer and the gaping astonishment of a tourist on the trail of a lost tribe. Because these days are golden; are so far from ordinary as shit from champagne.

Ordinary? Ordinary is scuffed shoes a size too small and a decade out of fashion but you have to wear them anyway. Ordinary is scraping together the bus fare to Plymouth to spend your five-pound Our Price voucher – your only Christmas present, aside from socks. Ordinary is own-brand biscuits and knock-down yoghurt and a breadline that's economy sliced white.

This? This is *extra*ordinary.

And he, unbelievably, is part of it.

In the mornings, while his sister's still sleeping and his father's passed out, sweating off the bottles, he takes Bea out on *Dolly*, teaches her to hold her breath, to tread water, to stretch her doggy paddle into a cautious front crawl. Then, boat stowed, he sees out the midday shift until three when last orders are called and he slips back out to the fish cellar where she repays him with lessons in deportment. For, yes, she has taught him the words he can and cannot use:

Dessert, not pudding.

Sofa, not settee.

Supper, not tea.

The items he can and cannot own:

Handkerchiefs not tissues.

Chinos not combat trousers.

Desert boots not Nikes.

She has honed his accent, too, drawing out his vowels and clipping his 't's with precision so that, when she says 'be Julian', like a performing dog he can please her immediately, summoning up the same effete, affected boredom, the same silver spoon.

'What about Hal?' she asks.

He slips into an odd cod cockney, drops his 'h's and picks up a swagger. 'Oh, fack off,' he tells her.

'God, it's uncanny,' she says.

Hal catches them later, aping him. Wandering off with a spliff and a plot to solve he walks into the fish cellar and finds himself mirrored in this thin boy.

'What the fuck are you doing?'

Jason flushes, looks for an answer in his shoes.

But Bea doesn't falter. 'Spinning straw into gold,' she tells him.

Hal leans in, looks at Jason's face: the bruised eye, yellowing now, the scimitar of scar on his forehead. 'Where did you get that?'

Jason shrugs. 'Low-flying toy lorry.'

'Poor Jason,' Daisy says later when Hal recounts his discovery, forces a performance. 'You need another story though.'

'What sort of story?'

'You fought off a boar,' she tries. 'Or, the beast of Bodmin.'

'Or a tiger,' Muriel suggests. 'Tigers are far more glamorous.'

Hal groans. 'There aren't any tigers in Cornwall, you moron.'

'Whereas there are dozens of boars,' she scorns in return.

Daisy ignores them both. 'We should test you out,' she says. 'Our own Pygmalion.'

'He's not a laboratory monkey,' Bea insists.

Julian smirks. 'And he's definitely not Audrey Hepburn.'

But she turns to him, pleads with picture-perfect eyes, so that when she asks, 'Can we?' there is no other answer but, 'Yes.'

'It'll have to be in town,' she says.

'Really?' He thinks of the Varlows, of the boys from the comp; the jeers and the beatings and the sheer bloody ignorance that has him labelled 'gayer', 'homo', 'poof'. 'Only they . . . they know me.' Loathe me.

'They can't *all* know you,' Daisy tells him. 'And besides, we're running out of milk.'

'And vodka,' adds Muriel.

'And charlie.' Julian finishes the list.

Bea is indignant. 'We can hardly pop to the Co-op for that.'

'No,' agrees Hal. 'But I bet Jase knows someone.'

Jason – Jase! – feels belief run through him swift as a line. 'I . . . might.' Sadie does. Sadie knows someone and she'll help him. She has to.

'Good,' says Daisy. 'That's settled then.'

And he feels for all the world like he's been given an 'A'.

Sadie won't play though, won't hand the name over, not without something in return.

'Take me with you.'

'I can't,' he tells her. 'You're working tonight.'

'And you're not?'

He pauses before spilling the truth, and his lie. 'Said I was seeing a girl.'

'He'll swing for you when he finds out it's *her*.'

'Who's "her"?'

'Oh, don't play dumb. I know what you're doing. With Daisy.'

'And you're not sniffing round Hal?'

She shrugs. 'I'd be doing you a favour,' she says then. 'Taking him out of the equation. Unless it's the other one you're after.'

'Muriel?'

'No, the miserable one.'

Bea. 'God, no.'

'Then what's the problem?'

He's stunned for a moment, slapped by her audacity, her cruelty, her conceit. But she's not without her own charm, or attributes. And she is, after all, one of Hal's beloved 'people'. 'What if I put in a word?' he says.

Sadie hesitates. 'You think he'll listen?'

He nods. 'Definitely.' Maybe.

She shrugs. 'Go on then. And tell Julian it's Darren Banner he wants. Tall, lazy eye, smells of petrol and Kouros. He'll be down the Lugger or round the Varlows'.'

'Why?'

'Does their garden.'

Jason nods again, a bobbing dog. 'Thanks.'

'Tell Hal I'm in all night.'

'He's barred.'

'He can come round the back.'

Jason shrugs assent. Though he's not convinced Hal will bite. Why would he? Why would anyone when they had Daisy? Though their father shagged Lorna Dawson when their mam was still around so who's to say what men will and won't do with their dicks when someone hands them candy?

'Thanks,' he says again. 'Really.'

And he *is* thankful. Because every hour with them is an hour with her. And an hour of being someone thrillingly, brilliantly different.

He rows them over in *Dolly*, much to Julian's distaste and Daisy's delight.

'There won't be room,' Julian insists, as he takes in the paint, thick and peeling, the motor held together with gaffer tape and faith. 'Is it even watertight?'

'She,' he says, pleased at his brief superiority, at knowing a fact that marks him out as being 'in'. 'And yes.'

'I still don't see how six of us will fit.'

'Five,' Daisy declares. 'Bea's not coming.'

'Is she ill?' Muriel asks, then turns to him. 'She was terribly ill once, you know. Cancer,' she mouths at the end, as if the word is filthy, or dangerous: might conjure curse.

He flinches at it all the same. Hadn't known it was *that* kind of ill. 'I—' he begins.

'She's just being difficult,' Hal interrupts. 'Leave her.'

The relief is sweet. He won't be tied to her now, carelessly paired off through his own sense of duty; this odd, annoying responsibility he feels for her, black sheep that she is. Sweet but brief, as he hears the 'c' word, feels it prick. She's fine now, he insists. Nothing wrong with her at all.

'You can get the ferry if *Dolly*'s that abhorrent,' Daisy carries on, oblivious to his torment.

The face Julian pulls is Polaroid-worthy. 'Fine,' he says, climbing in. 'But don't blame me if we all end up dead.'

'In Davy Jones's locker!' whoops Daisy.

'Who's Davy Jones?' asks Muriel as she is lifted into her seat. 'And why does he have a locker?'

Julian raises an eyebrow. 'Remind me how the fuck you got into Oxford.'

'Well I didn't pull in favours from some cock-waving old boys' club,' she retorts.

Daisy hoots in approval.

'It's the sea,' Jason explains patiently. 'The bottom of the sea.'

'Oh.' Muriel pulls a face. 'Should we be doing this?'

'It's only a bloody estuary,' says Hal. 'No one's drowning.'

Jason wants to correct him, tell him, again, that they *do* drown, sometimes. Caught in the tide or on the rocks or just out by their own drunken incapability. But he needs to stay on side. Wants to fit. And so he rows on silently, their own pet ferryman.

Or, as he tells it in his head, the Pied Piper himself, leading his band to town.

The evening is a whirligig, a merry-go-round, and Fowey a fat fairground for the first time in his life.

In the King of Prussia he talks to the weather-battered barman as if he is royalty himself. Orders a gin and tonic and drinks it without irony.

Along Fore Street he walks with a confidence he's borrowed from Caine's Alfie, but a laugh that's all Hal.

At the Lugger, there's no Darren Banner, but he sees Steve Creasy from sixth form snug in one corner, so he slips back to being just Jason. But then, out on the harbour, regatta-packed and reeling with pint-swilling city boys and girls drinking Pimm's, he's a charlatan again, a cheat, a sneaky thief who can magpie your accent as deftly as your smile.

'It's weird,' says Hal.

'I like it,' says Daisy.

'So do I,' says Muriel. 'Can you do Jagger?'

He brims, unseen, with pride. 'Maybe.'

Julian, though, remains unswayed. 'Where's your mate?'

'He's not my mate,' says Jason swiftly. 'He's my sister's ex.' One of them. And directs him and Hal to the Varlows' back garden, with a note saying Sadie sent them.

'I want to come too!' Muriel begs. 'Can't we all go?'

But Daisy doesn't want to leave the buzz and bustle of the quay and, besides, she's seen an aquarium, she tells them, a relic from the seventies advertising the world's biggest squid. 'It's a lobster,' Hal tells her, 'and it's not even alive.' But she calls it a 'creature', anyway, says it's more interesting than sleazing some dealer and so Jason, valiant, gallant, desperate, offers to go with her. And that's how they part: three up bunting-hung cobbles and two to the turquoise hum of a backstreet museum.

The room is deliciously chilled and he sees her skin pimple, the fine down on her arms stand upright. He wonders then if Hal still sees these things, or if they're forgotten now, or, worse, were never cherished at all.

The advertised lobster, it turns out, is still a red herring. Caught in Fowey in 1931 but lost now to the world of freaks and marvels, displayed in a private collection or dust-heavy in a cellar.

'What a fraud,' he says, loud enough that the owner – a man with the charm and smell of an eel – can hear.

But Daisy sings, 'No matter,' and busies herself with the shrimp, talking to them as if they are small children or kittens. 'Aren't they marvellous?' she says. 'So strange and ancient.'

'I suppose,' he says, but finds he means it. Finds he can see in them a sort of pre-historicism, their articulations and armour more dinosaur than he'd thought. 'Yes,' he says then. 'Yes! Like swimming stegosauruses.'

And her laughter is a golden coin, a gift that keeps on giving as they riff on history, on the fine art of time travel and a future in which teleportation will be not just possible but passé.

They stay until the eel-keeper tells them he's shutting up shop, wants to get down the King for a pint himself.

'But we haven't had our photo taken yet!' She pouts, protests. 'Please.'

'Two quid,' the man mutters, pulling a dust-covered Polaroid down from the shelf.

Daisy grasps Jason, rests her head on his shoulder. 'Say cheese,' she urges.

'Cheese,' he says, a second too late, his crapness caught on slow-developing celluloid.

'Oh, I like it!' Daisy claims as they watch their likenesses colour into life. 'I'll keep it if you don't.'

He shrugs to hide delight. 'Okay.'

And so, the photo slipped into her bag, her arm slipped through his, as casually as if they are lifelong friends or habitual lovers, they burst back out into the evening, the sunlight buttery now, turning the treetops of the Hall Walk a glowing golden green. And for one night only he sees it, the lure of his hometown – the salt tang; the lap of the tide, high in the harbour; the shanties and dancing and call of the water – not ordinary at all, but four shots of neat incredible.

Just like this girl.

Back in the Lugger, though, sits Hal, trolleyed and wet and tap-tapping his feet.

'Where've you been?' he asks, his breath booze-soaked, his pupils fat and black as coal. 'I looked bloody everywhere.'

'Where I said I was going,' Daisy replies. 'And why are you wet?'

'I swam the harbour,' he declares. 'Won a bottle of Bacardi.'

'That explains it,' she says.

'Don't I get a winner's kiss?'

She sighs but obliges, and the irritation in Jason is swift and needling.

'Where's Muriel?' she asks when they part lips.

'On a yacht I think,' says Hal vaguely. 'She pulled.'

'How terribly Muriel.'

'Did you find Darren?' Jason asks, eager for completion on this task at least.

'They've gone to St Austell. Julian said not to wait up.'

'Oh I don't want to go home yet!' Daisy says. 'We're having far too much fun. Aren't we, Alistair?'

Jason smiles.

Hal smirks. 'Alistair?'

'He's down from Fettes, don't you know. And Christ Church awaits.'

'Right.' Hal is obviously bored of this game. 'Well, when you've done with Alistair, I'll be back at the house.'

Daisy pales. 'Hal, don't be like that.'

'I'm not.'

But Daisy doesn't buy it. 'What's this about?'

It's not that Jason doesn't want to hear, more that he doesn't want to stop it, this row, defuse it before it can blow. So he pushes his way to the bar and orders two gin and slimlines with pink bitters dripped in.

'You staying in town?' asks the barman.

A Lucifer sparks, sulphur-bright. 'Pencalenick,' he says. Then, one better, 'Rashleigh.'

The barman sits the drinks on the counter, his 'nice' a slice of lemon, or cocktail cherry, perhaps.

And so taken with this is Jason, so amused to be confused with the visiting hordes – this sea of people from the gravel-drived suburbs – that he doesn't register the swell as they part to let out an angry young man, sodden with seawater and a half-pint of rum. It's not until he pushes his way back to the table with two spilling gins and a story of glory, of Alistair's triumph, sees one seat empty and Daisy seething that he realizes quite how successful he has been.

'Was it me?' he asks. Hopes.

Daisy, defiant, assures him it's not and he's almost disappointed until she tacks a 'Well, not entirely,' on to her chorus

of 'no's. 'It's more me,' she says. 'And all of it. The future!'
She says it again as if it's glittering, as if it couldn't be
anything but. But isn't that the joy of her? That she sees the
best in everything, sees rainbows in downpours, roses in
cowshit, diamonds in the pavement where others see glass.

'Do you want to go after him?' he asks, barely able to
fake willing.

But she shakes her head, pats Hal's still-warm seat, and,
faithful dog – tail-wagging, tongue-lolling dog – that he is,
Jason sits.

He asks her again, when he's rowing her back, when
they're six gins happy and singing, inexplicably, 'Mull of
Kintyre'. 'What's happening?' he says.

'Does it matter?' she asks.

And though it does, he denies it, lets her dip her fingers
in the water, disturb the glimmer from the moon.

But back on the slipway she takes his hand, holds it tight
as a once-lost coin. 'Don't turn into him,' she says.

'Hal?'

She nods.

'But—'

'I mean it.'

Emboldened by alcohol, and the hour, perhaps, he touches
her face. 'I won't.'

But before he can think of kissing her, before he can even
appreciate the sheer humming, thrumming possibility of this
moment, she is gone, back into Rashleigh, and back, bewil-
deringly, to Hal.

And all his brilliance, his Alfie-bravado and Alistair swank, seeps out onto the slipway like so much oil. He has failed, he thinks. She has made her choice and marked her card and his name – his real name – is not even on it. He is a fool to have thought it an option at all.

But then it comes: a whisper and a giggle and the sound of someone spilling through the side door of the pub.

Sadie, he thinks. And a boy, or a man. Some tourist bored with the bustle who ventured over the water for a quiet pint and got more than they bargained for. Or just Barry Ransome, collecting his dues.

But the door is in shadows and he down on the dock and he cannot peer, cannot sneak a peek without giving himself away, and so he resigns himself to enquiring in the morning, a casual, 'Who was the prince, then?'

Until the prince moves, and heads, in deck shoes, not up the hill to the main road, nor down to the ferry, but soft, across a shorn lawn. And over the threshold to Rashleigh.

Hal. Prince fucking Hal.

Who must be fucking his sister.

23.

James, 2018

Sleep, what little there is, is fitful, for James is menaced by memory. By the disquieting now that threatens to haul him back there, trap him in amber like a curious fly. And by the unknowable tomorrow, with all its skittering possibilities.

Here, in this outhouse – in a room he has lain in when it was no more than mud on the floor, when the windows were cracked and smeared or put out entirely – the past, he discovers, is not foreign but a landscape he can trace and tread without even opening his eyes. The smell of it – the clay taint of the estuary, the organic damp of the woods, the petrol stench of the car ferry that still soils the water along with the air – and the sounds – the awful squawk of chip-greedy herring gulls, the croak of cormorants scavenging the shallows – conspire to drag him back to a time and a boy he would rather forget. And yet, without him, without this place, that week, that girl – Daisy – he would not be here, would not be James at all.

His watch tocks softly through two, three, four in the morning. And at somewhere around then he abandons his counting and tries, instead, to install order in his thoughts, to clarify his intent.

What does he want?

He wants a story for Lydia, wants a book that will sell not just well but make every top ten list, make Waterstones' window, make Daisy the star, once again, that she must always be.

But he wants something else now – someone. Can hardly dare say it. Can hardly dare think it. But every time he blows out the flame it reignites, a joke birthday candle for persistent wishes.

He wants Daisy.

At first it sounds absurd, impossible even, in that dead of night depression that turns molehills to mountains, diamonds to paste, that dampens even the most dazzling of plans. But, pragmatic, he measures the fissures, counts the faults in their stars. Hal's affair for a start.

It was a tip from a stringer. He'd ignored it back then, hadn't wanted to so much as tiptoe near the pair of them let alone march in brandishing black and white photos, a quote from a Soho showgirl who saw them down Berwick Street at four in the morning: her pushed against a shutter, him drunk and grunting. A party aide – how textbook – with none of Daisy's grace or acumen, and barely half her allure, but who was younger and gullible and told Hal, James assumes, that he was magnificent, a wonder, and that Daisy didn't know how lucky she was. And he probably fucked her and told her that his wife didn't understand him, that she no longer cared. Isn't that how the lie always goes?

Then, smaller, but by no means insignificant, there is Hal's sheer blistering ignorance of Daisy: not merely taking her for granted but belittling her, bullying her in increments.

And finally – he can think of it now, can retrace the steps – his and Hal's – there is that night. That terrible mess that ended, and started, it all. Because Hal was with her, with Bea, when it happened and there is surely something in that. Something that will offer him everything: a secret, a story, the – dare he think it? – girl.

These things, these glints he now notes and stores like shells in a jar, along with the eye-rolling glances, the snapping, the distinct lack of contact. These slivers of light, of hope, he now counts like so many sheep until, at five, he succumbs.

She wakes him at eight with a knock at the door. He answers in shorts and a sheet – a necessary tent, aware of his bareness, the faint tang of sweat – but, emboldened by his abacus that counts him in with a chance, he doesn't apologize.

'Daisy,' he says, affecting nonchalance as deftly as Luna.

'Oh, God. I'm sorry. I woke you, didn't I?'

He laughs, generous, forgiving. 'It's fine,' he tells her. 'Really. I should have been up an hour ago.'

'Oh. Well . . . good then.'

There is a pause in which – to his, at first, ill ease and, moments later, thrill – she catches herself staring and has to look away hurriedly. 'I thought we could go for a walk,' she suggests. 'Before breakfast.'

He's starving now, off-schedule as he is, but the lie slips out in a blink. 'Great.'

'Really? Well, I'll wait outside. Oh, and bring your thingy. Your recorder.'

As she closes the door to afford him his privacy, he feels a needle of indignation, then the swift drip of disappointment that her first thought – her only thought? – at coming here, at calling for him, was work.

But he is not to be dissuaded today, he decides. Not now he has a plan, three-pointed, and balls after all. And so, without even showering, he pulls on a T-shirt, swigs Listerine, spits, and slips his feet into shoes that can barely be called sensible but which will have to do.

'Oh, you could have showered,' Daisy says when he walks out to meet her. 'I'm not in a hurry.'

He stiffens, sniffs. 'God. Do I smell?'

'Oh, no! Not at all. I only meant—'

'It's just . . . I was just going to wait until later. Until after—'

'Really. I didn't mean it. My poor attempt at a joke, I suppose.' She smiles. 'Shall we?'

He nods, and follows her through the newly hung gate and across the well-tended garden. 'Are the others—'

'Asleep. Well, Luna's on Netflix but I doubt the rest will be conscious for hours. Hal didn't come to bed until gone four.'

'But you?'

'I don't sleep so well these days. Age, I expect.'

Or dissatisfaction. God, let it be so.

But he says nothing, not yet. He has two days, after all, and this one has only just begun.

*

The morning is glorious and the view from Hall Walk god-like in its breadth and abundance. Too early for walkers, and, in the absence of a clock-watching father, it's as if he's seeing it through new eyes— He *is* seeing it through new eyes: the trees odd, spongy miniatures from a train set, the boats made of matchsticks and paper, the water itself a sliver of foil stuck down with a brush and glue. At the stone cross they collapse on the granite all the better to appreciate its extravagance, and their small place in it.

'Shouldn't you be asking me questions?' she suggests after their silence has stretched from seconds into more than a minute.

'Of course.' He fumbles in his pocket for the recorder, switches it on. This time, though, he does not dance around the issue, does not toy with its skirts. There is no time left to pretend, he must simply plunge in. 'Why are we here?' he asks.

She peers at him over outsized glasses that, along with her thin, shimmering top, give her the appearance of some sort of insect. 'Is this an existential question or do you mean more in Cornwall?'

'I mean at Rashleigh. This is where . . .' He peters out deliberately, so that she will sense his apprehension, his empathy.

She looks back out at the valley and for a moment he worries he's pushed it too far, too soon. But then she gestures for the recorder, to bring it in close.

'Hal doesn't understand it either,' she says eventually. 'But it's been so long now, it's as if someone is rubbing her out and I needed . . . I needed to feel her again.'

It never gets old, the moment they open up, let him in. And here he is, toe over the line, the crackle and snap of it singing before him. 'And do you?' he asks. 'Feel her?'

'Not yet.'

She's lying, he thinks – knows – but says nothing, sensing she's weighing this all up, working it out as she talks, making sense of it *by* talking, so that he, an ersatz therapist, is almost doing her a service.

He is not wrong.

'We tried telepathy once. Did you know that? It was my idea. I forced her to stare at me, to "see into my brain".' She flourishes the words like a bouquet, then slips back into solemnity. 'I thought she could tell what I was thinking if only she tried.'

'Could she?'

'Not once.' She sighs. 'Sometimes I get blindsided by it,' she continues. 'That she's still dead. Does that make sense?'

He ignores the murmur, the unfurling of wings. 'You thought she'd come back?'

She nods. 'At first I think I did.'

'But you knew that couldn't happen?'

'Yes. God, yes, of course.' She flaps a hand at something, a fly, or in that absurd affectation of wafting away tears.

He is used to this, the crying of confession, of catharsis, but this time it matters, panics him. 'Oh, God. I've upset you.' And he wonders, absurdly, if he has a handkerchief, plunges his hand in his pocket to check, even while knowing it will come back bare.

But before he can disappoint, she reaches out a hand and places it on his arm. 'No, you haven't. Really. I didn't mean like that.'

The sensation of her skin on his is electric: compelling and terrifying at once. He dares not move. Doesn't want to move. 'You . . . you mean ghosts or . . . reincarnation?'

She laughs, not hollow but bell-like and genuine. 'Not ghosts. Christ, that's the sort of woo-woo Muriel goes in for. You know she once had a priest exorcise her studio?'

'Did it work?'

'Well, her painting didn't improve.'

She lets go of him then, of his goose-pimpled skin, the air pressure lowering with a hiss of release. 'I think she's in me,' she says. 'Or was. Perhaps it's a twin thing.'

He nods, then, aware she's not watching him, and berating himself, echoes, 'Perhaps.'

She turns, smiles. 'What about you?'

He steadies himself. 'What about me what?'

'Do you believe in that stuff?'

'In ghosts?'

'In all of it. Ghosts. The great beyond.'

He thinks of the pub, with its cheery gingham, its glass granola jars that jostle for space with Bridgewater china but still fail to keep out the grime and the lino and the swaggering man who drove it into the ground. 'No,' he lies. 'It's hokum. I think when you're gone, you're gone.' He pauses. 'I'm sorry, that's probably not what you want to hear.'

She shrugs. 'Shame. I always thought I was Marlene Dietrich in a past life.'

He laughs, helping settle the heave. 'Why do people always assume they were famous?'

'Who would you have been then? Not Waugh or Faulkner? Or . . .' – she scrabbles to disinter dead celebrities – 'F. Scott Fitzgerald? You could be channelling Gatsby right now.'

'I'm flattered.' He is, stupidly so. But, 'God, no. A nobody, I suspect.'

She smiles, a thought dropping like a ripe cherry. 'You must have done something wonderful then.'

'What?'

'To come back as you.'

He starts, runs the line again to check he's not conjured it himself out of desperate want, but her eyes are on him, the pressure between them building minutely again, so that he could, if he wanted, reach out and touch her face. He's going to do it. He's going to—

She turns away. 'Well I shall no doubt come back as a Kardashian.'

Back at Rashleigh, Hal has ignored the noticeboard warnings and is halfway across the harbour, thrashing out a half-decent front crawl while Julian sits on a lawn littered with Saturday supplements.

'Where did you get the papers?' demands Daisy.

'That woman.' He gestures at the cottages up from the pub.

'June.'

'Probably. She knocked and asked and I said yes.'

'Did you pay her?'

'Of course. I'm not a total heathen.'

She turns to James. 'Breakfast?' she offers.

He nods, still mute with confusion.

Luna sits on the mooring wall wearing a string bikini and a scowl, a crab line dangling from one hand, her phone gripped in the other.

'Where's Muriel?' she asks as they pass.

She doesn't look up from the screen.

'I think she's rather the worse for wear,' Julian offers. 'I heard someone puking at stupid o'clock.'

'Julian!'

Smiling malignly he turns to an unmoved Luna. 'Apologies. I'm sure it's food poisoning.'

Daisy says nothing. Instead sighs, and leads James into the cool of the kitchen, where she opens a packet of croissants, finds butter and jam, pours hot black coffee from a gleaming machine that he knows from his own purchase cost a small fortune, though markedly less than a day's rental here.

'Will you swim?' he asks at last, half to puncture the bustle, half rent with concern. 'With Hal, I mean.'

She shudders exaggeratedly. 'Too cold,' she says. 'And I'm too old. You go though.'

He shakes his head quickly. 'No, no. I'm the same.'

Though it's not that, just as her aversion isn't anything to do with temperature or age. But rather that they both know what the tide can do.

He pushes out the thought – the thundering rush, the haul of the water, the hurtling rocks that seem to hit from above. 'I'd rather talk.'

210

'Good,' she replies kindly.

And talk they do.

They talk over their food, then more back out on the lawn.

They talk about Bea and her addiction to literature, about the slips of paper Daisy used to find with quotes written out in italic hand, about the book she thought Bea would write one day, if she'd only been given the chance. They talk about ghosts, and gods and monsters and she asks him, at one point, what he's thinking right now, and the first words that come are, 'Of aurochs and angels . . .' and he prays she will know them.

And know them she does. 'The secret of durable pigments,' she continues. 'Prophetic sonnets, the refuge of art.'

'Nabokov,' he says.

'*Lolita*,' she qualifies, then goes on to quote some more, her voice stretching long and lazy, like a languid cat. Unafraid of being ignored, she lingers on every vowel, doesn't even need to meet his eyes and instead shuts them against the sun, sure of herself, and her place in this world.

And, for all his lack of sleep, his four in the morning self-doubt, right now he feels it too: that belief; he knows he is worthy and, more than that, that his place is, somehow, with her.

24.

Bea, 1988

Bea's unsure, exactly, why she does it. Why she ducks out again and again. Desperation? Defiance, maybe.

Or deliberately drawing attention to herself. So Julian has it.

'Why are you so bloody determined to be difficult?' he'd demanded before he left.

'Why do you even care?' she replied.

'Leave her,' Daisy had told him, then turned to Bea. 'Really, though, why don't you come?'

But Bea just shrugged.

And so leave her they did, abandoning her to her own devices and apparent plans.

But she has no plans and now they've gone she's not sure she wants it at all – this solitude, this stagnant silence that seems to swell around her, carrying with it the Kodak moment snapshot of Hal and her sister, hand in hand along Fore Street in the afternoon sun.

She wanders the hall, her fingers dragging across the cracked door jambs and flock-papered dado.

She reads for a while, plucking a well-thumbed Dickens

from its place on the shelf. Though someone has been in here, Goldilocks-like, has shifted the stacks to leave a gap that needles until she shuffles the rest to fill it.

She eats, fashioning a sandwich from a strange array of leftovers, including half a boiled egg, a pickled beetroot and a slice of tongue. But, four bites in, she gives up, more bored than revolted, and, pulling on a cardigan against the creeping breeze and slipping *Great Expectations* into her voluminous pocket, she slinks out to the slipway, the foot of the ferry.

And waits.

And waits.

She hears the slam of a car door as that man from the pub makes off up the road.

The call of the daughter – Jacko! – to a dog or a cat or perhaps even a child.

The clank of the ferry as it takes its last fare before mooring up for the night, revellers left to taxis or begging favours from those with boats.

By ten it is too dim to read and, besides, she is shivering now, September heralding its imminent approach. So, blue-fingered and goose-pimpled, she retraces her steps, telling herself she's a fool for even thinking he might come back – that any of them might come back – and that they are right, she *is* deliberately obtuse, diffident and difficult and no wonder he doesn't want her. That no one sodding wants her.

Except, perhaps, one.

In the kitchen she sits on the counter drinking tea from a jam jar – the only receptacle left clean when he walks in:

Julian. Julian, who is always fucking . . . there. Listening. Pricking like a gadfly.

'Oh, it's you,' he says.

'Who else would it be? The others were with you.'

He is high, she can see it: his pupils wide; his smile the wrong side of leering. Though it's not mere chemical courage that makes him step between her dangling legs.

'Nice of you to wait up for me.'

She leans back. 'I didn't.'

'No.' He nudges up closer, so she can feel him – it – press against her thigh. 'You were hoping for him, weren't you? Still. How sad.'

'Fuck off.' She hovers hot tea over his crotch.

He snorts, but does not move. 'You wanted it once.'

'No I didn't.'

She didn't. But she'd let him all the same, through boredom or hormones. Let him fuck her on the floor of his college hall dorm. His breath thick with garlic; his freckled skin speckled with sweat; his unbearable weight pressing down on her so that for days she would have the landscape of the floorboards etched invisibly into her back.

'This won't make you him,' she'd said afterwards.

'Well, you're sure as shit not her.' Bullseye. Then, the icing on the cake. 'You tell anyone about this, you're dead.'

'The words every girl longs to hear,' she'd countered. 'As if they'd believe me anyway. Everyone knows it's Hal you want.'

He'd slapped her then, sharp and fast, then staggered back, horrified.

But she didn't even flinch. 'Point proven,' she'd said, then picked up her knickers and dignity, and popped the morning-after pill two days later just to be sure.

This time they both recoil, like north ends of magnets. He stalks through the door he came from, slams it, while she remains in the kitchen, stiff, still, silent.

Ten minutes later the beehived handle twists again and she braces herself for a second attempt, blames herself for not going to bed. But the voice that calls her is softer, is syrup for her soul.

Hal is back. And glowering.

'What happened?' he asks her.

She thrills to his vision, to his ability to see when she needs him. But he, it is clear, needs her more. 'Nothing,' she lies. 'What happened to you?'

'Doesn't matter.' He slumps in a chair, fumbles for a fag.

'Yes it does.' She slips down from the counter and up onto the table, facing him. 'Tell me.'

He holds out the packet and, for once, she takes one, if only for the closeness of cupping her hand around his as he lights it.

'Your sister,' he says at last.

'What about her?' Please let her have ended it.

'She doesn't . . . I don't know.'

'She doesn't understand,' she finishes for him. 'Or even listen.'

Hal nods, though reluctantly.

'You have to tell her London will kill you. Suffocate you. That you need to stay in Oxford for now.'

215

'I don't even want Oxford,' he snaps. 'All dreaming sodding spires and cunts in punts. Ha.' He laughs, then, as if impressed by his accidental assonance. 'Fuck graduation. I might just jack it in now. Who needs a degree anyway?'

Bea blanches, panicking at this new, too-soon prospect. But she will have to put that aside for the moment. Persuade him later, when he's more vulnerable, when he's begging for her shoulder to cry on, or more.

'If she loved you, she wouldn't ask you to leave.'

'If I loved her, I'd go anyway.'

She quickens. 'You don't love her?'

'I didn't say that. That's her talking.'

'But do you?' she pushes.

He looks up at her then, his eyes filmed with tears, or gin. And such is her visible pity, her sworn adoration that, when she puts her hand to his face, he grasps it, holds it tight to his cheek.

She teeters then, giddy, on the brink of possibility, willing him to pull her in.

But as swift as it started, he drops it, a hot rock. 'Of course I do.'

She hears them later, in the stairwell, rekindling their row.

'You kowtow to everyone,' Daisy tells him.

'Like who?'

'Julian. Your father.'

'Like fuck I do. Why would I want to drop out? Why would I want to move to–to Manchester, wherever, if not to escape him?'

'But that's just it, don't you see? You're only going *because* of him. Not because *you* want to.'

He snorts. 'You're wrong. I'm going because that's where—'

'The "people" are?' Daisy's voice is twisted with drink, riven with bitterness.

'God, you're arrogant at times. You and your sister.'

Bea sucks in a stunned breath so quick it forms a pebble in her throat. But what comes next offers no lozenge to dislodge it.

'The privileged Hicks twins,' he continues.

'And you're not? Hal fucking Hemmings, heir to an earl?'

He ignores that, counters, 'You do it too.'

'Do what?'

'Kowtow to your sister. Why else would you insist on staying down south?'

'It's about *me*. Fuck Bea. It's nothing to do with her.'

Fuck Bea?

'I want to be in London. I *need* to be in London. That's where everything is. Everything. You can't change the world from fucking Huddersfield, Hal. Even you know that.'

'A few hours ago you wanted to move *here*.'

'That was . . . just talk. I wasn't being serious.'

'It's hard to tell, you so infrequently are.'

'Well, sorry to disappoint. Sorry I'm not Barbara fucking Castle.'

'That's not what I want. Jesus!'

Silence lingers for seconds that stack into a minute. Then Daisy, indignant – and, Bea suspects, pouting – whines, 'It's my birthday tomorrow. No, now, in fact. Right now it's my birthday and you're determined to fuck it up for me.'

'I'm not,' Hal insists. And that's when it happens. The softening, the giving in to her. Just as everyone gives in to her. 'I'm sorry.'

'Kiss me,' she begs.

'Daisy, we need—'

'It can wait.'

And wait it does, as she listens to them fuck above her, Hal's 'Happy birthday' coming just before Daisy does.

But this time something hardens in her, ossifies; the pebble in her throat slips and wedges deep in her chest. Because she is tired of standing aside. Because she is sick of pity, sick of second place, sick of being the sickly one. And because it's *her* birthday, too. It's her twentieth birthday, and she wants a present. She deserves a present.

And there, on the lawn, is where she finds him.

25.

James, 2018

It is all-pervasive, this obsession with nostalgia. No longer an infrequent indulgence, the province of once-a-year Christmas dinners or once-in-a-lifetime school reunions, but a quotidian activity, a way of life, almost. Monetized and marketed and bought in the basket-load by the gawping hordes. It's there in the rotary phone on the mantel, its dial reminding us of bygone conversations, omitting, of course, the interminable time to enter a number, the indignity of party lines. There too, in the vintage children's annuals, the Ladybird learn-to-reads that sit in neat piles on Lloyd Loom bedside tables, intended merely as decoration, corralled as they are in the rooms for the grown-ups. And there in the Cath Kidston kitchenware stacked in the plate rack, that the owner probably thinks 'quirky' or, worse, 'quaint', failing to realize the same cups, the same saucers sit in the same fake Shaker wood in Basingstoke as well as Tokyo. Nostalgia is accepted, necessary to the point that, if you choose to avoid former colleagues, class companions, even the bullies from behind the bike sheds – the cigarette elite who could count on two hands the number of town girls they'd fingered – you are seen as an oddity, as somehow wrong.

But this ghost-hunting – because that is what it is – disturbs him. He has no desire to timeslip; doesn't want to remember, still less to relive. If the past was so glorious then people should never leave, while he has not merely moved on but slammed and bolted the door.

Or so he thinks.

The village is one thing – a single hillful of houses, half of them empty, it turns out, at this tail-end of the season. And in four hours on the lawn not one figure on the slipway has any ring of familiarity. No Alan Ransome in the phone box. No Fat Man Morris in the ferry queue. No Minnow Rapsey pushing his petrol mower down the battered tarmac, though, James suspects, he might find him stone cold and six feet under in St John's if he could be bothered to look. And the pub's only occupants are a family of four with a slavering Alsatian, its spit all over Luna's adoring hands, its shit on their lawn until Julian shouted at them to 'fucking clean up'.

No, in the village, though surrounded by phantoms of his own imagination, James remains safe, secure in his new self. But over the water lies no-man's-land; uncharted territory on which a hapless cartographer has warned in large, alarming letters: Here be dragons. And Hal, it seems, brave knight that he is, wants to explore.

'So, are we going to town?'

His insides slip.

'I wouldn't mind,' says Daisy.

'Christ, yes,' agrees Julian.

Muriel, pallid as ashes, groans. 'I'll get seasick,' she insists.

'It's a chain ferry, darling,' Daisy tells her. 'You can barely feel it moving.'

'Can't I just stay here?' she pleads, affecting the pout of a four-year-old. 'You can take Luna.'

Hal shoots Daisy a look but, before she can parry it, Luna excuses herself.

'I'd literally rather die?'

'Well, that's that sorted then.' Hal beams.

'I might stay, too,' James suggests. 'Catch up with some work.'

Daisy turns, apparently appalled. 'But you *have* to come! They'll only force me to drink if you don't. Besides . . .' She smiles, a card player about to lay down aces. 'I *am* work.'

So what else can he do but nod and follow? Nod and follow. Nod and follow wherever she leads.

Town resembles nothing more than a model village, retro living made large. What was once a grocer's is now a gift shop, hawking the same generic seaside tat as the three others over the road: striped hats and jerseys; faux driftwood daubed with vaguely nautical epithets or trite truisms, the three-dimensional equivalent of a sunset meme; hand-thrown mugs emblazoned with anchors, fish and, inexplicably, chickens. This is not just packaged nostalgia but the presentation of a bucolic ideal that never really existed outside of Hampshire or Hampstead. Where, he wonders, are the balaclavas, worn not for crime but against the relentless rain and cold? Where is the gaffer to tape up the holes in their boats as well as their shoes?

Where are the Barry Ransomes, the Steve Creasys, the Varlows, even, with their battered Land Rover? If they're in town, they're in hiding, away from the roil of regatta weekend. And he finds himself thanking that false idol 'fuck' that the crowd is so thick, the music so loud, and all eyes, if you catch them, fall only on Daisy.

They're halfway up Fore Street, pushing their way through toddlers toting ice creams like weapons, when Hal stops.

'What?' demands Daisy, then notices The Globe, dim and low-ceilinged, spilling drinkers onto the pavement. 'Already?'

Hal checks his watch. 'It's four o'clock, for fuck's sake.'

'Okay.' Her voice is low and her smile fixed. She is aware, already, of the stares, the hissed 'is she?'s and 'omigod's. 'Just—'

'He'll be fine,' Julian interrupts. 'I'll mind him.'

'That's what I'm afraid of.'

But she doesn't dissuade him further, doesn't suggest joining them, so that now, at least, it is just the two of them; a sop to James's increasing discomfort at being seen.

They head to the harbour, but, finding it heaving, double back on themselves and end up on the corner where, to Daisy's delight, and James's astonishment, the aquarium still stands.

'Oh!' she exclaims. 'Shall we?'

The world's largest lobster is still lauded on a hoarding, but they both know, of course, that the creature is long dead, that this is no more than a record of its monstrosity. However, her memory, it seems, is short or clouded, and when she pleads with him to indulge her, he can only say yes. Because perhaps, perhaps, she will remember a boy who came with her one time.

Inside there are dogfish and pipefish and pink-tentacled anemones. Transparent prawns and ugly tub gurnard. But no giant lobster, or even an outsized squid. Though a conger eel by the unlikely name of Columbo glides by, fat with menace.

'How marvellous!' she pronounces, thrilled at the eel. 'He hasn't changed a bit. Though I don't suppose it can be the same one, can it? How long do they live?'

James shrugs out his ignorance. 'You've been here before?' he prompts.

She smiles, her teeth lit by an indiscriminate ultraviolet glow. 'Bea and I came every year when we were small – too small to see above the tanks even. Daddy had to lift us in turn.'

He wonders then, that he never saw them – two flax-haired schoolgirls, illustrated in his vivid imagination by Mabel Lucie Attwell. He recalls himself and Sadie, sticky-fingered, lolly-gagging at the lobster board, their wonder in proportion to its bold boast. Remembers, too, a profound disappointment to find it not just missing but never here at all.

'How old were you?' he asks. 'When they died, I mean.'

'Eight when our mother went. Nine for our father.'

'How awful for you,' he says, meaning it.

She nods. 'It was. But it was a long time ago. I've survived.'

He tries again. 'So when did you last come here?'

She pauses at a tankful of tompot blennies. 'Adorable,' she deflects.

He doesn't tell her they are common, two a penny on the shore. He doesn't say anything, waits instead for her memory to jog, for her to admit it. But she is not playing ball.

'Like I said, we must have been tiny.'

She moves on, her fingers trailing now in a tank of rays that rise up and sway as if performing purely for her. 'It all seems so much smaller now.'

'We've just outgrown it.' She looks at him and he hears his slip. 'I mean the world has outgrown it,' he corrects, quickly. 'We can swim with dolphins, for God's sake. London Aquarium has sharks.'

'I suppose.'

They wander a while, her enchanted in turn by cuckoo wrasse, by sea snails, by dogfish egg cases. '"Mermaids' purses",' he tells her. 'Or "devils"', depending on your view.'

'I feel sad for the hermit crabs,' she announces then. 'Everyone hates them but the poor buggers never developed a shell of their own so what choice do they have but to steal?'

He stills, steadies his breath. This is no passing comment, surely, no flip remark. It is too clever, too probing. But when he steels himself to snatch a glimpse she is engrossed in the eel again and humming, absurdly, the theme tune from *Jaws*.

'Excuse me.'

They both turn now, him in alarm – on alert as he is – her slowly, expectantly.

'Of course,' she says reaching to accept the notebook and

pen, signing her name for a man in a Chelsea cap and his goggle-eyed son.

'Can we have a picture?'

'I don't know,' she says, genuinely bemused. 'Are cameras allowed? Will they upset the fish?'

'You could do it outside,' James suggests.

And so out they troop into squint-inducing sunshine and he watches from the sidelines as she smiles obediently for selfies, then stands sentinel for the aquarium owner, her hand on the lobster sign, endorsing the counterfeit, the sneaky conceit.

'James!' She beckons him over. 'Be in this one.'

But he shakes his head, has no intention of being papped and pinned up for all to see. The prodigal son standing out like a pauper in a sea of c-list celebrities, local heroes, and her.

She flaps a hand in fake irritation. 'He's just camera shy,' she explains, then poses for one more before accepting the man's bear hug with astonishing grace.

'Is that normal?' James asks when she's released from the fray.

'The mobbing?' She laughs. 'No. In London they take pride in pretending you're nobody. It's only on holiday they seem to find the balls.'

'Or the beer finds them.'

'Touché. I'm hungry,' she says then. 'I need cake.'

The tearoom is on Fore Street, an old Georgian thing, double-fronted, with the fading air of a former bank. Though, whatever it was, he doubts he would ever have dared go in, nor had the money to.

Inside, it is more time travel, this time to an elderly aunt's drawing room, or the ersatz version. All genteel detail: the scones on tiered cake stands, the china sprigged, and, if the odd cup is cracked, it is artfully so. It is packed, too. From the yachty tourists herding broods of Boden-clad catalogue models in matching sandals, to the coastal path backpackers with their sensible Merrells, to the middle-aged middlebrows down from suburbs like Solihull or Penge, all trying to cut themselves a fat jam-filled slice of home-grown paradise.

'It wasn't always like this,' she says. 'The town, I mean.'

'No?'

'But then where is? Everything changes, I suppose.'

He bristles, again unsure if this is a dig, a hint, or mere coincidence. 'Does it?'

Tea arrives. Lapsang Souchong that smells of the cork tiles his father drunk-laid on the toilet floor, where they stunk up the corridor and soaked up piss like a sponge and his mother had to pull them up again and lay lino herself. He doesn't mention this; doubts she even knows such a thing exists, let alone has smelled such an atrocity. He wonders, then, at the small, scorn-worthy things her glittering life has managed to skirt: polystyrene ceilings and nylon carpet; bags of scraps soaked in vinegar because chips are ten pence too dear; shop-bought Battenburg for a birthday treat, its heavy yellow jacket bearing as much resemblance to real marzipan as Dream Topping to cream.

Daisy strains the tea, drowns it in a quantity of milk that

makes him wince. Though the ceremony affords them time in comfortable silence. And they remain so for minutes, her sipping, appreciatively, while he works out what his next question is, what his next move will be. In the end, it is Daisy who offers it, leaning in, out of lip-reading distance of the nose-pokers and earwiggers.

'Do you want to know a secret?'

He nods, expectation quickening his breath.

'It was a mistake,' she tells him. 'Me and Hal.'

He feels his throat constrict, sets down his cup in case he is tempted to drink and finds himself choking. 'What do you mean?' he manages.

'You're not recording this, are you?'

He shakes his head.

'Good.' She places a hand on the linen tablecloth, sweeps invisible crumbs onto the floor. 'Bea knew him first. They were friends – close ones. And he saw her in the bar one night and kissed her. Only it wasn't her, of course. It was me.'

And then, swift and sharp and needling, it is Bea's voice he hears, her own hissed indignation at the awful unfairness of it all. 'I— How do you know?' he asks.

'He told me once. I'd threatened to leave. He was drunk and angry and wanted to hurt me.'

'He wasn't just lying?' He has to check her strength of feeling, though he knows it is gospel.

She shakes her head. 'I think it's one of the few times he's been utterly truthful. He apologized next morning. Took it all back. But I still think about it sometimes.'

'So . . . so why did you stay with him. If you knew?'

She smiles, pulls at an invisible thread on the tablecloth. 'You need to have known him back then to understand that. He was . . . brilliant. Driven. Everyone wanted to be Hal. Or fuck him.'

He swallows, prompts. 'Even Bea?'

'I think she knew she wasn't the one.' She gazes at him, eyes hollow with something. Sorrow? Regret? 'Not long term. He would have broken her, I suspect. Cheated.'

'But . . .' Say it. *Say it.* 'He cheated on you, though.'

Daisy lifts her tea, her left hand trembling, then thinks better of it, the cup clattering as it lands. 'He did.'

Shit. She knows. He isn't prepared for that. Was so sure he'd unearthed a landmine.

'So why stay?' His voice is indignant with it, and he blurts out a 'sorry' to soften it quick.

She shakes her head. 'It's all right. Because he believes in me.'

'But . . . tens of men must believe in you. Hundreds.'

She laughs, then, a dismissive ring. 'But they don't *know* me. It's easier to forgive someone who knows the bones of you, who forgives you your own faults.'

He pauses, then says, soft but bold, 'You're wrong.'

Her eyes meet his. 'Am I?'

And it's there, again. That flicker, that spark. He's not imagining it. And, cheered on by her apparent want and his desperate need, he lifts his hand and places it on hers. Not clasping, but not feeble either.

And she does not move.

Time stills then, and the world shrinks in on their fingers. And he thrills to it, to her touch, and to something else too – this intimacy that invites him in and begs him to press for more. If he can only find out what happened that night. What Hal's story was. If he can find the fissure and weaken it, or forge one of his own, then he can, perhaps, wrest her from her husband.

He tightens his fingers around hers. 'I—' But he is interrupted by the ping of a text.

She pulls away, grasps at her phone, grimaces. 'Hal's getting tetchy. He wants us to go.'

James wants *her*. 'He's a big boy,' he counters.

'He's *my* boy,' she replies.

He reddens. 'Of course.'

Hal and Julian stand packed in the crowd outside the King of Prussia, empty pint glasses a testament to their torment.

'It's like fucking Calcutta,' Julian declares.

'Kolkata,' James corrects, unable to help himself.

'Whatever. You know what I mean.'

'So let's leave,' Daisy suggests.

'You don't want one in the Lugger?' Hal pulls her in. 'Come on. For old times' sake.'

A snapshot flashes, of Hal and Daisy couched in the corner – his hair wet, eyes wild, words raging – and he wonders what it is Hal's hoping to recreate.

Perhaps she does too. 'I'm tired,' she tells him.

'You're always tired.'

She ignores him. 'Besides, someone has to pick Clementine up.'

'Can't she get a fucking cab?' Julian suggests.

'No, she can't.'

'Muriel can fetch her,' Hal declares.

'Muriel doesn't drive anymore. You know that. She's not allowed.'

'Remind me why we invited her?'

She shoots him a look, an in-joke or long-standing scold.

'Whatever,' Hal dismisses. 'Fine. Go. But we're staying.'

'I'll see you at home.'

'The house,' he corrects.

'Whatever,' she echoes, a belligerent teenager now. Luna. Or Bea, even.

'I'll come back with you,' James offers, or almost insists, he thinks.

But Daisy thinks differently. 'No, no!' she says. 'Stay. Drink. It's the weekend.'

He looks over at Hal, hoping – expecting – he'll dissuade her, suggest he should work, given what little time is left.

But, astonishingly, he nods. 'Up for it, James?' he asks.

And, bewildered, James nods, watches her walk away to the ferry, and instead treads behind Hal six steps to the Lugger.

And walks straight into a ghost.

And this one is no fleeting apparition, no harmless will-o'-the-wisp.

But a chain-clanking, wailing reminder of everything he left behind.

26.

Jason, 1988

He's not thick. He knows which sister is which now. Can tell them apart by the straightness of Daisy's back, the slump of Bea's; the way one of them fiddles with her hair and the other tosses it; the smell of them, even: one cloaked in perfume, the other in herself. So he knows it's not her. But when she says 'follow me' he goes anyway, across the lawn, through the gate and into the woods where the little house lies.

He's itching to blurt it, this secret that burns in him brimstone-bright and hot and all, the truth about Prince Hal and shag-happy Sadie. But there, in the dimness and dank, something switches, the blue gloom tamps down the flame, so that when he goes to open his mouth not a word comes out, just an odd, truncated 'yaw' like the mewl of a kitten or a baby bird.

Does it start then? When she puts a thumb on his lower lip? Or was it before, in the water, his hands on her skin, his stomach slipping with the intimacy of it? He could stop, he supposes. Push her away and say it's not right, not what he wants.

Only he does want it, doesn't he? And, according to the thickening cock in his trousers, it doesn't matter so much which one after all. So if he teeters it's for no more than a second, then he steps off the cliff and drops straight and swift as stone.

He marvels at her. At the taste of her – all saltwater and sweet biscuits. The shape of her naked – or almost – even in the half light. The fact she's letting him do this at all.

He's on his knees, desperate, his dick rigid, but his tongue tied, his fingers pitifully fumbling, unschooled, despite Dave Maynard's back-of-the-bus advice that included a poorly scrawled diagram and the instruction to 'treat it like a Creme Egg.'

'Slow down,' she tells him. 'Here.' She pulls down her knickers – Saturday, they say – so he finds himself staring straight at it. Not a neat *Club* centrefold, nor Dave's four-lined drawing with its ten-pence of a clitoris and a gaping hole arrow-marked 'come in here', but real, live— What does he even call it? A pussy? A snatch? A—

'Christ, it doesn't bite, if that's what you're worried about.'

'No . . . I . . . I'm, just. You're beautiful,' he says then, for want of anything better.

But that only seems to irritate her further. 'For God's sake.' And she pushes him so he has to put his hands out to the side to steady himself. 'Go on,' she urges.

So he does, sliding so he's the prone one, splayed on his back in the filth and grit.

She straddles him so quick he's barely thought about a

condom before his dick's in her hand and then inside her and— Jesus. Fuck!

And in an instant he gets it. Gets Sadie's addiction. Gets the brags behind the bike sheds, and the swagger in the bars.

This is it.

This is everything.

This is the secret of the universe and the meaning of life.

This is ambrosia and alchemy and the ark of the fucking covenant all in one. And he is humming with it, buzzing, every cell of him resonating. With her.

Her eyes are closed, he notices, so he shuts his as well. All the better to see *her* with. And then they're rocking, riding in almost silence, his hands on her backside, pulling her up and pushing her down, or so he wants to think, though she was the one that slapped them there.

Fuck, this is good. Is it good? Well, she's not told him off yet, and she's not stopped, so he must be doing something right and besides, he's close now, too close—

Oh, shit. Shit! He grabs at a memory, slumps back on the bus to listen in to Noel Rhodes, an improbably short boy, telling the assembled to name stuff to stall it. 'The 1979 Arsenal line-up, or Kings and Queens.'

'Pan's People,' said Brian White.

'Don't be a moron,' Noel told him. 'That's guaranteed to end it.'

But Jason couldn't name Pan's People anyway, nor has he got any clue at football, but monarchy might suffice. 'William,' he begins to himself. 'William, Henry, Stephen, Henry, Richard, John—'

'Hal.'

'Huh?' He starts and opens his eyes. She's staring at him. Was he talking out loud? Shit, was he—

'Be Hal,' she repeats.

He doesn't get it at first and tells her.

'Say something,' she hisses. 'Like he would.'

He gets it then. Only he's not sure he can. Not now. But she's sitting on him, poised, the tip of his dick at the lips of her. Teasing. Taunting.

'Tell me you want me,' she begs.

'I want you,' he says.

'In his voice.'

'I want you,' he repeats. But this time he drops an octave as well as the 't', though it doesn't feel right, doesn't—

She slides down a centimetre.

'Oh.'

'Again,' she tells him.

'I want you.'

Again she slips down.

He lets out a groan. Fuck it. Who's to know? Or care. It's not even a lie. He wants her. Whoever she is and whoever he has to be. 'I want you,' he says, his voice rich with breeding, and he slams her down onto him.

'I want you,' he says again, pushing her hips back.

'"Bea",' she says. '"I want you, Bea."'

'I want you, Bea.'

Eyes shut, head back, she groans this time as he pulls her down.

'I want you, Bea,' he repeats with every thrust. 'I want you, Bea. I want you, Bea, I—'

And as she quickens, he comes, in one shuddering wave from his toes to the tip of him. And only then does he call her by her true name. Gasped out, if only in his head.

'Daisy,' he yells. 'Daisy.'

He is glowing, giddy with it when he walks into the pub, his legs trembling, his heart fat and fast. So high is he that he doesn't clock the bulk of his sulking father until a hand grabs him by the front of his shirt and sends him slamming into a door jamb.

'Where the fuck have you been?'

He's panicked, strangled, can't get anything out but a whine.

Disgusted, his father drops him and he sinks, a stringless puppet, onto the flags.

'I told you,' he says. 'I was out with a girl.'

'Until four in the morning?'

'I—'

'Which girl?' interrupts his father.

He flails, weighing up the cost of a lie. 'Bea,' he picks.

'Swimming, were you?'

'No?'

'Fucking?'

He doesn't answer. As good as a yes.

'Good was she? Posh maid like her?'

He stays stoppered. Isn't going to dignify that sort of taunt.

235

But there's more where that came from. 'You think that makes you one of them?'

Jason shrugs.

'Think you're too good to wash pots, is that it? Think you're something else. Think you're better than me?'

'I am.' He's blurted it, let the words burst out before he can tame them. Might as well have poked the beast with a fiery stick and stuck out his tongue besides.

The creature steps back. 'You what?'

Jason pauses, teetering on the precipice for the second time that night like he's on an old rollercoaster, then, arms up, mouth gaping, plunges down. 'You heard me.'

Because he knows it, then. Doesn't need the drugs or the drink to believe it, feels it in the bones of him as if it's as real and vital as his own blood.

He *is* better.

He's a hero. A knight. Bright and brilliant and bound for better things than this shithole of a pub in a shithole of a village.

He'd go now if he could. Pack his bag and light out for the territory like a latter-day Huck Finn. To Paris, perhaps. Or London. Or just anywhere where he's not trapped like a caged monkey or preserved like an egg in a jar.

'I'm not stopping you,' his father says then.

'What?'

'You heard. You wanna go? Go. If you bloody love the high life so much then fuck off into it. But you listen up, boy.' He's back up in Jason's face now, so close the boy can see the veins in his father's jaundiced eyes like a scoop of

236

raspberry ripple. 'You walk out that door, you don't come back, you hear me? Not ever. Not tomorrow. Not when they drop you—'

'They won't,' he snaps.

His father laughs, an ugly, exaggerated sound, slaps his leg. 'Oh, they will. Scrawny little Cornish boy like you? They'll be gone by Monday. Fucked off up country where they belong.'

The words are meant as a slap. But instead they fall soft on his face as his mother's own touch. Maybe they will, he thinks. Maybe they will fuck off. But what's to stop me going with them?

Yes! That's it! He can go to school in Oxford. Or London, even! He can stay with Daisy, sleep on the sofa – or the floor if he has to. He'll get a job to pay his way, of course, as soon as he can. It can't be that hard. Christ, even Barry Ransome gets a wage packet. But until then she'll help. It was practically her idea after all, all this play-acting and pretence.

'All right,' he says, and he doesn't even flinch.

'All right what?'

'I'm leaving.'

His father barely skips a beat. 'So go.'

He makes for the stairs to pack his things but a hand grabs him, yanks him back.

'No chance,' says his father. 'Whatever it is you think you're getting, that's mine. My stuff, my house, my money.'

Mam's money, he thinks. But fuck it. There'll be other clothes – better clothes. Other boots and shoes. Other books – shelves of them, brand-new and with not a single page scrawled on or missing or torn out of spite.

'Tell Sadie I'll see her,' he says.

'Tell her yerself.'

And that's it. The last words his father will say to him. No 'good luck, son'. No 'I love you' – not that there was ever an 'I love you'. Just a throwaway remark for a relationship that's as disposable as a crisp packet, garnished with a grunt and belch as the man staggers up the stairs.

He stands in the silence, then. Lets himself steep and soak in the poverty. The ceiling stained with tobacco, the floor sticky with spit and spills, the sheer stink of it: of old smoke and stale beer and cracked ambition.

Then, without a word, he turns and walks back out the door. And he doesn't even care enough to slam it behind him.

27.

James, 2018

Has he spared a thought for Sadie? For his bar-tending, boy-loving, beer-swilling big sister.

Of course he has. But only to hope she got out, and not on the back of some townie's XT500. Anything else he's shoved under a rug, or to the far back of the larder, has repeated the mantra that they were barely related, only close for a moment, only clung together because two against one might stand them both a better chance. Because he is as far from the Pengelly mould as she was thrown from it and in the end the only two things they had in common were their father, and the need to leave.

But now there is this.

The girl – no, woman – behind the bar isn't Sadie. She's too plump, too young.

She is, though, the spit of his sister.

'You want ice with that?'

He's offered to get them in – has had to, because how can he not?

'I should charge a fiver a stare,' she says then.

'God, sorry.' He comes to. 'You . . . you look like someone I used to know.'

'Sadie, yeah? My mum.'

He's astounded. And not one iota surprised. 'Yes.'

'I get that a lot. Don't tell me, you've come back to declare undying love.'

Jesus. 'No.'

'You're too late anyways. She's gone. Off up country with some bloke off OK Cupid.'

He feels his heart brim with relief. That she's gone, yes. But more than that, that she's alive. 'Not your dad then.'

'Christ, no. This one's got a flaming moustache. And he's from Wales.' It is unclear which is the worst misdemeanour.

He tries to find the right way to say it, without malice or menace or sounding like a creep. 'So, is your father still here?'

'"Father"?' She laughs, mimicking him. 'I wouldn't know.' She holds her hand out for the twenty. Rings up the till. 'Why, you're not him, are you?' Smiling, she hands him change, which slips through sweaty fingers and scatters onto the bar.

'No,' he says scrabbling for pennies, then thinks better of it and writes them off to the charity pot or scavenging hands. 'I just . . . knew your mother . . . mum, back in . . . school. You really don't know? Your dad, I mean.'

She shrugs. 'Take your pick. Whichever one of your shag-happy classmates she was doing back in the late eighties.'

She is every bit Sadie, brash and swaggering. But someone else, too. 'When, exactly?' he blurts.

'Are you for real? Jesus. It's like sodding *Pointless*. Or the police. You're not the police, are you?'

'God, no. I'm sorry,' he says. And for once he is. Though more at his own ineptitude. He's had decades of training; he should know better than this.

She shrugs. 'I was born in May eighty-nine,' she says. 'You do the maths.'

'August,' he says, without missing a beat.

She shrugs. 'Whatever.' She looks at the pint of lime and soda he's sipped to stop it spilling. 'Definitely not my dad then. Nor a cop.'

And she's on to the next customer before he can even mutter a thank you.

And he *should* thank her; should throw his arms round her and tell her she's a godsend, a saviour.

Not just because Sadie is alive.

But because Sadie had a daughter. A daughter conceived that summer.

The summer she shagged Barry Ransome as well as half of the harbour boys, hoping one of them would take off into the sunset.

And the summer she fucked an Oxbridge prince, down for the holiday and drunk one night after a row with his girlfriend.

The summer she fucked Hal.

He is blazing with it – this new silver bullet. It sits, red-hot in his pocket, burning so that he fidgets on the bench, so eager is he to see her in him and him in her.

'Thanks,' says Hal, not bothering to look up.

Though it's one better than Julian who's engaged in conversation with a man whose skin is so livid and lotioned it appears blowtorched and eggwashed. James recognizes him from the back benches. A former trade secretary, now forced to beg for select committee scraps.

Hal is nodding and 'right'ing and, as he does, James tries to trace the connections, plays a strange game of pairs, but comes back disappointingly short. They are both dark-haired, but so was Sadie. Their mouths, perhaps, match, but then didn't their father have that too? Those swollen lips—

'James?'

He comes to, focuses on Julian, then on the MP.

'Ed Merritt,' he says.

James shakes his proffered hand, which has the temperature and consistency of boiled sausage. 'James Tate, and I know.'

'Oh, all bad, I hope?'

Practised, polished now, James humours him. 'Of course.'

'And you do . . .'

'I'm a writer.'

'Some pet of Daisy's,' adds Julian.

'Right, right. James Tate . . .' he ponders. 'Should I have heard of you?'

'I—'

'He's a ghost,' Hal interrupts. 'You're not supposed to.'

Hal hates him, James decides; he's only saying it to get one better.

'Of course.' Merritt roars with laughter, a fleck of spit

hitting James's collar, and it takes every fibre of him not to flinch in disgust. 'Well, best be off. Bunny's doing some bloody barbecue for supper and I'm supposed to be fetching the fish.'

'Nice to see you,' Hal lies. 'Dick,' he confirms, the minute he's gone.

'Why *haven't* I heard of you?' Julian is musing.

'Like Hal says—'

'I don't mean now. God, journos are as ubiquitous as rats. There must be hundreds I haven't had the misfortune to come across. I mean before. At Oxford. I find it hard to believe our paths haven't crossed.' He gets out his phone. 'Tate. How do you spell that? "I-t" or a "t-e"?'

'What are you doing?'

'Googling you.'

'Jesus.' Hal snatches at the phone but Julian's too quick, holds it aloft.

But James isn't concerned, not really. Knows Hal's done the same. And Julian will find exactly what he did: nothing. Because he has erased his past to secure his future. There is no trace of him in the ether save his byline. He has no social media accounts, bar the fake ones he uses for work purposes. He does not post photos of his avocado breakfast or update his status every time he takes a piss.

For the purposes of the internet he does not exist.

Julian drops the phone in disappointment. 'Where did she find you then?'

'You mean Daisy? My editor's a friend, I believe.'

'Lydia,' Hal explains.

Julian shrugs. 'They're all the same to me. Thin women.'

'Eyelids,' details Hal. 'Married to someone from Gerry's chambers. Or was.'

'Oh, *her*,' Julian summons. 'So you're *her* pet, as well.'

James sets his jaw. 'Or just good at my job.'

'You should send me your CV,' Julian says then.

He glances at the bar, at the business in hand, affecting well-practised nonchalance, before coming back to Julian. 'To check I'm not a charlatan?'

'Touchy. In case we ever need a speechwriter. Hal could use all the help he can get.'

'Fuck off,' Hal tells him. 'I can write.'

'As can many politicians,' James says quickly. 'But they don't have the time.'

Julian smiles, obsequious. 'And that's where you come in?'

'Precisely.'

'Like a body double,' adds Hal.

'Hardly,' says Julian.

Though, given James's gym visits and Hal's predilection for booze and biscuits, he suspects that, for once, it's not him Julian is belittling.

She appears then, next to the table, collecting empties with the same cocksure bustle as her mother.

'These dead?' she says.

'Yes, I . . .' But he trails off, mesmerized again by this likeness.

'Your round.' Julian nods to Hal. 'Perhaps she can fetch them.'

'*She* is the cat's mother,' snaps the girl, and he hears Sadie in every word. 'And no she sodding can't.'

'So what *is* your name?' Julian persists.

'Stella,' she says. 'Though I might be lying.'

'Well, Stella, or whatever your name really is, could you be a doll and get us three more in? And make his a gin this time.' He gestures at James, who makes to protest but then thinks better of it.

Stella leans in so Julian is forced face to face with her chest. 'What's *your* name?' she demands.

'Lord George Foulkes,' he tells her. 'No word of a lie.'

Hal snorts.

'Well, Georgey boy. One, you're full of it. Two, you can get up off your spoilt arse and get your own drinks. And three don't even think of reporting me to the landlord; it's my name above the door.' And, to a round of applause from the rest of the tables, and Hal, she leaves.

'Frigid,' declares Julian.

'You still would,' says Hal. 'If you hadn't, you know, turned.'

'Would what?' Julian's nostrils flare in disgust. 'Her? Hardly. Far more your type.'

Hal turns to James. 'Maybe she's *his* type.'

'What?' Already on edge, James feels the surge of adrenalin, quick and giddying.

'Christ.' Hal laughs. 'Your face.'

'I need a piss,' he says.

*

245

On the way back out of the lavatory he catches her eye again – Stella.

'Friends of yours?' she asks.

'Sorry,' he says. 'And no. Not really.'

'Good.' She smiles, every inch of it Sadie.

And, now he sees the disappointing truth: she's not Hal's. There's no evidence. Just a single willed memory from a fucked-up night thirty years ago. And that wouldn't stand up in court without DNA evidence, still less when flung at Daisy in desperation.

No, he must stick to plan A. To highlight Hal's shortcomings. To place him at the heart of the disaster with Bea.

He arrives back at the table to find Hal staring in exasperation at his phone. 'She wants us to fetch supper. Fucking fish and chips.'

Julian pulls a face. 'Does she know what that stuff does to your insides? And, more importantly, your outside?'

'It'll be stone bloody cold by the time we get it back, more to the point.'

'So tell her.'

He keys in a message.

One pops back by return.

'We can reheat it,' he reads out. He begins typing again, one-thumbed, but is interrupted by it ringing.

'Just do it, Hal,' James hears. 'I can't be bothered to sodding cook and nor can Clementine. And Muriel's not to be trusted with an oven.'

Hal rolls his eyes at James.

He replies with a smile, a lie.

'Fine,' Hal relents. 'What do you want?' He gestures at James for pen and paper.

'I'll text,' she says. 'See you in an hour.'

'More like two.'

But she's hung up. Gone back to Clementine, or Muriel, whoever needs her more – the latter he suspects. And so to the chippy they go.

It's complicated before they've even ordered, as fish supper for seven turns out not to be, of course. Luna is vegan and will only eat chips and only if they're cooked in oil that hasn't seen a haddock or a saveloy; Muriel wants pollock but the closest they have is cod or rockfish.

'Get her cod,' Julian tells him. 'She won't taste the difference.'

'It's not the taste, apparently,' explains Hal. 'It's the over-fishing.'

'I thought she was anorexic,' says Julian.

'Luna?' Hal peers at the menu again.

'Muriel.'

'Probably. Pair of them are a fucking liability.'

They settle on five cod, four chips, a haddock as backup, and some kind of pie for Hal, who would have demanded gravy, James suspects, if he could. But there is more trauma to come: they miss the ferry by moments.

'How long till the next one?' Hal asks.

James feigns a glance at the timetable. 'Twenty minutes.'

'If we're lucky,' Julian adds.

'Fuck that.'

'What are you going to do?' Julian demands, amused. 'Swim?'

'Hardly. Hey!' Hal calls to a boy hauling a Troy-class into the water. He looks up. 'Tenner to take us across.'

The boy screws up his face. 'In this? Must be joking, mate.'

'I'll do it.'

They turn in unison to see a kid in a dinghy, its tacked-on outboard hanging awkwardly. He's no more than twelve, James thinks, but kids are older now, and always were down here. Probably been working the taxis all summer.

'Great,' Hal says without hesitation. 'All aboard.'

The ferry ride over was bearable, steadied as they were by chains, surrounded by estate cars, so that he could imagine, when he tried, they were standing on a B-road.

But this is different. This is *Dolly*, all over again. The rattle of the outboard, the lap of water so close he can smell it, so close he can see shoals of silvery small fry and, beneath them, the brown blades of bladderwrack that tangled round his ankle . . . His stomach lurches and he clutches the side.

Hal frowns. 'You all right, mate?'

He breathes deep, knowing it's harder to vomit with air in his lungs. 'I'm fine, really.'

Julian looks appalled. 'I could have sworn you were born to it back there. All that "tiller" and "stern".'

'No . . . I . . .' But he can't finish, has to close his eyes and suck air in again.

'It's like a bloody millpond,' Julian says.

'Not tomorrow,' says the boy. 'Weather's breaking.'

James opens his eyes.

'What are you?' demands Julian. 'The Weather Whisperer?'

The boy holds out his phone. 'Met Office.'

Hal snorts. And, despite his nausea, James joins him. He's being paranoid, he tells himself. It's ghosts, that's all, the past trying to haunt him, taunt him. But he is not that boy. Just as that girl, though Sadie's she may be, is nothing to do with Hal.

And he tells himself that as they trudge up the slipway.

He tells himself that as they walk through the door.

He tells himself that all the way to the table, where he sees her. Again.

Those eyes. That mouth. That burnished brown hair.

'Clementine?' he says.

And his doubt evaporates like piss on a hot tin roof.

For though she is not a twin, not Bea to Daisy, she is something to that girl in the pub – to Stella.

She is her half-sister.

And his silver bullet sings.

28.

Bea, 1988

She doesn't know precisely why she does it. She only knows there's no other way. The inevitability of it as predetermined as height or hair colour or choice of public school. Perhaps it's to provoke Jason into admitting the truth – that it's not her he really wants at all. Or perhaps it's Hal she hopes to goad into some sort of admission. Yes, perhaps it's that. Though will she admit it? Not now it's done. Not after she made Jason . . . No, that's not right, she didn't make him do anything. He played that part eagerly, and, besides, it was Daisy's lips, Daisy's tits, Daisy's bits in his hands the entire time. She's neither vain enough nor stupid enough to think otherwise.

Afterwards, they lie silent, both on their backs now, so that she can feel the tin ridge of a ringpull in one buttock. But she doesn't shift – doesn't want it to be over, not quite yet. But, Hal despatched, Jason is fumbling, awkward again, even for his, what, seventeen years? Sixteen? Christ, she's a cradle snatcher. And a cherry taker too, going by the look of disbelief on his face when she finally took him inside her.

'Did you . . . you know?' he asks.

Jesus. 'Did I come?'

He doesn't reply.

She turns onto her side, feels for the tin thing, and pulls it off, a paperclip after all. 'What do you think?' she says.

'I don't know. I've never . . .'

She touches her fingers to his ribs, feels the bones of him. 'Yes,' she says. And it's not a lie, though he had little to do with it.

'Oh. Good? Are you . . . are you on the pill?'

She remembers him then, coming high inside her, feels the thick trickle of it now onto her thigh. 'Shouldn't you have asked that earlier?'

His face falls.

Her own contorts in humour. 'It's fine,' she tells him. 'Really.' Though that *is* a bloody lie. But Muriel's on Minulet so she'll just take two of hers – Daisy's done it before and lived. The poor man's morning-after pill. Or party girl's.

She wonders, then, if he's thinking about trying again, wonders if he's capable. The thinness of him: he looks as wrung-out and pale as a dishcloth. And her pity spills over like scalding milk and she kisses him. Though it is soft, sexless almost.

The silence that follows widens with time, it seems. Is no longer taut, fraught with the possibility of *it*, of them, but slack, blanket-like. She bathes in it. Drinks it in, thinking about everything and nothing at once.

'Do you believe in souls?' she asks, all of a sudden.

'I don't know,' he says. 'I suppose so?'

She ignores his hedging. 'I used to think they were an

actual body part. Slippery and thin. Translucent. Like a sliver of soap or something.'

He smiles, won over, she decides. 'And where was it? This soul?'

'Beneath my liver,' she tells him, matter-of-fact.

'Even though it wasn't on any anatomy chart?'

'Did you ever see a clitoris on a school anatomy chart?'

He flushes, shrugs.

'Well, there you go.'

'You think they're related?'

'Perhaps. What about God?'

'What about God?'

'I mean do you believe in him?' She recalls one of Muriel's more lucid rants. 'Or her.'

'No?' he answers. Although it isn't really, is it – an answer? It's another test; he's hoping to gauge her own reaction, hoping his tallies.

'Nor me,' she replies, kind, though it's not far from the truth. She'd like to believe in something, willed it for weeks. But God refused to comply with the sign she demanded and so she swore not to invoke him again. 'What about life after death?'

'Doesn't that rather depend on a god?'

She sighs, pointedly. 'Probably. How disappointing. I'd like to have come back as someone else.'

'Really? Who?'

As if she'd tell him. 'God, I don't know. Marie Antoinette.'

He frowns. 'But she's already dead. You couldn't come back as her.'

'Oh. Well, maybe I'm her now. She's reincarnated in me.'

'No she's not.'

'Why? Am I too tedious?'

'You're too nice.'

Nice? Nice isn't something to aspire to. Nice is cats and cake and cucumber sandwiches. Daisy isn't 'nice'. Muriel is definitely not nice – Christ! She reaches for her knickers. 'We should go,' she says. 'I'm tired.'

She doesn't sleep though. Sits, instead, on the doorstep with one of Daisy's fags, weighing up the worth of a fuck. Because what if he gets attached? What if he comes back begging for seconds, like a tiresome spaniel, all wide eyes and desperate for attention?

But would that be such a bad thing?

Yes, she tells herself. It would be bloody awful. This wasn't supposed to happen. As it is, it's a one-off. He's not the point of it, after all. He's a distraction. Barely a friend, even.

No, that's not true. It can't be.

Because when he saw her swim – really swim – for the first time, his smile was guileless and her own unbidden and wide and fat with gratitude.

Because when she fucked him she felt benevolent.

And because when he walks back across the lawn just ten minutes after she left him, a kerchief-less Dick Whittington, she stands, takes his hand, and leads him up the stairs to bed.

29.

James, 2018

Such a strange, dangerous game this, the one of atavism, of inheritance. Like a reverse photofit, trying to match eyes, noses, even a love for green sweets, with mothers and fathers, and theirs, beyond.

In Clementine he can trace Daisy's long neck, her refined jawline, the pronounced curve of her cupid's bow. But so much of her – the mahogany gloss of her hair, the deep beech of her eyes, the twin creases on her forehead when she's astonished or irritated or just concentrating – is surely all Hal.

But all that girl – all Stella too. And he quickens as he thinks it, brims full with horror and promise.

Oh, there are differences, because she is Daisy's, not Sadie's. She is still adolescent thin, her legs gangling like a colt, her breasts small and high. But it's there; the truth of it, of that night – of Hal's first fuck-up – is stark and, while half of it pulls pints on the harbour, its mirror is sitting opposite him on the lawn, picking batter from a haddock and swilling a Pimm's.

'It wasn't so bad,' she tells a bemused Julian, who cannot

fathom how she can have spent so long on a train, of all things. 'I had a book.'

'At least tell me you came first-class.'

'On my salary? It was bad enough in standard. Nearly two hundred quid, can you believe it?'

'Cattle,' corrects Julian. 'How much do they pay academics these days?'

'Not enough,' Hal replies.

'Too much,' contests Julian. 'It's only thinking after all.'

Clementine smiles. 'I know you're only saying that to provoke me and it won't bloody work.'

'I rather like trains,' Muriel decides. 'Perhaps we could get the train back? Luna?'

Luna looks up. 'Huh?'

'The train, darling. We could get the train back to London. What do you think?'

Luna gapes, an astonished frog. 'I would literally rather die?'

'Figuratively,' says Clementine.

Luna shrugs a 'whatever' and goes back to her phone and the Pimm's she's begged and been given, in spite of her age.

And all the while James pushes food around its paper wrapper, too dizzy to eat, as if he's back at St Austell fair, being spun on a Waltzer or whirled on a Rocket, and doesn't know if he's going to scream or throw up but he can't get off, not now.

'Aren't you hungry?'

Muriel's arm clanks with bangles and she's wearing a dress of Daisy's, he sees – that long one she arrived in. It drags on the ground on Muriel though, the hem of it already sullied, and he wonders if it's a gift or been magpied, and why.

'I'm fine,' he lies.

'I have tablets,' she tells him. 'If you need some. Or perhaps –' at this, her eyes widen, berry-bright – 'you need a lie-down.'

Julian's short snort is enough to tell him he's not imagining it, this attention, this unwarranted, unwanted come-on. 'I'm fine,' he repeats, grabbing a flaccid chip for good measure. He nearly gags on it, soused in vinegar as it is, soused in panic as he is, but, willing himself with bottomless want, he manages to swallow and smile, and turns, pointedly, to Daisy. 'So, how's your birthday so far?'

'Not yet!' she shrieks, checks her watch, rose-gold. 'There's still three hours to go.'

'God, fifty,' Clementine says, as if it's twice that. As if it's some unfathomable achievement, or perilous threshold to a dark netherworld. Which, to her, it probably is, just as it was to all of them once upon a time.

'Well, thanks for that.' Daisy raises her glass to her daughter.

'I didn't mean—'

'So has James buttonholed you yet?' she segues.

Clementine regards him, scepticism and curiosity weighted in equal measure. 'For what?'

'The book, of course,' explains Daisy.

Clementine wipes chip grease from her fingers onto a green plaid rug. 'Do I have to? I'd rather not.'

'Well, you don't have to, I just thought you might . . . be of use.'

She shrugs. 'No then.'

'I'm sorry.' Daisy has turned to him now. 'She's just being—'

Bea, he thinks. Another likeness slipping in.

'Difficult,' she finishes.

'*She* is the cat's mother,' says Clementine. 'And she's still right here. No offence.' She looks quickly at James.

He shakes his head, still half a sentence behind. 'None taken.'

'I just don't think I've got anything you'd want to hear.'

'Or maybe *I* wouldn't want to hear it,' says Daisy, her voice slipping into sulk.

'God, grow up, the pair of you,' Hal snaps, though it's softened by drink and the dregs of the sun.

Julian joins in. 'Fifty? Fifteen, more like.'

'I wish,' Daisy says. 'I'd give it all to go back.'

A surge of something lurches through him, and he pushes his food away again.

'Me too,' Muriel agrees brightly. 'Being grown-up is so . . . disappointing.'

'Thanks a fucking bunch.' Luna downs her Pimm's, holds her glass out for another.

'I didn't mean you, darling,' says Muriel, obliging. 'I meant the . . . the responsibility of it. It's so tiring.'

'Well, you can stop worrying then,' says Julian. 'Because you are the least responsible person I know.'

'Dick,' counters Muriel.

'He has a point,' says Clementine.

'Et tu, Brute?' says Daisy.

Clementine rolls her eyes, siding unwittingly with Luna.

'Anyway, Muriel has a point,' Daisy continues. 'It *is* all so bloody tiring. And boring too, half the time. All bloody blocked sinks and bills and dinners with people I don't even like.'

'But being a kid again?' demands Hal. 'It's not like you'd do anything differently. Study rocket science or become a fucking nun.'

'I might,' says Muriel.

'They wouldn't have you,' counters Julian.

'Who wouldn't?' Muriel demands.

'Either of them. The penguins or the geeks.'

James is staring at Daisy now, can see her walking towards the ghost of her sister, want to clutch her, bring her into the conversation. But then it's his eyes she catches when she opens her mouth to speak. 'At least we're here, I suppose,' she says.

He doesn't drop his gaze, doesn't flinch, knows this is something unspoken, something secret between them. That he, only he, knows the depth of her loss, that he is the one she opens up to, he is the one who understands.

And he will be the one she turns to, his the shoulder she cries on, when it all falls apart. Oh, God, this could happen. *Will* happen.

'Christ.' Hal punctures the silence, pours himself another glass of white. 'I wouldn't go back if you paid me.'

'Nor me.' Julian mock shudders, exaggeration expanding

in proportion to relief. 'I spent my fifteenth with some slapper called Stacey round the back of Oxford Street McDonald's.'

'How outré,' says Muriel.

'How revolting,' says Clementine.

'Prendergast,' he says then, plucking the name like a prize. 'Stacey Prendergast.'

'There's a name to conjure with.' Hal imagines.

'Probably still there,' says Julian. 'Flipping burgers.'

'You could Facebook her!' Muriel claps. 'Or Snapapp!'

At that, Luna laughs. Can't seem to stop.

'Christ,' Hal whines. 'How much has she had to drink?'

'Only a couple,' insists Muriel. 'Four maybe. But it's Pimm's – that's all fruit. It's practically Ribena.'

'Jesus. I topped it up with vodka.'

'I feel sick,' says Luna, as if to confirm his worst fears.

'Oh.' Muriel pulls a face. 'Really?'

'I'll take you,' Clementine offers.

'Take me where?' demands Luna.

'Bed,' says Clementine.

'But it's not even ten.'

'You're green,' says Clementine. 'Literally.'

And meek, defeated, Luna lets herself be led across the lawn by a girl – woman – who he now sees, to his delight, has the same strange gait as Stella.

'I put a bucket in with her.'

Clementine is back, clutching a cup of some sort of herbal tea.

'Will she be all right?' Hal asks.

'Why? Worried it might fuck up your chances?' Julian grins. '"Underaged drunk chokes on own vomit at would-be MP's coke-addled . . . whatever." James, you're the hack. What's the headline?'

But he doesn't get the chance to tell him where to stick his tabloid crap. Because—

'Julian!' snaps Daisy, and gestures to her left. 'Muriel?'

Julian rolls his eyes. 'It was a joke.'

But Muriel is, as ever, perfectly oblivious. 'She's been drunk before, you know,' she says. 'They all do it, these days. It's almost normal.'

'"These days"?' Hal laughs. 'You were always puking.'

'I was not,' Muriel insists. 'Julian, was I sick?'

'Always,' confirms Julian.

'Oh, God. So I was!' Muriel's face lights up. 'I was terrible, wasn't I? Good job we all grew up.'

Daisy's smile is weak. 'Not all of us.'

'Well, thanks,' says Hal.

'Speak for yourself,' adds Julian.

And James brims with it again. That only he can see Daisy's not talking about their persistent twittery; she's talking about Bea. But as he goes to touch her hand in empathy, triumph, the fading light enough of a cover now, Clementine edges a leg between them, insinuating herself like a jealous child.

'Do you believe in the soul?' she asks.

'Christ, straight to the serious stuff.' He glances at Daisy, wondering what the right answer is. But she's busied herself with a cigarette, so that in the end he has to search his own conscience and memory, for he's been asked this before somewhere, though he can't place by whom or when. 'No. You?'

'When I was small my mother told me mine was behind my liver,' Clementine tells him, then smiles at Daisy, indulgent. 'I imagined it like a cuttlefish bone, I think, or used-up soap.'

Daisy exhales, laughs. 'I did no such thing.'

'You did too. I think I confused it with a spleen for a long time.'

'And now?' he asks.

'Oh, there's no soul,' Clementine says, with no more emotion than if she were dismissing baked beans at breakfast. 'We're just here on earth – a bundle of nerves and connections – then we're gone. Poof! Like a dandelion clock.'

'How depressing,' says Daisy.

'I don't think so,' Clementine replies, matter-of-fact, still.

'What, so I've got some gaping black chasm then?'

'You will if you carry on smoking.'

'Charming.'

Clementine shrugs. 'I'm not saying that, I—'

'Bollocks. I've got a soul,' Daisy insists, waspish now. 'We all have.'

'Well, maybe not Julian,' James tries for light.

But they both ignore him.

'Whatever helps,' Clementine says. 'But I'm telling you it's not possible. There is no soul. Or self.'

'What do you mean?' Daisy demands. 'Of course there's a bloody self. Or I wouldn't be me.'

Clementine shakes her head, her sneer, queerly, all Sadie

now. 'It's an illusion. It's like . . . a story we tell ourselves about ourselves. There's no . . . no pearl of truth inside us.'

'I could have told you that.' Julian has joined in, smug as a judge. 'That's why this autobiography thing is such bullshit.'

Daisy frowns. 'Julian?'

But he ignores her, turns to James. 'You think you're going to unwrap her, don't you? Layer by layer like a bloody pass the parcel to find the real Daisy inside.'

'I—'

'Well you're wasting your time.'

Daisy's eyes narrow, cat-like. 'So what *is* there then?'

Julian smiles. 'Just more Haribo and sparkles, darling.'

'Oh, do fuck off.'

'God, Mother!' Clementine glares at her.

Julian holds his hands up. 'Joke,' he says again, though that's as deceptive as his hairline.

'It's true, though.' Clementine turns to her mother again. 'We're all just smoke and mirrors and self-tan.'

'Even me?' asks Muriel.

'Especially you,' answers Julian.

Hal nudges his daughter. 'That sounds like a line from a book.'

'Because it is.' Clementine pulls the teabag from her cup, drops it on the lawn. 'Mine.'

It takes Hal a second for this to register. 'That's . . . wonderful.'

Daisy's mouth gapes and she claps a dramatic hand over it for a moment. 'But why didn't you tell us?' she asks eventually.

'I'm telling you now.'

'Another writer.' Julian's smile is wry. 'God preserve us.'

James doesn't rise. 'When's it out?'

Clementine smiles. 'Next year. May, I think.'

'That's—'

'Bollocks,' Muriel announces, missing her cue, as usual, this time by several lines. 'That's what it is. Utter bollocks.'

'What is?' Clementine asks, hurt in her words. 'Me writing?'

'No, that . . . that stuff about the self. You're only saying it because you're scared. That's it!' She claps. 'You're scared of the truth. You're scared to be the *real* you.'

'What, and you're a bastion of bare-faced honesty? Christ,' exclaims Julian. 'You're not even wearing your own clothes.'

Muriel pouts. 'That's just the outside. It's what's inside that counts.'

'You're talking to a plastic surgeon,' Julian points out.

Muriel snatches Daisy's cigarette. 'And what would plastic surgeons know about souls?'

'Selves,' Hal counters. 'And that's what Clementine's saying, isn't it, Clem? That there *is* no real you, so the outside is all that counts.'

'Not exactly.' She sighs. 'But yes, appearance is the larger part of it.'

Hal leans back on his hands. 'Well, there you go. If you were looking for skeletons in Daisy's closet, don't bother. There obviously aren't any.'

'Really?' Daisy waves for her cigarette back from Muriel, takes a last drag, and stubs it out on the parched grass. 'Oh, darling, but surely you know by now?'

'Know what?' Hal is tired.

She laughs. 'I, darling, am all fucking skeleton.'

And with that, she stands and stalks back into the house, leaving the lawn party in abundant, stunned silence. Leaving James jiggling with pity and pathos and desperate want.

'Is she all right?' asks Julian after a moment, though he makes no effort to move.

Hal shrugs it off. 'She's fine. It's just . . .' But he trails off, unable to say it.

'All monsters and dust.'

All eyes turn to Clementine. 'What?' Hal asks.

'All of it,' she replies. 'All of this. Too many memories.'

Hal shrugs. 'I told her she was mad.'

'Helpful.' Clementine stands. 'I'll go then, shall I? Seeing as no one else seems to be moving.'

'We should all go,' James suggests, as if bringing the others in will absolve him, disguise his need. 'Besides, it's getting dark.'

'Oh, but I love the dark!' Muriel claps, happy again. 'And I thought we were skinny dipping?'

'You can do what you like.' Hal stands. 'But I'm not freezing my balls off in there.'

'Nor me.' Julian picks up the bottle and follows Hal, who follows his daughter into the house.

James wants to edge ahead of them, run to her, tell her he gets it, but it's not time, not yet. So he begins to clear up: fish-stinking papers and plastic cups while Muriel sits, still, resting on her elbows, legs splayed.

'What about you?'

'What about me what?' he asks, barely bothering to hide his sigh.

She stretches one foot out, runs her toes – ringed and painted – up his calf.

He stiffens, shifts.

'We could . . . *swim*.' She says it like it's everything but. 'You and me.'

'I don't think so.'

'Because you've got a girlfriend?'

He nods, to save her face. But it's not that. Not anymore. Though he's yet to muster the courage to end it. Can't do that over the phone, still less text. No he will face her, when he gets back. But, Jesus, Muriel. That borrowed dress. As if she can just slip on Daisy's vestments and become a version of her when she's not even close. She's a fake, a fraud. The touched-up advertisement. Oh, she's not all bad, not by a long shot. But while Daisy, despite her enhancements, exudes truth, Muriel is a haphazard patchwork of paper and paint, all nipped and tucked, the cracks plastered over. She is a wannabe. An also-ran. And Daisy? She is Botticelli's Venus, Delacroix's Liberty, the true Mona Lisa, while Muriel is pathetic and desperate; a cheap copy stuck up to fool the hordes.

And so, laden with litter, he leaves her in a fug of Diptyque and self-pity and walks back into Rashleigh, to tell Daisy she is the real thing, whatever her daughter claims. But when he gets inside he discovers she's taking herself straight to bed and no level of complaining by Hal or concern from Clementine can sway her.

'It's nothing,' she insists. 'Saving myself for the big day, that's all. I'll see you in the morning. Bright and early.'

'Not too early,' pleads Julian. 'Some of us have a decent Sauternes to get through.'

She shakes her head in disbelief, but without malice now, indulging him as one would a child, though God knows he doesn't deserve it. 'Good night,' she says.

And then, like a dandelion clock – poof! – she is gone.

'I might hit the hay, too,' James says.

Julian snorts. 'Could you be more obvious?'

He glares now, belief turning his fragile carapace to brass armour. 'Actually, I've got a lot to do. We've only a day, after all.'

'You can't make her work on her birthday,' Clementine intervenes.

'Well, not too hard,' he replies.

She smiles – a strange, wary thing that is part Daisy, part Hal, and – oh, God – part Stella, and he wants for a moment to kiss her for gifting him this golden ticket. But he steadies himself, is ready for this, will not throw it all away in a foolish, flippant minute.

'Good night,' he says.

And he is gone too.

But not to bed.

Back in the outhouse he sits and listens.

To Daisy telling him he has a way with words, a way with her, and that she's so glad Lydia found him, that he agreed.

To Daisy telling him she's surprised he hasn't thought

about office himself, or at least a career in front of the camera – a new Paxman, perhaps, or younger Humphrys.

To Daisy telling him she tires, sometimes, of life and that he is medicine, a tonic.

But this isn't work. None of this will make the final cut. This is for him alone. He needs to steep in her, to catch every nuance, to believe that she believes in him.

Because tomorrow he has another job to do. Tomorrow he is all about Hal.

And Stella.

He needs to take measure, to see her again. And to see Hal's face when he gets it. Then he can make his play. Finally. Show Daisy who Hal really is.

And why he is so much more.

Because, whatever Clementine claims, there is a core to him. Unwrap him and there is no sweet treat or glitter, but no poor Cornish boy either. His own modern Prometheus, he has remoulded not just his manners and glad rags, but his entire inner being.

And all because Daisy told him he could.

30.

Jason, 1988

He walks widdershins in his sleep, tossing as snapshots flash and fragments catch in his vague memory and wild imagination: the inside of a thigh under his fingers, the skin thin and pale as skimmed milk; a hank of hair in his hand, salt-dirty and sand-gritted; a lip against his, swollen with want and sticky with cherry ChapStick and spit. Wakes sweating and spent to the hiss of his name and blue eyes squinting.

'Daisy?' he says, still in the haze of sleep and heat of a hard-on.

But it's Bea's eyes that widen now. 'I think we've played that game enough,' she says.

Fuck. He reaches down, lands on a floor-laundered T-shirt and pulls it on.

'Don't mind me,' she says. 'Not like I haven't seen it.'

'What time is it?' he asks.

She looks at her Timex. 'Half one,' she says. 'Or thereabouts.'

'I should—' But what should he do? Go? But where, then? He's been kicked out, hasn't he, and not before time. So this

268

– he looks around – this narrow back bedroom, with its slant wall and skew window and single bed, is his last hope of shelter because, Christ knows, no one from school will have him, and the Varlows have long washed their hands after his father's performance at the funeral.

'I . . .' he repeats, but gets no further.

'It's all right,' she says, 'I told you.' She puts a hand on him then, wraps skinny fingers round his wrist.

He looks down, wonders if he should take them in his, what it might lead to. But quick as a flick she drops it and stands, the distance between them stretching like dough until it's estuary-wide.

'Coming?' she says.

'Where?' he asks. 'Swimming?'

She shakes her head. 'It's clouding over.'

He's relieved, glad he won't have to face his father, or Fat Man or Alan, to get to the boat. Only . . . 'Where then?'

She laughs, a tinkling, crystal thing. 'The kitchen,' she says. 'That's all. It's breakfast.'

The room falls Sunday silent, all eyes on him.

'He slept in the back room, before you ask,' Bea announces as she slumps into a seat.

'Wasn't going to,' says Hal through a fug of skunk.

Julian, up on the counter with a bowlful of cereal, smirks. 'Right,' he says.

'We're not *all* a sack of walking hormones,' Bea retorts.

'Speak for yourself,' says Daisy and, catching his eye, smiles.

Something in him twitches and he clatters a chair out, sits quick.

'Perhaps I have too many hormones,' says Muriel, all charcoal eyes and ennui. 'Perhaps that's the problem.'

'What problem now?' Hal asks, as if he's totting up a long list.

She leans in, conspiratorially. 'Julian says I'm a sex addict. And he's a doctor.'

Bea snorts. 'Julian's a third-year med student. It's hardly the same. Anyway, he's staying for now. So get used to it.'

'Who is?' Muriel asks blithely.

'Jesus.' Bea seethes. 'Jason.'

'Imagine if he *was* Jesus!' Muriel claps. 'Like in that film. They found him in a hay barn. The children.'

'But he wasn't Jesus,' Julian explains, less than patient. 'That's the whole point. He was Alan bloody Bates. He was a criminal.'

'Perhaps Jason's a criminal,' suggests Muriel, hopefully.

Julian rolls his eyes, takes in Jason. 'Hardly.'

Jason feels himself fade in his gaze, become blurry and vague. 'I can go,' he offers, though tinges it with unwilling.

'Please do,' he replies.

'Fuck off, Julian,' Bea tells him.

'What? You can't just . . . just invite anyone.'

But Bea pours milk onto Rice Krispies, which snap, crackle and pop a response. 'It's my house. I can do what I like.'

'But it's not supposed to be a bloody free for all. Tell her.' He kicks at a chair. 'Daisy.'

Daisy pushes Jason a bowl, hands him a spoon. 'That's exactly what it's supposed to be or *you* wouldn't be here.'

And with that the faded haze of him becomes tight and precise again, and a neat, strong arm reaches out for the cereal box, shakes cornflakes into pale green Pyrex.

Hal leans back, strangely satisfied. 'Doesn't bother me,' he says. 'Besides, we're going home in two days.'

At that, that almost-last-orders, Jason flinches, and he has to force a swallow. He can't ask yet, though. Will wait until he can get Daisy alone. Or Bea, even. Tell them the mess he's in, wait for one of them to throw him a lifebelt.

Julian stacks his bowl in an overflowing sink. 'You always did have a thing for waifs and strays.'

Hal snorts. 'Me or Daisy?'

Julian sighs, dramatically. 'I meant Daisy, but if the cap fits.'

Daisy turns to Jason. 'You know what a waif is?' she asks him.

He shakes his head.

'A lost boy.'

Muriel claps. 'Like in Peter Pan?'

'I suppose,' she indulges, then turns back to him, back to her story. 'If a child is found but unclaimed they fall to the Lord of the Manor.'

'Who told you that?' demands Bea.

'I read it,' says Daisy. 'I can't remember where.'

'Well, that would be Hal, anyway,' Julian says. 'Surely.'

Hal bristles. 'I'm not a fucking Lord.'

Daisy stiffens – only slight, but he sees it. But then smiles, beguiling. 'Well, then, he can fall to the Ladies instead. Can't he, Bea?'

Bea looks at him, distance thinned, benevolent again. 'Of course.'

And for a brief, glittering moment, he soaks in it, in the attention of the pair of them, in their dappled light that catches him, makes him shine as if he's the golden one, diamond bright. But—

'Haven't you forgotten something?' Daisy says then, eyes expectant.

Shit. 'Thank you?' he says, tentative.

She laughs, shakes her head. 'Happy birthday,' she says. 'Happy birthday to us.'

'Happy birthday!' He blurts it, like a four-year-old or a fool. Turns to Bea, quickly. 'Both of you,' he adds, tempered this time. 'But I didn't get you a present.'

'None of us did,' admits Julian.

'Speak for yourself,' Hal says. 'Gave Daisy hers last night.'

Julian groans. 'Really?'

Jason looks over at Bea, catches embarrassed eyes and a flicker of – what? Guilt?

'I got you both a present,' Muriel announces. 'But I can't remember where I put it.'

'What is it?' Hal asks.

Muriel thinks, smiles. 'You know, I can't remember that either!'

'It doesn't matter,' says Daisy, twirling a strand of Muriel's hair in her fingers. 'You being here is the present. The party is the present!'

'We should have invited Dempster,' Julian says then. 'And that ginger girl with the massive tits. What's her name?'

'Harry something or other,' Hal obliges.

'Harry McAllister,' Daisy explains. 'And we would have, only you screwed that one, Julian. Literally.'

Julian holds his hands up. 'Touché.'

'Dempster's in Crete, isn't he?' Hal says then.

'Thank fuck,' says Daisy. 'He'd try to turn it into some Bacchanal.'

'What? It's not going to be a Bacchanal?' Hal feigns horror.

Daisy shoves him. 'You know what I mean. All that club bollocks. There'd be initiations. He'd make Jason run naked round town.'

Even the spurious suggestion sends his dick shrivelling. 'Are *your* friends coming?' Jason asks Bea then.

Julian laughs, a cold hard stone of a thing.

'They're already here,' she tells him, her throat tight as if each word is lemon-bitter.

And so they are.

They stay in the kitchen for gone two hours, or so the sloth of a clock has it. Smoking and drinking tea and eating toast from the table because no one will wash up, not today, not on a birthday. He offers to do it himself at one point and Julian stands aside, opens his arms, says, 'Be my guest.' But Bea tells Julian to fuck off and Daisy says no, he mustn't, it's not his mess, after all.

'Shouldn't we get some air?' someone says at some point.

But the first rain has hit the window by then, the weather

breaking after all. 'Bollocks to that,' Julian decides. 'What could we possibly want out there that we don't have in here?'

And even Jason has to admit the truth of that.

It's Daisy who caves eventually. Stands and says she's done.

Hal pulls her back to his lap, squealing like a piglet.

'Stop it!' she shrieks, pulling herself free.

Hal pouts.

Bea stubs out a cigarette. 'Where are you going anyway?'

'To get ready,' she says.

'It's not even four,' Hal protests.

'It takes time to prepare.'

'Not that long.'

'You don't know even know what I'm coming as.'

Jason turns to Bea. 'Is it . . . fancy dress?' he blurts, his words edged in panic.

'Of course.' Muriel is swaying to The Doors, a tinny Jim Morrison singing from her Walkman.

'What kind?' he asks, not wanting to know the answer, not needing to, as what the fuck can he do about it now? And who has fancy dress parties past primary school anyway?

'The Beautiful and the Damned,' Bea says, scorn spread thick as jam. 'Like the book?'

'I know that,' he snaps, then softens, sorry not even touching it. 'I didn't . . . I—'

But Daisy – part Glinda, part Fairy Godmother – waves her magic wand and his heart fair sings with it. 'Hal will sort you out with something,' she says quickly. 'Won't you?'

Hal shrugs. 'Fine.'

'Then that's settled.' She turns to Bea, pulls at her hand. 'Come on, then.'

Bea frowns. 'Come where? Why?'

Daisy stifles a sigh. 'You'll see. Just . . . come.'

And so it is settled. Slowly, one by one, they drift up the stairs and scatter to bedrooms to prepare, the others carrying their first charged glasses of champagne, him piled high with Hal's hand-me-downs – a jacket in emerald velvet that gleams in the light like the shell of a beetle, black trousers with a strange stripe sewn on the side, a pair of patent shoes two sizes too big but he can stuff them with toilet roll. Though he can't pack out the jacket. That will have to hang off him – does hang off him – but he tells himself she won't notice, will be beguiled besides, because, even several inches too short and several more too skinny, he is different, a vision, a thing to behold.

He practises the accent. 'Hello, Daisy,' he says.

'Hello, Jason,' she replies.

No— wait. Not Jason. Something else. Something better. 'Charles,' he says. 'Call me Charles.'

And so he stands at the window, awaiting his entrance, the rain hammering, his fingers tapping the sill and his lips whispering his newness.

31.

James, 2018

He wakes twisted and pinioned, must have tossed clockwise in his sleep, sheet-wrapped as he is now, a poorly thought-out Egyptian mummy, or – and the absurdity does not escape him – an ill-suited ghost. Something feels askew and for a brief, gloating moment he thinks Daisy has been watching him, scans the expanse of the room, but both chairs are empty, at the table just a laptop, its lid open but black eye closed to the world.

But when he wrestles himself free, rises, he sees he's not mistaken after all, or not completely so, because she's there, on the lawn, the cigarettes she's failed to give up clutched in her hand like a talisman.

'Don't tell Clem,' she says, holding one out as an offering.

He hasn't smoked since student days, and even then it was a ploy, a practised thing to play the game, to pull in potential customers as he handed out Camels, but now he accepts it as part of the invitation, settles on the bench, next to her. 'I shan't,' he says, then forces himself to take a drag, tries to ignore the stale biscuit taste, the health warnings. But he manages not to sputter or cough, and, relieved, wonders if he could still blow a smoke ring, if she asked.

But that's not the question.

'You don't have children, do you?'

He pauses, not inclined to lie, but wondering where she's going. 'No. I don't.'

'"I"?'

'We,' he corrects reluctantly. 'Or it was. It's . . . complicated.' All but over in name.

'They change you,' she tells him. 'Not all for the bad. But something happens and you begin to . . . to lose yourself.'

He says nothing. Cannot say anything, because who is he to correct her? Though he cannot see what is lost about her, cannot see a lack, a hole.

'Do you think she's right?' she asks.

'Who?'

'Clem.'

'About what?'

'All that stuff last night. About there being no real me. Or you for that matter.'

'No,' he tells her without hesitation, because of this he is convinced. While he plays at performance, appears malleable as an actor, this itself is the pretence. Because, for all his fabrication, now he has made himself anew he is as much truth as the next man, as any man. Inside him *is* a pearl formed from the grit of simply being alive and, while souls he decries as so much desperation, this small seed he can grasp as if it were a piece of pea gravel: hard and real.

But she doesn't hear him, or doesn't listen. 'Maybe she's

right,' she muses. 'Maybe I'm just a sort of hotchpotch. Maybe I'm just bits and bobs of everyone I ever knew. And what about all the parts I played? Perhaps I'm part Marilyn and part Marlene and part . . .' She clutches at a name.

'Mrs Dalloway?' he suggests, recalling a playbill.

'Yes! And Mrs de Winter.'

'And Princess Di.'

'Oh, God. Don't remind me. But yes, maybe even her. And Muriel, too. I must be part Muriel. And part . . .' She stops short, but he knows without question who she was going to name. And knows she is right.

'You contain multitudes,' he tells her.

'Sorry?'

'Walt Whitman. "I contain multitudes."'

She smiles. 'Perhaps.' Then, emphatic, 'Yes, I do. Does that make me a fake?'

He shakes his head. 'You seem perfectly genuine to me.'

She takes back the cigarette. 'Ah, but that's because you don't know me.'

'But I do,' he says, without even wavering. 'You're –' he thinks of the word – 'inimitable.'

She laughs, as if coughing out a pip. 'But not, apparently, irreplaceable.'

He starts. 'Hal?' he asks, hopes.

She shrugs. 'Not especially. We're all on a conveyor belt though, aren't we? And behind us come newer, shinier, better-made versions. I'm the old guard as of today. Can you imagine?'

'Oh, God,' he says as the significance hits. 'Happy birthday.'

She smiles. 'I wasn't angling. But thank you.'

'I didn't even get you a present,' he admits, mentally slapping himself for his omission, for Isobel's insistence that that was 'just too weird'.

'Don't be silly,' she says. 'Why on earth would you? You being here is enough of a gift.'

And it's there again, a sun-bright spark of a thing. And so he doesn't argue his case, doesn't say a word. Instead he sits looking out under glowering clouds and over grey-metal estuary, feet in the damp lawn, bench pressed into his back, one knee pressed against hers. And he cannot shift even an inch, despite his stale breath, despite his swelling bladder, despite the desperate ball of want inside that is screaming at him to cup her face and kiss her – not yet, not yet – because right now he needs this moment to defy time and tock on for ever.

And on it tocks, for ten more seconds, until the first fat drop of rain hits.

'Fuck,' she exclaims.

'Fuck,' he echoes.

And then they run.

Barefoot and yelping like dogs or children they burst into the hall and run smack into Hal and Julian, who appears, improbably, to be setting the table.

Julian smirks.

Hal doesn't flinch. 'Happy birthday, darling,' he says. 'I wondered where you'd got to.'

'I thought I said no work.' Clem is trailing down the stairs, still in some sort of night attire, though not the silk kind – the kind Daisy favours – but slobbish cotton.

'It wasn't work,' Daisy assures her daughter. 'Not properly.'

'You should be lying in.'

'Perils of getting old,' she tells her. 'We need less sleep.'

'Is that what it is?' Julian asks.

'Tell that to Muriel,' Hal adds. 'She's out for the count still.'

'Really? Julian, go fetch her, would you.'

'I'll go,' says Clem and turns on her heel, pyjama legs dragging so that he wonders she doesn't trip.

'I should shower,' he says. 'Before . . .'

'I wasn't going to say anything,' she taunts and for a moment he thinks to flinch. But sees, then, that it's entirely lacking in malice, a suggestion, instead, of their proximity. A whisper of conspiracy.

'Ten minutes,' he says.

'Make it twenty. Muriel's notoriously slow.'

'Twenty,' he confirms. 'I'll shave.'

'Are you capable?'

'Julian!' Daisy protests.

Julian conjures bemusement. 'I meant because he's so young.' He turns to James. 'What are you? Barely forty?'

'Forty-six,' he says, subtracting a year for safety, as he's always done.

'Exactly. A baby.'

'Old enough,' he snaps back, then curses himself for rising.

Julian raises an eyebrow – a feat in itself – and stalks out of the room, Hal wandering behind.

Daisy flaps her hands as if to break the butter-thick tension. 'Go on, shoo. Shower.'

'Twenty minutes,' he repeats.

And her smile as he walks backwards is beatific.

It takes him less than fifteen, but he spends the last five perfecting his plan.

He will tell Hal he needs to interview him. Not for the book – he'd hardly agree – but for a feature piece, a spread in a Sunday supplement ahead of the campaign. Guaranteed run and copy approval – he can't turn that down. Then, when he gets his 'yes', he'll say perhaps they could do it in town, though, away from Rashleigh. Away from the party prep. Get a pint, make it a casual thing. Talk about his community pub ideas. Getting him to the Lugger, specifically, well that may be harder. But he's prepared to pub crawl if it comes to it. Prepared to tip pints on the floor when he's taking a piss just to stay sober and secure this story.

Yes, that is how it will go.

Like clockwork.

And so, miraculously, blissfully, it does, until Julian lands, a giant fly in the ointment.

'Actually I need to go over, too,' he says.

'For what?' James asks.

He taps his nose.

'Where the fuck—'

'Hal!' Daisy yells at him.

He clocks Luna. 'Sorry, where are you going to find that?'

'I know a man,' Julian claims. 'A bloke.'

James almost snorts at his attempt to down-class, but the very thought of him skewering this is needle-sharp and just as jolting.

'Bloody hell, mate.' Hal holds his hands up, his croissant flaking on pristine linen. 'You could score in a fucking nunnery.'

'Hal!'

'Seriously? She's not even sodding listening.'

'Who isn't?' asks Muriel.

'Doesn't matter,' says Daisy, patting her on the arm. 'The boys are going to town, that's all.'

'Oh!' Muriel claps. 'Can you take Luna?'

Julian groans. 'What for? I thought she'd "literally rather die".'

For once, even James agrees. But they are outnumbered, and outmanoeuvred.

'Someone called Flick is there,' Muriel explains.

Luna looks up. 'Fliss?' she corrects. Adds a muttered 'God' at the end for good measure.

'Maybe Clem can come,' James suggests quickly. 'To chaperone?'

'I'm not a fucking child?' Luna whines, proving, of course, she is exactly that.

Besides, Clem has other plans. 'I'll stay with Mum.'

'Since when has she been "Mum"?' demands Julian. 'I thought it was Daisy, Daisy all the way.'

'Since *Mum* gave up arguing,' says Clem, as smug as a plum.

'Life's far too short,' says Daisy. 'Anyway, you don't have to stay, darling,' she adds. 'I'm only going to sleep.'

'I thought you didn't need sleep,' Julian points out.

'God, you really are a bore at times,' she retorts.

Clem shrugs. 'Whatever. I've got proofs to read anyway.'

Daisy laughs, soft, as if to herself. 'That's more like it.'

And so it's settled. They will leave at three – Hal, Julian, Luna and he – take the ten past ferry.

'Have fun,' says Daisy as they troop out the door, in an assortment of plastic macs and laden with umbrellas. Except, of course, for Luna, who, despite the promise of more downpours, a storm even, is dressed in a crop top and hot pants that suggest to James that Fliss is entirely manufactured and it's a boy on whom she's calling. 'Be back by six for supper,' she adds.

Hal turns. 'That's a bit bloody early. I thought we were eating at eight.'

Daisy raises her hands. 'You're supposed to dress up.'

'That doesn't take two hours.'

'If I say six you'll be back at seven. It takes an hour to shower and dress. Just do as I say for once, Hal. Please? It's my bloody birthday after all.'

There's a tightness to her suddenly, a rawness, and James wonders what's brought it on – if it's just the age thing, or if the absence of Bea is beginning to bite harder, become more of a black dog than a strange, sullen cat of a thing. He's struck, then, with the urge to abandon the whole plan, to stay with her, hold her, tell her everything is perfect, everything is going to work out.

But it isn't, is it? Not unless he goes. Unless he proves this theory and presents the evidence. Otherwise she's stuck, still, with this gibbon of a man, this cheat and charlatan who's lied for years, for decades. And it's hours, now, not days, until they abandon Rashleigh.

And so he goes, off down the rain-slicked slipway and onto the ferry, as the first clamour of thunder rumbles in electric air.

On deck, Luna stands several feet away, disowning the decrepit old men, then, ashore on the Fowey side, sneaks as swift as a phantom, disappearing into the Pac-a-Mac'd crowds, the only sign of her an occasional glimpse of a pink lion's mane bobbing amid bright-coloured hoods. 'Half six at the ferry!' Hal had roared after her. But her headphones were in and her attention, as ever, elsewhere.

They stop at a cash machine, to get a tonne for the dealer. But Julian's card is declined, and withheld, swallowed into the machine like a pill down a gullet.

'For fuck's sake,' he exclaims. 'What's that about?'

'Something you're not telling us?' Hal smiles.

'It's not funny.'

'Here.' Hal pulls out his wallet, flips through the card holder. 'Use mine.'

'Thanks,' says Julian, though barely gratefully. 'What's the PIN number?'

It's just PIN, James thinks. The 'n' stands for number. But he doesn't say it, doesn't want to rile him further.

Julian takes out a hundred, hands the card back to Hal. 'Come on then,' he says. 'Shopping.'

James pales. 'What?' he asks. 'What about a pint?'

'Can't,' says Julian. 'Meeting a man about a dog in twenty.'

'But . . . do we all need to go?'

'I think we're the henchmen,' Hal says.

'Precisely,' Julian replies.

This isn't supposed to happen. 'Are you . . .? Should you—'

'It's all right,' Julian interrupts. 'I'm hardly going to be papped in fucking Palookaville. You can wait on the wall or something if you're worried.'

They pass the Lugger, already thick with drinkers. 'Who are you meeting?' he asks, his words half disappointment, half fear.

'Remember that kid?' He's talking to Hal. 'From before. He's still here. The twat.'

James stiffens.

'What kid?' Hal asks.

'Darren Banner.' Julian spits out the name like it's a maggoty apple, and a pock-faced teenager slips into James's mind, dressed in acid-washed denim and stinking to high heaven of dog and Kouros.

'How the fuck did you remember that?' Hal demands.

'I'm good with names. And faces.'

James flinches, rights himself. It's not a dig. Just a coincidence. That's all.

'Still dealing then,' Hal continues, oblivious.

'Everything,' confirms Julian. 'Asked if I wanted ketamine and an unlocked iPhone as well. That's ambition for you.'

'At least he's employed,' Hal says. 'Of sorts.'

'Oh he is. Still doing that big house at Readymoney. We're meeting him there.'

The Varlows. The bloody Varlows. His stomach is a sudden churn of salmon and eggs and over-buttered sourdough.

'I might stay here,' he says suddenly. 'Get prepped.'

'Bollocks,' Hal grabs him – good-natured though it is – and steers him along South Street. 'I'm not henching alone. You're my collateral if we get caught. You can spin it.'

And so they go, three middle-aged men – a politician, a surgeon and a seasoned ghost – to buy drugs from a townie his sister once fucked, at a house he once played in, the son of the char.

But someone is half smiling on him, so that the Varlows – whoever is left of them – are away 'up That London', so Julian is told, who retells it with scorn. But there is still Darren Banner, who saw him enough waiting up for his sister, or being dragged down the road by the staggering old man.

Only Darren is late, still fixing a thing, and so they must wait, must suffer on, on the wall above a beach that is, despite the drizzle, heaving. A teetering child walks behind them, a plastic crab in his hand, smacking their backs as he passes.

'Oh, just fuck off,' Julian barks eventually.

The child squawks, bird-like, mother gape-mouthed as a fledgling herself.

'What?' Julian demands. 'He started it.'

'Fancy a Mivvi?' Hal asks then.

'Do they even make those anymore?' James asks, though he can't eat, can't even think about food.

'It'll be brown bread ice cream and goji fucking sorbet,' Julian moans tapping out another text. 'Where the fuck is he?'

His phone beeps an answer.

'Finally. Wait here.'

His mouth fills with saliva, and he begins to sweat as Julian stands to head for the electric gates of this cliffside castle, this Georgian fortress cut into the rock. But before he's gone a few paces they swing open, and his man – their man – comes out.

Or *a* man. Because this Darren Banner isn't skinny-limbed and slick-haired. Not sauntering in his Fila jacket, a poor man's Tony Manero, Hi-Tecs two sizes too big. No, this one is bald and barrel-bellied, bursting out of an unbranded T-shirt and sweatpants, the limbs in them so swollen his walk suggests some sort of disorder, or an ape.

He is unrecognizable.

And so, of course, is James.

He is a nobody, another tourist on the du Maurier trail. Of no more interest or concern than the sad-sack dads on the beach in their floral shorts and faux-mariner shoes. And so the swell of his insides shrinks and flattens and his heart ceases its desperate race, and he doesn't even wince when Julian shakes Darren's hand and hands over his cash as neatly as any Camberwell pro. He doesn't pale and sweat when Julian pockets the proceeds and slips into the public toilet, taking his place in a queue of jiggling kids, too full of

lemonade and too prudish to piss in the sea. And he doesn't
hesitate for more than a second when, done with his business,
Hal slips the wrap in James's pocket and tells him it's his
turn.

He deserves this.

He needs this.

It's only one line.

'So which pub?' Hal demands as they swagger back along
Esplanade.

'King of Prussia,' says Julian.

'No,' he says, in a strange new voice that is not-to-be-
messed-with cocky. 'It has to be the Lugger.'

'Oh, does it?' Hal is amused.

'There's a woman,' he blurts. 'I want to . . . to see her.'
He steels himself to effect some sort of nudge and wink.

'Right.' Hal raises his eyebrows in recognition. 'That
barmaid. You should have said.'

'Dirty fucker,' Julian decides.

And, though it is all he can do not to slap his smug pucker,
he smiles wide and wise as the Cheshire cat, shrugs, and,
like the Pied Piper himself, leads his minions up four short
steps.

And into her lair.

32.

Bea, 1988

Bea sits, hip to hip with her sister at their mother's satin-wood dresser. The mirror is hairspray-sticky, the glass tarnished, the top scattered with the evidence of Daisy's brilliant existence: a Coty compact, a bottle of Dior, a packet of Durex, 'ribbed for her pleasure'.

'You don't have to be like this,' Daisy tells her. 'You can be—'

'Like you?'

'I didn't mean that. You can be anyone, Bea. Anyone at all.'

Bea stares, then, at their dim-lit asymmetry – the incremental difference in length of haircut, neatness of eyebrow, thickness of kohl. By a slow process of accretion they are growing apart and one not-so-far-off day no one will confuse the two, call either by the wrong name. Rather, she thinks it will be, 'Really? You're sisters?' And the injustice hits swift and bitter.

'What if . . .' she begins, then pauses, panning for, and catching, her confidence like gold. 'What if I do want to be you?' And weary with it, with the wanting, she rests her head on Daisy's shoulder.

The Daisy in the mirror frowns and Bea feels her sliver of soul thin out, wear down. She's fucked up again and Daisy will only tell Hal, whisper it, giggling. And the pair of them will laugh at her bravado, at her pathetic desperation, dine out on it in their marvellous lives. She stiffens, lifts her head.

But as she does, she sees the mirror Daisy's lips twitch and slip into a grin. 'You want to be me, Bea? Then be me you shall.'

The transformation is intricate, immaculate: their bobbed hair bathroom-bleached and Brooks-short, their fringes nail-scissor-snipped. Bea tweezes her eyebrows, conceals a small spot, then they match glitter and lipstick and red-lacquered toes, and in their ears pin two pairs of identical pearls. Their outfits are less easily achieved but in Muriel's silk slips and swathed in lace from the linen press they fashion themselves dazzling flappers, Waugh-worthy Bright Young Things with feathers in their nylon headbands. So that when they sit again at the dresser, the effect is astonishing. Paper dolls they are once more, the distance between them no thicker than tissue.

Bea touches her neck, tilts her head left and right. 'I'm you,' she says, incredulous. 'I'm actually you.'

Daisy laughs, presses her shimmering head to her sister's. 'Or maybe I'm you.'

Bea shivers, squints. 'Why would you want that?'

'I don't know.' Daisy strokes her arm then, as if she is a child or a cat. 'All those clever thoughts, all those books stacked pile-high in your head. You know everything.'

'I don't.'

'You know more than me.'

Bea pulls her arm away, blistering with irritation. 'Well, you *have* more than me.'

'What about Jason?' Daisy demands.

Bea thinks of him then, wide-eyed and bucking beneath her, and is instantly sickened. 'That's nothing,' she says.

'But didn't you—'

'Really. It's nothing. He's in love with you, you know.'

'Is he?' Daisy smiles. 'Poor boy.'

'Poor Hal,' Bea counters. 'Doesn't he tire of it?'

'Poor Hal nothing. He'll survive. He has his precious "people" after all.'

It courses through her then, scorching and sore. 'What do you mean?'

'Oh, buzzy Bea. Did you think we'd go on forever? We'll be lucky to make it through the next year let alone Hull or Halifax or whichever . . . grim city he's determined to conquer.'

'But—' Bea is twitching with it, practically stamping her foot – with indignation and incredulity and something else besides. 'But you said! You said you loved him!'

'And I did. I do, but—'

'But what?

'But he's got a chip on his shoulders the size of Wales and I haven't the wit or the will. Besides, I'm twenty for fuck's sake. And this isn't . . . nineteen fourteen.'

'What do you think happened in nineteen fourteen?' Bea demands.

'God, I don't know. Marriage I suppose. Babies. My point is, life's too sodding long to get stuck now.'

And swift as a snip, Bea's rage gives way to golden opportunity, her mind tick-ticking, outstripping the clock. 'When will you end it?' she asks quietly. 'Tonight?'

'Oh, God, no!' Daisy pulls a face. 'I'm not that barbaric. It'll run its course by Christmas I think. And thank God. I don't want to spend another bloody Boxing Day with his obsequious mother. All that "Poor orphan Daisy" nonsense. Poor bloody nothing.'

'I rather liked her.'

'Portia? Christ. Though I don't mind his father. At least he drinks.'

'His father's a bastard.'

'So Hal says.' Daisy lights a cigarette, takes a drag. 'You're welcome to them.' She holds out her cigarette.

Bea takes it, stares at the pair of them in the blurred glass. Twin sisters they may be, and identical, too, but inside, their souls or selves or whatever you call them are as unalike as carob and chocolate.

And on that precarious foundation, Bea hatches a plan, on which hangs a future so gilded that princes would blink. 'Swap,' she says. 'Let me be you.'

'What?'

'You said you were me, so be me. Be . . . clever and full of books or whatever it is you think I am.'

Daisy turns to her. 'And what will you be?'

But Bea doesn't lose focus, doesn't flinch from the mirror.

Simply smiles, lifts her chin. 'Amazing,' she says. 'I'll be bloody amazing.'

Daisy laughs. 'You already are, but fine. For one night only you can be me.'

'For one night only,' Bea repeats.

But that is all she needs.

33.

James, 2018

He is four gins pissed and five lines high and King of the Fucking World.

And he's a dick, he knows. A dick for doing it but he needs chemical courage. Because it's today. It's now. He didn't know it before but everything, everything – the back-room bar deals, the Fleet Street years, the moulding and managing and making of him – has been building to this. He is sick and dizzy and sitting in that rollercoaster teetering on the brink and any moment it's going to roll over, roll over, and then there's no going back. He will plummet or fly.

'You're actually not such a prissy little shit once you've had a few,' Julian concedes.

'Thanks,' he says, corralling his coke-born sarcasm.

'De nada.'

James is suddenly suffused with an urge to punch him. Slam his fist up into his nose so it snaps and splits and sends him sprawling. But he doesn't, of course; he is not that sort of man. No, he is disciplined, restrained, despite the drink and drugs, despite his birth, his lack of breeding, and so manages to refrain from trigger-happy scrapping and the dickish misogyny that goes with it. In any case, he needs to keep Julian on side if only to get rid of him because time is rolling on.

He looks pointedly at his watch. 'We should start,' he says.

'Start what?' Hal asks.

He quells the tremor that ripples his insides. 'The interview.'

'Fuck!' he exclaims. 'I'd forgotten. Isn't it too loud in here?'

'Aren't you too trolleyed?' adds Julian.

'I'm fine,' James lies. 'It's fine.'

Hal nods, shrugs. 'Fine,' he echoes.

He flips his phone to record, sets it down on the table.

'Don't I get the machine treatment?' he asks. 'Not worthy?'

'I forgot,' he admits, though not why – the prospect of outing Hal clouding out necessities, accessories.

'Really?' asks Julian. 'A professional like you.'

'It happens,' he snaps, though knows, only to amateurs. Then waits for Julian to make a move, to fuck off for a walk at least, but instead he settles back against the liver-coloured vinyl as if spectating at some indoor sports fixture. 'Do you mind?' he hints.

'Yes I do, rather,' Julian opines.

He looks to Hal, raises a brow at his newfound buddy – oh, yes, they're buddies now, mates: hugging, laughing 'maaaate'ing mates. Bonded not just by Hendricks and charlie, but by words: by Keats and Yeats and old Smiths' lyrics; by Kennedy and Kinnock and King Fucking Lear.

And, of course, by Daisy.

'Go on.' Hal nods at Julian. 'I'll be fine. I've got copy

approval anyway so if I flop my cock out – metaphorically of course – then we just click delete.'

'And do what? Browse the fucking tat shops?'

'Find Luna?' Hal suggests.

'But it's not even six,' he whinges. 'And it's pissing down.'

'And you know what she's like. She's probably halfway to St Austell by now and Muriel will go spare if we come back empty-handed.'

Julian wavers then, weighs up the losses and gains, the strength of the rain. But then, to James's surprise, he leaves.

'Well done,' he says, and for once he means it.

Hal laughs. 'He always caves. Rumour has it she's his.'

'But—'

'Sperm donor. You know, the old turkey baster.'

'Oh.' The image is as unsavoury as the thought that Luna might be Julian's. 'Shall we?' He presses the red button. No going back now.

'What about . . . You know.' Hal nods towards the bar, towards her, towards Stella.

'Maybe later,' says James.

'I can put in a word,' Hal offers.

'Like I say, maybe later.' Because he's not ready, can't launch into it, not yet. He needs . . . He needs . . .

Another line.

'I'm . . .' He nods to the toilets.

'Save some for later, will you?' asks Hal. 'I can't do dinner straight.'

He nods and is gone, racking up a fat one on a lemon-scented cistern lid, rolling up a twenty. He hesitates before he leans in, weighing up the risks himself now, working out how quickly it will slip out of his system. But of course there's no angel on his shoulder anymore, no wise, white-winged abstainer to whisper words of caution, just the whirling glitter-stippled memory of Daisy urging him to try anything and everything and dancing with him when he does.

And so he inhales.

Back in the fray, the saloon side is heaving, the crowd downpour-swollen and dripping onto thin carpet; their hooting relief tempered with the realization that the kitchen is shut and there's nowhere to sit. He glances at the bar then, but can't seem to see her, assumes she's glass-collecting or barrel-changing or restocking snacks.

But when he finds his way – fights his way – to their corner, there she is. Her hands flat on her table, Hal's hand on her arm, and their heads pressed together over the phone.

'What are you doing?' He snatches at it, see it's still on record.

Stella pulls away from Hal, puts her hand on James now. 'Leaving a message, that's all, love.' Then she winks at Hal – winks at him, for fuck's sake.

Jesus, can't he see it?

But no, apparently he can't.

'She likes you,' he says as James slams back into the seat. You should—'

'No.'

'Woah, okay? Christ, what happened back there? Some local fag try their luck?'

He snorts, though it's mirthless.

'I thought you wanted her anyway. What changed your mind?'

'Nothing, I—'

'Because she's "common", is that it? Not the right class? Bit of rough?' He's grinning now, still oblivious. 'I get it, I do. We don't like to slum it.'

'Jesus.' He's flailing now, his heart a drum roll, his head trying to keep pace, but the world that a few seconds ago seemed poker-straight and perfect now struggles and skitters like a trapped rabbit.

'Or is it the age thing?' he tries. 'Is that it? Is it because she's young enough to be your daughter?'

And he feels it rising like bile then, like word vomit, a stream of stinking invective and he knows he should stop it, knows what it means, but he can't, he can't. 'No,' he spews, a hissing stage whisper, mindful even now of prying eyes. 'Because she *is* a daughter. *Your* daughter.'

Hal frowns. 'What?'

He takes a breath. 'Look at her. Don't you see it? Your eyes? Your mouth? Jesus, she's the spit of Clementine. They could be twins.'

But still Hal can't joint the dots. 'James, mate. I think you've fucking lost it.'

'Deny it,' he says, quieter now. 'Go on, try. I know you fucked her mother.'

At that, Hal's grin slips and his face sets like wax.

'Summer of eighty-eight, remember?' he continues. 'You stormed off and went home alone, only you didn't go home, did you. You went sniffing round the pub, round Sadie Pengelly.' He stiffens as he says the name out loud – the first time in more than thirty years – but it's necessary, the only way he'll admit it. 'One-night stand was it? No strings? Some kind of revenge on Daisy? Well, you fucked that up, didn't you. Because nine months later . . .'

The silence that follows is absolute, electric. And he almost wants to take a bow, wait for the applause.

But the show, it seems, is not quite over.

'Fuck me,' says Hal. 'You're him, aren't you? You're that kid.'

And with those words something gives in him. That hard seed, that pearl he's fashioned, wrests itself free from its anchor and begins to drift. Because he's let the charlie do the talking and fucked up royally, been found out. Or rather, revealed it himself. And not brilliantly, no Barnum or Goldin or Carter the Great. He didn't pull back his disguise and cry 'ta-dah' as glitter showered down and the crowd gasped, then applauded his accomplishment, the Great Pretender. But in a schoolboy slip based on his own desperation. Dick, he tells himself. Dick, dick, dick, he sings.

Hal's staring, sizing him up like a prize bull. 'Unbelievable. It really is you. But your name wasn't James. It was . . .' He digs for it, strikes gold. 'Jason!'

He winces at it but still says nothing, keeps his teeth tight and his mouth clamped, scared his very self will slip through his lips and sail out the door like a screaming demon.

'And all that time we thought you were dead.' Hal shakes his head. 'You want to know something? That barmaid? Not my daughter. For one, I never slept with your sister. Not that fucking desperate.'

'But I saw—'

'You saw what?'

'I . . .' But what did he see?

'Nothing,' says Hal. 'You saw nothing.'

He trawls through the snapshots – Sadie laughing. CLICK! A man. CLICK! The trawl across the lawn back to Rashleigh. CLICK! But that's it, just his sister and someone from the house – Julian most likely. He fucked everyone then. Even he admits it. But . . . but the likeness . . .

'Clementine. She looks like—'

'Daisy. Clem looks like Daisy. And that girl – Stella, is it? – she looks like her mother, I assume. So they both have dark hair. Brown eyes. Big fucking deal.'

'No, there's something—'

'There's nothing. And you, mate, are deranged. You want the truth? The skeleton?' He waits for a beat, ever the playwright. 'I can't have kids.'

And so leftfield is that, so unplanned for, that he flounders, seem to spin in dark water, tries to grasp something, anything solid. 'But—'

'Clem? She's not even mine. Me and Daisy broke up for a while after . . . everything. She probably fucked her way around half of RADA. And can you blame her? Her sister was dead.'

He sways then, pained. The thought of Daisy blindly, mindlessly fucking is an image he cannot concede.

'Oh, what? You're jealous? Because she screwed some toff

called Monty but she wouldn't screw you? Oh, wait! That's it, isn't it?'

'No—' Yes.

'I know you sniffed around her back then. But you had to settle for second-best, didn't you. Poor little Jason.'

He flinches, at the insinuation and the insult. 'Bea wasn't—'

'Oh please. Don't bother.' He leans in, so James can see his eyes, bloodshot, feel each beery breath hit his face. 'What were you even thinking? That you'd wangle yourself this job and then wangle her? You really are something, you sad little twat. You actually think she's going to want you? Just because you've filled out and dropped the accent. Just because you're wearing fucking, what?' He snatches at James's shirt. 'French Connection instead of Marks and Sparks now?'

He pulls away. 'It's not French Connection.' It was never even Marks back then.

'Whatever. You think she gives a shit? You think she's going to welcome you with open arms?'

He clutches at a straw, at the vestiges of his belief. 'Maybe. I don't . . .' But he trails off. He hasn't thought about it, hasn't planned this far ahead. Stupid, stupid boy, useless dick of a kid. And he feels his father's fist hit his lip for the umpteenth time.

Hal shakes his head, laughs mirthlessly. 'The thing is, *Jase*, you told Bea she could swim. It's your fault she was in the water in the first place.' He smiles with the riling pride of a man who has laid down an ace.

Something in James slackens, heaves, and he has to swallow, breathe, to stop it surging up. That wasn't . . . He didn't . . . Only he did, didn't he. He told her she could swim.

Jesus. He's messed it up now, all of it. He should have kept his mouth shut. Or should never even have come, because now all of it – the last thirty years turning Jason to James – is for nothing. Is a waste. He might as well have stayed after all, life sentence that it was. Or better, he should have drowned, should have let himself be sucked under along with her. No one to pull him out. No one to even try.

They didn't try. They left him for dead anyway, just like Bea.

And then he remembers it, a small straw to be clutched at, a seed of possibility he'd planted and then forgotten, but now it's green and growing. 'You were the one with her,' he says, almost incredulous himself. 'You were with her before she fell or jumped or whatever. You could have stopped her.'

Hal's face sets, and for a second James thinks he might hit him. But then he hisses, loud and low. 'You think I didn't try? You think I didn't tell her to stop? No, this is on you. All down to *you*. And when Daisy finds out you're back, she's not going to hang out the fucking banners, she's going to lose it. And, mate, I wouldn't want to be you when she does.'

No. No. No. 'You don't know that,' James insists. 'You don't know anything about me and her.'

Hal laughs. 'I know she kissed you once.'

And the pearl of his self drops into his stomach and begins to dissolve like a milk tooth in a glass of Coke.

'You know why she did it?' continues Hal. 'Because she felt sorry for you. That's all. She pitied you.'

The fickle world stills then, seems to cease its inexorable spin, as the grim truth of this sinks in: that she never wanted him, that he was her pet, her waif, handed to her like a runt pig or weak kitten because his mother had died and his own father disowned him.

A nothing, a nobody to toy with on holiday then leave behind on the beach like a lolly stick or chip wrapper. He is a fool. A fucking fool, founding his hope on a flimsy fairy wing.

But wait. A green light flickers and Tinkerbell appears.

He isn't Jason.

He's not that lost boy. Not the boy who fumbled around with Bea. Who fucked up with kindness, by assuring her she was more of a swimmer than even she imagined.

Not the boy who trailed round after Daisy, dog-like, taking whatever scraps she would throw his way.

Nor even the boy she kissed, whether it was from pity or something else, something right and guileless.

No, he is not Jason Pengelly.

He is James. He is everything Daisy ever wanted then and will want for in the future.

And more than that, he is better than Hal, he thinks. Hal, who is a parasite and a cheat and a coward besides, for, whatever he claims, he could have saved Bea if he'd acted quicker, acted at all.

Oh, he sees it now the mist is thinning. He just has to get to Daisy before Hal does. He has to tell her the truth – all of it. So that she will see he's not some desperate, clawing stalker. One of the dirty mac brigade or online porn bores who have wanked themselves to sleep over skin pics and are hoping for a shot at the real thing.

No, he is her white knight, her shining-armoured saviour, and it's time for him to act.

And in three short seconds he does. He stands and snatches up his phone and Hal's – a precaution. Then he turns on his heel.

And he runs. Heart dancing, feet slipping in the tipping, pissing rain.

Not for the ferry, half a mile or more away through squeezed streets.

But past the King of Prussia, across the square, and onto the dock.

34.

Jason, 1988

Jason checks his reflection, this bricolage boy, this pastiche dandy that Hal has rendered him. At first, he fidgets, ill at ease in his borrowed skin; a hermit crab in a gilded cast-off made for a creature with far better breeding. But Hal is a playwright, a director, no less, adept at the alchemy that can conjure kings of paupers and gods of men.

'Stick your shoulders back,' he tells him.

Jason does as he's told.

'Better. Head up.'

He drops his shoulders, inflates his small chest.

Hal nods, pleased at his achievement. 'You'll do. Now come on, I'm gasping.'

He treads down the staircase as if onto a stage, and well he might, as the hallway is glorious, playing dress-up itself in tinsel and tea lights.

'What the fuck?' demands Hal.

'Don't you love it!' exclaims Muriel, draped in a paper chain. 'We found it all in a box.'

'It's not sodding Christmas,' Hal says.

Muriel ignores him. 'There are fairy lights somewhere,' she adds. 'But the bulbs are all blown.'

'Fused,' corrects Julian. He climbs down from a stepladder where he's been fixing a string of silvery trinkets, clocks an eyeful of Jason. 'What the fuck have you come as? Heathcliff?'

Dick, he thinks.

'Ignore him,' says Hal.

But he can't. He's too full of it – of himself and something else besides, brimming over so he can't help himself. 'Maybe,' he blurts, then switches his intonation. 'Or maybe I'm you.'

'As if,' Julian replies.

But Hal – the Belasco – is having none of it. 'You should be on the stage,' he says. 'You've a gift.'

Julian snorts, but Jason's heart dances, sweeps onto centre stage. 'As. If.'

Muriel claps. 'Again!' she begs. 'Again.'

And he, prince of mimics, obliges. Again.

And again.

And again.

'You're a performing seal,' Julian says after one rendition. 'That's all. A clown.'

Jason might stumble at that, mumble a struggled apology. But Jason's long gone, discarded on a bedroom floor along with a Smiths T-shirt and odd socks. And someone else is here: a brilliant boy who gives not one shit what this tit of a man thinks. So he seal-honks himself, claps flapping hands in place of flippers. 'Happy now?' he demands.

'So the court jester's grown balls,' Julian laughs. But it's a half-strangled thing, and his irritation is clear.

'Well I think . . .' begins Muriel.

But no one gets to hear Muriel's considered opinion because, as if by magic, two fairies appear at the top of the stairs, their hair spun with silver, their dresses with silk.

And the ersatz Christmas panto falls pin-drop silent.

'You have got to be kidding,' whispers Julian.

Muriel gasps, claps a hand to her mouth.

And Hal, Hal is staggered, his mouth caught halfway between grimace and grin.

Because there, on the landing, are two perfect Daisys. They are as indistinguishable as a litter of snow-white kittens, alike as two peahens; as if the Great Botticelli or God himself had cloned Venus or Eve in flesh and blood and beautiful, beautiful bone.

They descend to ovation and Muriel's kiss.

'*I* want to be you too,' she pouts. 'What about me?'

'We ran out of lace,' says Daisy.

Or Bea.

Fuck, he cannot tell them apart, their likeness extending beyond the hairbands, beyond the dresses and into every gesture, as if, by some prior arrangement, they have taken Daisy's gait, Bea's tilt of the chin and topped it with a coquettishness that is pure confection.

'What are you playing at?' asks Hal, going to grasp a hand, but stops short, unsure, as he must be, whether he has the right one.

'Wouldn't you like to know,' she replies, fondling his face before slinking to the gin.

Definitely Daisy.

Definitely maybe.

'What's the matter?' asks the other. 'Scared you might make a mistake?'

Bea, he decides, this one has to be Bea.

But then she laughs – a high, ringing thing – and his surety slips; he's convinced he's mistaken.

But he doesn't feel sick or scared or defeated. No, this is fairground stuff, pure exhilaration, for he wants them both. Is that possible?

Yes, he sees it now.

He wants Daisy's bravado but Bea's slant eye on the world. Her way of seeing through things. Where Daisy's stage is dappled and dazzled, kaleidoscope bright, Bea slips into dark corners, pinpoints bleak truth. Where Daisy sees what she wants, paints pure possibility, Bea holds on to the bones of him, and doesn't complain.

He wants Hal too, wants his way of walking through the world like it owes him.

Yes he wants all of them, all of this. Wants late-waking days in a house with a history, wants to sit round a table and talk Coleridge and Keats. He wants nights, diamond nights like this one, with the Polaroid clicking, capturing them in instant colour, with the champagne flowing as if it's cheap as bitter, and coke that replenishes itself, an everlasting gobstopper for the grown-ups. It's unfair, he thinks, to have lived so long – more than seventeen years – not knowing this existed, that life could be lived in the light. And now he's tasted it, drunk from the fountain, how can he ever go back?

It would be like giving up breathing.

Giving up sex.

Fuck. Sex.

As soon as he thinks it, his dick kicks and stiffens, a silent agreement, a plea. Maybe he could.

Maybe Bea would.

He stares at the pair of them, dancing now, their glasses carried aloft to be sipped as they spin. He thought he'd got it for a moment, one of them branded as she was with a slick of thick lipstick, a smack on the cheek from Muriel's coral mouth. But now they both carry the smear and so he is back to his guessing game, to a wing and a prayer.

Eeny, meeny, miny . . .

'Bea?' He grabs at a hand.

She pauses, smiles. 'Yes,' she says. 'Well done.'

And elated, intoxicated, he grins with achievement. 'Do you want . . .' he begins, but Jason slips in, second guesses the answer and catches his tongue like a cat.

'Do I want what?' she asks.

Sod off, Jason, he thinks, and he squeezes him down, slips him back in his box like a cackling Jack. 'Do you want to go for a walk?'

She turns to her sister, sees her clamped onto Hal. 'Yes.' She turns back to him. 'I do.'

And quickly and quietly they slip into the Christmas of the hallway, with its tinsel and glitter, and trip out the front door.

'Shit!' she yells. 'It's pissing down.'

'Not where we're going,' he tells her, and takes her already damp hand.

Then they run, their steps even and sure, but his heart fairly racing, across the short-shaven lawn and into the shelter and hum of the water's-edge woods.

35.

James, 2018

He is a committed thief, a dazzling magpie. Has stolen so many things over the years – penny chews from the corner shop; a pair of shoes from the disinfectant-smelling cloakroom at school; an accent, a CV, a self – he's lost track of what is rightfully his at all. But it's only through necessity. Only because he is owed. It's not his fault, after all, that he was born a pauper, born to the wrong man, in the wrong town, at the wrong time. Why should he have been denied a chance to shine? To share in all the glories this world has to offer.

And this – this isn't even stealing. He doesn't want to own a boat, after all, has no use for it after tonight. He only needs to beg a ride. But there's no one left to pester for a favour. The rumble of thunder has sent them scuttling for shelter – emmets and ferrymen alike. And so he has no choice. Not really. Besides, everyone does it: town drunks stuck over at the Russell Inn; pissed-up village kids stranded at the Safe Harbour. You can hotwire an outboard soon as you can swim round here and he's no exception. He needs a shoelace, that's all, tied tight, twice round the kill switch.

He doesn't know whose it is. Not the Varlows' *Merry Penny*, moored halfway round to Readymoney, nor his own old *Dolly*, pea-green and peeling and probably driftwood by now. No, this is nobody's boat. Nobody that matters anyway, nobody he needs spend a second fretting over when they find it gone in the morning and have to traipse up and down the estuary to trace its dumping ground.

Thunder rumbles as he fumbles with the knot in his deck shoe, starts to unthread the lace, thanking God and fuck that he wore these and not wellies or slip-ons. Wondering why anyone would invent a safety switch that doubled as a do-around for the light of finger. He yanks the lace free with silent triumph, is sliding it round the red disc when he hears it – him.

'What the fuck are you doing?'

He turns his head, peers into the heaving rain to see Hal on the harbour wall, arms wide and wild as he walks towards the ladder.

'You can't just nick a boat, for God's sake.'

The cagouled heads of two foolhardy tourists turn to investigate, but he doesn't have the time to deny anything, still less to fight, so he goes back to his work, winding the lace once, feeling it slip in the slick-wet, then winding it again, and again, until he has it right. He glances up again. Hal is halfway down the ladder now, ready to drop to the pontoon, leaving only ten yards between them.

'Come on!' he wills the wretched thing. 'Just sodding start!'

And, to his relief, and Hal's obvious astonishment, it does.

And James is off the mooring and out as he staggers, then stands, agog on the dock.

'What the hell do you think you're going to achieve?' Hal calls after him.

But James lets the wind take his words, lets the rain dissolve them like powdered aspirin, like so much cocaine, while he steers starboard across the gunmetal estuary, back to Rashleigh.

Back to her.

The thought calms him, controls him for a moment, but then enormity sinks in, reality bites. The motor is coughing, protesting at its pillage, like *Dolly*'s before, while the boat itself is filling with bilge, the rain hard and fast and the wind whipping the river so that it spills over the sides. He is buffeted and lashed, a child's toy, a spinning top, a paper yacht at the mercy of the storm. His fingers tremble with adrenalin, his stomach churns and contracts, coke and panic unsettling its contents and sending them sliding into his bowels.

I do not need a shit, he tells himself. As if thinking will make it so.

But it does, doesn't it? Every impulse, every action, every function of our body is carried out only because our brain has commanded it. Painkillers are a confidence trick, fooling nerve endings into believing we're fine. Just as the self is a story we tell ourselves: malleable, mutable, chooseable. So he is James Fucking Tate and he does not need a shit in the middle of a fucking estuary only fifty fucking yards from home.

What he needs is Daisy.

What he deserves is Daisy.

What he's getting is Daisy.

He repeats it and repeats it, a mantra in his head above the buzz of the engine and the roil of the water.

But then come the questions. Where's Hal? Has he gone for the ferry? Will he get to her first? But he can only hypothesize, and pointlessly so, because he can't stall Hal any more than he can quicken his own pace or take a short cut; the distance and circumstance is set. He can only beg that lightning holds off, that the boat holds up as well as his will, cutting its flailing furrow in storm water.

He's close now. Close enough to see the flicker of light from her bedroom window. Close enough to abandon ship and fuck bothering with a mooring. Close enough to wade through the churning shallows to cross the last nine yards or so.

Fuck. Fuck! The water is cold, and deeper than he thought, the undertow snatching at his coat and trousers, dragging off a shoe. Something catches his ankle – a strand of bladderwrack or fat, flat-bladed kelp – and he jerks in panic, then flails as he tries to right himself, as he tries to focus on the slip. For a terrible second he is snapped back there, to that night. To the clatter and crack of the storm, to the haul of the water, pulling him down.

But back then he was feeble, thin-limbed and skittish as a cat. Weakened by years of cheap meals and beatings. But now he is built for better. Now he is sculpted and spun as if from gold. Now he can do this; he *is* doing this, he is King of the Fucking Water and Hal is nothing. He is drowned like an unwanted puppy, or soon to be.

And this thought whips him, drills him, thrills him so that he is electric; buzzing and humming as he scrambles up the slip. And then he is there. Standing on the sodden lawn, staring up at her window. One foot bleeding along with his hand, his arms numb, his heart aching with panic and pain.

But he has never seen clearer, never been sharper, never felt so fucking strong.

Can you see, Daisy? he pleads. Can you feel me out here?

I'm coming. I'm coming to tell you.

To get you.

To claim what you promised.

Do you remember what you promised, Daisy?

36.

Jason, 1988

They stand in the outhouse. Facing each other. Waiting. Her skin is shimmering; her eyes wide with mascara black as soot, running now in inky trails down glitter-stippled cheeks. Her hair, starkly shorn, clings to her head like a gilt cap and her dress is as see-through as a moon jellyfish and slippery as an eel.

But, fuck, Bea is beautiful.

He sees it clearly now – sees how she conjures up charisma when required to render herself splendid as her sister. Sees that she, and she alone, perhaps, can be his saviour. Not Hal, who is too caught up in his theatrics, and too beholden to Julian. Not Daisy, who is too caught up in Hal, at least for now. But Bea . . . Bea wanted him, still wants him, clearly. Standing here as she is, breathy and wet.

'Bea—' he begins, then lunges almost, his lips crammed against hers in such urgency they almost hurt, his hands clapped to her face as if she might otherwise escape.

But slowly she opens her mouth, lets in his tongue, kisses him back with a passion that she appears to have magicked up along with the charm. She pulls him to her then, pushes the bone of her pelvis against his stiffening groin so hard he groans and grabs at the lace she's draped in, drags it from her so it falls in the dirt. Then his hands are on her, palms pressed at her waist, then rising higher and around, finding unfettered breasts.

He lets his fingers brush over them, his dick kicking, then slips his thumbs under spaghetti-thin straps, lets soaking silk drop from her shoulders.

She's not wearing any knickers.

'Jesus,' he says out loud, a prayer and a thank you in one, as he takes in her nakedness: her nipples, harder than before and darker too, the triangle of hair he swears is clipped, neater somehow, and can only be so for him.

He yanks off his jacket, wrenches the shirt high over his head, and, still half-blind, is rewarded by her hands fumbling with the buckle on a belt borrowed from Muriel to keep Hal's trousers up. 'Please,' he begs in his head, but to her now, not some false god.

And she listens, lets the unfastened belt drop with a clink and unzips his fly so that they fall to the floor, helps him stagger out of them so that now he stands, straining against Woolworth's best that, while clean and not yet moth-holed, were never intended for such occasions as this. But she doesn't see it, or doesn't care, reaching for him, her hand inches from him, hovering, teasing. And he goes to help her, pushes her hard against his want, the chill of her fingers a thrill to the heat of him. 'Please,' he begs again, this time out loud. 'Please,' he repeats. 'Please, Bea.'

But at that, something snaps, and she is startled, skittish, as if shaking herself from a strange dream. 'No,' she says, and pulls her hand back. 'Shit. I'm sorry.'

Bollocks. Shit-fucking bollocks. 'Why are you sorry?' he asks, his voice tinged with more bitterness than he'd aimed for. 'What's the matter?' And, he goes to hold her, to pull her hand back to its rightful place.

'No,' she says again, wrapping whip-thin arms around her ribs, all the better to keep him off.

He baulks at that, mumbles a sorry of his own.

'Don't be.' She stoops then and picks up the dress, the silk limp and filthy, pulls it on over hunched shoulders with a shiver.

'Here.' He offers her his jacket – Hal's jacket – but she shakes her head.

'Keep it.'

Hurt, he hauls it on, its still soaking sleeves catching on his elbows. 'Why . . .' He tries to find the right question. 'Why did you stop?'

'Because this isn't . . . It isn't what you want.'

'It is,' he insists. 'It's exactly what I want.' He moves towards her again.

'Then it's not what *I* want,' she says quickly, then trails into a muttered, 'not really.'

'But . . .' He flails, grasps for words, for reasons that will not come. 'Why not?'

She pauses, seems to take a steadying breath. 'Hal,' she says.

What the fuck? And he feels it then, that hornet-heat buzzing inside him, blistering at the injustice of it, so searing that he slaps her straight back. 'Hal doesn't want you,' he spits. 'Christ, you know that. He'd fuck my sister before he'd fuck you. Has done.'

She lets out a sound and her eyes brim, but brief, before she wipes them, taking two lines of coal-black up to her hairline. 'He wouldn't. He . . .' She trails off, because she knows it's true, must do.

'I—' He's about to apologize, to try to reel her back in somehow, but then he sees it, a shift in her, almost imperceptible, but there nonetheless. Least to those that know her.

Know them.

Fuck.

'Daisy?' he asks, hardly daring to believe it.

Her face is a sudden flush. 'I'm sorry,' she gushes. 'I shouldn't have.'

He goes to speak but finds his words stoppered up, so thrown is he. He is giddy with it, reeling, 'I . . .' he manages.

'You're disgusted,' she finishes for him.

It's a wash of cold water, a wake-up slap. 'What?' he blurts. 'God, no. Not that at all. Just . . . why did you do it? Start it, I mean.'

She shrugs, which is less than he hoped for, but better than 'a bet' or 'a dare'. 'Because I could,' she says at last.

'Then why did you stop?'

'I . . .' She looks at him, lets him see into her.

'Hal.' The name is a pill, too big and bitter and stuck on his tongue.

'I know. I know it was stupid of me.'

He shakes his head. 'No. No it wasn't,' he tells her. 'I . . . I'm glad.'

She frowns, a crease appearing on her forehead. 'Are you?'

He reaches a hand to her face, thinks to kiss her again to prove it. But she tilts her head, rests a cheek on his palm.

'Did he really . . . you know?' she asks.

'With Sadie?' He could lie, could insist it's all gospel. But maybe the possibility is enough, the chink he needs. 'Maybe. I don't know.'

She laughs, a short, snorting thing. 'It doesn't matter anyway. The whole thing's a mess.'

Hope swells in him, fresh. 'Is it?'

But she's silent now, still. Thinking.

He wishes, for once, that his sister was here, could tell the truth, and tell him what to do besides. Because he's rigid with not knowing, with not understanding the rules or what game is even being played.

'Have you got a fag?' she asks.

'No, I—' But then he stops, thinks, shoves his hands into the pockets of the jacket, pulls out a packet of Camels from one, from the other a lighter, a transparent pink Bic.

She laughs again, but softer now, pleased, as if he were a magician and she the dumbstruck front row. 'Thanks.'

She sits then, lights one, offers it to him, but he's too wired for nicotine and shakes his head, but sits beside her anyway, grit in his pants and between his toes. 'Are you . . .' he tries. 'Are you going to break up?' Christ, let it be so.

She blows out a lungful of smoke. 'Perhaps.'

A bell rings in victory, the ball hits the net. 'But I thought—'

'You thought we were, what, fated?'

'I—'

'That's Bea's thing, not mine. Too many novels, and biblical guilt.'

'I just thought you . . . you were in love.'

She smiles. 'I was. Maybe I still am. I don't know. I don't know who I bloody am or what I want. Does any of us yet?'

'I do.' And he does. He wants her. And he wants to be someone wanted by her. That is all. And everything.

But most of all, right now, he wants to kiss her again, knowing it's Daisy.

He inches closer, rests a hand on her leg, taut with cold and, perhaps, anticipation; lowers his head so that he can hear, can feel each shallow breath she takes. And for a moment, as their eyes meet, as a look of something – understanding? – passes between them, he believes with all his shrivelled being that she is going to let him.

But instead she touches his face, shakes her head. 'Don't,' she says.

'Because of him?'

She nods.

'But . . . but wouldn't it be a good thing? I could be—' he grasps for it, 'revenge? I could be payback for . . . for everything.'

She laughs, throaty, theatrical, head back, so loud it stings.

'What? Aren't I good enough for that?'

'No. No, that's not it.'

'I can be anyone,' he blurts then. 'Anyone you want. You know I can. I . . .' He hesitates, then lets it come anyway. 'I can be him if you want. Hal, I mean.'

'Oh—'

'Fuck me, Daisy,' he hiss-whispers at her in his stolen voice, dropped an octave and all glottal stop 'Go on. You know you want to.'

But she doesn't, he can see it sooner than he's said it, and he falls back, defeated, slumped like a discarded toy.

'Christ, he's the last person you should be.'

'Who then?'

'Be you.'

'I hate me.'

'Then be someone else. Someone . . .'

'Better?' He snorts.

'I didn't say that. I'm not the one who hates you, remember?'

He thinks hard and fast, knowing time is ticking, his chance slipping. 'If I do . . . If I change, will you . . . have me then?'

She smiles and he tries not to see the pity that tinges it. 'That depends.'

'On what?'

'On who you become.'

He's blindsided by this . . . this hope, fat and spangling; snatches at the advertisements of men he's seen in magazines or on TV or strolling down Fore Street on a regatta Saturday. He could be anyone: a banker in pinstripes, a Jagger in skin-tight jeans, a modern-day Jesus himself with long hair and faded corduroys, beads clacking at his chest and the waft of patchouli dogging him like an aura.

But she stalks into his thoughts, shakes him from reverie. 'What's your middle name?' she asks.

'Patrick,' he tells her, and not without reluctance. 'Patrick John.'

She frowns, pushes still-sodden locks from his brow the better to get the measure of him, he reckons. 'No,' she says. 'You're not a Patrick.' She pauses. 'Nor a John.'

A weight lifts, the name of his father discarded like she's reversing a curse.

'So, who are you?' she asks.

'Rafe?' he offers, borrowing a braggard from school, all fat neck and sweating.

She pulls a face. 'God, no. Louis?'

He laughs, despite himself. Recalls an insipid first-year with wisp-thin hair and a birthmark on his face in the shape of a sock. 'Not Louis,' he begs.

'Sebastian then.' Her smile is wide now, wicked.

'Sinjin,' he offers, a name he's heard only in mocking.

'Benjamin?'

'Or Benedict?'

'Or Hilary.'

'Or Valentine! Or—'

'Rumpelstiltskin!' she yelps, triumphant. 'It's perfect. It's so very . . . you!' She rests her head on his bare chest, and it's his turn to kiss her, his lips pressed on her hair, tasting shampoo and salt and want, he is sure of it.

She lifts her head. 'Perhaps not,' she says. 'But there must be a name. Jason.' She sounds it out, stretches it, testing it for possibility. 'Jason . . . Jason . . . James—'

'James.' He catches it, a neat-fitting glove of a name, a peach.

'Yes, that's it!' She beams. 'You are every bit a James.'

'James,' he repeats, as if it's nothing, as if he owns it. But of course, he doesn't, not yet. 'And when I'm James, will you kiss me then?'

She laughs, guileless. 'Yes,' she replies. 'Then, I will kiss you.'

And half naked though he is, he slips the promise in his pocket like a pound from the floor, to be stored in a jar and saved for later.

For a few months from now, or a year at most.

When Hal is gone up North, and Daisy free, and he the man he's supposed to be.

37.

James, 2018

He imagined this moment once – the catharsis of confession – played it out over and over in every which way, to see if anything could be gained. But so absurd it seemed, so Grand Guignol, that he buried it away in the box marked 'never' and spent a life he once hoped would be devoted to Daisy avoiding her instead, staying away from plays, turning off the television until in the end he got rid of it altogether. So that now he watches only what he needs through subscription or a set-top box, where adverts are few and accidents rare.

But here he is, on the edge of the precipice. Pushed by Hal and his own false step, his drug-loosened tongue, his panicked imagination. His one slim advantage being that Hal isn't back yet, hasn't the wit to borrow a boat, and the ferry – thank fuck – the ferry will be suspended for the duration of the storm. Hal will blag a cab, of course, but it will have to go right upriver to the bridge at Lostwithiel before it can drop back down, which gives him forty minutes, maybe more, to spin his story into something salvageable.

He has had to waylay the daughter of course. The sight

of an at best bedraggled, at worst half-drowned man slopping blood and seawater along the tiles raises more than eyebrows.

'God.' Clementine looks up from laying the table. 'What happened?'

'Nothing. Really. I tripped . . . Where's—'

'Let me get you something. A towel.'

'I'm fine. I just need to talk to your mother. Is she . . .'

He waits for an answer while Clementine eyes him, Hal's features slipping quickly, leaving only Daisy and the semblance of some one-night-stand stranger. But it doesn't matter now. There is still something to be said, something to be done. Has to be.

'Upstairs,' she answers at last. 'Where's Dad?'

His throat closes and he's forced to swallow. 'With Julian I think,' he manages then turns swiftly to go, to find himself face to face with a bedazzled Muriel, her eyes ringed in glitter and hair glinting in the light.

'Is Luna with them?'

'I . . . Julian went to fetch her.'

'So Dad isn't with Julian?'

He jerks his head back to Clementine. 'He went to fetch Julian. To fetch them both I think. I had to . . . it's a long story. They're fine.'

'You need a drink,' Muriel decides and grasps his arm.

Jesus. He shakes her off sharply. Too sharply. 'I . . . sorry. I just need a word with Daisy. Something's come up.'

'Said the actress.'

He doesn't answer that. Just mumbles an apology, and manages, at last, to leave, thumping along the corridor and up two flights of stairs. Then he is there, outside her door, his heart a-dance, his head alight with the certainty that, in a few minutes, everything will change, the world will shift on its axis and their new lives will begin, for better or worse.

He knocks – absurd, given the urgency, but his manners are intact, his dignity not entirely deserted him.

'Clem?'

'No, I—' he begins, cuts himself short. 'It's me.'

She's silent for a moment and he wonders briefly if she knows, if Hal has somehow called her, warned her. Or perhaps she's naked, searching for a robe. And he hates himself for hoping that, even now.

But when she eventually bids him enter, when he pushes the door, she is fully dressed in floor-length crepe and absolute black, the back low, the front ruched over pale cleavage. She's seated too, facing the dressing-table mirror so that their eyes meet in glass as he walks in.

'James,' she says. 'You're back. And wet.'

Her tone is flat, even, and he knows then Hal hasn't rung, can't have done.

'I know. It's . . . I needed to talk to you,' he says.

'Can it wait? I'm not quite done.'

'No, I . . . not really.'

The shallow crease in her forehead disappears and her voice softens. 'You're dripping everywhere,' she says, as if she's only just noticed. 'Go and dry off.'

'But—'

'You can use our bathroom.'

'I'm fine,' he insists, all too aware of the clock tick-tocking down.

'Don't be absurd.'

He's thrown, but in no position to argue.

'There's towels in there.' She nods at the door. 'And . . . whatnot.'

'I . . . okay.' And so, obedient, still, he goes.

He doesn't understand it. This effort to dry him, to tidy him. But perhaps she has plans. He hopes she has plans.

'You'll need dry things,' she says, when he emerges. 'Here.' She pulls out a dresser drawer, takes a pair of boxers, some socks. 'There's clothes in the cupboard.'

'I . . . I should get my own.'

'And you'll get soaked fetching them. Besides, Hal won't mind.'

Hal will mind. Hal will spit feathers and damn him to all hell and back. And, more than that, *he* minds. A hand-me-down child, he doesn't understand the vogue for vintage. Even washed several times, the smell, the stain of second-hand clothes lingers in the wear of threads and minute moth holes, marking one out as a charity case. To be pitied, at best; at worse mocked and maligned.

But, fumbling, faithful, he opens the door to the wardrobe, pulls out a clean shirt, fresh linen trousers that should almost fit. Then retreats into the en suite to change.

She looks up when he enters again. 'Perfect,' she says. 'Who needs a suit?' Then turns back to her make-up, coating mascara on lashes that can only be false. 'So what is it then? Do spill.'

He opens his mouth, but finds it gapes like a gurnard, unable to say it – to say anything – after all.

'Here.' She holds out a string of pearls. 'Can you?'

'Yes . . . I—' Hands clammy now, shaking, he takes them and drapes them round her neck, his fingers slipping as he tries to fasten the clasp. 'Sorry.' He tries again and manages to snap it. 'Done.'

Her hand goes to her throat and their eyes meet again, caught in the glass. And then something comes. 'He's having an affair,' he blurts. 'Another one.'

Well, he could be. Is probably.

The clock ticks; dust motes float in the air.

'I know,' she says. 'I'm not stupid.'

His legs, his will weaken still. 'But . . . but he's standing for office.'

'Which is why he will end it. He, or Julian, will pay her off, like they did Della or whatever the last one was called.'

Fuck. Fuck! 'I don't understand.'

'Why I forgive him? Or why he does it in the first place?'

'Both,' he says quickly. 'Why *does* he do it?'

She shrugs. 'Why does any man, or woman for that matter? Because he's scared of getting old. Because he hates me in that moment. Or hates himself.'

'But you don't need him.'

'Oh!' she laughs, high and clear, like the ring of a teaspoon on crystal. 'You've said that already. But the thing is, I do. Who else would love me in my darkest days? And who else would love him? You of all people should know that, Jason.'

He doesn't hear it at first. Then, when realization hits, has to replay it in his head to check. But her wry smile, her wide eyes echo it.

Jason, they tell him. *You're not James. You're Jason.*

His stomach slides, his legs lose sensation; he has to prop himself, one hand on a chair. 'You know?'

He flicks through possibilities in his head, tries different lies for size, different versions of truth, perhaps. Hal got hold of a phone. Or Julian. Must have—

'Oh, I've known for a long time.'

He starts, ceases the guessing game. 'How long?'

She pushes a single-drop pearl through her right lobe, admires it. 'I saw you in a cafe. On Fleet Street. It must have been, oh, twenty years ago.'

'I . . .' But words will not come.

'I followed you,' she continues. 'Back to your rag. The *Chronicle*, was it?'

He nods, staggered, but then is bathed, suddenly, in a shaft of bright light. Because she followed him. She wanted him. She waited all this time.

Why all this time? Because of him? Or because of— He wavers, must steel himself. 'But you said nothing.'

'Because I didn't need you then.'

'And . . . you do now?'

She nods, her smile beatific.

And his unbodied hope and the vestiges of coke dance their merry way to his heart, tell him it's the sign he has waited for, the nod, the promise paid. And he leans down and kisses her.

Violins do not play.

Enchanted bluebirds do not sing.

Instead, she swivels and his lips slide, dog-like, across her face. Then, to his horror, and shame, she slams her hands into his chest.

'Oh God.' He staggers back. 'I—'

She wipes her cheek. 'What the fuck?'

'But you said. You said—'

'I said what? What did I say?'

He is reeling. 'You held my hand,' he pleads, then plays back through soft focus snapshots, Instagram-filtered to fit. 'And you gave me clothes.'

'Because you were wet. And it's nearly dinner.'

But there's more, isn't there? Not from this week, fortnight, perhaps. But from this house, this same week, thirty years ago. 'You told me you'd kiss me again,' he says triumphantly. 'When I was done.'

She pulls a face. 'Done with what?'

'With changing. With being a better person. Well, here I am, Daisy. I'm changed. I'm better. God, I'm better than *him*, anyway.'

'The conceit!' She stifles a laugh. 'Though perhaps that's to be admired. As for the other thing, I don't know what you're talking about.'

He's flailing again, panicking, plucking at anything that might be ripe, regardless of variety. 'He's a dick,' he says. 'A liar. You know . . . you know he probably killed your sister. Have you asked him about that? Have you? He was the one with her, wasn't he? He could have saved her.'

'He was drunk,' she replies. 'Jumping in would have been stupid. Suicide even. Then I'd have lost both of them.'

'But—'

'It doesn't matter what happened.' She shakes her head, her eyes wide now, a rabbit caught in headlight glare.

'I . . .' Is that it? 'But that's all that matters, surely?'

'No.' She is irritated. Insistent. 'I'm here now. And so is Hal. And we're tied. Don't you understand? Tied.'

'But you didn't love him.'

'I have always loved him.'

And the truth bruises, purples as deep as a plum.

'You did want me,' he says again, a plaintive child now. 'You told me to be someone. Don't you remember?'

Please remember, he wills her. Please don't let his life, his very self, have been founded on nothing more than a whim of a comment, a frippery that disappeared like spilled ice cream in drizzle.

She pauses, then nods. But there is no glimmer of recognition. There is nothing there.

'I . . .' He had thought to apologize, to beg leniency, or another lie, to let him keep, at least, his secret. But something is awry, and he cuts himself off, peers for it. Then, a dropped coin caught in a torch, he sees it, bright and damning.

Oh fuck.

'Where were we?' he asks.

'What?'

'Where were we when you said that?'

She laughs again, but this one is fake, forced. 'Good God,

that was thirty years ago. I can't be expected to remember everything.'

'But you do. You remember the shape of the walls, the smell of it all. You remember what you were wearing the night you arrived.'

'I—'

'What was my middle name?'

'I don't know. David?'

'Wrong. Try again.'

'You're not fucking Rumpelstiltskin.'

And she's no sweet miller's daughter after all. But here she sits, still spinning straw into gold.

'What's my middle name?' he repeats.

'I honestly don't know.'

'But I bet you know what biscuits we kept in the tin.'

'What?'

He ignores her 'I bet you remember the name of my boat. Where we took her.' He pauses. 'Where I taught you to swim.'

'I . . .'

And that trailing off is all it takes. And he trembles as he says it, as it clarifies in his mind, hardens like a seed in the sun.

'Hello, Bea,' he says. 'It's been a while.'

38.

Bea, 1988

Bea feigns not to notice them, pretends she is engrossed in Hal's story – the tale (oft-repeated) of how he came to be in possession of signed vinyl, David Byrne's felt tip scrawl across the cartoon blue sky of 'Little Creatures' – but she sees, from the corner of her beady eye, her sister slip out the door and across the lawn, Jason goggle-eyed and panting in her wake.

Who does he think she is? Bea wonders. Perhaps he doesn't care. Perhaps any sister – any sex, any screw – is enough. Perhaps if you're born to nothing, born to thin-sliced white and own-brand cans and discount biscuits, then you take what scraps you're given. Perhaps that's why he fucked her at all. Because she was there. Because she was willing. Nothing more.

But who bloody cares? Who cares about Jason? Jason is nothing, a nobody, at least right now.

While she? She is, at last, somebody.

'Hal!' she says, flinging her arms around his neck. 'Hal, dance with me, darling.'

The track stutters and scratches. 'Jesus!' he exclaims, peeling off skinny limbs. 'You'll ruin it.'

God. 'Sorry.'

She stands impatient while he rescues it, lowers the trembling needle with the same reverence he affords playscripts and cocaine. And, once upon a time, Daisy.

'There.' Hal stands back as jangling guitars pick up their post-punk riff again.

'Now will you dance?' She pouts, pretty pleasing him with wide eyes, half snide at her sister's tactics, half glad of the pathetic obviousness of men.

He kisses the neat cap of her hair. 'I need a piss,' he says. 'In a minute.'

Her head tingles and sings. 'In a minute,' she repeats as he slopes to the stairs.

She spins, glimmering, a disco ball herself, to see Muriel dancing, arms wild with abandon in the manner of a child or an idiot, Julian slumped on the sofa, eyeing her with something that veers between lust and disdain.

'Where's the pauper?' he demands.

She stops. 'What?' She holds up her arms, as if deaf to his request.

He beckons her over, and sighing, she complies.

'The pauper?' he repeats as she perches, precarious. 'Where is he?

'Jason?' she asks haughtily, as if it could be anyone else. But the guilt, the irritation is weak and erasable. 'With Bea,' she replies, adds, a decorative 'of course' to better embellish, embed her lie.

But Julian is not so promptly fobbed off. He peers at her, as if inspecting a prize cow or a corpse, perhaps, forensically checking for evidence. 'You're Bea,' he says.

She forces a laugh. 'I'm Daisy, you dick.'

His expression is set. 'Liar.'

Indignation colours her cheeks but she is not letting him have this. 'I'm Daisy. What do you want me to do, show you a bloody birthmark?'

He smiles, a malign Cheshire cat. 'You've a mole on your left tit. Daisy has an appendectomy scar.'

'And how would you know?' she says, goading but quick, picturing the thin, pink line, touching her own pelvis for effect. 'Anyway, the scar's almost gone. Vitamin E oil.'

He leans into her then, his breath syrupy thick but sour. 'You know how I know.'

She starts, stands, swipes at a spinning Muriel and pulls her out of orbit. 'Muriel, who am I?' she demands.

Muriel's eyes are unfocused, her smile sliding. 'You're my darling,' she says, staggering, and kissing a print of pink onto Bea's cheek. 'My darling Daisy.'

'See?' says Bea. 'Daisy.'

Julian shakes his head. 'You are utterly fucked up. The pair of you.'

Bea shrugs, unsure who 'pair' refers to, uncaring. Because she is a step closer, two ticks nearer, now that Muriel and Julian are scored from her list. As long as Daisy keeps Jason away. Absurd that, of all of them, he can tell the pair apart better than any. But Daisy will play whichever role is required – she is nothing if not a born actress.

336

So now, there is only Hal to convince. And he is drunk and high and halfway there already.

And upstairs, alone.

He's still in the bathroom, the stop-start tinkle of piss ringing through the half-open door. She walks in anyway, emboldened, determined, desperate.

'What the—' He looks up, startled, a spray of urine splashing the back wall. 'Fuck, Dais. I'm not done.'

'I know.' But instead of backing out, she leans against the door, shutting it with a thudding clunk like a full stop.

She watches him finish, watches it. Such strange things, dicks. So sad when flaccid, then reddening into aggression, almost.

'What are you doing?' Hal shakes it, goes to put it away.

'Don't,' she says suddenly, grasping his arm.

'Don't what?'

'Don't . . . don't you want to . . . do stuff?'

'"Do stuff"?' He snorts. 'What are you? Fourteen?'

She bristles, corrects herself. 'Fuck,' she says, mustering her best Daisy. 'Don't you want to fuck?'

'Now?'

She is thrown again, panicked. Doesn't he want Daisy perpetually? Christ, he was half-hard in the car. But she has one chance, and he is literally dick out, so she is not letting this slip. 'Yes, now.' She snakes her arms around his neck, presses her lips into his shoulder blade, then up into the rough stubble at his throat. 'Come on.'

He lets her kiss him then, lets her push her tongue into

the wet cave of his mouth, each breath a prayer. God, please let this be right. Please let this be how Daisy does it. Please let him fall for it. For me.

So taken is she with the precision, the play by play of it, she forgets, at first, to enjoy it. But then, the thrill of it, the victory, is a shot of vodka and buoyed, brilliant, she reaches down, grabs at his belt, brushing his – oh, shit – still limp dick.

She drops her hands, her gaze. 'What's the matter?' she asks.

Hal tugs at it, gloomily. 'Coke,' he says. 'Let's go back down.'

'No!' It comes out louder than she expected and Hal frowns.

Fuck.

Fuck fuck fuck.

'Wait,' she says, and drops, desperate, to her knees.

This is not how it's supposed to be. None of this is. But this is the only way, she tells herself. The only way, because he can't see her, can't begin to tell, and can't complain besides, not with her lips round him.

It sits, a slug in her mouth, and again she invokes Daisy, wonders, disgusted, how her sister gives head? Hopes they both read the same *Cosmo* column, remember the same dorm talk.

And then she begins.

Within seconds he's hard, within minutes he's in her, she bent over the sink, watching him, dazed, in the mirror. 'I am fucking Hal,' she says to the strange Daisy. 'I am fucking your boyfriend.' She closes her eyes, slips into a grin. 'I am fucking *my* boyfriend.'

He comes, high and hard inside her, and, while the earth may not move for her – not this time, not yet – rockets go off to herald her success.

'Shit,' he says, panting, leant over her back. 'I meant . . . I didn't mean to—'

'It doesn't matter,' she insists. 'I can take the morning-after pill.' Has to anyway – still – from that time with Jason. She shudders at the thought, stunned that she thought he could replace Hal, even for a minute, even with fancy clothes and fine words.

'Are you okay?'

She looks up, sees concern, confusion. 'Yes, of course, I—'

Still staring at their reflection, he snatches her slip, pulls it down to reveal her tits, and a dark brown dot the size of a pea.

'Jesus!' He pulls out of her, pulls up her dress. She fights him, trying to right herself, but it's too late, his fingers are on her stomach, fumbling for the ridge of a scar that isn't there. He yanks her round to face him, shakes her. 'Bea?'

'I—'

He staggers back, slapped, sucker-punched. 'What the fuck?'

'I'm Daisy!' She clutches at straws, at will-o'-the-wisps.

He shakes his head, pale as skimmed milk, so pale she thinks he might throw up. 'You're not,' he says, cold, dead to her.

She puts her hands on his chest, clawing, desperate. 'I am. I'm Daisy,' she repeats. 'I'm exactly the same as Daisy.'

He hits them away, pulls up his trousers, puts his dick back in his pants. 'You're a fucking psycho. Julian was right.'

'Julian's a prick. He doesn't know anything.'

'Personality disorder, he said. I don't think even he thought you'd go this far.'

'But what's the difference?' She's crying now, gobs of snot running down her face. 'What's different about us?'

'You want a frigging list?'

Her rage is red and razor-sharp. 'I'm every bit as good as her. You only kissed her by accident. Remember? It was supposed to be me.'

Hal acts incredulous. Has to be, acting. 'What are you talking about?'

'That night in the bar.' He can't have forgotten. 'In Oxford. You thought it was me when you kissed her.'

'No, Bea. I really didn't.'

'But you must have,' she insists. 'You didn't know her then. Hadn't even met her before.'

He snorts. 'Jesus, Bea. I kissed your sister *because* she wasn't you. Because she wasn't so fucking . . . po-faced and pious. Because she was a breath of fresh air and you were so . . . stifling. Clinging like a limpet. You know that's what Julian calls you? "The limpet."'

'I'm not a–a limpet,' she spits. 'I can do everything she can do. Haven't I just proved it?'

He snorts. 'Anyone can fuck.' The words spray like bullets. 'All you've proved is you need sectioning.'

'I can act. I can sing. I—'

'Bullshit. And anyway, who cares? You've just fucked your sister's boyfriend.'

She laughs, short and hollow. 'And you've just fucked your girlfriend's sister.'

His face contorts and he raises a hand, then, as she flinches, drops it. 'You're nothing, do you hear me? Nobody. You can't act, not like her. You're too scared to sing. Too pathetic to swim even.'

His words hang in the air, lit like neon. A come-on. A dare. And she is going to take it. 'I can fucking swim,' she declares, as triumphant as if she'd found gold at the end of a rainbow. 'Jason's taught me.'

'Bullshit.'

'Watch me,' she says, and grabs at the handle.

'Now where are you going?'

'To swim!' Her words are left, luminous, on the landing as she thumps down the stairs, her hairband askew, her lace long-forgotten.

'Bea!' he yells after her, then, to her delight, follows it with thuds of his own.

He is coming for her after all. He will watch her, and then he will see.

She flies out the front door, out into the pissing rain and rumble of thunder. She's soaked in seconds but what does that matter? In a moment she'll be deep in saltwater. Her feet sink into mud as she slaps across the lawn, heading for the high wall.

'Stop it.'

The voice snaps at her heels, but can't catch her.

Sheet lightning shatters the sky like a camera flash, flooding the rising water with electric blue.

'Bea, stop. You can't.'

But she's there now, teetering, toes on cold granite, rain slicking her feet, her dress, her hair. She raises her arms above her head. 'No? Watch me!' she calls. Then looks down.

The sloe-black water is rolling now, its once still-as-a-millpond meniscus shattered and sweeping quick out to sea.

Thunder claps again, a volley of gunshots applauding its power.

Bile rises, a sour sting at the back of her throat. This is not how it's supposed to be.

'Bea!' A hand grabs at her – Hal's – but she is slippery as a seal and nimble as a cricket.

'I'll jump,' she insists. 'Touch me again and I'll jump.'

'You're not making sense.' He's close, but not touching, two feet away.

'I . . .' But she trails off.

This is not how it's supposed to be.

Her arms drop, and she turns to face him, trying a different tack. 'I'll tell her,' she says. 'I'll tell her you fucked me and knew it was me. Not that she'll care. She's dumping you anyway.'

Hal laughs, but its ring is as fake as a tin coin. 'Liar.'

Bea is bursting with it now, blurting. 'She told me tonight. She's bored of you. She doesn't even love you anymore. Not really. Not like I do.'

'You are fucking mental.'

'Am I? Or am I the honest one? Am I the loyal one? The one who stood by you when everyone else said your Macbeth was "amateur", when . . . when the *Isis* said you were a "sheep in wolf's clothing"? Where was Daisy then? In bloody London, that's where.' She is glorious, a triumph, can hear the ovation in her head even before her final line. 'Probably fucking some RADA brat.'

It happens in an instant. The hand slams into her side, winding her and sending her flailing, grasping at arms but catching nothing but air and rain. 'Hal!' she tries to call, but no sound comes out. No hands try to rescue her.

This is not how it's supposed to be.

The fall takes seconds and forever, and she sees herself in slow-motion, the drape of her arms as she arcs through the air. But when she hits the river it's with the full force of a flat body, sending dark water up into wet sky, even as it gushes down her gullet.

She cannot scream. Cannot breathe.

Cannot swim.

The pain is terrible: a piercing of lungs, and scraping of limbs on rock underneath. The sound is terrible: a hurtling gurgle like a drain being emptied; the roar of her blood and drum of her heartbeat, a battering fanfare as she battles for breath; and – Jesus Christ – above it all, the rhythmic lilt of David Byrne, 'Road to Nowhere' on looping, anodyne repeat.

This is not how it's supposed to be.

But this *is* how you drown.

39.

James, 2018

Her face is a picture, her smile sliding like cheap make-up under spotlights. Though his can hardly be camera-ready, his world not merely tilted but savagely wrenched. And he can't decide if he's devastated or thrilled. That they're both counterfeits, frauds. Him, the pauper who dared to dream; she, the shadow of her twin. And, despite his bristling disappointment, he wants to applaud her, her feat of achievement so much the greater because, while he fled his past – found an entirely new cast to help play out his life – she immersed herself in hers.

'How?' he asks. 'Why?'

'Because I had to,' she snaps. Her right hand clutches her throat again, pearls twisting round rigid fingers, the other, white-knuckled, grips the dresser as if the room is spinning or rising on the swell of a tide. 'I had no choice.'

'We all have a choice,' he replies automatically.

'Oh, please. You know damn well that's not true.'

He does, of course, but does she? 'You could have been brilliant,' he tells her. 'Come into your own with her . . .' He can't finish it. Shouldn't have started it.

'With her out of the way?'

He reddens, caught. 'I didn't mean—'

'Yes, you did.' She closes her eyes, takes a breath, opens them, and is steady again, composed. 'Because I thought it too. For a moment. Out there in . . . in the water. But even then I knew it was bollocks. She'd still have upstaged me. I'd end up the poor pathetic sister, the one who should have died.'

'No, that's not . . .'

But it is, isn't it?

'You always did try to humour me,' she says then. 'Pretend I was special.'

'You were— *are.*'

'Oh, Jason. You were only doing it to get into my sister's knickers, I knew that.'

'I—'

But this time he's interrupted by a racket in the hallway, the thud of size tens on bare floorboards, a desperate, yelled-out, 'Dais?'

Fuck.

The door is flung open so hard it knocks into a chest of drawers, dislocates a figurine that clatters and falls. And then he's in there with them, damp and haggard and ragged with rage.

James backs up against the wall.

'You little shit.' Hal steps towards him.

'Hal!' Daisy swivels, smiles, doesn't skip a beat. 'What do you think? Will he pass muster?'

Hal stops, turns to her. 'Whatever he's said about me, it's

345

bullshit. You know who he is? *Really* is? He's that dick from the pub. The pot washer. He—'

'Hal, drop it,' she interrupts.

'But—'

'I know,' she says. 'I know who he is and it's fine. It's in hand.'

Hal stares at him then, agape, then swings back to her. 'What the fuck?'

'I'll explain later. But please, a moment?'

He turns back to James, fronts up to him, a TV villain, a spitting Bill Sikes. 'This isn't over.'

James says nothing. He does not move. He does not breathe until the door is shut and Hal is gone. Then, 'Jesus!' He exhales. 'How do you *do* that?'

'Do what?'

'That!' He jabs a finger at her. 'This. Play the innocent?'

'Oh, I'm pretty sure Hal knows.'

'What?' For the second time he is stunned, and yet, now, somehow unsurprised. 'So . . . why doesn't he say anything? Why doesn't he—'

'Out me? Leave me?'

He nods.

She turns back to the mirror, fixes an invisible kink in her hair. 'Because I know things too.'

'About him?'

She nods. And there it is, a crease, a split, a chink, only what can he want with it now? What can he do with it now that . . . that Daisy is gone? Now that this world has been tipped up like a box of spillikins and scattered wide and indiscriminate.

Yet, still he has to know. 'What do you mean?'

'It's not important.'

'Yes it is.'

'Really—'

Then he sees it, as precise as if he'd witnessed every whisper, every kiss, a mirror image of his own messed-up scene. Only this one wasn't cut short, aborted. 'That night. You and Hal. You fucked. He thought you were Daisy and he fucked you.'

She pauses, then drops her head into a nod.

'And then what? He found out? He worked out the scam? Got angry? Tried to, what? Hit you?'

'Yes— No. I was showing off. Parading around claiming I was as good as Daisy. Claiming I could swim.'

Guilt pricks him again, needle-sharp and deep. 'I shouldn't have told you that.'

But she shakes her head. 'But I *could* swim. He just didn't know it.'

'And, what? You jumped in?'

'No, I . . .' She shakes her head again. 'I didn't jump. He— he—'

'He pushed you? Jesus, that's it. He thought you couldn't swim and he pushed you.'

'He pushed *Bea*,' she blurts. 'Not me. Bea.'

But he's not listening. He's there again, on the edge of the sodden lawn, on top of the mooring wall. A rattle of thunder, a smack, a cap of gold hair pulled under the water. Then—

'But Daisy jumped in,' he says. 'Daisy tried to save you.'

'And so did you.'

'But I didn't die. Daisy did.'

'No— No! Don't you see? It was *Bea* who died that day. Bea . . . Bea who's gone.'

But he's not listening to her justifications, the absurd calculations she's made to make this mess seem plausible, good. He's too busy piecing together his own story in this, to fashion truth from the soup of spin and segue she's cooked up for him – for all of them. Because she's not the girl who pulled him into the outhouse, who pulled away before they fucked, who named him James and offered a promise she couldn't possibly keep.

She's the girl who threw stones at his window.

She's the girl he snuck out to the beach.

She's the girl he kissed in the outhouse and then fucked on the floor while he called out Daisy's name in his head.

Oh Jesus. He fucked her.

He fucked Bea that night.

He fucked Bea and nine months later she had a kid. She had—

'Clementine,' he blurts. 'She's mine, isn't she?'

There is a ballooning silence, and then she nods and the truth is both a kiss and a slap.

It makes sense, now. It all makes sense. Clem and that girl from the pub. Sadie's girl, Stella. They look alike not because of Hal, but because one is his niece, one his daughter and he sees them then, side by side, and with them, his mother, his mam, her own kind likeness feeding down. 'Were you ever going to tell me?' he demands.

She looks away. 'At first I thought you were dead. Then I assumed she was Hal's. And now . . .'

'But—' He's spinning, giddy as a dervish, high and terrified and desperate for something, anything to come good from this. 'But . . . now that I know, I can raise her. Or help.'

She laughs. Laughs! 'She's twenty-nine, not a child. There's no raising to do. Just doling out cash and platitudes.'

'But . . . but it should have been me.'

'Really? And that would have fitted in with your – what – drug deals and fake essays and bar work? Oh yes, I found out some things,' she adds, to answer his incredulous gaze. 'Besides, how would I explain that to Hal?'

'But he knows.'

She shakes her head. 'He knows she's not his. Not that she's . . . the—'

'The pauper's daughter?'

'No—'

'It's all right. I know what I was.' Was. Not am. 'But now I'm . . . changed, don't you see?'

She sighs. 'It's not about that. Not anymore.'

There's a silence then, thick as dripping, sliceable. Then she turns again, takes his trembling hand in her chilled fingers. 'So, are you going to tattle tale?'

He pulls it away. 'Are you?'

She shakes her head, sets her jaw. 'And nor will you if you're half the man I hope you are. Besides, what possible gain could there be? We all invent ourselves, even Hal. Those flat vowels took years to cultivate. His man of the people schtick? All fake. Besides, it's him I did it for.'

349

'Him?'

'He needed me. Well, he needed someone and Daisy was leaving, or going to. He needed someone who would stick with him, who would help him shine.'

'For Christ's sake, Bea.'

'It's Daisy.' Her voice is cold. Even. 'And, yes, Hal needed me, and now he needs you. We both do.'

'What?' He fishes for reasons, grasps at something glinting, hopes it's no milk bottle top. 'Are you . . . leaving him?'

She laughs. 'Oh, it's better than that.'

'What then?' He's losing patience now, losing hope.

'Oh, James, haven't you guessed yet?' She frowns, a neat crease cleaving her forehead. 'I'm dying.'

40.

Jason, 1988

This is how you drown.

You're sitting half-naked in an outhouse with a girl who's rechristened you, and promised to kiss you, when you hear a name – her sister's name – being hollered into the wind, rain catching it and sending it seaward.

You scrabble to your feet, haul on still-soaked clothing that scrapes and sticks and struggles to fit, then flee from the scene through woods and a gate and across sodden lawn, following the girl who adds, 'Bea? Bea?' to the loudening chorus.

'What happened?' you beg the assembled, lined up on the wall like a creche of penguins. 'Where's Bea?'

But Julian, his face awkward, contorted, says nothing, while Hal, frantic, carries on yelling her name.

'Hal?' Daisy demands. 'Hal, where is she?'

'She jumped,' he says. 'Right in.'

'But she can't swim,' Muriel says, calmly aghast.

'She can,' you insist.

But not well enough.

Lightning picks out a head in the water, gold cap of hair,

gasping mouth. You panic, scrabble for an anchor, a rubber ring to throw her, come up only with the boat.

'Bea!' yells her sister. 'I'm coming.'

'Wait for the boat,' you tell her. 'Wait.'

But before you can convince her, before Hal can catch her, she is arcing into the water as slick and pale and shimmering as a fish.

'The rocks!' you call. 'The storm!' But your words are moths, drowned on the wing, already dead when they hit the ground.

And out there, in the inky swill of the water, are two girls, your only admirers, your tickets out. And you are not letting them go. And so, you see, you have no choice. You have to follow them.

You have to save them.

You have to jump.

41.

James, 2018

In every practised scenario, every permutation of their future that he has played out, not once did he imagine this: that he could lose her through something so ordinary, so arbitrary and inevitable as death.

It seems unfair. Laughable almost. But the joke is on both of them.

'What— I mean . . . You're ill?'

She nods. 'The cancer came back. Poor, pathetic Bea's body, still weak, still diseased after all.'

And he sees it now: how pale she is. Etiolated, almost, starved of light and something else. It's not just the perpetual thinness of vanity and acting. It's more. Worse. How could he have missed it? 'But can't they . . . do whatever they did before?'

'It's spread,' she says, decisive as a knife. 'Nothing to be done. Or nothing that I will tolerate. I'm not having chemo to buy a few months lived in misery.'

'But—'

'No.' She cuts him off.

'So . . . what now?'

'Tonight? Tonight I'm going to go to dinner, and celebrate my birthday, and mourn my sister with the people I love. And who loved her.' At that she takes his hand and this time it is he who flinches, but she who does not let go. 'And then I will tell them all what will happen. I will tell Hal the only truth he needs to know: that he is going to lose me. But that he has Clementine, and Julian, and Muriel. And you.'

'Me?' He feels the tears threaten to spill.

She tightens her fingers round his, shakes him. 'Didn't you wonder why you were here? Why I was so desperate that you got the job that I'd go begging to bloody Lydia?'

'I—' But he stops short. Because he didn't wonder at all. Never thought for a moment it was anything other than coincidence, cruel or divine.

'Because I knew you were capable of keeping a secret, a secret so huge, so looming it could ruin me.' She pauses, squeezes his hand again, her eyes a-glitter. 'Because you understand, don't you? What I'd stand to lose.'

Oh, God, she is good.

He rubs at his eyes. 'But why not just die quietly,' he asks, 'without me as a witness?'

'Precisely because I *need* a witness, don't you see? I need it on record: who I am. I'm Daisy. Fucking glorious Daisy. For all time. And I need the money. Or Hal will.'

'Anyone could have done it, any half-decent ghost.'

She shakes her head. 'No one else loves me like you do. No one else even looks at me like you do, not anymore. God, the need in you, I can feel it. Anyone else would have at best done me no justice, at worst sold me off to the *Sun*.'

354

He cannot deny it. Instead plays his last chip. 'And how do you know I won't drop the project?'

She stands, grasps his shoulders, pleading. Or so she plays it. 'Because you need it, too. You need *us*. Think of the moment when I tell Hal I'm dying, imagine writing that – the drama of it!' For a minute he thinks she will clap, delighted, Muriel-like. But she steadies herself. 'Hal needs to be painted a hero, you see. People must see how he rallies.'

He touches her face without thinking, remembers who she is and feels a short shock like static, drops his hand. 'And what if he doesn't?'

'Then you will make him. Because that way people will love him – the widower of an already tragic wife. Imagine how they will vote for a man like that.'

'You think he'll stand? After this?'

'He has to,' she snaps. 'I stopped the cogs of it, thirty years ago. I eclipsed him. And now he has to make his mark, find his own place in history.'

Her devotion is as astonishing as her delusion.

'Not all of us have to . . . to stand out.'

She places a palm on his cheek, cold as it is calculated. But he doesn't remove it. 'Not all of us want to be a ghost either. Slipping invisible through life. Leaving no trace, no legacy. Don't you want to be known?'

He shakes his head. Yes.

'Think how perfect it will be if you stand by him, write for him, guide him, make him the best Hal he can be.'

'He has Julian for that.'

'Julian's a liability and you know it.'

'I . . .' He nods. 'And you really won't tell him?'

'For what gain? Unburdening? That's so terribly selfish, don't you think?'

She smiles then, and he sees it, suddenly. Sees it in brilliant technicolour and marvellous detail: she *is* Daisy. Everything about her is calculated to convince and it does. She is brighter and more brilliant than the original. None of the wavering, none of the cracks and doubts of either Bea or her sister. She is a Disney Cinderella, a Las Vegas Liberty; a rendition so perfect she has become more believable, more lauded than the real thing.

'Kiss me,' he pleads.

And this time she doesn't falter; doesn't slap him or scorn him or reel in disdain. She slips her hand round to the nape of his neck, and, eyes wide open, she parts her lips and pulls him in.

It lasts seconds, and is a lie, he knows it is a lie. But it is everything he remembers, too, and everything he sought and tried to deny. 'I'll do it,' he says. 'I'll do what you want.'

And, satisfied as a cat, she smiles.

42.

Bea, 1988

She is hauled from the water by Hal in the end. Her white knight, her handsome prince. He has summoned a boat, or stolen one, and pulls her, peels her from the buoy she has clung to.

'Daisy?' he shakes her.

Her reply is a cough, a spew of saltwater over his shoes.

'Daisy,' he repeats.

And then he's holding her, as if she were as fragile, as precious as a fledgling, and so she cannot correct him, cannot tell him the truth. Not yet.

In a minute. In a minute she'll confess. When her breath is back.

When the real Daisy is safe and sound and smiling at the joke.

In a minute.

In the early hours of the morning her sister is found, pulled up by police divers from where she has snagged under a boat. Her eyes dead as a herring, her body bloated and blue.

'She couldn't swim,' Hal tells them. 'She thought she could, but . . .'

'She could have been a Channel swimmer,' says one of them, his dry suit creaking, stinking of rubber. 'Lightning would still have got her.'

'I told her,' says Hal, his voice dropping into a sob. 'I told her not to do it.'

'Tell him,' someone urges – a voice in her head. 'Tell him now.'

But she cannot speak, cannot get words past the grief that has sewn up her throat. And look at him, look at him! If she explains it's Daisy down there, savaged and cold, then that is the greatest cruelty of all, surely. This, this is kinder. Yes, she is being benevolent.

Just like Daisy.

'It's all right,' she whispers, grasping his hand until her own knuckles whiten. 'No one thinks it's your fault.'

And no one does.

Death by misadventure, they're told to expect, though they're warned there'll be interviews, statements to be made, a body to identify, officially.

Hal offers to do it, but she insists it has to be her. Insists she will be fine.

Muriel goes with her, but stays in the corridor, says she'll throw up, and she's greenish already so Bea has no reason not to believe her.

And there, on the mortuary slab, is where it all ends, the soul of one sister slipping into the other, the name handed over, the life stolen for good.

'Yes, that's her,' she says. 'Beatrice Elisabeth Hicks.'

Later, she signs papers, inks her borrowed name in black Bic in a small oblong box: Daisy Clementine, the loops long-practised, the mimicry precise.

'I'm so sorry,' the officer tells her.

'Thank you,' she replies. 'Me too.'

And she is sorry, and sad and ravaged. So that she has to take pills to sleep and others to stay awake, has to balance vodka with Valium to get through the day.

But through it she gets. And then the next. Until she no longer forgets to turn when Hal calls out, 'Daisy?'

Hal.

She has him now, in the palm of her hand, licking her shoes if he could.

But she can't let him touch her, not yet. So she tells him she needs time. To think, to grieve, to 'process'.

'But I can help you,' he insists. 'You need me.'

But she pushes him, gently, away, tells him to give her a month, maybe two, promises to call him when she's ready, if she's ready.

Then, that night, the house abandoned, the lock on the communal bathroom tight, she soaks her stomach, her chest, with surgical spirit, takes the scalpel she's found in a toolkit and sterilized twice, and chops the head off a mole, then slices a line above her appendix, an inch long, and deep.

43.

James, 2019

The next year is as mapped out and curated as their very selves. Every eventuality planned for, every argument anticipated, every diversion blocked off and re-routed until they are on course again, true.

That night, at dinner, James watches her practised announcement, the sudden solemnity, the catch in her voice – deliberate – when she says the word 'cancer'. He watches Clementine, sobbing; Muriel hysterical so that Luna, brought back half-cut and skunk-smelling by a livid Julian, slaps her own mother. He watches Hal holding his changeling wife, not knowing that he is already mourning the wrong girl for the second time.

Just months later, he will carry her coffin, though ranked at the back, behind Julian and Hal and an actor he once saw in *Hamlet*; throw damp soil on oak at a South London cemetery while the press keep a respectful distance, the clicks minimal, the flash off. Later, he will hand Clementine a handkerchief (not tissue), fresh-pressed and monogrammed. He will confiscate Hal's sixth wine, reminding him who he is, who he has to be now.

In the spring, he will stand at Hal's side as he signs copies of her autobiography – the autobiography he's credited with finishing, of course, when she got too weak. Then again, weeks later, when Hal is elected to office, an MP for his home constituency, an undersecretary in the new coalition. She was right, of course. The public – the people – love him; he is a young Tony Benn. This self-proclaimed upper-class traitor. This Daisy-made man.

Then, in September he will seal a cheque in an envelope: £10,000 of his own – her own – cash, stamp it and send it over the Tamar.

Did she guess that? That the first pub he'd help save would be Stella's, Hal's co-op keeping the doors open and the optics stocked beyond the regatta and into the thick of the winter, when the weather is bleak and the businesses boarded until tourists come calling again.

Perhaps Julian is her father, perhaps not, but, whoever it is, she doesn't deserve them. Nor an uncle who disowned her own mother three decades before. But this he can do now. As a stranger he can play a part, however small, in her life.

And then there's Clem.

Does he once say a word? Does he let slip to his daughter that she is just that?

Of course not. But then she knew he wouldn't – couldn't. Because then he'd have to tell her who *he* really was. And he is not that boy anymore.

That boy was left behind on barnacled rocks, thirty years or more ago.

His socks, his soul, his name washed out to sea.

44.

Jason, 1988

It's been hours, or maybe just sixty long minutes, when the current's hold on him seems to slacken, and he is able to wrestle himself to the edge of the estuary. Is it still estuary? For the filthy silt has turned to sand here, the forest leaf-fall to flotsam and jetsam – tin cans and tampons and a child's plastic animal, all caught on the rocks. No, it's a beach, he thinks, *that* beach. He's been washed out to sea and then in again, a bobbing bottle himself, landing at Lantic, far round the bay. Too far now to save her, to save either of them. And at that he collapses, passes out for what might be a moment or a night and a day.

When he comes to, the sky is still glowering but the rain has eased to a steady pitter-patter and the thunder has cleared, leaving space for herring gulls and cormorants to call across the water. His leg is bleeding but nothing is broken, nothing snapped. He can walk, albeit a slow stumble, can breathe, albeit ragged and sore. He is, above all, alive.

But wait. Who is alive?

*

In sagging trousers he staggers to a stand, then scrambles, heading for Rashleigh.

Four hours, maybe more, it takes him, but in that time the sun comes, dries him out like a kipper, salt leaving white tidemarks he has to brush off with ferns. In that time he rinses splintered fingers in Mal Dennett's cow byre, blood mixing with trough water meant for the herd. In that time he ducks into the porch at the Polmears' where he knows he'll find boots and a Barbour and a bottle of gold top besides. In that time he stops in seventeen places to keep clear of the raincoated and wellied, drifting into the woods or onto false paths. But at the Quiller-Couch cross he cuts back onto Hall Walk before dropping down through the trees to the back of the house.

They're there, all of them, gathered on the lawn and spreading onto the slipway. Muriel and Julian and Hal and— which one of them? Because neither wore a sweater and leggings, neither was shod with Docs.

'Daisy?' calls Hal, as she's helped into a car. 'Wait.'

Daisy, he thinks, relief thick as treacle and twice as sweet. But where is Bea?

Muriel is sobbing, he realizes, her cries raw and repeating, the plaintive caw of a gull or a fox. Julian hands her something – a tissue? No, wait, a handkerchief, embroidered no doubt. But she refuses, goes on wailing.

'Someone shut her up,' comes the voice.

His heart quickens and his eyes slip over the scene, trying to find him.

There, sitting on a concrete bollard, grey-faced as stone,

slack-jawed as a moron: his father. And, holding on to his shoulder, a trembling Sadie, still dressed for the dance floor in a boob tube and heels.

He opens his mouth to call out, to comfort her. But then it comes to him, a gleaming vision, a pleading Tinkerbell that prances, flits in and out of his peripheral vision, beckoning, begging, beguiling.

'Come with me,' she insists. 'You're a lost boy now.'

And he is. Forgotten in no time, if not already, least by those that matter. Some kid that hung around like a bad bloody smell, like a stray, sniffing round girls he couldn't hope to have, a life he couldn't hope to lead.

Alive, he is consigned to this. To slink, tail dragging back to his father, handy with his fists; back to Fat Man Morris and Alan Ransome, all brag and swagger; back to Sadie with her braying and her men. Back to under-poured pints, and past-sale-date crisps and never quite enough of anything.

But dead, he can go anywhere.

Can be anyone.

Can be a hero or a villain.

Can be the Wonderful Wizard of Oz.

Can be Smaug.

Can be Peter Pan, or Hook, or the tick-tocking crocodile.

Or be merely a boy worthy of her, one day, not so long from now. When everything has settled, sunk in, moved on.

And so, instead of walking across the lawn, handing himself in to the police for his part in this tragedy, he doubles back, takes himself back up through the woods, to the Polmears' old potting shed to wait out a night. Then the next morning, he heads out across fields and farmland, a Huck, a pioneer in borrowed clothes, but, in his sights, a new life; in his pockets, a novel he's itching to finish, John Polmear's wallet fat with fifties from a bookies' win, and a Polaroid of a bob-headed girl.

He walks as far as Polperro then catches a bus up to Plymouth, the driver clattering his change and nodding him on without even a glance; the passengers oblivious, in their post-holiday world, heading to Dingles for sensible shoes and school uniform and a sundae if they're lucky.

The queue for the bridge is half a mile long and two cars deep and he feels sweat beading his brow and back, twitches in irritation. But he conjures her up, whispers her words in his head, encouraging him, promising him, and within the hour he is out of the county; crossing the Tamar no bigger a leap than a step across Fore Street, no wrench at all. For he's not leaving Wonderland, Narnia, at all, but heading into it.

In Plymouth, he buys a hat and a bag, fills that with new socks, a jumper, a toothbrush and paste. Then back at the station he catches a train, clacks along the coast-cut tracks of Teignmouth and Dawlish, through Exeter's red Devon soil, then up into a patchwork of honey-hewn villages, the wide sweeping crescents of Bristol and Bath. At Didcot he changes, waits on a bench with his back to the power plant and his hands wrapped round a cup of stewed tea.

'All right?' says the man who sits next to him, sawn-off shorts and smelling of Brut. His name badge – Debenhams – reads 'Pete'.

Joanna Nadin

'All right,' he replies, his words clumsy and catching, his accent awry.

Pete pulls a KitKat from his pocket, runs his finger down the foil before cracking it in half, offering him a finger.

He nods, takes it. 'Thanks,' he says, steadier now, more sure.

'Where you off to, then?' Pete asks, chewing, a concrete of chocolate coating his tongue.

He swallows, looks up at the announcement board, checks for the fifth time he's right.

'Oxford,' he says, the word a pearl in his mouth. 'I'm off to Oxford.'

45.

James, 2018

He asked her, near the end, if she ever worried she'd be caught.

'At first, perhaps,' she said. But days turned to weeks and those to months and no one once questioned her claim, her signature.

'Not ever?' he asked.

'Only you.'

Clementine was right: we are all works of fiction, all smoke and mirrors and self-tan. Some of us staking a claim on a single ideal identity; others moth-like, butterflies, dancing through an array of curated faces as fickle and fast-changing as status updates.

So is it deception? Or do we just adapt to survive, to better ourselves, to improve on God and genetics and circumstance, which are, after all, no fault of our own.

And does it matter? A lie gets halfway round the world before truth's even buckled its shoes. And who wants truth these days? Give them the old razzle-dazzle. Isn't that how the song goes?

And Jesus, Bea, you razzled-dazzled them all.

Acknowledgements

With thanks to Judith Murray at Greene Heaton and Sam Humphreys at Macmillan for giving me free rein to write what I wanted; to the Placers and Friday Writers for advice, tea and sympathy; to Julia Green, who urged me to start the doctorate that led to this novel; to James Coggan (and the actually very impressive Leonard) at Fowey Aquarium for nautical guidance; to Tom Varcoe for the blagged boat ride to Ferryside; to Polruan Reading Room for allowing me to become a temporary member; and, finally, to the people of Fowey and Polruan for being so generally welcoming. If my topology appears irritatingly inaccurate, I apologize – I admit I altered it slightly to better fit the plot. If my characters are indifferent at times to this fictional version, I want to be clear it's not a view I share or have ever entertained. I still dream of the real thing, as rich and glittering as Manderley.

Have you ever wished for a different mother?

Joanna Nadin's first novel for adults, *The Queen of Bloody Everything*, is about mothers, daughters and how we can make many choices in life but can't choose where we come from.

As Edie Jones lies in a bed on the fourteenth floor of a Cambridge hospital, her adult daughter Dido tells their story, starting with the day that changed everything.

That was the day Dido – aged exactly six years and twenty-seven days old – met the next door neighbours and fell in love.

Because the Trevelyans were exactly the kind of family Dido dreamed of. *Normal.*

'A must-read' *Independent*

'You're in for a treat with this one' *Red Magazine*

Discover Joanna Nadin's second novel,
The Talk of Pram Town

'Beautifully written and deliciously clever – the characters
will stay with you for a long time and you'll find joy on every
page. Really can't recommend it enough'
Matson Taylor, author of *The Miseducation of Evie Epworth*

It's 1981. Eleven-year-old Sadie adores her beautiful and
vibrant mother, Connie. It's always been just the two of
them. Until the unthinkable happens.

Jean hasn't seen her daughter Connie since she ran away
from the family home in Harlow aged seventeen and
pregnant. But then Jean gets a life-changing call: could she
please come and collect the granddaughter she's never met?

Jean and Sadie are worlds apart, but could a second
chance at family bring them together?